Defender
of the Flame

Sylvia Engdahl

✳ *Ad* ✳
Stellae

Eugene, Oregon

Book design and layout by Sylvia Engdahl

Cover photo © by Nikita Vishneveckiy /
Dreamstime

ISBN-13: 979-8-9858532-0-9

FROM THE REVIEWS OF
THE CAPTAIN OF *ESTEL* TRILOGY

Book One: *Defender of the Flame*

"This book reaches back to the brio and speculation of Engdahl's classic books of the Seventies. . . The reader will be taken on an exciting and suspenseful ride. . . With an admirable protagonist and many interesting and well-drawn characters major and minor, *Defender* is satisfying on multiple levels. . . I expected to like this book; I was startled that I loved it. A must read."
—Literary critic Nicholas Birns

Book Two: *Herald of the Flame*

"A futuristic ride that has many parallels in today's society. This is a 'thinking man's' science fiction book—the type we need more of today!"
—*The Feathered Quill*

"These novels are not so much genre 'Romance' or even just 'Science Fiction' as they are Literature. These are novels about life."
—Jacqueline Lichtenberg, *Alien Romances Reviews 14*

Book Three: *Envoy of the Flame*

"This engrossing book explores the powers of mind (psi), alien contact, and a little romance, all with an optimistic view of humanity's future. A very good read!"
—Amazon verified reader review

Contents

Preface

This is one of five novels—the Founders of Maclairn duology and the Captain of *Estel* trilogy—that are tied together by the concept of a flame as the symbol of the evolving "paranormal" powers of the mind and by their setting in an imaginary future in which those powers are developed first by a small group of people, and later by their successors' influence on human civilization. It is the first book of the trilogy and is complete in itself, but starting with it will reduce the suspense of the duology's novels if you're planning to read either of them.

However, the trilogy is set two centuries later than the duology and is quite different in many respects. Unlike the first "Flame" novel, *Stewards of the Flame,* it does not deal with the controversial dystopian view of healthcare on which that book is focused. It is a faster-moving story about a starship captain destined to play a significant role in human history, and for that reason some science fiction readers find it more to their taste. It is also of special interest to adults and older teens who have enjoyed my Young Adult novels *Enchantress from the Stars* and *The Far Side of Evil* because it involves the interstellar Anthropological Service that appears in those books.

Each of the "Flame" novels can stand alone. When I wrote them, one at a time, I had no intention of writing another; the idea for the succeeding story didn't come to me until months, or years, later. They can be read in any order, except that each includes enough backstory to affect the suspense of the preceding one. Please note that unlike my earlier books these are adult novels and contain some material inappropriate for readers below high school age.

Sylvia Engdahl, June 2021

What then of the prospects of our evolution? . . . Are we stations on a not yet fully traveled road? Is there reason to hope, as so many have, that great leaps beyond still await us? . . . A growing store of remarkable facts declares the presence of unknown faculties in the species and unknown energies awakening in our midst. There is enough information for speculating on our possible psychic evolution— enough evidence to prove that marvelous breakthroughs are possible. The problem is that we fear breakthrough and are addicted to the known and the familiar.

—Michael Grosso, *Frontiers of the Soul*, 1992

There is no such thing as chance; and what seem to us merest accident springs from the deepest source of destiny.

—Friedrich Friedrich Schiller, *Wallenstein*, 1798

*Destiny grants us our wishes, but in its own way, in order to give us something beyond our wishes.

—Johann Wolfgang von Goethe, *Elective Affinities,</i>* 1809

Part One: Titan

1

TITAN! HE STILL couldn't believe it. How could he, Terry Radnor, a full lieutenant in Fleet and due to be in command on his next explorer mission, possibly have been sent back from Centauri Ops Center to the desolate training base on Titan? It must be a mistake. Fleet was, to be sure, a ponderous bureaucracy noted for mistakes when it came to personnel placement, at least in terms of young officers' preferences. He had been extremely fortunate to get explorer duty on receiving his commission instead of being assigned to a freighter crew. He was not willing to accept the thought that his luck had run out.

Gloomily, Terry stowed his gear under the bunk he had been assigned and then sprawled on it, wondering why he did not have a room to himself. He was entitled to one. Even aboard explorers, small ships with crews of four, there were private staterooms. On Titan instructors generally had them, and what could he be here for if not to instruct? He had had his tour as a trainee on Titan long ago, just after leaving the Academy.

He hadn't minded then—it had been exciting, his first trip to an alien world; he'd never before been further from Earth than Fleet headquarters on the moon. Titan's weird methane lakes, the strange murky sky, and the odd sensation of handling a ship in the thick air had been enough of a novelty to compensate for the cramped, uncomfortable quarters within the ancient domed structures. And while flying outside the atmosphere the overwhelming sight of ringed Saturn, huge against the blackness of space, had thrilled him. But he had since visited worlds of quite a few stars, and in any case you didn't see anything from inside the domes. It was unlikely that he would be able to do much flying; the only ships stationed on Titan were trainers, and he did not have an instructor's rating.

Nor did he want one, Terry thought bitterly. With a flying instructor's rating he might be stuck here for years, when he should be out exploring, collecting data on unopened worlds—possibly even getting rich. Fleet allowed crews a fair share of valuable finds, lest they turn to smuggling despite the draconian penalties they would incur if caught at it. Somehow he would have to wangle a transfer before anybody took note of his more-than-adequate academic qualifications for classroom instructing. That was a deadly job for a top-notch pilot and one not usually given to any officer so young. It was work for people near retirement. Either there was a glitch in a computer somewhere, or they were shorthanded.

The door slid open and a tall, lanky lieutenant appeared, presumably his roommate. "Hi, I'm Drew Larssen," he said. "Welcome to the dumping ground. Don't take it personally, but why they've sent us another warm body with nothing to do but kill time is beyond me."

"I just now got here," said Terry. "I won't be killing time for long."

"Yes, you will. Before the week's out you'll be stir-crazy like the rest of us."

This was not good news. Evidently the base was not shorthanded, and if it was being used as a dumping ground for superfluous personnel, his own performance rating might not be as good as he had assumed. "What do they claim we're here for?" he inquired.

"They don't. Oh, they'll find a job for you. I'm

babysitting engineering trainees myself, which their section leader would be doing anyway. They pulled me off drive maintenance on Alpha for this!"

"You're not a pilot, then."

"You are? God, if they're bringing in pilots it's worse than I thought."

"I don't suppose it does any good to apply for a transfer."

"What do you think?" Drew frowned. "It's a funny thing, though—the CO doesn't mind people asking. He acts like he doesn't know any more than we do why we're here."

Definitely a snafu then—if it were not, the CO would know. "Is he much of a pain to work under?"

"Oh, Derham is okay. If it weren't for him, things could be a lot worse."

"Derham?" Terry was astonished. Admiral Derham had been the CO when he'd been here before, and one of the best officers he had ever encountered; everybody had liked him. A man of his caliber should have moved on to a more desirable command by now.

"I've heard he took a three-month leave a while back," Drew went on. "The old-timers were afraid he might not return—though the XO acting for him, Commander Vargas, is all right too."

Two exceptionally good commanders at a base otherwise viewed as a dumping ground exceeded even Fleet's reputation for mismanagement. Terry was still puzzling over it when, the next morning, he reported to Administration to receive his work assignment. He didn't expect the CO to see him personally, but to his surprise Admiral Derham greeted him warmly and even remembered him from the ceremony at the end of his training tour, when he had been awarded top honors.

"I know you'd rather be flying, Lieutenant," Derham told him, "and I can't arrange that right now. We have more pilots than we can use. You'll be programming simulations for the time being. Just be patient, and something more to your liking may turn up."

Programming sims—well, that was better than instructing. At the Academy Terry had downplayed his very considerable programming talent for fear that he would be permanently assigned to AI maintenance instead of pilot training. Later he had learned that it was an asset, since all members of explorer crews were required to be proficient in at least two fields. Simulating emergencies at a training base didn't require much talent, since the AI was already programmed to do most of the work involved; but at least he would have direct access to the supercomputer.

Would he dare make creative use of that access? he wondered. He had not done any hacking since high school and his expertise had even then been carefully hidden. It had been his main interest for several years, making up for the lack of social life resulting from his reputation as a loner. He had never enjoyed social activities, not because he didn't like people but because he couldn't seem to connect with them. There was a gulf he'd never been able to cross, as if some bridge should be there that he didn't know how to step onto. In his relationship with computers he felt in charge. And so he had cracked many of the largest systems on Earth's Net, never doing any damage, never touching the data he could easily have altered, but simply taking satisfaction in his ability to get in. Now, though, if there were a way to assign himself to duty somewhere other than on Titan . . .

No, he decided. Derham would know. If it were anyone else he might have risked it, but he did not want to lose the respect of Admiral Derham.

Terry did, however, take a look at his own record to see if there was some error in it that might have led to this inexplicable interruption of his career. There wasn't. He rated high in just about everything, and there were no unfavorable notations.

That was why he was incredulous when a few days after his arrival he was ordered to report to the medical department for psychological evaluation.

2

TERRY DID NOT like psych officers. What spacer did? In his case, any such summons was particularly distasteful because he was aware that his loner status might be considered grounds for investigation. He had noticed hints of this during his entrance exams and training evaluations, though there had never been any complaints of discord with his messmates. He had been viewed as standoffish, but not disliked. And he had been too busy for his superiors to care that he was not especially eager to take part in the few recreational activities cadets were allowed time for.

Now, however, he was not busy. The psychiatrists were probably not busy either, which meant that they might want a subject to analyze who could be easily spared from work. He could see no other reason why they would have decided to test him again. And there were things he was not at all eager to have them pry into.

He was so preoccupied with this thought that he nearly got lost in the search for the office to which the med reception screen had directed him. Titan Base was old, having been established long before the development of interstellar travel, and by now it was a maze of cramped interconnected compartments under domes too small for the facilities it contained. It had not been thought worthwhile to replace them, since the only operations retained here were those connected with the training of new Academy graduates to live and work under less than ideal conditions, not only in the harsh outside environment but in quarters no more roomy than they would find aboard a ship. Thus every inch of space was utilized—but not effi-

ciently. Various departments had grown, others had
shrunk; and as a result, the compartments allocated to
them were not always adjacent. The office of Dr. Aldren,
to whom he was referred, proved to be nowhere near the
rest of the medical complex. It could not have been harder
to locate if it had been deliberately hidden.

The outer office was tiny, and was nearly filled by the
receptionist's desk. She was a tall, slender woman with
striking silver hair that must have been intentionally
changed from its natural color, for though she certainly
wasn't young, she did not seem old enough for it to have
turned gray. And she wasn't in uniform, which seemed
odd. He had not thought there were any civilian employ-
ees on Titan.

"Hello, Lieutenant," she said, smiling. "You can go right
in; Dr. Aldren's expecting you."

Resolutely, Terry entered the inner office. He hoped
this would be over quickly. He hoped he would not be
required to talk much; the inevitable AI interview would
be bad enough. "Lieutenant Radnor, reporting as ordered,
sir," he said.

To his amazement, the man who stood waiting for
him might have been the twin of the receptionist. He appeared to be ageless—tall, trim and full of vitality, yet
silver-haired and with penetrating eyes that suggested
years of accumulated wisdom. And he, too, wore civvies.
Quickly Terry realized that these two people were not in
fact alike; their features were quite different. Only build
and hair color had given that impression. Yet there was
something more, a warmth, a welcoming manner, that
made him feel some sort of affinity with them.

"You don't have to call me 'sir,'" Dr. Aldren said. "I'm
not a Fleet officer, just a friend of Admiral Derham. He
has asked me to do what I can to improve the morale here."

The morale at the base certainly needed improving,
Terry thought, but it wouldn't take a psychiatrist to figure out why. Any of the surplus officers could have told

him, and in fact Derham must already know. Was he so powerless to transfer them that he hoped an outsider could find some new way to keep them from dying of boredom?

The room didn't seem anything like a medical office. The desk was crowded into one corner, looking as if it hadn't been recently used, and there were two standard-issue chairs, also pushed aside. Filling most of the space was a blue mattress of the kind used aboard spaceliners, laid directly on the floor. "As you see, I'm not much for observing conventions," Dr. Aldren said. He proceeded to sit down on the mattress, inviting Terry to join him.

It was impossible to sit stiffly erect there, as he would have preferred to do. He waited, puzzled, as the doctor added, "Just make yourself comfortable. I'll have Roanna bring us some coffee." He spoke with a slight accent that Terry couldn't place, affecting not his choice of words but only their pronunciation. Where, he wondered, had Admiral Derham met him? On Earth during the admiral's long leave, perhaps?

Almost immediately the woman appeared, though Terry had spotted no form of signaling. Was there a hidden mike that would pick up everything he said? He took the steaming cup she offered him, realizing that since there was no flat place to set it down, he was effectively barred from nervously clenching his hands. To his surprise he didn't feel as nervous as he'd expected to. There was something about this man that inspired trust.

"I'd like to hear your impression of the problems here," Dr. Aldren said. "You don't need to tell me that you'd rather be someplace else; I'm aware that you and a good many others were brought to Titan against your will. I can't change that, but maybe I can find some means of making duty at this base more tolerable."

"Do you have any idea why we're here?" Terry ventured. "I've heard that extra people have been coming in for weeks."

"Well, Fleet's top brass doesn't confide in me," Aldren said, "and since for the present you are here, we've got to make the best of it. What do you do in your free time?"

"Not a lot. Work out in the gym sometimes, or read. Or play video games." He did not mention that he played them on the supercomputer when nobody was watching; he had covered his traces well. The rec room did not attract him; it was crowded and there wasn't much to do there if you didn't have friends to chill out with.

"How about chess? I'd guess that you're a good player."

Terry shook his head. He was *too* good at chess; he could always anticipate his opponent's next move, which took the fun out of it and did not make him popular. He had the strange feeling that Dr. Aldren knew this, and to change the subject he said, "On shore leaves I used to hike. But of course that's not possible here." For officers stationed on Titan there was no weekend escape because there was nowhere outside the domes to go. In any case, he'd had leave just before arriving; after a brief visit to his mother he had spent it camping in the Yellowstone Reserve, the chance to hike in Earth's remaining patches of wilderness being the one advantage to his recall to its solar system.

"What would you like to be doing, Terry, if you had a choice?" Aldren asked.

"Flying, of course. I've never wanted to be anything but a space pilot."

"You have programming skills, too, don't you? Very advanced ones?" At Terry's look he added, "I have access to your record, but nothing you say to me will be entered in it. Our conversation is absolutely confidential; it's not being recorded and I don't make notes of my own impressions, either. That's among the benefits of not being formally employed by Fleet."

"I'm a pretty good programmer," Terry admitted. "I could have gotten a job anywhere on Earth, even without college—during my last year of school I had offers. I chose

Fleet instead because I wanted to fly." He added, "I was a hacker, you know. I broke into a lot of systems, though nobody knew it was me—" He broke off, horrified. Why had he said that? The hacking was not on his record; there was no way Dr. Aldren could have found out.

The doctor didn't seem surprised. "I'm assuming you didn't do any black-hat hacking," he said.

"No, of course not—I only wanted to see if I could get past their security. And—and to kill time."

"School must have been a drag for you, since you earned high grades and still had time to kill. But I suppose you weren't one for partying."

"It wasn't that." Now they were getting to it, as Terry had known they would. "I'd have liked to hang out with some of the guys, only—"

"Only you never seemed to fit in. There was a wall of some kind between you, and it wasn't a matter of your intelligence. You reached out silently and they didn't respond."

Terry caught his breath, astonished. How could Aldren possibly have figured that out? It wasn't something that happened to other people; he had read enough in the knowledgebase to be sure it wasn't.

"Did your parents respond, Terry?"

Psychiatrists always wanted to know about your relationship with your parents. He had nothing to hide there; when he was ten his dad had died but he had gotten along well with his mom, largely because she hadn't pried into what he was doing with his computer. Only . . .

A picture came into his mind: His mom, putting her arms around him, saying how much she loved him, and he, then a small boy, hugging her and realizing for the first time that he *couldn't reach her*. He could nestle close and know that she did love him and that he wanted more than anything else in the world to tell her how deeply he loved her back, but words were too weak to express that feeling. There should be a way for him to reach her mind!

But there wasn't, and by the time he was six he had stopped trying. He had let it go with merely speaking his love for his parents and had shrunk from the embraces that seemed so inadequate. They hadn't noticed, because for them, speaking was enough.

"It hurt, didn't it," Aldren observed. It wasn't a question.

"Yes," Terry said in a low voice before becoming aware that he hadn't told him any of this, had not even answered the question.

"And so with women—"

This was what he had dreaded. With a psychiatrist, the subject of sex was bound to arise. And it embarrassed him, though not for the usual reasons. His relations with women were normal enough. He had never had any physical problems.

Nevertheless his experiences with sex had not been happy. Despite physical satisfaction they had left him emotionally drained—there was something missing in it, some connection that ought to be present beyond the mere joining of bodies. It was, perhaps, what was known as love; but other men did not seem to feel frustrated by not falling in love every time they slept with anyone. He did, and he had therefore avoided the situation when he could. On long expeditions that wasn't always possible; explorer crews paired off and he did not want his presumptive partner to think he didn't find her attractive. So there had been brief relationships, but never, to his disappointment, one that he found fulfilling.

"I'm not involved with any of the women here," he said, hoping to bypass the issue of past abstinence.

"Don't worry about it," Aldren said. "Most people settle for too little. It's better to hold off until you meet a woman you have a lot in common with."

"That's not very likely to happen, is it? I'm—too different."

"Not so different as you think. There are new worlds

of experience ahead of you, Terry, things I know about you but can't explain at this point. Aldren's smile was so genuine, and so empathetic, that Terry almost forgot he was a doctor. He was aware only that he was the most congenial man he had ever met—not so much in what he said but in what he intuitively grasped.

"For now, let's talk about your career goals," Dr. Aldren went on. "I assume you want to go back to exploring, but if that's not possible, is there any other assignment you think you could adapt to?"

"Not really. Freighters and even liners—they just make milk runs, and flying charters means you've got to take orders from the client. Exploring—well, you see something new, and you never know what it's going to be. Each planet is different. And I might make a rich find."

"You don't care about getting rich."

"No," Terry agreed. "That's what everybody else wants, so I say it . . . but I've always thought, hoped anyway, that someday I'd come across some tremendous secret out there, out near some star where no one has been before, something that *mattered*. . . ." To make light of it he added, "Aliens, maybe."

Aldren laughed. "Wouldn't it be great if we someday met some, after all the centuries humankind has waited in vain."

"I—I wonder if maybe they're a sort of symbol. What people imagine because they don't have a name for what I'm looking for."

"That's very perceptive. I think you must have read quite a lot, and not just science fiction."

"I know my way around the Nets and their knowledgebases at centers where I've been stationed."

There was a pause. Then Aldren persisted, "You can't command a ship with a crew of four forever. What's going to happen when you're promoted?"

"A terraforming expedition, maybe. Someday perhaps even a colonizer."

"What about cruiser duty?"

"God, no!" Cruisers had no real function beyond endless preparation for hostilities that their very existence
prevented. Back when the League was formed, the Uni-
fied Colonial Fleet had been established to make interplanetary war impossible. Its possession of armed cruisers was one of the two means by which it succeeded, the
other being its legal monopoly on ownership and operation of all but the smallest starships. Occasionally cruisers were called on for police action such as putting down
rebellions or dealing with pirates, but mainly the patrollers they carried flew practice missions. It was an
assignment no experienced officer wanted, and Terry
knew that even at the command level he would find it
deadly dull.

They talked on for a while, not saying anything very
significant, at least it seemed so at the time. Terry found
himself prolonging the discussion, feeling more and more
drawn to Dr. Aldren and not liking the thought that since
he wasn't psychologically disturbed they were unlikely to
meet again.

"None of what I've learned about you will reach Admiral Derham," the doctor assured him as he rose to leave.
"Except that with your permission, I will tell him that
you'd benefit from a more challenging assignment."

"Thanks. Not that I want any special consideration,
but I hope he'll take your advice."

"One other thing. You mustn't mention to anyone except the admiral that we've had this conversation, or even
that you've been to see me. I don't want people comparing notes."

"Okay," Terry agreed. He hadn't realized that the rest
of the newcomers were being called in, too. Perhaps that
was the solution: morale at the base was to be improved
one person at a time. Whether or not Aldren found any
other means of doing it, he had certainly improved *his*.

Later, lying on his bunk in the dark, he reflected on

this and was dismayed. His face burned. What had come over him? The man was a psychiatrist, trained to probe whether he was employed by Fleet or not. Yet somehow, without meaning to, he had told him all his most private secrets, all the things he had never intended to admit to anyone. Some of them, Aldren had known without being told. The connection he'd felt between them was uncanny. It was the sort of link that he had sought with others and never found.

3

LATE THE NEXT day, Terry was notified that the CO wanted to see him immediately. Elated, he changed into a clean uniform and headed for Administration, thinking that Dr. Aldren's recommendation of a more challenging assignment must have been taken seriously. Perhaps it had even precipitated correction of the error that had brought him to Titan.

"Lieutenant Terry Radnor reporting," he said to the intercom; there was no receptionist on hand after regular office hours. To his surprise, Admiral Derham himself responded.

"Come on into my office, Lieutenant," he said, "and close the door, please."

Terry complied, and stood at attention before the admiral's desk. "You have new orders for me, sir?" he asked hopefully.

"Not yet. Sit down—there's something I want to discuss." He waited until Terry was seated, then continued casually, "How did you get on with Dr. Aldren?"

"Fine, sir." It had been more than fine, and he was not sure what such a question was meant to accomplish. Knowing that Dr. Aldren was the CO's friend, he could scarcely have answered any other way.

"He's an exceptional person," Admiral Derham declared. "How would you feel about working with him for a while?"

Stunned, Terry burst out, "Sir, I liked Dr. Aldren very much, but I really don't think I need psychotherapy." Certainly Aldren had not implied that he did.

"That's not what I mean. There is some experimental work going on here of which Dr. Aldren is in charge, and he has told me that you have aptitude for it. Since I can't offer you a transfer soon, I think you might be interested in volunteering."

Terry's heart lifted. So he hadn't been under suspicion of social maladjustment after all—he had merely been interviewed for a special job. It didn't much matter what it was; any diversion would be welcome, and short of flying, to work under Dr. Aldren would be better than anything he could have hoped for. "Yes, sir, I would," he said.

"It's a spare-time commitment in addition to your regular work," Admiral Derham warned. He hesitated, assessing Terry's reaction. "This is a top secret project," he said soberly. "There's a good deal you need to know before deciding to participate, but I can't tell you any of it unless you sign an Extraordinary Secrets Acknowledgment."

Terry had heard of ESAs. Signing one was no small matter. If you leaked a secret covered by it, even accidentally, it meant dishonorable discharge from Fleet; if you deliberately revealed such a secret, the penalty was lifelong banishment to a penal colony. If the secret turned out to be some sort of cover-up that ought to be revealed, you couldn't blow the whistle. Yet he felt sure beyond doubt that any project run by Dr. Aldren would be aboveboard.

"I had to sign one myself," Admiral Derham said. "Only a few key officials know about this experiment; I was briefed at headquarters during my leave. And no one else other than the people we're recruiting must ever know. This ESA is binding for life, Lieutenant. You cannot ever, at any time in the future, mention what you learn about the project to anyone you are not specifically authorized to discuss it with. Is that understood?"

"Yes, sir." Drawing a deep breath, Terry took the stylus offered him and signed the input pad, then added his thumbprint. Once in the databank it was unalterable, he knew; even his most sophisticated hacking skills did not extend to top security Fleet installations.

"Okay," the CO said. "Now, this is difficult to explain, and it won't be clear to you until you've been told more by Dr. Aldren, assuming that you wish to proceed. Basically, a way has been found to give people—capabilities, capabilities that go beyond those ordinarily possessed by human beings. For instance, people who have had such training have full power over their own health. They control their inner processes so that they never get sick. They can heal minor injuries by mind alone. And they are immune to pain. Obviously, capabilities of this kind would be of use to Fleet officers, particularly to explorers."

Incredulous, Terry protested, "How can inner processes be affected except by drugs? Or—or do you mean with drug implants, sir?" He did not like that idea at all. And he hadn't thought Dr. Aldren was the sort who would like it, either.

"No drugs are involved," Derham assured him. "In fact, people trained in these skills don't need to take drugs for illness or risk factors. They don't need medical care at all except in case of serious injury. And if they consistently practice what they've been taught, they don't decline in old age."

It sounded too good to be true. "If this is possible, sir, why it is secret?" he protested. "It would be useful to everybody, not just Fleet."

"Yes, and the long-term goal is to offer it to the whole population, but it will take many generations to reach that stage," Derham said. "There are a number of reasons for secrecy, not all of which need concern you at present. But for one, the training is extremely challenging and requires a great deal of time and skill on the part of the instructor. The only people in the League currently qualified are Dr. Aldren and his wife. What do you think would happen if the public knew that it was possible and that only a privileged few were being given access to it?"

That was too obvious to require a reply. "Titan base has been chosen for the pilot project because it is small and isolated," Derham went on, "and because at present we have officers with free time on their hands. The training is being offered on a strictly voluntary basis; no one will be pressured in any way to take it. Whether you accept or not, it will not be entered in your record. Refusal won't have any adverse effect on your advancement. It's essential for you to understand this—we want only genuine volunteers."

There had to be a catch somewhere. "If these capabilities are for real, why would anybody refuse?" he inquired.

"Well," said Admiral Derham, "there are a couple of conditions that might put some people off. In the first place, as I've told you, those given this training gain permanent immunity to pain. But it's not a free lunch. The first stage of training is physically painful, extremely so. There are good reasons why it's got to be, most of which can't be explained to you in advance. You have to be willing to tolerate it."

Terry frowned. That everyone given this information would "volunteer" was a foregone conclusion, since the admiral must know that no young officer would let the CO think he, or she, was a coward. Certainly he himself wasn't going to be deterred by fear of pain. But he couldn't envision Dr. Aldren subjecting him to it. He was not the kind of man who would.

As if sensing this thought, Admiral Derham said, "One of the special qualities an instructor of these skills needs is the ability to inflict suffering on a volunteer without flinching, for the sake of what that person stands to gain. He or she has to be confident enough in judging people to be sure it's someone who will benefit, and who will later feel the gain was worth the price. It *is* worth it—I've been through the training myself, and I know."

"*You* have these capabilities, sir? Immunity to illness and pain?"

"I do, as well as certain other abilities to which the training often leads. So does my wife, who as you may know is a medical officer here under the jurisdiction of the Surgeon General's command. The ordeal essential to acquiring them is not something I would suggest to any-one without first experiencing it personally."

If Admiral Derham had done it, then so could he, what-ever it took, Terry resolved. He had never refused a chal-lenge or doubted his ability to meet it. There was no deci-sion to be made.

"Our XO, Commander Vargas, has also been through it," Derham went on. "He's the only other person here who's in the loop, apart from your fellow trainees, whose identity you won't know for the time being. And that brings up the other condition you need to consider. When pos-sible, only committed couples will be chosen for this train-ing because the changes it leads to would be impossible to hide from a partner. We don't have enough eligible couples on Titan, so we are accepting some singles, both men and women. But they've got to remain single, in all senses of the word, not just legally."

As Terry absorbed this, he continued, "I don't know what you've said to Dr. Aldren, that's confidential; but I assume, since he gave me the go-ahead to recruit you, that you're not in a current relationship."

Terry nodded. For once, maybe it was an asset.

"However," Derham said, "you'll undoubtedly want sex at some time in the future. And once you've had the train-ing, to be intimately involved with anyone who hasn't been vetted would be a violation of the ESA you signed."

Not knowing what to say, Terry was silent. "We will approve, and if possible train, any reliable person you ask us to," Derham went on. "But there can't be any impulsive liaisons, however brief. Again, I know Dr. Aldren would not have recommended someone to whom that restriction would be an undue burden. Am I making myself clear?"

"Yes, sir." The reason for Dr. Aldren's unworried reaction to his dislike of casual sex was now clear, too. What about explorer crews? he wondered. That might be awkward. But then, if he were able to do without medical care in an emergency, all members of the crew would know.

Again seeming to sense his thought, Derham said, "We will give priority to explorer crews when we expand the project, since they are among those to whom the training will be most useful. But what I'm telling you isn't just a matter of medical emergencies. I can't say any more now—in due course you will understand."

There was a great deal he didn't yet understand, Terry thought, and he had begun to suspect that there was a lot more to the project than had been revealed to him. He might be a fool to walk into it so blindly. And yet he trusted these two men, Admiral Derham and Dr. Aldren, above all others he had ever known. . . .

"You don't need to give me an answer right away," the CO said. "You can have some time to think about it."

"I don't need to think about it, sir," Terry declared. "I'm in."

"Okay, then. There's an opening in tonight's schedule, so report to Dr. Aldren at 2300, and don't eat anything beforehand, starting now." Admiral Derham added, "The first part is hell, but once you're past that, most of the training's fun. Good luck, Lieutenant."

4

THE TIME UNTIL 2300 dragged, and having been ordered to skip mess call, Terry was hungry. Why, he wondered, had he been told to report so late at night? The corridor lights had been lowered and he took a wrong turning before locating the remote office again. It occurred to him that with a secret project underway, they might indeed have hidden it deliberately.

He was greeted not by the doctor but by the silver-haired woman. "Hello, Terry," she said with warmth. "Welcome to the Flame project. We didn't meet officially when you came before, but my name is Roanna—I'm Aldren's wife."

Taking a closer look at her face, he realized that the silver hair, and Dr. Aldren's, might actually be due to old age, healthy and fit though they both appeared. Admiral Derham said that people who'd had the special training didn't decline—but that meant this couple must have received it long ago.

"Later, you'll be working with me as well as with Aldren," Roanna went on. Why, Terry wondered, would his wife refer to him by his surname when not including "Doctor"? Misinterpreting his puzzled expression, she added, "Both of us are qualified neurofeedback instructors."

"Neurofeedback?" He knew what it was, the real-time observation of data about one's own brain activity, but he had thought it was a therapy for specific medical disorders or, sometimes, for stress reduction.

"Yes, didn't Admiral Derham tell you? That's the technology we use, though of course there's more involved than technology. Most of our equipment is standard, but our input is more detailed and our software is far more sophisticated."

That was interesting. He had caught up on recent software development during his free hours on Titan, and had not encountered any techniques more sophisticated than what he'd been familiar with during his hacking days. If the innovative training had existed long enough for people to grow old, how could the software it required be advanced?

Roanna smiled. "You'll see what I mean when the output's shown to you. Right now, I'm going to take you back to the private lab—it's not quite as accessible as our main ones, which are next to the office."

The private lab proved to be not only relatively inaccessible but a mere cubicle with metal walls that looked all too solid. "Is that lead shielding?" Terry asked, growing more apprehensive by the minute as he noted the two large reclining chairs, equipped with straps, that nearly filled the space.

"Yes, but we don't use radiation," Roanna said. "This used to be part of the medical radiology department before that was expanded. It's ideal for the project because it's soundproof and has a control booth, so that someone can operate the computer without overhearing confidential conversations." She motioned for him to sit in one of the chairs. "Aldren will be with you in a few minutes," she told him, and left the room, closing the lead-lined door firmly behind her.

The few minutes turned out to be more like a few hours. There was no clock in the room and Terry had not looked at his watch when entering, but it was past 0130 by the time it dawned on him that his nerve was being tested.

That thought was a relief; he had been close to panic at the thought that he might have been forgotten and would remain trapped in this isolated cell forever. Well, if such tactics were to be used, he would be a good sport about it. He was sure, from his one short contact with Dr. Aldren, that whatever ordeals he was required to undergo would turn out well.

The pilot project was code-named Flame, Admiral Derham had told him, a name that had been chosen by Aldren. What was the significance of that? Probably none; code names were unrelated to the work to which they referred so as not to hint at what was going on. It was a clear indication that the pain ahead of him would involve neither actual flames nor heat of any kind. He swallowed, realizing that he was about to find out what it did involve.

Another hour passed before the doctor appeared, less casual than before, yet with the same underlying warmth. A thrill of confidence spread through Terry, close to what he always felt when about to lift off in a ship. The gloom of the past week fell away. It was all right that he was on Titan! Fate had brought him here to gain abilities he would never have acquired elsewhere.

"You've had time to reconsider, and so I needn't ask whether you're volunteering because you really want to," Dr. Aldren said. His voice was calm, but there was emotion back of it. As before, there was a connection between them, the thing he had never been able to feel with other people, the element that had been missing—as if their minds somehow touched.

"I know you're wondering what's going to happen to you," the doctor went on. "I can't tell you all of it yet. Part of it's secret even from participants, and besides that, there are phases of the initial instruction that depend on surprise. But I'll explain some of the theory. You may not be in a mood to absorb it right know; later we'll go over it in more detail."

"I'm aware that there'll be pain," Terry said. "You don't need to talk me into going through with it."

"The first few lessons are unavoidably harsh, and you have a right to know why." Aldren sat down in the other chair and continued soberly, "Terry, most of the things we wish our bodies weren't subject to—fear, sickness, and pain—are protections supplied by nature. They evolved because without them, animals and young children, and even primitive adults, wouldn't be able to avoid injury. There are rare cases of children born without pain receptors, and usually they don't live long; sometimes they even mutilate themselves. As for illness, most of what leads to it evolved because it was protective against more rapidly fatal illness, or is the result of processes vital in emergencies being continued when not needed. And so the physical reactions we experience as unpleasant are deeply embedded in our genes. Are you familiar with the concept of biological programming?"

"Yes— It's something like a computer program, I guess, though I don't know much about biology." He had almost said "Yes, sir," before remembering that with Aldren he was supposed to be informal.

"The point is that programming can be altered. Our biological programming, derived from our genes, determines our brains' reaction to stimuli—what neurotransmitters they produce, and so forth—and ordinarily we can't change that. But a way has been found by which we can learn to do it. How or when this happened I'm not at liberty to tell you, but it has been thoroughly proven. It is not experimental in itself; the only experiment here concerns its practicality for use in Fleet. The training you're about to undergo will teach you to override your biological programming consciously."

It made sense. "You mean so that my brain won't produce pain or sickness?"

"That's right. Suffering occurs wholly in the mind; it's an emotional alarm that makes injury impossible to ignore. It is not the same thing as the physical sensation produced by the injury. You will continue to feel the sensation, but it won't bother you any more than touching something harmless does. You'll be able to turn off the automatic alarm. And once you have learned to do that, you will be able to turn off other automatic reactions, such as a rapidly beating heart, when there is no good reason for them to continue. As a human adult, you can watch out for your body's safety without the built-in protections evolution gave to organisms that aren't equipped to judge."

"But if this is possible, why haven't adults been doing it for centuries?"

"There have been exceptional people who did do it—some yogis and shamans, for instance, and other practitioners of spiritual disciplines. And there have been cases where it happened spontaneously if a person had to function with seemingly superhuman endurance during a crisis, when action had priority over self-protection. That's the key factor—initially, it only happens during a crisis. So we have to create a crisis in order for you to learn."

"Pain?"

"Yes. In principle there are other ways of producing extreme stress, but pain is the fastest and safest. It can be stopped instantly when it has served its purpose, without lingering aftereffects. And since you'd want to be able to turn off pain eventually anyway, you have nothing to lose by dealing with it at the beginning."

"Will I really be able to turn it off? Permanently, I mean?

"Once you're past the learning stage, you'll be free of pain for the rest of your life, provided that you don't panic and fail to use the ability you've acquired. It's not automatic—you have to consciously shift into a special state of mind. That's because a person too sick or confused to do so might also be unaware of bodily harm."

"I'm ready to start learning, I guess," Terry declared, drawing a deep breath.

"I believe you are. But it's going to be a lot worse than you think, Terry. Long ago, way back in the twentieth century, researchers tried treating chronic pain with a form of neurofeedback. Their primitive equipment made it impractical, but that wasn't why the results weren't more spectacular. They only did it with relatively mild pain. One might think that the way to learn such a skill would be to start with mild pain and progress gradually, but that's not how it works. After all, for it to work with mild pain would defeat the purpose for which pain evolved."

Terry shivered. He'd been warned, of course, that it wouldn't be mild. . . .

"There are other things involved without which the earlier researchers couldn't have succeeded," Aldren went on. "Better brain scanning techniques, more advanced software, and some factors you're not ready to understand yet that make it essential for us to maximize stress. But there's no getting around the fact that the pain has to be truly extreme."

"Well," said Terry determinedly, "If other people have gotten through it, I can."

"Many have, and so have both Roanna and I. I wouldn't subject anyone to this if I hadn't been through myself."

That was what Admiral Derham had said. Despite himself, Terry was beginning to worry. He'd never questioned his own ability to face pain, and this would be a bad time to start. Nevertheless, he felt queasy and he was glad he hadn't eaten.

After removing his shirt as instructed, he sat silent while Aldren attached sensors to his chest, fitted a complicated-looking helmet over his head, and then fastened the chair's straps, immobilizing him. Finally, he brought forth an odd-looking metal device which he placed between Terry's left arm and the armrest, binding it tightly with more straps, padded ones.

"This is a neural stimulator," he said, "It's harmless— it won't injure you in any way. You'll doubt that when you feel its effects, but I give you my word that your arm won't be damaged."

With a rush of fear Terry grasped the import of what he'd been told. Suffering occurred in the mind, Aldren had said. A crisis would also have to take place in his mind. He would not be able to simply grit his teeth and endure physical sensations. . . .

"There are two kinds of fear," the doctor said. "There's rational fear, which we feel when we know there is danger of being harmed. You know I will not harm you, so you've been thinking that you won't be seriously afraid. But there's also emotional fear, which isn't dependent on real danger. All sorts of things can generate it; people with phobias, for instance, feel genuine, agonizing fear about things that don't bother normal people at all. One way or another, their brains have gotten rewired to produce it in those situations, and with the right kind of therapy, that can be reversed. The fear of physical pain, however, is part of the biological programming we were talking about, entirely apart from the dangers from which it protects. It can't be overcome just by deciding to be brave. You're going to feel it much more intensely than you can imagine beforehand, and knowing that the pain is harmless isn't going to help."

Abruptly, Terry became sickeningly aware that this was true. A wave of fear struck as if rushing in from some external source; his stomach heaved and he felt sweat drenching him and dampening his pants. Or was it sweat? So far, maybe, but if he couldn't get a grip on himself. . . . *Oh, God*, he thought. To be humiliated in the presence of the man whose opinion he most valued. . . .

Desperately he reached out with his mind, searching for the magical sense of a strange bond with Aldren—and it was not there. He felt a barrier more unbreachable than the one he felt with everyone else he knew. He was alone, confronted by terror he did not know how to combat. Surely it wasn't supposed to be like this! His mouth dry, he barely managed to get out words: "You—you're going to tell me some special way to deal with it, aren't you?"

"Absolutely. But not tonight, Terry. First you have to go through the crisis."

"It lasts *all night*?" He had assumed this instruction would be given to him at the height of the crisis, only a few minutes from now.

"I can't say in advance how long it lasts. That depends on data about your brain that's being recorded by the scanners in your helmet, and on the monitoring of your heart as a precaution. Of course it won't last any longer than you're willing to endure it. This training is entirely voluntary. I'll be here with you, and you can end the pain at any time simply by telling me to stop."

"I can?" He had thought he was willing, but if it turned out to be really bad, maybe he should take a short break before continuing. . . .

"You can end it," Aldren repeated. "But if you quit before it's over, you're out of the project. You won't get a second chance."

He had no choice, then. Terry felt almost glad. He was afraid of what he might say if given a choice.

The light in the little chamber dimmed, leaving only the bright glow of the LEDs on the remote in Aldren's hand. Then the pain hit him. It was so overwhelming that Terry nearly shrieked aloud. Never, never had he imagined anything like this! He gasped for breath. It couldn't be true that he would not be injured, because his arm felt seared to the bone—certainly it must be charred under the stimulator's metal plate. He had been misled somehow . . . yet Dr. Aldren *wouldn't*. . . .

Determinedly, he began a silent count. One . . . two . . . three . . . twenty-nine . . . thirty . . . By the time he reached sixty he could no longer keep the numbers straight in his head. There was a limit to the number of seconds this could go on, surely. Perhaps his time sense was distorted, perhaps he hadn't been counting seconds—it seemed more like minutes.

The pain didn't let up. It intensified.

Terry's mind was hazy; he was close to passing out, and wished wholeheartedly that he would. Yet what if that was considered quitting? He would *not* quit! Though being in the project didn't seem to matter anymore, his self-respect mattered. He knew he could not live with himself if he let this ordeal defeat him.

But in the next moment terror flooded his mind, because for the first time he realized that a time was coming when nothing would matter except stopping the pain. He wasn't thinking clearly; he lost touch with his surroundings and he was falling, falling into a dark whirlpool that was about to suck him in. In desperation he cried out silently, *Please, please . . . don't let me be destroyed this way, I can't quit, but what good will it do if my mind is destroyed?*

As if in reply, a new thought came to him. *You will not be destroyed, only changed. A mind-altering crisis is what we're aiming for.*

For an instant Terry felt reassured. And then the pain intensified again, and he lost control of whether he was thinking or screaming, but in the next instant the burning stopped abruptly and he realized with despair that though he had not knowingly given in, he had gasped aloud that he'd had enough.

5

THE AFTERMATH WAS agonizing, not physically, for the pain was completely gone, but emotionally. At first Terry was conscious only of rage—rage at Dr. Aldren for betraying his trust, at Admiral Derham for talking him into volunteering for a manifestly inhuman experiment, at Fleet for sending him to a planet so deficient in scope for his abilities that boredom had led him to volunteer. But once he calmed down a little, he became aware that what he was really feeling was rage against himself.

He knew underneath where the blame lay, and it wasn't with Aldren or Derham, both of whom had given him clear warning. Terry was engulfed by regret and shame. He hadn't suspected that he might fail. It hurt to know that he had lost his chance to gain capabilities he now saw as infinitely desirable, and that he would no longer have the companionship or even the respect of Dr. Aldren. It was still worse to realize that his concept of himself had been false.

He had never doubted his own courage. He had been confident that he could do anything he set out to do, whether it was gaining entry to a secured Net installation, landing a spacecraft, or jumping a starship to an uncharted system. That confidence had been the only thing in his life he could count on—and now he could never count on it again.

He lay back on the now fully reclined second chair, on which he'd collapsed after using the sealed room's screened-off lavatory facilities, unmoving, staring up at the low lead-lined ceiling. He had been left alone again, and he no longer cared if he was ever found. There was nothing ahead to hope for. He'd been told that neither success nor failure in the Flame project would go on his record, but whatever reason had caused him to be pulled off explorer duty still existed; he might never have been able to return to it in any case. Now, he was no longer sure he wanted to. He might not trust himself with command of an explorer now. There was no way of knowing what sort of crisis might arise on an explorer mission, and he had learned that he was not very good at getting through crises.

After a long time Dr. Aldren came back and sat in the chair beside Terry, turning to face him. "It's natural to be disappointed in yourself," he said, as usual grasping feelings that hadn't been purposely revealed. "The important thing now is what you're going to do about it."

"There's nothing I can do," Terry said bitterly. He could sense that Aldren was genuinely sympathetic, that amazingly, his cowardice had not changed the man's previous approval to scorn. But sympathy was not what he wanted.

"You'll get another flight assignment before long. And after all, until yesterday you never expected to gain any extraordinary capabilities."

"I'm not the same as I was yesterday."

"No. Will you be happy once you get back to flying, Terry?"

"I think you know I won't. You know what I feel—you always have." The lost connection between them was back in full force. He found that in spite of what had happened, he still trusted Aldren, and if it had been possible to wish for anything, he'd have wished to know just what it was that made contact with him so special.

"The worst thing wasn't the pain, was it? It was finding out that you couldn't handle it indefinitely—that you're not sure you could handle it at all a second time."

Terry nodded miserably. What good could it do to put this into words?

Slowly, thoughtfully, Dr. Aldren asked, "What would you do if you ever crashed a ship? Would you stop flying, leave Fleet?"

"Of course not. No pilot worth his salt would stop flying after a crash. You make another flight as soon as possible, before you have time to lose your nerve."

"Like getting back on a horse."

"A horse?" Terry had never paid much to historical vids involving horses.

"In ancient times, it was common knowledge that a rider should get on a horse again soon after being thrown."

"Well, it's too bad it doesn't apply to things like last night's crisis."

"It does apply, Terry."

"What? You said I wouldn't get a second chance."

"It's true that no one who quits during the initial session can continue in the project. But you're not thinking about the project now. You're simply afraid that if you ever had to face severe pain again, you'd crack up before it even started."

This was undeniable, so Terry said nothing.

"It would help, wouldn't it, if you were free of that fear—if you knew you *could* face it, that you could take on whatever fate threw your way, even if it didn't always turn out well?"

"But I can't know, because it's over and done with. Unless— Oh, my God," Terry burst out, sensing more than had been stated aloud. "You're saying I should let you subject me to pain again just to prove I'm capable of consenting."

"It would a wise thing to do," Aldren agreed. "It would take only a few minutes out of your life, and you've seen that it doesn't harm your body. It couldn't make you feel any worse than you already do."

The idea was appalling. He must be out of his mind to be seriously considering such a thing. Yet if he didn't do it, he would lose what remained of Aldren's respect for him. And it was true it couldn't make things worse. Even if he broke down again, he would at least know that he wouldn't retreat from whatever might arise in the future.

In a daze, Terry found himself getting back into the chair, sitting still while the sensors and helmet were attached, and the neural stimulator. He didn't much care what was done to him. He would probably pass out this time, or even scream; but it would make no difference. The point of this was simply to consent to it, not to display courage he now knew he lacked.

Relax, he told himself, and it seemed as if the thought came from outside. He was detached from it. *Relaxing will help. This will be easier if you let go and quit trying to be heroic. The sooner you reach your limit, the sooner you'll know you can trust yourself not to stop short of it.*

The pain wasn't as bad as before, which was, Terry felt, misplaced mercy on Aldren's part. If it was made too easy he would never be sure he could have stuck it out even as long as last time. "Don't hold back," he said, finding he had breath enough to speak.

"I'm not going to," Aldren said. "But this time I want to show you some neurofeedback. Roanna's in the control booth operating the computer."

To Terry's amazement, the entire metal wall opposite the chair lit up in a blaze of color. The image wasn't a brain scan; he knew what those looked like. Rather, it was a complex, hypnotic pattern of moving lines.

"Our software interprets the brain data," Aldren went on. "It shows a symbolic representation of the mental state you're in. But this one isn't real-time—it's a recording from last night. The intensity of the pain is shown by the color, in rainbow sequence starting with violet."

"Then why is it yellow instead of red?" Terry asked. He was sure that last night's pain had been close to the maximum that could be produced.

"Last night was in the mid-range," Aldren informed him. "I'm going to switch to a real-time display now. What color do you think it will be?"

"Green, maybe even blue."

"You're wrong, Terry. Take a look." The image faded and was replaced by a new pattern in brilliant, glowing orange.

"That's got to be wrong," he gasped, feeling himself weaken at the thought that it might not be. "There's less pain today, not more."

"There is more in terms of physical stimulation. But you are not fighting it now, and your brain is reacting differently. This is lesson number one—fighting your biological programming does not work. Accepting your feelings does."

"Why are you telling me this when it's too late?" Terry demanded.

"Because it's something you need to know in order to absorb the training."

Bewildered, Terry whispered, "But you said—"

"I said that no one who quits gets a second chance. But you didn't quit, Terry. You simply cracked up after your brain had reached a state where you no longer had the power to decide. The data readout on my remote showed that."

"You left me here for hours, blaming myself?" Terry burst out angrily.

"I hated to," Aldren told him, "but it was a necessary part of the crisis. You had to reach the point of not caring what happened to you in order to stop fighting for control long enough to discover that pain lessens when you let go. That's something no one with any power of endurance can grasp without a demonstration."

"Yet there wouldn't have been a demonstration if I hadn't decided to come back."

"No. Coming back was the real test, the one you've just passed."

"You mean you planned it this way all along? But then how do the rest of the trainees learn, the ones who don't crack up the first time?"

The pain ceased instantly as Aldren turned off the stimulator. "You're missing the point," he said. "It works the same way for everybody. The first session continues until the brain data shows me that no further reaction will be voluntary—and there is always a second session, though some people aren't as easily persuaded as you were. With most of them I don't have to use such high intensities as I did with you, because they can't tolerate as much to begin with."

"What if someone refuses to go through it again?" Terry asked grimly.

"That never happens. To leave a person with the memory of intolerable pain, not knowing how to prevent suffering in the future, would be psychologically damaging. It would violate my promise to do no harm."

"You just force them, then?"

"Of course not. But for a volunteer to back out would

mean I'd done a poor job of choosing trainees," Aldren said, smiling. "I don't begin the process with anyone I'm not already sure of."

6

AFTER A SHOWER and four hours of sleep in a room adjacent to Aldren's office, Terry felt better, though still somewhat depleted by hunger—and still very confused. How could the doctor have been sure of how he'd react in a crisis when he hadn't known himself? "I—I'm too stirred up to know my own mind, I guess," he'd admitted.

"Yes. Your brain has been jarred into a state in which ingrained mind patterns can be broken, which facilitates this kind of learning. So it would be better to go straight ahead today than to wait. The more stress you're under, the easier it will be to let go of old habits of thinking."

"I've got to report to work," Terry had protested. "I've already been away from my quarters overnight, which is going to be hard to explain."

"That's been taken care of. As far as anyone knows, you have been admitted to sick bay with a new virus that's going around, which only Admiral Derham's wife, who's the medical officer in charge of the isolation ward, is allowed to treat. It won't be questioned."

"Okay," Terry had said. After all he'd been through, he wanted to find out as soon as possible what had been gained by it.

"The next session will be different," Aldren had declared. "You'll be given feedback and other kinds of help. You're ahead of the game because you held out longer than average the first time, so that by now you're already able to deal with pain severe enough to trigger a breakthrough. And you happen to have other qualities that not all trainees possess. I can't promise, but I believe that for you it will take only once more to master the trick of not suffering."

Roanna provided him with clean clothes and offered him coffee, but no food; he was shaking by the time they got back to the small hidden lab. He tried not to think ahead while he was being strapped into the chair. What was about to happen would happen, and there was no use worrying about how he would meet it.

"You're going to be fine from now on," Aldren told him, "as long as you remember what you've learned about relaxing. It's a paradox—in order to gain voluntary control of processes that are normally involuntary, you must be willing to lose control in the sense most familiar to you and use your mind in a different way."

"Like switching to another computer program?"

"There's an analogy, but minds are not computers. The key to entering the necessary state of consciousness is volition, which is something computers don't have."

"Neither do people, according to what I've read. Free choice is just an illusion," Terry pointed out, glad to be distracted from his apprehension.

"That theory has been dominant for a very long time," Aldren agreed, "which is one reason why the skills you're about to learn weren't developed sooner. It's true that living beings are biologically programmed, but as I told you last night, what we do here overrides that programming. Only volition makes this possible."

With a sigh, he added, "The notion that we don't have volition is not merely false—it is potentially dangerous. There are people who don't want to believe that human minds have abilities beyond those that fit their theories. Some of them are powerful people. Some might resort to violence to suppress any evidence that they are wrong. I hope you'll never encounter such a situation, but it's conceivable that you will. One of the reasons for the secrecy of this project is to minimize that possibility."

Sensing deep feelings in Aldren, Terry burst out,

"There's more to it than I've been told, isn't there? The Flame project, I mean."

"Yes. You are not yet authorized to know its full purpose."

A plan that will give us a chance to help spread these abilities? Terry wondered. To do more with our lives than just hope there'll be something to discover if we fly far enough?

Aldren continued fervently, "Picture a time when nearly everyone is free of pain, when there is hardly any sickness, when people of all worlds sense and respect each other's inner feelings. When they have full use of all the capabilities humans are born with, some even greater than they're now aware of."

Puzzled, Terry asked, "Why would abolishing pain and sickness make people respect each other's feelings? I'd think it would be the other way around. If they don't care about all the suffering there is now, which a lot of them don't, why would they if there were less of it?"

"Well," Aldren said, "altering the brain's programming has far-reaching effects. People who've learned to do it discover more powers within themselves than the ability to control their physical reactions."

Awed, Terry whispered, "Will I discover . . . more powers? Besides those I know about?"

"Yes, I'm sure you will. Right now, though, we'll focus on proving that you do have volition, because it is the key to all the rest."

To Terry's astonishment, Aldren proceeded to sit down in the second chair, put on a helmet of his own, and rest his arm casually on what looked like a second stimulator. "This is what we call working on dual," he explained. "Most of your training, with me and with Roanna, will be done like this. The aim is for you to make your neurofeedback pattern match mine."

"You mean so that my brain's reacting in the same way?"

"That's right. How much do you know about altered states of consciousness, Terry?" Aldren asked.

"Well, I know drugs produce them."

"Yes, but so do many other things. Not all states are as dramatic or as destructive as those produced by drugs. Whenever your brain is operating in a different way from the ordinary rational mode of thought, that's an altered state, and there are far more distinctions than are traditionally considered separate. For example, sexual arousal is an altered state—you are not fully rational while you're having sex. Severe pain also alters the way your mind works, and so do other crisis situations."

"But in a crisis, I can't stay in control, so how does a crisis help?"

"It shakes you up, makes your brain receptive to new patterns of functioning so that you become familiar with what they feel like and can later reproduce them. Essentially that's what drugs do, which is why people sometimes have bad trips long after the drug has worn off. The states you experience with our guidance, however, will be good ones."

Terry frowned. "How can I experience good ones if I'm in pain?" He was resigned to the obvious fact that he would be; his arm was already hurting just in anticipation.

"You'll see. I will lead you into a state where you don't suffer from it, which you'll later be able to enter at will. And that will teach you how to switch states so that you can learn others without needing to be in a crisis."

"Merely by somehow making my neurofeedback pattern match yours," Terry said skeptically.

"Exactly. Our software portrays states of consciousness symbolically, using data from brain scans that would not be visually distinguishable without processing. That's needed not only for matching, but to remind you how specific states feel. Eventually you'll be able to enter them by visualizing their patterns in your mind."

That seemed unlikely, Terry thought, but he resolved to do what he was told to do without trying to figure it out. At first he was shown only his own pattern—fascinating, like a fractal music visualization but without motion. Following instructions, he switched between tension and full relaxation, induced by the memory of a happy afternoon during his Yellowstone camping trip. And the distinctive shapes of the image on the wall shifted, so that after a few minutes of watching he would have been able to tell from a recording how he had been feeling from one moment to the next.

"These are ordinary, normal states of consciousness," Aldren said. "Do you remember, from this morning, what the pattern looked like when you were in pain?"

Terry nodded. It had been jagged and less steady, especially in the recorded one, and of course differently colored; the normal patterns were multicolored instead of the monochrome used to indicate intensity of neural stimulation.

"Okay, we'll try that again, starting on blue." The feedback pattern turned briefly to gray, and Terry steeled himself for what was coming. The pain was mild when it hit; still the sharp jagged lines appeared, and the harder he tried to alter them, the more erratic they became.

"Can't you make it look more like the normal pattern?" Aldren said. "This isn't very much stimulation; in a minute or two you'll have to deal with a lot more—"

He'd never be able to do this, Terry thought. There wasn't any *way* to do it, and worse pain was coming . . . what if he cracked up again. . . .

The pattern went crazy.

As it shifted from blue to green, he gritted his teeth and swore to himself that he *would* master himself, he would not let Aldren see that he was close to panic; it was only pain, after all, and he'd been able to stand it last time. But he could see from the pattern before him that he was failing.

"Terry," Aldren said quietly. "You've lost sight of what you learned this morning. Stoic endurance doesn't work, remember."

He struggled with the thought. No, you weren't supposed to be stoic, you were supposed to let go and stop caring what happened . . . but he *did* care. He was no longer in despair, and now learning to do what was expected of him mattered a great deal. He tried to calm himself, tried to believe some magical way of controlling the pattern would be revealed to him. It steadied a little, but not much.

"Make it look like the normal pattern," Aldren commanded.

"I can't," Terry admitted.

"No, you can't. Nobody can directly control these patterns. This is lesson number two, Terry. Brain functioning cannot be changed by force of will. Willpower is, in fact, counterproductive. You have to decide what you intend and then just *let go* and allow it to happen."

"But it won't happen if I'm not trying."

"Yes, it will, once you grasp the concept. We'll go on dual now, and I'll show you."

A second pattern appeared beside his, similar but not so erratic. "Just watch," Aldren said, "and imagine your pattern being as much like it as possible. But don't *try* to change it—just envision it already happening."

As Terry watched, he began to feel very strange. He sensed that he was drawing on some inner source of guidance. He didn't know how he was doing it, but as the color brightened to yellow, the similarity between his pattern and Aldren's grew.

"It's—awesome," he said. "But . . . there's still a lot of pain . . . am I supposed to be getting immune?"

"Not yet; that's the next step. Immunity to pain is a whole new pattern, unlike the one we're in right now. It is a different state of consciousness."

"But you—you're immune, aren't you, and your

pattern's like mine," Terry protested. He had assumed that the stimulators were cross-connected and that Aldren was in the state that prevented suffering.

"I have the ability to enter that state," Aldren said, "but it's a matter of volition. I'm not in it right now because you would be unable to match an abrupt change. We have to do it gradually."

"You mean you're *feeling* the pain? Like a normal person does?"

"I'm used to it," Aldren said calmly. "It's part of an instructor's job. I don't mind because it's not being forced on me by internal programming—I'm free to choose."

The pain intensified as the patterns crept toward red. "Keep your eyes on them," Aldren ordered. "You're doing fine, you've learned to follow while we've been talking. If this doesn't work the first time I shift, don't worry—no harm will be done if we have to try again."

Terry was dizzy with pain; he felt on the verge of cracking up again. "It's okay if you do," Aldren continued. "You'll reach a point where you *have* to escape somehow. When that happens, don't fight it. Just watch the patterns and go where mine leads you."

He was falling, falling into blackness, but though he could no longer see the room surrounding him, the patterns stood out as if tangible, so bright that he had to struggle to keep his eyes open. He could no longer hear Aldren's voice, but somehow he knew what was being said to him: *You're okay. Nothing terrible is happening to you. Follow me, and we'll be changed, the pain won't hurt anymore. . . .*

It was as if he were suspended in space outside a ship, the familiar stars surrounding him, but with an instrument panel glowing before his eyes, demanding attention. He was supposed to dock somehow. When the pattern on the two halves of the panel matched he would be docked, and safe. It was a shifting pattern now and desperately he reached out with his mind, trying not to lose it, trying to bring it back in focus, like gaining clear sight again after a spell of double vision. . . .

And then, abruptly, the pain was gone.

Not gone, exactly; he could still tell his arm was afire, but it didn't seem to matter. He was no longer suffering from it, in fact he felt *good*. Terry's spirits soared. It was like being high—not that he had ever been high on drugs, but this was how he imagined it would feel. Except that his mind was clear. He was back in the small room and could see the patterns as they were, just images on a wall, but different, now, still red, but not shaped like any he'd previously been shown. As he watched, the red monochrome broke into a thousand shades of color covering the whole spectrum, and he realized that his arm was no longer being stimulated, although it made no difference to him one way or another. He knew he would not suffer if it started again.

Does this make up for the bad part, Terry? Aldren didn't speak aloud, but the question was clear.

Oh, yes! I've heard people can get high on pain—

It wasn't the pain that did it. It was ending *the pain simply by shifting gears, so to speak. By using the power latent within human minds.*

He looked at Aldren, knowing from his face, and even more from the emotion he sensed in him, that he too felt elation. *Will this last?* he asked hopefully.

"The high will fade, but you'll be able to reach it again. Not just by ending pain, but by using some of the other skills we'll teach you once the focus provided by pain is no longer needed."

7

BACK IN THE office, Roanna laid out an enticing variety of food. Nothing had ever tasted so good, Terry thought. He was still floating, and even the fact that he was on Titan no longer seemed depressing. It was even better than flying; more than anything else he wanted to learn what his mind was capable of.

And yet. . . . "I don't understand *how* I learned," he said. "Just watching a pattern—it can't be as simple as that! The computer could generate those patterns, and people wouldn't stop suffering just by looking at them."

"No," Aldren agreed. He paused thoughtfully. "Terry, I'm going to tell you something I don't mention to other trainees this soon. Some of them would find it frightening, but I don't believe you will, and I think that in view of your past problems in relating to people, you have a right to know."

Terry waited, puzzled.

"The skill you've just grasped, and the other controls over your body and brain that will follow, can't be explained in words," Aldren went on, "and so they can't be learned from ordinary methods of instruction. The preliminary stress and the neurofeedback are necessary, but alone they're not enough. There is a third factor."

"There's got to be," Terry agreed. "It was strange, almost uncanny—I found I could make some sort of adjustment in my mind that I can't describe."

"That's because you learned not from the patterns, which are only symbols of the state you're in, but from what I communicated to you."

"But I didn't hear you talking."

"I didn't say anything out loud," Aldren told him. "Knowledge of this kind can be transferred only directly from mind to mind. By telepathy."

"Telepathy? You mean ESP?" Terry said incredulously. "But that's just fantasy—there's no such thing."

"So modern society would have you believe. As soon as scientific researchers started to zero on psi powers, the repression of their existence increased—but that's a long story. First you need to know that the training is based on a telepathic link between instructor and student, without which it could not be made to work. That's why these extraordinary skills are not more common, and one of the reasons why they must be kept secret."

"Keeping that part secret isn't going to be hard. People would laugh at anyone who claimed to be telepathic."

"Or worse."

"Worse than being thought crazy?"

"People with psi abilities have often been persecuted, Terry. During some periods of history those suspected of witchcraft were burned alive."

Aldren meant this to be taken seriously; Terry sensed that he was deeply troubled, unbelievable though the whole idea seemed. "I don't see how we could have been in contact by psi," he protested. "You're saying you're a telepath, I guess—but *I'm* not."

"Oh, but you are. You are exceptionally psi-gifted, as I have known since the first day we talked. That's why you were able to match patterns much faster than average."

Terry was speechless.

"Everybody has latent telepathic ability," Aldren stated. "It's had a far greater influence on history than is widely known. But most telepathy occurs on an unconscious level. In modern society conscious awareness of it rarely arises spontaneously. Because Roanna and I are aware and can use it purposefully, we're able to provide silent help during training, as I did during your second and third sessions. Without that help, you couldn't have grasped the new way of responding to pain."

"You—*read minds*?" It must be true, Terry realized with awe. All along, Aldren had shown an uncanny ability to understand things that had not been said.

"'Read' isn't the right way to put it. I can't invade people's privacy; it is always two-way communication. If consciously or subconsciously a person wants to tell me something, or vice versa, it doesn't have to be expressed in words."

"How can it be two-way when the other person isn't doing it?"

"As I said, it's unconscious. But under certain circumstances, in contact with a strong telepath, the ability to use it consciously can be awakened. The degree of aptitude varies, and yours is very close to the surface. You have always sensed a connection between us, haven't you?"

Yes, Terry thought, beginning to understand. The mysterious link that had so perplexed him . . . the thing he had never experienced with anyone else . . .

But you wanted to experience it with them. And when you didn't, when they didn't respond, you drew back, feeling a lack you could not define. It hurt, and you avoided situations where you might be hurt again.

Aldren had not said this aloud.

"The isolation is nearly over for you, Terry," Aldren continued. "Others who receive this training will become aware of their telepathic ability, though they are less ready to acknowledge it than you are and it won't happen as quickly. Stress enhances it; that's one of the reasons why we use stressful methods, because without the telepathic connection it would be impossible for anyone to learn the rest of the skills."

Slowly Terry absorbed this. To feel connected to others, at last. . . .

"Another thing that enhances it," Aldren said, "is sex. That's why we don't allow you to have sex with anyone not cleared for the secret. A person in whom telepathic ability has been awakened could unknowingly reveal it to a partner, since during sex telepaths fully merge their minds."

"Merge them? Know what each other are thinking?"

"Yes, and feeling too, even in the physical sense. Having once had this experience, few people have any interest in partners incapable of it."

With a surge of excitement Terry pieced things together. This must be what he'd sensed was missing. . . .

"You had too much latent ESP not to feel the lack of a link where it should have been strongest," Aldren agreed. "And because you did, you pulled back from even the ordinary unconscious sharing that couples in love—or mere friends, for that matter—take for granted."

Terry drew breath. He had always believed there must be more to it than what he had felt.

"Has the ability to use telepathy consciously been—awakened in me, then?" he asked. "By communicating with you under stress?"

Aldren nodded. "Some people would be disturbed by knowing this about themselves," he declared, "but I think to you it will be a relief. And there are more psi powers than telepathy. You'll be taught more, such as remote viewing, and possibly some a bit further advanced."

"Why would these powers disturb anyone?" Terry asked. "Surely, if they're latent in everybody, they can't be harmful."

"They can be misused, just like any other human ability, so I'm careful who I train," Aldren said. "Psi isn't something to play around with, and its effects when used for destruction can be very terrible—legends about evil sorcerers have a basis in reality. But that's not what people are afraid of. The average person in this society, especially a scientifically-oriented person, has a deep-seated, innate fear of possessing psi powers, which is why the evidence of their existence has been rejected and suppressed."

"I don't understand," Terry said, perplexed. He could sense that this wasn't just a casual conversation; he was being told something that for Aldren had deep significance.

"People's impressions of their relationship to the world, and of control over their own actions and interactions with others, depend on being confident that things work in the way they've learned to depend on since babyhood," Aldren explained. "If they are forced to recognize that reality is fundamentally different, they lose that confidence—and that's scary, so scary that some among them will go to any lengths to keep from having to acknowledge that the beliefs they grew up with were wrong. The secrecy of our project is a necessary protection from such fanatics. If it becomes generally known that a group of us are actively developing psi capabilities, we may someday be in danger."

"Physical danger, you mean?" Terry exclaimed in astonishment.

"What people fear, they often try to destroy. The further the project is spread, the greater the chance that the secret will get out. In the future, if you choose to stay involved later in life—" Aldren broke off. "It's too soon to talk about that. But not too soon for you to learn something about the crisis humankind will soon be facing. You told me you read a lot, that you're familiar with the standard knowledgebase available on every world's Net, so you've probably come across information about ancient cultures that took things we'd call paranormal seriously—magic, spirits, and so forth?"

"Sure, all kinds of superstitious stuff. In some cultures people really believed in that sort of thing. In fact even in our society, as recently as a couple of centuries ago some used to believe in nonsense like witches and ghosts and mediums who could communicate with spirits."

"A lot of it was nonsense, but not all. Some such things were actual manifestations of psi. Mediums, for instance—those who weren't frauds—were gifted telepaths who genuinely believed they obtained information from spirits when actually it came via unconscious telepathy from their clients. And a lot of so-called magic involved psi capabilities with which you're not yet familiar. The various metaphorical explanations used to describe them, though not literally true, represented real phenomena."

Fascinated, Terry listened as Aldren continued,

"Throughout history belief in the paranormal was common, though it was a minority outlook in modern Western civilization, which dominated Earth. Then during late twentieth century and early twenty-first, more and more people began to get interested in it and a few scientists pursued it to the extent of gathering evidence that became increasingly difficult to ignore."

"I've never seen any mention of that," protested Terry.

"No. Because by the end of the twenty-first century, a strong reaction had set in, something that had happened on a lesser scale many times before. When it began to look even to mainstream researchers as if psi might be real, people's unconscious fear of losing confidence in their orientation took over. The majority became even more vehemently opposed to the idea of ESP than before, and suppressed all knowledge of it—not through censorship but through denial and ridicule. Researchers dared not go public lest it destroy their careers. It was said that such experimentation as had seemed successful had not panned out. Psi was dismissed as an immature notion that had been outgrown, interesting only as an element of fantasy fiction."

Terry admitted uncomfortably, "That's what I always thought it was, from what I read."

Aldren went on, "It was a good thing that for hundreds of years the planetary civilization of Earth did focus on technology to the exclusion of psi. That was essential for attaining interstellar travel, without which our species couldn't survive when conditions of Earth get even worse than they are now. But over the long term, human progress requires development of both technology and mind powers—neither is sufficient without the other. Creating a technological civilization that incorporates psi is the next step in our evolution. It's going to be a slow and painful process, Terry—and as I said, dangerous for those of us involved. There will be resistance that may turn violent. We must begin in a very small way, and it may look like a hopeless cause. Yet if no one takes the first step, humankind will stagnate and eventually die out. And so some of us have committed ourselves to making a start."

8

FROM THEN ON Terry spent an hour a day using neurofeedback, either on dual with Roanna or alone to practice, in one of several more accessible rooms that were similarly equipped. No pain was involved in these sessions after he mastered the skill of shifting states on his own. He was now capable of matching an instructor's mind-pattern without it, though his mind tended to wander at first when not forced by suffering to give the patterns his full attention.

He missed working with Aldren, who was busy teaching less talented trainees who needed his guidance the most. Roanna was not quite as strong a telepath. But while the instruction itself was on an unconscious level, Terry found he could sense her feelings and sometimes her thoughts, just as she was sensitive to his. To interact with someone in this way was a joy to him. In the past he had been comfortable only with computers and ships, from which he didn't expect the response that had been lacking in his human contacts.

From Roanna, he learned to regulate his temperature so that it no longer depended on whether his surroundings were hot or cold—this, she said, was one of the simplest skills. After that he learned to control his heart rate. And he learned to enter other states he could not detect except through the mind-patterns, which she said controlled the production of neurotransmitters by his brain and thus would affect his health. "Often neurotransmitters that enable the body to handle stress keep on being produced after the stress is over," she told him.

"And when continued too long, they cause changes leading to illness and aging. If you purposely turn them off, so to speak, whenever you're not facing a crisis, your body won't develop chronic disease. In time, this will become nearly automatic, so that you don't have to keep thinking about it. A new pattern will replace the biologically-programmed one."

At first Terry feared that his frequent absences from his quarters would be noticed, but he soon found that a system had been set up to make them appear normal. Neurofeedback therapy for relaxation was offered to everyone and since most people on Titan felt stressed, many took advantage of it; going to the lab wasn't considered strange. Even his roommate Drew Larssen went sometimes, though he more often stayed late in the rec room with an attractive fellow-officer named Mikaela Orlov. Terry didn't know which people were in the project, for by an unbroken rule, neurofeedback sessions were strictly private.

Life on Titan became bearable even between his sessions, for the crowding had been relieved by the arrival of a cruiser, which remained in orbit while many of the current ensigns and their instructors lived on board. Drew said they were giving it a thorough maintenance check in preparation for a long training cruise. It was unusual, he added, for this to be done anywhere but at a major ops center; evidently it had been arranged because there were so many extra people at the base. Cruiser duty was a common first assignment for ensigns upon completing their tour on Titan, though normally such a large ship would not have come to pick them up. Terry had seen no sign of the rest of its crew; perhaps the lack of recreational opportunities on Titan had kept them from taking shore leave.

Seeing Terry's fascination with the neurofeedback software, Roanna allowed him to study the source code. This was not secret, and he was able to route it to the computer in his quarters. Soon he was running it with simulated brain input, which became nearly as great an obsession as hacking had been in his younger days. He had plenty of time free, since with much of the ensigns' training taking place aboard the cruiser, there were not many simulated exercises to be programmed at the base. Terry had stopped wondering why he had been sent to a planet where there was little if any meaningful work for him, mainly because he was no longer sorry that it had happened.

He had an occasional neurofeedback session with Aldren, and became more and more curious about his past. It was obvious that he and Roanna had considerable experience in teaching the mind skills. There must have been a previous project elsewhere—but not in Fleet, to which he'd been told it was new and experimental, and what other organization could have been in a position to keep it secret? He was so used to Aldren's slight accent, which Roanna shared, that he no longer noticed it; but it suggested that they'd come from some backwater colony.

He still felt closer to Aldren than he ever had to anyone else. It had been explained to him that a permanent bond existed between people who had been in contact during extreme stress, and that it was even stronger with telepaths than with others. This had begun to form as far back as his initial training session, Roanna said; Aldren had literally suffered with him through their unconscious link and had found it agonizing to withdraw all telepathic support, which he'd done purposely to prevent the session from being unnecessarily prolonged. Terry fervently hoped that their contact wouldn't end when his training was complete, unless, of course, he was sent back to exploring—which he'd begun to think was unlikely to happen soon.

After several weeks, during one of their infrequent sessions together, Aldren said. "Do you want to try something a bit scary today?"

"Sure," Terry said. He was long past feeling any nervousness about such suggestions.

"I'm going to teach you to control bleeding," he said, "and then to heal minor cuts."

Without hesitation Terry held out his hand while Aldren slashed a finger with a small knife. Control of pain came easily to him now; he felt the stab but it didn't hurt. It bled profusely into the towel he held in his other hand, but once they were on dual neurofeedback the flow quickly ceased.

"I stopped it for you," Aldren said, "so that you could see the pattern of the state needed for healing."

"You can heal other people, not just yourself?" Terry asked in surprise. He had always assumed that so-called psychic healers were charlatans.

"I can," Aldren admitted, "and if there were any people on Titan who weren't receiving adequate medical care, it would be very hard to refrain from it. But think what has happened historically whenever someone was believed to have such a power."

"They were idolized," Terry realized. "They were turned into cult figures."

"Exactly. Are you beginning to see how complicated this project is going to get, Terry? Healing is a natural ability and it would be wrong never to use it, but it has to be done with discretion. Someday you too may be able to heal others besides yourself. If so, you will bear a heavy responsibility."

What have I gotten into? Terry thought with dismay. *It's bigger than I bargained for, I never wanted to be superman. . . .* Yet he did want to—at any rate, to use all the powers within himself that were emerging. Until it began to happen, he had never felt whole.

"For now, you just need to be able to heal your own body," Aldren said. "Let's see if you can match my mind-pattern."

Since Aldren was helmeted in the second chair it was

necessary for Terry to cut a second finger by himself. Unflinchingly, he did so. This time it took longer for the bleeding to stop, but once he succeeded in matching Aldren's mind-pattern he gained control over it. "Keep your eyes on the feedback," the doctor told him. "Something else is about to happen." To Terry's amazement, the two cuts healed while he watched, so that only scars remained—scars that Aldren assured him would be gone by the next day.

"This is not something to practice alone in your quarters," he said, "but if you ever need to call on the skill, you'll have an underlying memory of the state of consciousness it demands. Later you may be taught to heal deeper wounds."

"How much more will I be taught?" Terry inquired, wondering what was left to come.

"Soon you'll start on remote viewing," Aldren said. "That's actually easier to learn than what you know already—it requires less telepathic skill on the part of the instructor, and some people were doing it as far back as the twentieth century. But here, other things have higher priority."

Remote viewing, he explained, involved seeing at a distance, even a long distance like the other side of a planet. It wasn't practical on Titan, where it was rarely possible to go outside the domes to find out whether what had been seen was accurate. And it wasn't always reliable, for not all viewings were true ones, even when made by people who were exceptionally psi-gifted. On the whole, however, it was a useful skill—especially, Terry thought, for explorers. He eagerly looked forward to it.

But the next morning a priority message appeared on his phone. With incredulous dismay, he read it: "To Lt. Terry Radnor: You are ordered to report to the cruiser FHS *Shepard* at 1900 tonight for immediate deployment."

9

THE *CRUISER?* IT must be a mistake, Terry thought in anguish, just as his original transfer to Titan had been a mistake; there was no possible reason why he would be sent on a training cruise. He had too much experience on explorer missions to be demoted to cruiser duty. Unless . . . maybe they were correcting the original error by getting rid of some excess personnel. But Admiral Derham would hardly include him among them, not when he was in the Flame project.

He requested permission to see the CO, feeling sure that Derham would apologize for the routine order that had somehow reached him, and would rescind it. That was not what happened.

"I'm sorry, Lieutenant Radnor," Admiral Derham said. "But you're needed on this cruise, and I can't excuse you from it."

"Needed, sir? How could I be needed on a cruiser?" The captain and a few watch officers would do whatever piloting was needed to supplement the AI.

"You'll be a patrol leader. You wanted a flight assignment, didn't you? I know it's not like commanding an explorer, but it's what is available right now."

Patrollers were fun to fly when you were new at it, and despite his more advanced experience he wouldn't mind flying one on an actual mission. But there were no missions for them other than occasional police operations or sorties against pirates, which were rare since no pirate in his right mind would venture anywhere near a cruiser. In reality, patrollers were used mainly for pilot training. And after all, they weren't starships, nor were they able to land on a planetary surface, which was only challenging part of flying within a single solar system. As a patrol leader, he would be mainly concerned with teaching ops protocol to ensigns.

But that wasn't the major issue. "Sir," he protested, "I haven't completed my training with Dr. Aldren. It was my understanding that once I agreed to participate in the Flame project, I'd be obligated to see it through."

"That's true, but your regular duties have priority, as you were told when you volunteered."

In desperation Terry burst out angrily, "Any pilot could fill a patrol billet on a cruiser! You told me you have more people qualified for flight status than you can use! It's not fair to send me away before I've had a chance to develop the skills I was promised."

With uncharacteristic coldness, Admiral Derham replied, "It's not for you to judge what's fair, Lieutenant. Either follow your orders or resign your commission—we've no room in Fleet for officers who don't want to do the jobs they're given."

Unbelieving, Terry managed to say "Yes, sir," and leave the office before succumbing to the impulse to ruin his career with an ill-considered retort. His face was hot with rage. If it weren't for Fleet's monopoly on interstellar transport, he thought, maybe he *would* resign! Aldren wasn't employed by Fleet, after all, and might be willing to keep on teaching him. There being no way a civilian could pilot a starship except outside the law as a smuggler, it was not a real option. But to be pointlessly pulled away first from exploring and then from the one other thing that was important to him. . . .

He was not ready to give up. Dr. Aldren had made plain that he had exceptional aptitude for mind training and that his participation in the Flame project was valued. He had said that his initiation into the use of psi powers was only beginning. And Aldren was Admiral Derham's friend—surely he could pull strings to keep him on Titan.

But Aldren was occupied with scheduled neurofeedback sessions, and Roanna said it would be 1700 before he could see him. That was cutting it close, leaving only two hours before he had to report to the cruiser, and the last shuttle would leave half an hour before then. Maybe a phone call from Aldren to Derham would be all it would take. Or maybe he could be sent back from *Shepard* before it departed.

Nervously Terry packed his gear, telling himself that it was wasted effort because he would just have to unpack it. Drew had also been ordered to *Shepard* and appeared to be equally unhappy despite having complained constantly about his make-work on Titan throughout the weeks since their arrival. In the mess hall, Terry found that this feeling was prevalent. "It doesn't make sense," said Mikaela Orlov. "There's not one of us who needs extra training, and there aren't nearly enough billets for full lieutenants to account for the number who've been called."

Terry scowled. Never one to make casual conversation with messmates, he had not realized that *Shepard* would have more than the usual complement of experienced officers. Normally its crew would be composed almost entirely of sublieutenants and ensigns, preparing for their eventual assignments to the working ships of Fleet—freighters, transports, liners, explorers, and colonizers. There was very little actual work to be done aboard any ship, and apart from service personnel everyone aboard was commissioned. The function of junior officers when not flying was to oversee the functioning of the AI, and in an emergency, to assist with troubleshooting. The specialists in charge were of higher rank; though Terry had enough basic knowledge of AI maintenance for it to be his secondary role in an explorer team, he could hardly be needed on a cruiser for that.

In any case it had been stated that he would be flying patrollers. Yet Mikaela was as good a pilot as he was; in fact she had an instructor's rating and had been one of the few newcomers giving flight training on Titan. If she too had been assigned to *Shepard*, perhaps he had not been singled out. Which made Admiral Derham's attitude all the more puzzling.

"Maybe Titan's short on consumables," Drew suggested.

Terry supposed that was possible. Bases in Earth's solar system were amply supplied, but it was true that this one had been overcrowded for many weeks. Still, if they were running low on life support there would be enough warning for a supply ship to reach them. Not unless there had been emergency damage to a dome would it be necessary to send people away.

"*Shepard* came in with a skeleton crew," Mikaela said, "and they're due for annual leave, even the captain. Vargas is taking command. That's some help—he's fair, and he'll do the best he can by us."

That was what he'd thought about Admiral Derham, Terry reflected bitterly. He hadn't had much contact with Commander Vargas, the XO on Titan, but he'd heard only good things about him. He might have had no voice in picking the new crew, in which case he would be in sympathy with their dissatisfaction; but a ship full of malcontents would have to be ruled with a firm hand.

When he finally got in to see Dr. Aldren, there was no need to explain what he was there for. Aldren knew. Whether he'd picked this up telepathically or had been told earlier, he greeted Terry with a silent surge of concern. *It's going to be all right*, Terry thought with relief. *He understands what it means to me to stay.*

Aldren was more formally dressed than usual; he and Roanna, he said, were going to the reception for Commander Vargas's promotion to captain. Terry noticed with surprise that he wore a tiny copper lapel pin in the shape of a flame. Was that a symbol of the project? Would the people who completed the training receive such pins?

No, Aldren told him silently. *It symbolizes something else, something in my own life, a commitment that I honor.*

Motioning Terry to sit beside him on the familiar floor

mattress where they'd talked in the past, he continued, "I know your reassignment is a blow to you. I wish I could say something to make it easier."

"But—I thought—"

"That I could talk Admiral Derham out of sending you away?"

In anguish, Terry became aware that Aldren's mind had been abruptly closed to him; he couldn't connect even with the emotion he was sure the man was feeling. "I don't want any special favors," he said, although that was exactly what he wanted. "But you're his friend—"

"His job requires him to make command decisions. I'm just a civilian outsider. It's not my place to interfere."

"You're a psychiatrist. You could tell him it wouldn't be good for my mental health."

Aldren gave him a penetrating look. "Is that true, Terry?"

"Well, not exactly," Terry admitted. "I'm not going to go off the deep end."

"I trust not. I'm sure there's a good reason for your assignment."

"Good enough to make up for my not getting all the training you promised me? You said I'd be taught more than how to control the involuntary functions of my body— that I'd learn new psi capabilities. I'm just about to start with remote viewing!"

And he would lose more than that. There was the rest of the Flame project, the part he wasn't yet authorized to know. It had been implied that it was something he would care about. That he'd be involved in action of real importance, maybe for years to come. To put him through the hard initial sessions and then deny him a chance to take part in whatever the training was leading up to . . .

"Terry," Aldren said seriously, "doors in your mind have been opened that can never again be closed. Here or elsewhere, whether or not you receive more formal training, you will go on developing your inborn capabilities.

Over time they will grow. That is what happens to human beings who don't retreat from new experiences, and you have never been one to retreat."

Terry bowed his head. Put that way, he couldn't argue. But how could he live without the inner contact with Aldren and Roanna on which he'd come to rely? All his life he had been cut off from people, never knowing what it was for minds to touch. To go back to that, to be alone, unable to reach anyone . . .

He had been told that sooner or later more people in the Flame project would become conscious of telepathy. Possibly some would be aboard *Shepard*, but would it be awakened in them without further guidance from Aldren? He recalled that Commander Vargas had received the mind training, but he could hardly expect a close telepathic relationship with the captain. Would he be able to find out who the rest of them were, given the secrecy by which they all were bound?

Aldren knew. Perhaps that was why his mind was barricaded; he might fear that he'd unconsciously reveal too much. After all, he, Terry, was no longer even in the project now that he had been ordered to drop out of it. If only there could be one last moment of mind-touch. . . .

"I can't tell you any official secrets," Aldren said, "but there is something else I will tell you, against my better judgment." He paused, then continued hesitantly, "Incredible though it may seem, in remote viewing we sometimes see the future. This has happened to me occasionally, though I never can be sure whether it's precognition."

"Precognition? Knowing about events before they happen?"

"Not reliably. It's often so vague that we can't make out exactly what we're seeing." Slowly he continued, "Last night, Terry, I saw your face in such a vision—not as you are now, but older—and deep in my mind I knew that if the vision was true, you have an extraordinary destiny somewhere forward in time. This may be a false viewing, as many of them are. On the other hand, you should not be discouraged about your future, for there is a real possibility that there's something crucial ahead that neither of us can foresee."

Stunned, Terry felt his anger drain away. His eyes burned with tears, and he knew he must leave before the doctor saw them. Their farewell was silent, but he knew that what he had gained from Aldren's friendship would stay with him always.

10

LIKE ALL CRUISERS, *Shepard* had living accommodations even more cramped than those on Titan, and it appeared to be equally overcrowded. Drew, again Terry's roommate, arrived declaring, "We're in luck to have this stateroom. Couples, even sublieutenants, are getting most of the double ones, so some of the single lieutenants are being crammed into ensigns' quarters."

"What's being done with the ensigns, then?" Terry inquired.

"There don't seem to be many, oddly enough. Nearly all those who did the maintenance work have gone back to Titan."

The purpose of training cruises was to train ensigns; the role of full lieutenants was merely to supervise. Was it indeed just a way of getting them off Titan, then? For many couples to be assigned to a cruiser also suggested this. Considering the distances involved in Fleet operations and the fact that it was primarily a merchant rather than a military service, it would have been impractical to separate married officers; but they could not serve under the same unit commander and it would thus complicate scheduling.

No one had mentioned their destination, which in itself was strange. They had been told, however, that they should expect a long deployment. The ansible office had been mobbed, with nearly everyone trying to send last-minute interstellar messages to loved ones. Terry had been able to avoid the crowd since his mother was on Earth and could be contacted via ordinary comm channels, which he had done earlier in the day. He'd been glad, for once on board he had wanted only to retreat to his bunk before he found himself venting his rage on others who were no happier than he was to be aboard. Though his anger at Aldren's refusal to intervene had faded, he was still furious over the unfairness of Admiral Derham's stubborn unwillingness to reconsider.

To his surprise it was announced that *Shepard* would jump at 0800. That meant almost immediate departure from Titan and full-speed transit in normal space to get far enough out from the sun. Usually time was allowed for the crew to settle in first—not that the crew had much to do with jumping, as it was an AI-controlled maneuver handled almost entirely by the captain. And the pre-jump checkup had already been done. But the whole idea of a training cruise was for the ship's crew to practice the entire process. What point was there in boarding them at the last minute, like passengers?

Terry slept poorly, his heart aching at the knowledge that he was being transported farther and farther from the telepathic contact he craved. Did telepathy work over distance? he wondered. Not interstellar distance; Aldren had told him that. Usually it could be used consciously only when people were near each other, though on the unconscious level, it could reach across an entire planet. Emergencies enhanced it. He was not sure how great an emergency it took, but if there proved to be no telepaths on the ship except maybe the captain, what did that matter?

He wondered why Aldren had seen him in a vision, and if there could be anything in the interpretation he'd put on it. An extraordinary destiny . . . that did not seem likely. He appeared to be destined for relegation to the ranks of officers who never had opportunity to achieve anything significant. Fleet was full of them: freighter crews, staff officers at headquarters, aides to the captains of liners whose main function was to socialize at dinner with the paying passengers. Many were capable people who had simply gotten stuck in the merchant branch of the service; but there were others initially assigned to exploration and terraforming who, through no fault of their own, had somehow fallen off that path. He had never thought this could happen to him . . . and now it was more vital than ever to stay on it, for he *cared* now, cared about more than just wanting to fly into uncharted regions. Having discovered more powers within himself than he'd been previously aware of, he felt his life would be empty if he could not make use of them in some way that mattered.

At breakfast he ate sparingly, too depressed to feel hungry. He had not been assigned any duties yet and it would certainly be some time before the patrollers were flown. He expected the day to drag.

Notice had been given that all hands were to report to the messdeck for briefing immediately after the jump. This was odd, Terry thought. Ordinarily the senior officers and patrol leaders would be briefed about planned exercises before anything was said to the rest of the crew. He sat glumly in the wardroom until the klaxon signaled that the jump had taken place and that *Shepard* was now in some other solar system, light-years away from Titan— he had no idea where. Then he made his way to the messdeck. It was so crowded that late arrivals had to stand, and he observed that "all hands" included even the cooks and other noncommissioned service personnel.

Captain Vargas entered alone, and at once there was silence. "I'll get right to the point," he said. "I know some of you are unhappy about being sent on a training cruise for which you feel you are overqualified. Well, I have good news for you. This is not a training cruise. It is a mission so secret that only a handful of top officials are aware of its true nature. The orders were that no one on board except myself was to be informed before we jumped."

A murmur of excitement spread through the gathering. Not a training cruise? Whatever it involved was almost sure to be an improvement.

"You are bound to keep this secret in the future by the ESAs you signed—" the captain continued.

But he had never signed any ESA except the one covering the Flame project, Terry thought. His being here *was* wrong; there'd been another snafu. . . .

"—when you volunteered for special training. I can now tell you that everyone aboard this ship has had at least the first stage of that training, and you are free to discuss it among yourselves. Those of you not already on Titan were sent there specifically to learn the mind skills required to qualify you for this mission."

Terry gasped. His original transfer hadn't been a mistake, then. Had he been chosen for some special reason, or just because any officer whose ambitions were put on hold would be sure to volunteer out of boredom?

He sensed that many were wondering about this, and when Captain Vargas replied as if to a spoken question, Terry realized that he was indeed telepathically sensitive.

"Dr. Aldren and I chose the candidates together," Vargas said, "he from psych profiles and I according to your proven skills. The central databank at Headquarters was made available to us. You can count it an honor to have been selected, for we picked only the best of the best. To those of you with experience, I won't apologize for the frustration you felt at being transferred from your former posts without apparent reason—we need people who can handle themselves in unpredictable situations that may involve long periods of inactivity. The responsibilities you will be given demand a good deal of maturity."

But we didn't finish the training, Terry thought. If we're to use it, why were we pulled away too soon?

"You can stop regretting that you were reassigned before completing as much training as you'd anticipated," Vargas went on. "You will have opportunity to continue it. When we reach our destination, neurofeedback facilities and qualified instructors will be brought aboard."

But there were no qualified instructors other than Aldren and Roanna—Admiral Derham had said so. Perhaps he had meant just with respect to the initial stage, the stressful one needed to produce the breakthrough.

"There are no ansibles where we are going," Vargas was saying, "and for security reasons we won't be installing one. You will be out of touch with the League for at least a year. But you'll have no cause to complain, because you will have frequent shore leaves on a world that Admiral Derham has described to me as virtually idyllic. It is a world where the entire population possesses the mind skills you have gained, and more."

Terry sat frozen, unbelieving, as Captain Vargas announced, "The name of that world is Maclairn. Our mission is to guard it from discovery, and if necessary, from harm."

Part Two: Maclairn

11

MACLAIRN, CAPTAIN VARGAS told them, was an unauthorized colony that had only recently been discovered. It had been founded more than two hundred years back by emigrants fleeing persecution on their home planet of Undine—all of whom had possessed the capabilities in which *Shepard*'s crew had recently been trained. The method of teaching these capabilities had been developed in secret by a highly gifted neurologist named Ian Maclairn, who formed a group pledged to resist Undine's tyrannical medical policies. On Undine, the government was literally run by medical officials and treatment for even minor abnormalities was enforced by law. Dead bodies had been kept on "life support" indefinitely, and still were, as far as Vargas knew. All residents were continuously tracked by implanted heart monitors and imprisoned in the hospital at the slightest sign of any health problem. Just before this last provision went into effect, Maclairn had died and his followers had managed to escape. They did it by hijacking the starship they chartered, ostensibly to take them to a legally-open world.

"We learned all this just a few months ago," said Captain Vargas. "They deliberately isolated themselves on the world they named Maclairn, without any more supplies than the emergency pods routinely carried by a charter transport. There were only three hundred people and they nearly starved in the early years. The planet is dry and mostly rock; nothing edible grows on it but what they planted. Without their special abilities they would have died out. As it was, they established a thriving culture unlike any that has existed in human history. That was their goal—they aimed to prove that humans can move beyond the old norms by creating a society that people elsewhere would someday want to emulate. But they knew they couldn't do it unless they were left alone to develop their mind skills and pass them from generation to generation, because the effects aren't limited to good health and self-healing. They extend to psi powers. The people of Maclairn are telepathic, and they can do other things with their minds that you won't believe until you observe the results."

There were murmurs of amazement; most members of the crew didn't yet know what he knew, Terry realized. Consciously telepathic—*all* the people on the planet! He'd been aware that Aldren and Roanna were not unique, but he hadn't imagined there could be a whole world where such things were normal.

"Ian Maclairn planned all this," Vargas went on. "He believed it was the next step in human evolution. But it could affect evolution only if the new world was someday found and observed—so he revealed their destination to a friend on Earth with instructions for his successors to seek it out after two centuries had passed. The legacy was held in trust by an institution called the Maclairn Foundation, which spent that time accumulating enough capital to buy a starship—"

"Buy one, sir?" someone questioned. "But there are no private starships capable of such an expedition. Not unless you count smugglers."

"The existence of civilian transports isn't widely known," the captain agreed, "but since ownership of jump ships with minimum cargo capacity that carry no more than twelve people isn't illegal, occasionally they are built. It's not economical to own one if you've got to hire a full-time crew; that's why companies charter ships from Fleet. The Maclairn Foundation didn't care about economy. Their funds were dedicated to one purpose only, the discovery of the planet the followers of Ian Maclairn had headed for. Four months ago, they succeeded. They were awed by what they found.

"But they knew, and the Maclairnan leaders knew, that it had to be kept secret. Just as there would be an outcry if your own training were publicized, there'd be trouble if people were aware that such powers—and, I can tell you now, lengthened lives—are accessible on an unopened world. The planet would be invaded by hordes seeking the Fountain of Youth. Besides that, there are dogmatic scientists and their followers who won't acknowledge the existence of psi and would feel threatened by proof of it, maybe even to the extent of resorting to violence. The Maclairnans have always intended to pass on their abilities to other worlds, but it has to be done under carefully controlled conditions.

"So when the Foundation's expedition returned, they had to think of a way to avoid questions. A privately-owned starship is unusual enough to rouse curiosity at whatever port it comes into, and it was obvious that it had jumped; the natural supposition would be that they'd made a rich find worth the underworld's effort to seek out. There was also some danger of attracting pirates. And so with the help of their hired crew they made it look as if they were crackpots—that they'd been hunting for an alien base that they were sure the government has been hiding."

Aliens? They really said that? Terry thought, amused. The notion that that the government had been concealing alien contact had been cropping up ever since the twentieth century, and by now, since no aliens had ever appeared, even its adherents were becoming convinced that there weren't any. If you wanted to be dismissed as a crackpot, it was a good story.

"The CEO of the Maclairn Foundation has connections," Captain Vargas went on, "and he was able to get them a meeting with a few higher-ups at League headquarters. They had photographic proof of what they'd seen, of course, and a good deal of data—most members of the expedition were young scientists. And as to the psi powers, they had Aldren and Roanna."

Oh, my God, Terry thought. No wonder they're so special. . . .

"Aldren and Roanna are natives of Maclairn," the captain announced. "They are the first of many who will come to the League worlds and teach their mind skills without revealing their origin. There will also be small groups of League citizens chosen by the Foundation to visit Maclairn and observe its society; Admiral Derham and his wife were members of the initial one. The goal is to gradually, over many years, spread the Maclairnans' capabilities throughout civilization until possession of them by trustworthy individuals is so widespread that revelation of their existence won't result in culture shock.

"But none of this can happen without the protection of Fleet. Maclairn has no wish to join the League; it will remain politically independent. However, a contract has been signed. In exchange for training given League citizens, Fleet will keep a cruiser in orbit at all times to make sure that no unauthorized ships approach the planet. No person who has not been given personal experience with its people's abilities will be allowed to know it exists.

"We are privileged to be the vanguard, and a great responsibility has been entrusted to us. A continuous watch will be maintained throughout this solar system, and it goes without saying that the keeping of the secret hinges on the vigilance of every patroller pilot among you. But beyond that, every member of the crew will have shore leaves on Maclairn, during which it's essential that its people be viewed neither as freakish nor as superhuman and that the differences between their culture and ours be respected. This is one reason why you have all been given mind training, so that you will feel that you're their equals and will share their belief in the importance of what they have achieved. Fraternization will be not only permitted, but encouraged. A secondary aim of our presence here is to learn what future problems, if any, may arise in the course of contact between psi-capable people and those who lack such powers."

Commander Dorene Hastings, the ship's XO, rose and said, "Sir, if Dr. Aldren and his wife are typical I don't believe anyone will have trouble adjusting."

"I'm sure they won't. In some ways Aldren and Roanna are exceptional, however—they're what are known as mentors. 'Doctor' is a courtesy title we have given them on Titan; the Maclairnans use neither honorifics nor surnames, and their vocations are different from ours. Mentors hold the highest rank that exists in their society. Only mentors are qualified to conduct the stressful phase of mind training, as well as to serve in a number of other roles, some of which we don't yet understand. And only they are eligible to hold the top positions in Maclairn's government."

Shepard's jump had been precisely calculated, so that it had emerged in Maclairn's solar system only two days out from the planet, one of which had extra hours due to adjustment from standard Fleet time to the colony's. Terry, like most others aboard, could barely contain his excitement during those days. Work assignments were made and patrols were organized; he inspected his ships with a new respect for their functionality. A watch was to be kept by a ring of satellites in high orbit, of course; and unmanned sensor stations would also be placed elsewhere in the solar system. But only manned patrollers could turn away any intruders that the sensors detected.

"We don't expect any," the captain had said. "Only once in Maclairn's history, less than fifteen years after its founding, did an explorer come upon it, and the odds against that happening again are great since League charts show nothing of value here. Nevertheless, because the stakes are high, we must be prepared. And after training of citizens on other worlds begins, there will be a chance that the secret might get out. Then the danger will grow."

Once close enough to Maclairn to see its features, everyone was eager for a turn in *Shepard*'s small observation dome, though the image on the viewscreens was equally spectacular. It was a beautiful planet from a distance, dry and barren as it was said to be. Golden, adorned with the green ribbons of planted areas and the sapphire gems of small ancient seas, it shone brilliantly against the black backdrop of space. Terry's heart swelled and he felt a shiver of anticipation. He had seen many worlds, but never one that aroused the emotion this one did.

Destiny, Aldren had said . . . was this the place of his extraordinary destiny? Aldren had been born on this planet; he wouldn't perceive it as extraordinary. But somehow Terry was sure that he too was *connected* to Maclairn. If there was such a thing as precognition, he thought, perhaps he was experiencing it now.

12

AS SOON AS *Shepard* was in low orbit, Captain Vargas and several of the senior officers went down to meet Maclairn's leaders. Meanwhile, the pilots took their ships out for brief test flights. Terry hadn't flown a patroller for some time; explorers carried only shuttles. It felt great to be back in control of a fast ship, although in actuality it was AI-piloted and, except in the case of emergency maneuvers, very little skill was involved in flying it. He devoted most of his attention to the gloriously bright planet he circled, marveling not only at its beauty but at the thought of the telepathic contact he might experience there. He could hardly wait.

As it turned out, he didn't have to wait long. The first task for *Shepard*'s crew was construction of a ground base for a satellite communications system, which the colony lacked because their original comm satellite had failed only a few years after their arrival. Technical experts were sent down with the equipment, and to his joy, Terry was assigned as their shuttle pilot.

Before leaving, they were given the briefing that would be required of every crew member prior to his or her first trip to the surface. "You'll be treated as honored guests by the Maclairnans," Captain Vargas said, "but Aldren and Admiral Derham warned me that some of their customs are unlike ours. I don't want any of our people showing surprise or disapproval."

The landing pad for the shuttle was ancient but recently resurfaced, Terry saw as he hovered over it. It was flanked by two others occupied by ships that belonged in a museum. One of these, he saw to his surprise, was a grounded explorer, apparently the source of the automated beacon he had homed in on. Explorers were the only jump ships that could land; he had done it for practice, though shuttles were used except in emergencies where a long-term ground base was needed. He recalled that once, long ago, an explorer had come to Maclairn— and he realized with mixed feelings that its crew had been stranded. The colonists would not have allowed them to leave, any more than future intruders would be released if they got close enough to see habitation. But the colony had had no weapons; this ship couldn't have been forced down. Why had it landed? Was it disabled, so that not even the officer on watch could have escaped? That seemed unlikely; explorers rarely failed in flight.

Slowly he settled the shuttle vertically onto the pad,

an easy landing compared to those he had made on the rough ground of undeveloped worlds. Once assured of the ship's stability he gave the okay for his passengers to unstrap, wishing, as he did so himself, that he didn't have to wait for them all to disembark before setting foot on the surface. When the hatch opened, a wave of heat struck. Maclairn's climate was intolerably hot in the daytime, Captain Vargas had warned. One of the main reasons they had been given mind training was so that they could adjust their body temperature, as even small Maclairnan children were able to do. Otherwise they couldn't be outdoors without flight suits.

By the time Terry had secured the ship, Commander Chiang, the officer in charge of the landing party, had introduced himself and the team to the group of people that had come to meet them. Terry noticed that the Maclairnans were all quite tall and slender, distinguished from each other mainly by hair and skin coloring; he knew from the briefing that this was an inheritance from the genetic perfection enforced by law on their ancestral planet Undine. All appeared to be young—but, he realized, that might be merely because of slowed aging. Age was not an appropriate topic for conversation, the captain had said; until a person was over a hundred, as many were, it was considered an entirely private matter.

Immediately he was aware of the warmth of these people, just as he had been impressed by Aldren's. As he joined the group a distinguished-looking older couple turned to him and smiled. "Welcome," the man said. "I'm Corwin, and this is Kamila. That was a smooth landing you made." He spoke with a slight accent like Aldren's, which Terry now knew to be due to the long isolation of Maclairn from the League.

"Thanks," he replied. "I'm Terry." He didn't add "Radnor," for it had been decided that with Maclairnans crew members would use only given names, in accord with local custom. The colonists didn't omit surnames just for informality—they didn't have them. Aldren's name was his only one, just as Roanna's was hers. In the first generation many IVF children had been born to single women, and because of the small population there had been relatively few surnames in any case, most of them arbitrarily assigned by the crèche system on Undine; so it had been decided that family names would be pointless. A computer kept track of names to prevent duplication, though recently it had been decided that reusing a name would be allowed if it had been at least twenty years since its former bearer's death.

There wasn't a lot of talking in the group, which seemed unnatural until Terry realized that speech wasn't needed. Telepaths didn't make conversation just to fill silence; their friendliness didn't have to be demonstrated with words. Though no specific telepathic communication with him was occurring, he found that he felt more comfortable among them than he had ever felt among his fellow Fleet officers. There was no need to ponder what he thought of them or what they might think of him, and he turned his attention to his surroundings.

This, Corwin explained, was the Old Settlement, the area where the colony had originally been established. It was on a high plateau between the mountains and Lake Hari, a long narrow body of water that had been created by damming the river at the bottom of the adjacent canyon. Terry had seen this from the air, and had seen the canyon's terraced wall with many planted levels, green against the yellowish rock that covered most of the planet's surface. "The terraces were the only place they could grow crops in the early years," Corwin said, "after a flash flood wiped out their first field on the canyon floor. They'd lost most of their robotic farm equipment and had to plant and cultivate by hand."

They had also built stone huts by hand, he continued, since originally there was neither wood for lumber nor straw for making brick. Clusters of such huts remained

in the level area near the landing pad, domed like bee-
hives, but augmented now by wood and brick additions.
Groves of trees surrounded them, terragenic trees that
had not been there originally. They were genetically engineered to be fast growers, but wood had been needed for
too many purposes to let them stand while the settlement was young.

"Of course no one lives here now," Kamila said. "The
wells have run dry, so the old homes and prefab shelters
are preserved only for their historic value. But your captain decided this is the best place for Fleet's base. The
power plant is operational, and a limited supply of water
can be piped up from the lake. The land around our
towns is all cultivated; there'd be no place near them
for a spaceport."

The six original prefab shelters, like all colonial structures carried by Fleet colonizers, were of virtually indestructible material and were still standing after two hundred years. Terry marveled at the fortitude of the people
who had first settled here on a desolate rocky plateau,
with nothing at all for life support but what they brought
with them. During the past few days he had heard the
outlines of their story—their hijacked ship had been so
low on air that they'd had to land fast, without exploring,
and had been stuck with the inadequate site onto which
their supply pods had been dropped. They'd had only one
qualified shuttle pilot; the courage it must have taken for
him to set down time after time near the rim of a canyon,
knowing that any damage to his ship would mean the death
of them all, was awesome. And the hardships they must
have endured when forced to devote years to hard manual
labor while facing starvation did not bear thinking about.
The brief dangers and discomforts of his own explorer
missions paled beside what Maclairn's founders had gone
through.

"We'll be staying in one of the prefabs while working
here," Commander Chiang announced. "But on leaves, we'll

be guests in the modern towns, and we're invited to a cookout tonight here by the lake."

Terry set to work helping to unload equipment from the shuttle. The Maclairnans had offered one of the historic stone huts as a foundation for a satellite tower. Primitive as they were, they had electric wiring; the early settlers had had power, beamed from their starship and later from windmills like those still in use.

Carrying heavy boxes in the intense heat was an effort at first, though before long he had gotten so used to adjusting his body temperature that he didn't need to keep thinking about it. At dusk it got cooler, and before long, cold; the relatively thin atmosphere of Maclairn made for extremes. The team had brought flight jackets, but that wouldn't have been enough protection for long exposure without the ability to physically adapt.

Just before dark Corwin escorted them down the terraces to the lowest one, which formed a pebbly beach by the lake. A row of standing torches at the water's edge illuminated the area, casting rippled reflections. Maclairnans were there tending cookfires, evidently having come in the boats tied up at the nearby dock; and a larger boat was approaching. Its lighted upper deck was crowded with people, including some older children—though, Terry realized, they might not be children by the local standard, for Captain Vargas had said that Maclairnans were considered adults at thirteen. As it came in to the dock, Terry sensed the happy mood of the group and felt his own soar to match it. To be here, within a gathering of telepaths, exceeded all he had wished for during his lonely times.

He watched the new arrivals come off the boat. Again, they were uniformly tall and slender—except for one. His eyes were drawn to her because she was different; at first he'd assumed she was one of the teenagers, but when she was closer he realized that despite her lesser height she was a woman somewhere near his own age. She was blond, with short wavy hair, and as she passed, the light of a torch shone briefly on her face. Though he could not see her expression, he somehow sensed that she had noticed him.

Terry knew at once that this was a woman he wanted very much to meet.

13

WHEN THEY GATHERED informally around the cookfires, Terry held back until he saw where the blond woman went. To his relief, unlike most of the Maclairnans she did not appear to be with anyone in particular—even the teens had paired off, but her group was composed of older people and members of his team. As he was debating whether it would be permissible to sit beside her uninvited, a vibrant white-haired woman approached him and motioned him to it. "Join us, Terry," she said warmly. He wondered how she knew his name.

Once the circle was formed and the members introduced themselves, it became apparent that these were some of Maclairn's leaders. The woman who'd spoken to him, the first person he'd seen who despite her vitality looked truly old, turned out to be Jessica, head of the Council. The Council was the ruling body, he knew; that meant that in League terminology she was Head of State, the equivalent of a monarch or planetary president. Yet she was sitting on the ground with the rest of them, and no one appeared to be paying her any special respect.

Terry did not spend long thinking about it, and scarcely heard the other people's positions. He was waiting for the woman beside him to speak. Finally when her turn came she said, "I'm Kathryn, ambassador to the League." Ambassador! She couldn't be as young as she looked, then. But did it matter, when ages weren't supposed to be mentioned?

There was a silence, and she turned to him, smiling expectantly. It was a moment before it dawned on him that it was his own turn. "Terry, pilot for the landing party," he said, finding his mouth so dry he could scarcely form the words. Her eyes met his, and now he could see that they were blue.

Mugs of ale were passed around, then plates, and the chickens roasting over the fire were carved and served along with thick slices of bread. "It's good to have you here," Kathryn said to him. "Fleet, I mean. For a while I was afraid the League wasn't going to agree to the terms."

"Why wouldn't they? It's not as if there were too many other jobs for cruisers."

"They wanted Maclairn to join the League and be subject to its government. To all the bureaucracy other worlds have to put up with. They weren't happy about the first colonists having gotten away with hijacking a ship and establishing an unauthorized colony."

Well, that was no surprise, the central government of the League being what it was. "Why did they give in?" he inquired.

"When we held out for independence, they decided to grab the chance to keep an eye on us. They were torn between not wanting to acknowledge that psi powers exist and fearing what Maclairnans might do with them. I didn't go out of my way to be reassuring."

Do with them? What harm could they do, except perhaps spy on undercover operations? Terry wondered. And why had this attractive young woman been chosen as their ambassador when the other leaders were obviously much older? "You must be a good diplomat, especially since you couldn't have known anything about League affairs beyond what you'd studied in texts over two hundred years old," he said. "Nowadays colonies don't usually get much say about their status."

"I'm not a native Maclairnan," Kathryn said. "I was a member of the Foundation's first expedition. My grandfather's the CEO of the Foundation and as an attorney I specialized in League law, so he sent me to negotiate the contract."

"You won't be staying?" Terry was surprised by the depth of his disappointment. Even in these few minutes, he had felt she was someone he could truly connect with.

"Not all the time, but I'm a citizen of Maclairn now. I didn't return with the expedition—I chose to receive mind training, and then went back to Earth with the first group of observers, the one that included your admiral. I'll be taking messages to and from the mentors who go to teach. I don't want to be away from here, but I believe in what they're trying to do, and considering the sacrifice they'll be making—"

"Sacrifice? Don't they like teaching?" Aldren had seemed to enjoy it, except for the painful stage.

"Earth's society is a mess compared to this one. Besides, to be exiled for years from their homes, their friends and relatives, unable to communicate with anyone except their partners in the way they've been doing since they were born—"

God, was it like that for Aldren and Roanna? They'd shown no signs of being unhappy on Titan, even though nearly everybody else there had hated it.

"We all cried the night before Aldren and Roanna went," Kathryn told him. "I was new here then; they left on *Promise*, the first time it returned, and I didn't understand why everyone was grieving for them—or why, if it was such a sad parting, they wanted to go. They did want to, of course. They'd been preparing for nearly a century—"

"A *century*?"

"Yes, they'd known since they were kids when the two hundred years would be up, and mentors are exceptionally psi-gifted in childhood. The best ones all hoped they'd be chosen when the time came, after a lifetime of serving as ordinary mentors here."

"But Aldren can't be older than seventy at the most," Terry protested.

"Oh Terry, he's over a hundred, and Roanna is nearly that. Maclairnans don't age, remember. The average age at death is a hundred and twenty, and it comes on quite suddenly. Some who go to Earth won't live to see Maclairn again."

Then why? Terry wondered, trying to adjust to his astonishment. *Why does anyone go to teach on other worlds, when the League doesn't appreciate it and they have to keep it secret so as not to put Maclairn in danger?*

"Because that's what it's all been for, the creation of a psi-based culture here that will someday advance the evolution of humankind. That was Ian Maclairn's dream. Without that goal the early colonists couldn't have survived." There was an intensity in her reply that he sensed rather than heard . . . and she had answered his unspoken thought.

Yes, I'm beginning to pick up thoughts, though only with Maclairnans . . . never before with anyone else. I didn't know I could do it with people not born telepathic.

"Aldren said I'm psi-gifted," he confided. "But so far I've only been able to communicate with him and with Roanna."

"That's it, then. For it to be conscious, both people have to be sensitive." *They told me I wouldn't become a full telepath until* . . . She broke off, for some reason flustered, and he sensed that this thought hadn't been meant to reach him.

To cover her unexplained embarrassment Kathryn said quickly, "It wasn't just that Aldren and Roanna knew they'd be homesick. They were terrified that it might not work out, despite all they'd studied in the old records."

"Aldren was terrified?" She must be mistaken, Terry thought. If there was anyone immune to fear, it was Aldren. *Though he did mention some future danger. . . .*

"Not that. Of course it's terribly dangerous, what we're

doing, for the long term—we're inviting opposition that may eventually turn violent. But what scared Aldren was not knowing whether he could get adults through the stressful phase of training. Jessica hadn't yet done it with me, you see. I was the first adult given the mind training since almost two centuries ago—and even then, it was done only by Ian Maclairn and his successor Peter, who was the first leader here and the first mentor. Peter recorded his advice, but there was no knowing if anyone else would be good enough to pull it off."

"I don't understand," Terry said. "Aldren seemed to have had plenty of experience."

"Yes, but with the kids—starting with the first generation born on Maclairn, everyone has received the initial training at thirteen. It's easier than with adults because the kids are telepathic from birth and because they don't have years of past experience telling them that volitional control of their perceptions is impossible. And they look forward to the ordeal because it's how they gain adult status. So though the steps are the same, they don't suffer as much as an adult does. Especially," she added, "not as much as a Fleet officer. It must have been much worse for you than for me."

He had been told that it was permissible to discuss the training with anyone on Maclairn except children too young to have been through it, from whom it was vital that the secret of the second session be kept. "Well," he said, "I suppose Fleet officers do suffer more from thinking they've failed than civilians—we're not used to failing."

"More than that," she pointed out, "you're hardened to stress. You don't lose control so quickly in the first session, so the mentor has to inflict far worse pain than with the average person. At least that's what Jessica explained after I'd been through it and asked why Aldren had been afraid he might fail. He wasn't sure he could get a non-telepath to volunteer for a second session if the pain was more severe than what's usually needed. Peter had trained only a few Fleet officers, the captain of the ship that brought them here and the explorers who were stranded, and he warned that it was horrible having to be so hard on them."

"I wondered about those explorers when I saw their grounded ship," Terry said. "I'm an explorer pilot myself, at least I was until I was sent to Titan. So I couldn't help thinking what it must have been like for them. Do you know why they brought their starship down instead of just a shuttle?"

"That's a key event in Maclairn's history," Kathryn said. "They were bounty hunters when they arrived—there was a price on the heads of Peter and Jesse, the captain, because they'd left Undine illegally and hijacked the starship. They'd have been executed if captured, and the colony would have been exposed and taken over by the League. So Jesse gave himself up to the explorer crew, planning to blow up the ship before it could jump, but he couldn't do it because his son and Peter's foster daughter Ivana were brought aboard. In the end Ivana—who was only thirteen and pregnant—saved them by disabling the hyperdrive—"

"Wait a minute! You're saying a thirteen-year-old girl without any engineering experience disabled the hyperdrive?" Terry protested.

"Terry," Kathryn said seriously, "have they told you anything about psychokinesis yet?"

"I don't even know what that is."

"Affecting things with psi. Moving them, or in this case, heating them to the point of burning or melting. Ivana was extremely psi-gifted. She wasn't aware of the extent of her own power, but when she found out what was going to happen to Peter and Jesse—and to her unborn child—if they were taken to Earth, she focused on the hyperdrive's control panel and melted it past repair."

Speechless, Terry felt the world around him spin. He

had thought he knew what psi was, what had always been hidden within himself, what he would find on this world that attracted him far more than any other he had visited. Now everything he had ever believed was shaken, not because what Kathryn had said was incredible, but because he knew inside that it was true.

It's not an evil power, she assured him. *It has never again been used for destruction. Once they saw it was possible, they did constructive things with it, like melting copper or glass. . . . And healing is based on psychokinesis, too.*

Aldren had said he might someday become a healer.

Struggling to regain his composure, Terry said, "So the crew couldn't leave the solar system. They had to become Maclairnans. But why not keep the starship in orbit?"

"It was needed—it was the colony's salvation. The settlers had lost their own ship when its AI failed; they'd sent it into the sun. They didn't have enough power or equipment to jump-start manufacturing. And they lacked the technological expertise the explorer crew could provide. Peter had trusted in fate, and he turned out to be right. What started as disaster for them proved a blessing."

"What happened to the girl—to Ivana?"

"She became a mentor, and when she was old she succeeded Peter as leader. She was Jessica's great-great-great grandmother."

"The leadership is hereditary, then."

"Not officially, but psi talent is to some degree. The Council elects the most gifted of the mentors, and Jessica was chosen. She's been the only leader since Ivana, because they live so long—she was already twelve when Peter died."

"How large is the Council?" he asked.

"It has eleven members. Not all of them are mentors—they're chosen for expertise in particular areas. It's an administrative body, not a legislature. The original colonists set it up that way and when the population grew nobody saw any reason to change. Maclairn doesn't have formal laws. People are free to do whatever they want as long as they don't intentionally harm anyone, and most telepaths have too much empathy to harm others. The mentors can usually deal with the few deficient in it. In rare cases the Council has to step in, but its main function is just to coordinate everyday public affairs. There's a Forum elected by the people that can override its decisions, but that hardly ever happens."

She went on giving him information as they finished eating, but after a while Terry's mind wasn't on it. Still shaken by the awesome psi powers these people possessed, he fell silent. He looked around the circle at them, seated casually on the ground near the fire as if it were one of the camping trips he'd enjoyed during his boyhood, and he knew—knew inside, through the telepathic sensitivity he had gained—that their world was one he wished that he could belong to. He had never felt any allegiance to Earth, much less to the various planets where he had been stationed. Now it was as if he had come home.

Around one of the other fires, soft singing began. It sounded familiar—the colonists' lyrics had been set to the tune of an ancient Terran alma mater—and the impact of it came not just from the music but from the feeling that everyone shared. As the group around him took it up, Kathryn squeezed his hand.

I never want to leave here, she was thinking. *People everywhere else go through the motions, they try to get close to each other, but inside they don't really* connect.

You felt that way too?

Not while I was living on Earth. But ever since I found out what it's like to be with people here. . . . Imagine what a difference it will make if someday the whole human race gains our powers—if our descendants can not only banish pain and sickness, but truly communicate. . . .

He could not describe the void in his former life, or explain how already the emptiness was being filled. But it did not need to be stated. Their exchange of thought was not in the form of words—telepathy, Terry perceived, involved only meaning. It was translated in his head to words because that was the only way his mind could process it.

I'm glad you've come, she told him again, *and not just because we need Fleet to protect us. But oh, Terry, keep this world safe!*

14

THAT NIGHT IN the Old Settlement shelter where floor mattresses had been placed for the landing party, Terry could not sleep. His mind was too full of what he had just seen and felt, and what he was beginning to understand about Maclairn's peril. It was no wonder that the League was wary of its people if they could melt metal by mind alone!

But that was not the main reason why secrecy must be maintained, Kathryn had told him. The mentors knew that as Aldren had said, many humans had an innate fear of psi, one they didn't allow themselves to recognize and which therefore led them to ridicule the concept—or sometimes even seek to destroy the evidence. Unconsciously, they feared that their way of dealing with life, their orientation to the world around them, would crumble past restoration were they to suspect such powers within their own minds. He had found this incredible when Aldren spoke of it. To him, having psi powers had seemed wholly desirable. But now, at the thought that if he was psi-gifted he too might be able to burn things, he felt a touch of the same apprehension.

He would get over it, he knew. It didn't affect his belief that for more people to become telepathic, or even to gain more spectacular uses of psi, would be a major advance for humankind. What it did do was to make him all too aware that such a reaction might pose a real threat to the mentors who went to serve other worlds, and possibly even to Maclairn itself. To Aldren and Roanna . . . to Kathryn . . . to this world where in so little time he had come to feel he belonged. And he was glad that he was among those chosen to defend it.

Restlessly he tossed on the mattress, until finally he got up and went out into the cold dawn. Nothing was moving outside; the Old Settlement was deserted except for the presence of the sleeping landing party. There was, he knew, no visible native animal life on Maclairn other than crawly creatures that lived in water or in dry seasons, underground. The planet was mostly rock and no complex ecology had evolved on it; it was an environment alien to the biology of Earth. There had been none of the terraforming that preceded establishment of authorized colonies—the settlers had introduced genetically engineered plants by enriching the soil, but these had not spread past cultivated areas. As he moved away from the trees he came to barren stony land in the short space between the settlement and the landing pads.

Beyond them, the rising sun struck the hull of an old damaged ship, a large shuttle that he'd been told had crashed on the night of the colonists' first landing. Its interior had been stripped of useful materials, but like all ships, it was composed of an alloy impervious both to recycling and to the ravages of time. After two hundred years it was still intact.

There were three other old shuttles, smaller ones, on one of the pads; these might still be operational, assuming that enough power was available to recharge them and present-day Maclairnans were knowledgeable about maintenance, although the colony would have little use for them now that land transport facilities had been developed. They were dwarfed by the ship on the third pad, the grounded explorer. It towered above everything else in the settlement, gleaming in the sunlight, and Terry's heart began to race at the sight of it. Though an ancient model, it was not very different from those he had served on; explorers didn't change much over the years.

Seen from the surface instead of in space, it looked awkward and unnatural; still it roused memories of the life from which he'd been torn. As he approached he could make out the name emblazoned over the hatch: *Picard*. It had served the colony well, according to Kathryn. Without it, Maclairn would have been unable to develop the technology that made its society fit to be emulated rather than dismissed as an anomaly by modern civilization. Yet he hated to see such a ship stuck here like a beached whale. Happy though he was to be on Maclairn, that saddened him; he had spent the past few months longing to be back aboard an explorer, and it was possible that he would never fly one again.

Unless . . . was it possible that this one could still fly?

Its AI must be operational, for it had provided the beacon that guided them in; evidently the Maclairnans had planned ahead for their rediscovery and set it to hibernate on minimum power. The interior of the ship itself would not have been gutted even if they had taken out all the equipment that could be used apart from it. Passage of years wouldn't have caused any deterioration if it had been depressurized, as it surely would have been when placed in hibernation. The hatch was sealed, he found on investigation. No doubt the Council knew the code for the lock.

Of course, *Picard* could not jump—with its hyperdrive controls destroyed, it could no longer be called a starship. But if it had enough power remaining to lift just once, it could dock with *Shepard*. Then, after a thorough maintenance overhaul, it could fly in normal space within this solar system. And that, Terry thought with excitement, would add considerably to the safety of Maclairn.

Shepard's patrollers had limited range. They could intercept an intruder, but not before it got quite close to the planet, whereas a ship jumping into the system might emerge anywhere. The plan was to deploy unmanned sensor stations at various distances from the sun, but putting them in position would take many months if they had to be sent out under their own power. An explorer, on the other hand, was fast. And it could be used to place sensors on asteroids or other planets, which *Shepard*'s AI was incapable of doing.

Why, Terry wondered, had the planners of the mission not thought of this? Why had Headquarters not sent an explorer in addition to the cruiser? To save money, no doubt; according to Kathryn protecting Maclairn had not been high on the League's priority list. On the other hand, perhaps that was an unfair assumption—perhaps they had felt that to protect the secret, it was best not to provide a ship that would be able to leave. Not all explorer crews were totally trustworthy, and news of a hitherto-unexploited colony might be worth a good deal of money in some quarters. Neither of these considerations had any bearing on the use of *Picard*. But would he be allowed to find out if it could lift?

Power gauges and AI checks would tell whether it could, in theory. But theory wasn't a reliable guide when it came to ships. Whatever the instruments said, the attempt would be risky. Any pilot who claimed otherwise would be a fool.

He could go to Commander Chiang and explain his reasoning. And he would probably be told to forget it, after which he would not be free to pursue the idea. Fleet was not inclined to take unnecessary risks. To be sure, the value of *Picard* was not an issue in this case, since it was now useless on the ground. But the life of a fully trained, experienced explorer pilot would not be lightly endangered. Daredevils were generally disciplined, and any act deemed foolhardy might well result in his being grounded, or at the very least, demoted from patrol leader to standby status.

If, on the other hand, he could offer some evidence before raising the subject, the captain might then be persuaded to send down engineers and AI experts to evaluate the ship. He could do some preliminary checking himself; on explorer missions AI maintenance had been his backup role. But he did not have the code for opening the hatch.

Could Kathryn get it? Jessica was her mentor, and in fact she'd said she was living, while on Maclairn, in Jessica's house. Probably Maclairnans would come today, as they had yesterday, to make sure the Fleet officers had everything they needed. If he asked her, Kathryn might come with them; although the colony as yet had no satellite service there was a wired phone line between the Old Settlement and Petersville, the colony's capital. And she had given him her number.

15

TERRY THOUGHT ABOUT it all through breakfast. He had no duties on the surface; installation of the satellite phone equipment was specialized technical work. Officially, he was at loose ends. And so, he decided, the bold way was the best way. After all, the captain had declared that fraternization was to be encouraged. "Sir, I met a woman last night that I'd like to talk to again," he said to Commander Chiang. "If I'm not needed today, may I have permission to phone her?"

"Permission granted," Chiang replied, "as long as you don't leave this area." The phone was in the prefab known as the Commons, where they'd slept, and Terry hurried to it. He told Kathryn only that he was curious about the grounded explorer and that he'd like to show her its interior. That would be excuse enough if they were seen. And in fact it would circumvent the question of authorization that sooner or later would arise—the ship was after all the property of the Maclairnans, who had confiscated it after disabling its hyperdrive. Fleet had no right to enter it without their permission.

"Jessica thinks this is a good idea," Kathryn reported when she arrived on the boat that afternoon. "She said nobody has looked it over for many years and she's wondered if there's some way we could make use of whatever is left inside."

He got a pressure suit from the shuttle and while Kathryn watched, climbed the footholds leading to the hatch. He drew a deep breath as he opened it. The gauge in the airlock showed that the interior was indeed depressurized; feeling only a moment of apprehension lest power failure trap him inside, he put on his helmet and closed the outer hatch firmly behind him. The pump's normal soft whir reassured him. Once the airlock finished cycling he would be able to enter.

He would have to pressurize at least part of the ship, since Kathryn wasn't trained to use a suit and even if she were, it would be risky to reseal it while she was inside—or in fact, while he was; there was no knowing how long the power would last. It was unlikely that stored oxygen had been left aboard, but since the airlock's pump still worked, the intake pump probably would. He proceeded to the bridge, made sure that the intercompartment locks were closed, and set it in operation. While he waited for the green light to show that the air was breathable, he turned to the control console and gave the command to wake.

One by one the indicators lit up, until the whole board blazed with them. His eyes went first to the power gauges. There was power! Not a lot, but enough to keep the ship alive until, when docked with *Shepard*, it could be replenished. There was almost certainly enough to lift. Whether there was enough to reach escape velocity was something he wasn't ready to think about.

There remained the question of the AI. Ships were not designed to be controlled manually; the only time when the pilot had any influence beyond giving commands was during landing. The AI carried out the pilot's orders to lift, to reach the specified destination, and to dock. Or else it didn't. If it didn't, you were either helpless or dead. The original colonists had sent their starship to destruction in the sun when its AI began to fail; its mere presence in orbit had become a hazard. *Picard*, too, would present a hazard, and not only to him, if its AI could not be trusted.

Removing his helmet but not his suit, he went back to the hatch and called to Kathryn to come up. She climbed the footholds easily; as she did so Terry couldn't help noticing how full of life she was. A current of vitality passed from her to him, like a live circuit. They were not consciously communicating by telepathy, yet the connection formed last night between them was unbroken. He felt sure that it would never break. He knew he did not want it to.

"This ship's like *Promise*, the Foundation's ship," she told him as they went through the open airlock. "Except it's not quite as big. How many staterooms does it have?"

"Four," he replied. Now, close to her in the lighted corridor, he could see her better than by last night's firelight, and he liked what he saw.

"*Promise* has six. I've made three trips in it now, but I never saw the bridge. Our captain is a crotchety old guy who came out of retirement for us; he doesn't like to have passengers get in his way."

Terry showed her around, explaining what some of the controls did and what the lights meant. There were no active alarms, and the data he called up on his video monitor showed normal readings. As far as he could tell the newly-awakened AI was doing its job, but of course someone would have to perform a more thorough internal check.

"Where are the hyperdrive controls, the ones that Ivana destroyed?" Kathryn asked.

That panel looked normal; evidently all the damage was underneath. He found a wrench and removed the bolts. When he got the cover off and looked into the mess of melted metal behind it, he gasped in awe. That anyone's mind could have done this, let alone a teenage girl's, was past believing ... except that everything he knew about Maclairn and Fleet's mission here required that he believe in the power of psi.

He sensed that Kathryn, too, was stunned. "I've only known about this for a few months," she said, "so I'm not used to it yet. The children grow up on the story; Jesse and Ivana, and Peter of course, are their heroes. I think perhaps the ship was sealed to keep it from being turned into some sort of shrine."

"Is it sacred to them, then?" he asked. That might make things awkward.

"Not in a religious sense. But it's a revered historical monument, like the site of the first landing on Earth's moon or the dome on Centauri Prime where the charter establishing the League was signed."

Troubled, Terry said, "Kathryn, I think this ship may be able to fly. If so, we can guard this solar system a lot more effectively than we can without it. Are people going to be upset if we take it away?"

"Some, maybe. Not the Council, not if it contributes to defense." She frowned. "But Terry, it's been nearly two hundred years since it flew. Even if it looks functional, wouldn't taking off in it be dangerous?"

There was no use lying to a telepath. "It would," he admitted, "though of course experts would check it over first. There's risk in any explorer mission. I don't lose any sleep over it."

"You're saying you'd be the one to do this personally."

"Well, first I'll have to convince my superiors that it's worth trying," he said.

"You mean they're doubtful?"

"They haven't heard about it yet. It's my idea."

"Terry, I'm not sure I like it." He could tell that his safety mattered to her, and his heart jumped as he realized what that meant.

They locked the ship, leaving the corridor and bridge pressurized, and walked to the grove of trees that shaded some of the old stone dwellings. The heat was oppressive even in the shade, but Terry was by now able to adjust his temperature without effort, as Kathryn was. She wore a short-sleeved shirt and form-fitting pants that ended at mid-calf; seeing her for the first time without the warm clothes that had covered her at the cookout, he became acutely aware that their telepathic closeness wasn't the only thing that attracted him.

"I guess I should ask," he said. "You're not—with somebody, are you? I mean in a relationship?"

"No," Kathryn said. "Not anymore. On Earth there was a man I planned to marry. When I first got here and knew I wanted to stay, I wrote him a letter asking him to join me. It was never sent because by the time *Promise* left, the decision had been made to keep the existence of this world secret. We met when I returned and I told him as much as I could without giving too much away—Maclairn isn't going to allow immigrants, but the Council had agreed to make an exception. When we were together, though, I saw it wouldn't work. He's a musician and I'd thought he would be happy here, but he'd just signed with an interstellar distributor . . . and besides, when I hinted about psi, he was repelled by the thought of it. He was ready to break up with me rather than believe I might be psychic. That was when I grasped the extent of some people's unconscious fear."

"I'm sorry," Terry said.

"I'm not. I thought I'd be heartbroken, but in the end all I felt was relief. My God, Terry, I'd been sleeping with him for more than a year. I thought I knew him, knew what it was to be in love. But I didn't. When Jessica told me how it *should* be between lovers—"

"A joining of minds as well as bodies? I've always felt that . . . only I didn't know I did. I only sensed that there was something missing."

"Yes. Maybe there's not when two people feel like soulmates, but that kind of feeling comes from unconscious telepathy. The Maclairnans won't have sex with anyone who's not telepathic—I mean historically they wouldn't, when they lived on Undine among outsiders. Now, of course, they're all telepaths, but with observers coming, and Fleet—"

"When our captain briefed us on local customs, he said not to take it personally if friendships didn't lead to romance." *And he also said that when they do, it often happens much faster than it would with non-telepaths. . . .* "Most of the crew hasn't developed much of any psi awareness yet," he added.

But you have. Her thought, though not consciously intended for him to pick up, was clear. *And I have, except Jessica said I won't gain full telepathic sensitivity until I've been with a lover who has it. On Undine, that was how newcomers were taught—sharing minds during lovemaking awakens psi capability that carries over to other situations.*

Do you think we could teach each other? He could not say this aloud yet, not when he'd known her for less than a day. But they both knew it was just a matter of when.

16

TO TERRY'S SURPRISE, when he broached the subject of flying the explorer, Commander Chiang raised no objections. "It's worth looking into," he said evenly. "I'm no judge since my field is communications, but I'll pass your comments on to the captain."

The next morning a second shuttle arrived bringing Commander Linley, who was *Shepard*'s chief engineer, and two AI specialists. Terry spent all day with them checking over every detail of *Picard* that could be examined without more extensive disassembly than was possible while it was on the ground. When they finished Linley pronounced the ship spaceworthy.

"I see no reason why it can't get as far as *Shepard*," he said. "I wouldn't want to say it can patrol the solar system until I've evaluated results of a complete overhaul, but since that can't be done until it's docked, I'm willing to give it clearance. Naturally I can't guarantee that lifting a ship that's been grounded for two centuries is safe. You're the one who'll be flying it, Lieutenant. It's your call."

"I want to try it, sir," Terry said.

"You realize you won't have a crew."

"There's no need for one just to get into orbit." There was also no need to risk anyone's life but his own, a fact too obvious to require mention.

The attempt was put off a day because Commander Linley was scheduled to take two mentors up to *Shepard* the next afternoon and wanted to get that out of the way before returning to observe the liftoff. Also he said he'd be bringing a medical officer back with him, which struck Terry as pointless since the chances of needing one were virtually zero. If the ship crashed he wouldn't be injured, he'd be dead, a possibility that the senior officers were evidently unwilling to acknowledge.

He slept soundly that night but woke early with excitement rising in him like a bubbling spring. He wasn't sure which excited him most—the idea of flying *Picard* or the thought of seeing Kathryn again.

She was in charge of liaison between mentors and the League, so she would be coming to the Old Settlement with them. Two—a married couple—were to live aboard *Shepard* and continue the mind-training of the crew. Once used to working with outsiders they would go on to Earth in *Promise* and another couple would begin the process. And, he realized, Kathryn would be going as their official escort, a prospect he didn't like at all. He wasn't sure how long her trips would last; she would assist the Foundation in getting them settled and would bring a new group of observers back with her. Hopefully she would be able to spend more time on Maclairn than away.

Before long the comm technicians went to install satellite dishes in the towns, leaving Terry at the base. He spent the morning showing Commander Linley and the other newly-arrived officers around the settlement, then walked down the terraces to wait for the boat bringing Kathryn and the mentors from Petersville, which was located just below the dam. By daylight he could see more of the beach, which she'd said was a popular place for swimming. There was no spare water on Maclairn, which relied largely on wells for irrigation as well as domestic use. It rained infrequently; she had been vague about that, saying that some sort of rainmaking technology was used during dry spells but nobody would explain to her how it was done. The river dammed to create the lake had been periodically inundated by flash floods, during the first of which the colonists had lost their first crop and their leader Peter, trapped under a boulder, had lost his legs. He had been physically crippled for the remaining eighty-odd years of his life, but he was a superb mentor, and in fact the only mentor until Ivana came of age.

Terry pondered this with mixed feelings. The original Maclairnans had left Undine to escape its oppressive medical tyranny and so had not minded doing without the medical technology available on all civilized worlds—they hadn't needed it, for there were many healers among them. But healers could not restore lost limbs. Had Peter had any regrets, stuck on a world where he could not be given new legs? Was the commitment of the Maclairnans to reliance on mind power reasonable, or merely blind devotion to an abstract ideal? They intended to reject technological aid from the League, he knew, except for comm and power satellites. To be sure, in most respects they were now technologically advanced. They had no objection to technology itself, only to the price in loss of independence they would pay if they imported it. So they weren't sacrificing anything but what they valued less than what they gained. Yet it upset him in ways he couldn't define. He had never committed himself to anything beyond his desire to fly; it was hard to imagine feeling committed to a less personal goal.

And Kathryn had declared more than once that she was committed to Maclairn and its vision of humankind's future. That seemed to mean something more to her than the wish to make it her home.

He walked along the beach to an upright slab of rock at the far edge of the leveled area, on which to his surprise he saw that names were chiseled—first Hari, for whom the lake had evidently been named, then several columns of others. This, then, was a community grave marker. She had mentioned that Maclairnans buried their dead in the lake from boats, a custom begun on Undine where their ancestors had defied the law by secretly burying bodies in the sea. The few interred in Maclairn's ground before the lake's creation had been moved years later, at the time of the first death from old age.

What would it be like, he wondered, to be so attached to a particular location that you knew that you would someday be buried there, in a place you'd been coming to all your life? That was how it was on ancient Earth, of course, but he had never given it any thought. Insofar as he had considered death at all, he had assumed it would be on some distant world he had so far never heard of, if not in space itself. Now . . . what if *Picard* did crash on liftoff? Did the mysterious tie he felt to Maclairn rise from precognitive knowledge that this lake would be the repository of his own remains? For a brief moment he pictured his name on that marker as clearly as if it were real.

The thought didn't depress him; instead, it magnified his eagerness for life, a life filled with experience beyond just piloting explorers. He'd begun to sense it during the training for mind powers he had so far only begun to develop; it had grown at his first sight of Maclairn; and now, thinking of Kathryn, he felt his blood stir and he was nearly consumed by a mixture of longings. He would fly *Picard* and take joy in it, but there was more, so much more. . . .

He turned and saw that far down the lake a boat was approaching, barely visible in the shadow of the cliffs that rose from the opposite shore. It was the large boat; apparently friends had come with the mentors to see them off. Terry walked out on the dock to meet it. As the only Fleet officer present, he supposed he should offer some sort of official greeting.

Kathryn stood at the railing at the boat's bow and waved to him as it came in. Her flame-colored shirt and white pants were brilliant against the deep blue of the water, a picture he knew would be indelibly impressed into his mind. Dazzled by it, he found himself wishing that no one else was present so that he could take her into his arms.

With difficulty he turned his attention to the couple slated to work aboard *Shepard*—to his surprise, Corwin and Kamila, whom he had not previously realized were mentors. They looked no different from any other Maclairnans, and were dressed just as informally. Yet they had a certain presence, as Aldren and Roanna did, that made them stand out as special. It wasn't a matter of age, as they appeared to be younger than Aldren, though Terry reminded himself that Maclairnans' age couldn't be judged by sight. Nor was it anything they said. Telepathy, perhaps? He knew instantly that they were to be trusted and that they were aware of everything about him that he'd want them to know.

He and Kathryn went with them as they climbed the trail up the terraces, a walk undoubtedly familiar to them, accompanied by their group of friends as well as a robocart carrying boxes of neurofeedback equipment for installation aboard *Shepard*. When they reached the top Commander Linley introduced them to the other officers present and escorted them to the shuttle pad. There were no long farewells; there had been a gathering for that in town, Kathryn said.

The mentors were excited and eager to go, but at the same time sad to be leaving Maclairn. Sensing their feelings, Terry began to understand, a little, what dedication to a long-term goal involved. They couldn't hope to have any significant influence on Earth. They could help only a few individuals gain the new capabilities that might someday transform humankind. They were likely to meet opposition, even danger. And there was so much that they'd be giving up. . . .

Along with duffle bags, the departing mentors were carrying lightweight jackets, impossible to wear in the heat but necessary for meals in the wardroom aboard ship. Seeing the one draped over Corwin's arm, Terry noticed a flame-shaped lapel pin like the one Aldren had. Once the shuttle lifted and the other Maclairnans headed back to the lake, he asked Kathryn about it.

"Is it some sort of insignia for mentors?" he inquired?

"No," Kathryn said. "All mentors have them, but so do a lot of other Maclairnans. It means they are Stewards of the Flame."

"Aldren named our secret training the Flame Project," Terry said reflectively. "Does it have something to do with teaching mind skills, then?"

"More than that. The flame symbolizes enhanced human mind power. Originally, 'Steward of the Flame' was a password the group on Undine used for identification when they had to hide their abilities from the authorities. Then when they emigrated, they had to give a reason to ask for Fleet's help in leaving illegally, so they pretended to be a religious sect that was being persecuted. They didn't think of it as a real group designation—there wasn't any need for one when they all participated in the Ritual. But after the first generation not everyone chose to, so ever since then the name has been used to distinguish the people who do."

"The Ritual? Is that a religious rite?" Terry asked, surprised.

"No, though it's as solemn as if it were, I think. What happens during the Ritual is secret from everyone who hasn't been through it. I was told that knowing in advance would interfere with a novice being able to do whatever it is they do, some special kind of psi that Jessica says I'm not ready for yet. The ceremony involves formal commitment to using our advanced capabilities and spreading them to all humankind. It's how they kept that goal alive for more than two hundred years."

So the commitment she'd spoken of before wasn't just a vague feeling. As Terry pondered this, Kathryn added, "Only a mentor can lead the Ritual. It's their main responsibility besides giving mind training, though they also act as psychotherapists and healers."

At the rim of the canyon they paused. "Will you have to have more mind training before you're eligible for the Ritual?" Terry asked. He was eager to keep her talking because he did not want see her go.

"Yes, though I'm not sure just what kind," she told him. "Some people didn't think I should be ambassador when I wasn't a Steward and hadn't made their pledge, but there wasn't any alternative. I was the only person knowledgeable about League law and they didn't want to wait. Now, though, Jessica's hoping I'll qualify before I go back with the mentors."

"When will that be?" he asked, hoping it wouldn't be soon.

"Well, they'll work aboard the cruiser for several weeks

at least, but now that they've left home they're anxious to get to Earth."

"Several weeks . . . Kathryn, I may not get any leave sooner than that! I've had a chance to visit the surface and there'll be a lot of people in line who haven't—by the time I come again you may be gone." He didn't attempt to hide his dismay at the thought.

Her face told him that she had picked it up and that she shared it. "Oh Terry," she said. "I've been trying to forget about tomorrow, about you flying that centuries-old ship. I know you have to do it, any risk is worth taking to protect Maclairn—but it scares me."

"Will you come and watch?"

"If you want me to. I couldn't bear it if anything went wrong . . . but I don't think I can bear to stay away, either."

"I'll be lifting the first thing in the morning," he said, "as soon as Commander Linley gets back. Will there be an early boat?"

"I could come by myself in a water taxi. Only . . . I think I'd rather stay over. The abandoned stone huts are . . . used, sometimes. They're not considered private property."

"I've seen dim lights in a few of them," he said. "I wondered, because I thought no one lives here anymore."

"They don't. But the kids—the teenagers—don't have much privacy in town, and so it's sort of traditional for couples to come up at night from time to time."

The kids who were considered adults at age thirteen. Captain Vargas had warned about this in the briefing: adult meant fully adult on Maclairn and sex between young teens was not frowned upon. Since they were telepathic, fully sensitive to each other's feelings and taught from childhood to respect them, preventing it would be both impossible and unnecessary. Contraceptive technology was unavailable; most girls bore their first child at fourteen or fifteen, a holdover from the early years when rapid population increase was vital, though nowadays after a woman had two or three children her tubes were sealed by a psychic healer. Extended families were the rule, with grandparents and great-grandparents taking an active role in a child's rearing.

"If you're going to stay, let's sit under the trees again until the installation team's back and I have to go in for mess call," he said, rejoicing in the reprieve of a few hours. "Maybe Commander Chiang will let me invite you to eat with us."

"I brought some protein bars," she said. They walked further along the rim this time, to a clump of trees distant from the Commons.

He should be thinking about the flight in *Picard*, Terry thought. The most thrilling event of his life so far, a chance to do what no one else had done. He wanted desperately to do it . . . but right now, there was something he wanted more.

They sat in silence, sharing thoughts without words. Soon, somewhat to his surprise, he found that his arms were around Kathryn, pressing her close to him; and when they kissed, all other concerns fell away.

After a while, when he could speak again, he said, "I think I envy the kids who use those huts."

"You don't have to," Kathryn said.

He didn't need to ask what she meant. "I can't very well stay away after mess call," he pointed out. "The commander would send out a search party."

"No, he wouldn't. Corwin will have asked him not to."

"Corwin?" he said, astonished. "God, Kathryn, did you *tell* him—?"

"Not aloud, but he's a mentor, Terry. He watched us together, and I don't think you were hiding your feelings any more than I was. He knew before we did."

"But why would he speak to Commander Chiang?"

"Because he's studied Earth's customs and knows they're different from Maclairn's, that ours have to be explained to prevent misunderstanding. And because he knew it's your last night before—"

"Before I might be killed."

"Yes. Here, it won't be seen as rushing things. Couples who care about each other sleep together—it means so much more than just sex, you see. At least I've been told it does."

It means something to hold to, he thought—something indestructible that will last forever. He was not nervous about the coming flight, yet he sensed that a bond with Kathryn, a merging of their minds, would make him more than just a skilled pilot. It would give him the roots he had never had, a reason not only to keep exploring, but to return.

Chiang had been at the landing party's briefing, where the captain had made clear that on matters concerning Maclairn's customs the advice of mentors was to be respected. He would not disregard any suggestion Corwin might have made to him. And what the hell, Terry thought—even if he was disciplined for it later, he was not going back to the Commons tonight.

17

THE HOUSE THEY chose was one of the smallest, little more than the original beehive-shaped stone hut with an entry and small kitchen added at one side. The single room was dominated by a wide, thick mattress covered with handwoven blankets, leaving little space for the seating cushions and low table against the opposite wall. "We sit and sleep on the floor even in town," Kathryn said. "The early settlers had no wood, and by the time it would have been possible to build chairs and raised beds, people were so used to not having them that mattresses or futons were all they wanted. Most homes have Japanese-style dining tables with floor cushions."

The hut had cabling for electricity, but the power had been turned off; when it began to get dark Kathryn lit an oil lamp. "Sunflower oil," she explained. "There's no petroleum on this world." They sat munching the protein bars, drinking from a canteen filled at the settlement's central pump; the stone huts had no plumbing. It was rather like camping, Terry thought, the one thing on Earth he had really enjoyed. During leaves on other worlds he had rarely gone beyond the cities adjacent to spaceports, which were ultra-modern and all alike. Maclairnan towns were more inviting, Kathryn had told him; still he was glad that their first time together would be in this special place in no way like those where he had been less happy.

By the time it was fully dark it was also cold; the stone walls and roof were some insulation, but they had not brought jackets and despite their volitional control over body temperature, the pile of blankets on the mattress beckoned—offering a good excuse not to wait any longer. They left the lamp burning but undressed too quickly to take in the sight of each other's bodies.

Terry had thought he might be shy, that memories of the emotionally-frustrating earlier relationships might intrude. His expectations of what sex was like among telepaths had been built so high, by Aldren's comments and by Kathryn's own, that he feared he would be disappointed, or worse, that *she* would be. But when it happened it seemed natural and inevitable, leaving no room in his mind or hers for doubts or comparisons. Full arousal was almost immediate, and it came less from the touch of their bodies than from the merging of their inner selves.

He had thought he knew what telepathy was. He had known *nothing*, Terry realized fleetingly, but then he could not think at all, but only feel; and what he felt was not his excitement alone, but also Kathryn's. No gradual preliminaries were needed—he was as aware of her physical sensations as she of his, and astonishingly, he could not tell which were which. It was as if their two bodies were literally one, for when their hands explored each other's flesh he experienced pleasure in places his own body lacked.

But all this was as nothing to the melding of their minds. At the moment of climax he felt her rush of joy as if it rose from his own depths, and afterward, as the urgency faded, he saw through her eyes. As one, they stood first at the prow of the boat, the spray cool on their faces, and then on the walkway across the dam, looking down on the settlement where he had not yet been. Its sprawling stone and brick buildings, surrounded by clumps of trees, were a focus of comfort amid the green oasis of planted fields and the barren rocky land beyond. And within the house in which they next found themselves was warmth and firelight and the sound of singing, and he knew he could never be lonely again, for she was linked with him and would always be with him, no matter how far from her he might go. They were together, yet it was a connection, not unity; they lost no individuality by it— he was more fully himself than he had ever been while separate. He was flying, with all the stars of the galaxy in front of him and the expectation of something new and wonderful just ahead, and she shared the thrill, for she was as aware of his deep longings as he of hers.

He held her close, feeling the pulse of her heartbeat, as they absorbed the facets of each other's memories: at first perceived consciously, then dissolving into shared dreams. Some time during the night they woke and made love again. No words passed between them. There was no need for words when they were already sensing everything that might be said.

When it began to get light, Terry got up and put on his clothes. This was the day he would fly *Picard*. He felt no fear of any mishap; nothing could part him from Kathryn now, or ever again. They would be physically separated while he was aboard *Shepard* and she traveled to Earth, but that would not weaken their indissoluble bond. He was committed to something after all, he realized. He had wondered what that would feel like, and now he knew. It gave him a feeling of inner strength he had never experienced, despite lifelong confidence in his ability to excel in mere technical skills. He was no longer isolated from the essence of life; from today onward, he would be whole.

Kathryn rose and together they stood looking out at the cold dawn. *I'll be watching,* she told him as they kissed one last time. *I'm not scared anymore, Terry. I know you'll be okay.*

At breakfast in the Commons, no comments were made about his absence; fellow-officers who under other circumstances might have kidded him had evidently been instructed to ignore it. Just as Terry finished eating, the shuttle arrived and he went out to greet Commander Linley.

He had worried that he might be distracted while doing the preflight inspection, unable to concentrate on the job at hand, but it did not work that way. His mind was totally focused; his awareness of Kathryn was an undercurrent too thoroughly integrated to interfere with conscious thought. Once his checkup of the ship was complete he got into his pressure suit, sealed the airlock, and settled into the captain's seat on the bridge. The familiar vibration as he put on power was reassuring. He paused, making the inner adjustments he'd learned through neurofeedback for lowering his level of stress hormones and calming his heart.

In the instant before he gave the command to lift, he called out silently, *I love you Kathryn*, and recalled with dismay that he had never told her so. They had sensed their love, not declared it in the way non-telepaths would do. But now, even at this distance, her reply came back to him: *I love you, Terry. . . .* From Commander Linley, too, came a strong send-off—*Go for it, Radnor*—and he understood that through last night's experience his telepathic sensitivity had indeed been permanently enhanced.

Power surged through *Picard* as its antigravs raised it from the pad where it had rested through two centuries. It hovered briefly and then, stirring a ring of pulverized rock beneath, it lifted.

Within seconds Terry was looking down on the plateau and the blue sliver of the lake. Before he had time to locate the grove of trees where he and Kathryn had first kissed, he was in space.

He took a deep breath. There might yet be trouble—the ship might not reach orbit, or its AI could fail during rendezvous or docking. But *Picard* was free of the ground, and his spirit soared with it. *His* ship, for surely he would have chances to fly it after it became operational. This was what he had always wanted, to fly, and keep flying as far as his ship could take him. But now he would not feel the letdown that had saddened him at the end of his previous flights. From now on he also belonged to a world.

Within a few minutes *Shepard* loomed ahead of him and docking, handled efficiently by the AI, went smoothly. Captain Vargas and several senior officers were waiting at the airlock. "Well done, Lieutenant," the captain said. "With this ship we can set up surveillance much further from the planet than with patrollers alone."

"Yes, sir. It would have been too bad to let it sit on the ground when it was salvageable."

"So Admiral Derham thought when he was here," said Vargas, smiling. "But he advised me that the idea should come from you. He said you'd jump at any flight assignment we offered you, and wouldn't give enough consideration to the risks unless you took the initiative in evaluating them."

Stunned, Terry said, "He foresaw that I'd suggest it? But I might not have been in the Old Settlement long enough if I'd only gone down on leave."

"Why do you think you were assigned as shuttle pilot for the first team sent there? For that matter, why are you aboard *Shepard*? You've known all along that you're overqualified for cruiser duty; the admiral said you expressed yourself very strongly on that point."

Oh, my God, Terry thought. "Sir, are you saying I was pulled off explorer duty in the first place because—"

"We needed an experienced explorer pilot rated fit for command. Aldren and I considered several, and he said that based on your psych profile he considered you the best bet, as well as the one with the most aptitude for mind training. If this ship proves functional you'll be its captain, and you'll be responsible for deploying unmanned sensor stations on asteroids and on the system's other planets."

"I'll be very happy to do that, sir," Terry declared, thinking with remorse of how he'd inwardly cursed the admiral for assigning him to what appeared to be a routine training cruise.

"Commander Chiang tells me that congratulations of another kind are also in order," Vargas continued.

Terry felt his face burn. He hadn't thought the captain would be told.

"Don't worry about it. We want to establish ties with the Maclairnans, and they are very pleased by this particular one. I assume, from what the mentors have said to me, that it's of the kind likely to last." He hesitated and went on, "I'm not married, but Admiral Derham and his wife are my close friends, and they've given me to understand that relationships between couples who have had mind training are more—intense than others. That's why we recruited couples where possible, and why we care with whom our single people become involved. Such relationships aren't taken lightly here." *And I trust you don't intend to take it lightly.*

He's warning me not to break it off! Terry realized. *Sir, I wouldn't. . . .*

I know that. I'm enough of a telepath to sense your feelings. But you'd better see Corwin as soon as possible, because until he senses them himself he'll wonder whether he was right to intervene.

But Corwin had already sensed them, Kathryn had said. If he wasn't sure, why would he have spoken to Chiang?

All at once Terry saw why, and why she had known that he would. Jessica had told her she wouldn't gain full telepathic capability until she had sex with another telepath, and that she wasn't yet ready for the Ritual that apparently required well-developed psi powers. Until she was, she couldn't make the formal commitment they expected of their ambassador. No wonder the mentor had taken action. . . .

Just as his own telepathic sensitivity had been increased by their union, so had hers. She was truly Maclairnan now, fit to formalize the commitment that meant so much to her and become a Steward of the Flame. But in doing that, would she be creating a barrier between them? Terry wondered. Aldren had told him his psi powers would grow, and inside he knew that this was true. He would surely develop all those Kathryn had gained. Yet he was not free to pledge lifelong loyalty to Maclairn while he remained an officer in Fleet. And only in Fleet could he fly.

18

TERRY WAS SCHEDULED to meet with Corwin that evening to resume his neurofeedback training. Immediately he felt a strong rapport with him, even stronger than with Aldren—stronger, he realized, because his own telepathic capability had dramatically increased. There was no need to discuss his feelings for Kathryn; Corwin knew. Nor was it necessary to tell him anything about his past. Terry was not sure how much he drew from their link and how much he had learned from the recorded report on the trainees that Aldren had sent in care of the captain, but he could tell that the mentor was aware of everything that mattered.

After a dual neurofeedback session during which he demonstrated that he could follow a visual mind-pattern into different states of consciousness and that he could consciously control his heart rate, blood pressure, and various internal states perceivable only by a skilled healer, Corwin announced that the next step would be to learn remote viewing.

"I want to—but it's hard for me to believe it's possible," Terry admitted.

"It's easier than it sounds. As Aldren may have told you, a few people were doing it systematically back in the twentieth century, before the reaction set in that made public advocacy of psi powers disreputable. We can't be sure how many continued to do it in private. But since you are psi-gifted and already trained to enter altered consciousness, you'll probably get good results."

"Well," Terry said, "I guess if I try I can see Kathryn—where she is now, I mean, not just memory." He paused, a picture forming in his mind. She was in Jessica's house, a rambling stone building like those he had seen when their thoughts merged. . . .

"That's just what you *mustn't* do," Corwin declared. "If you were advanced enough to perceive the surface from orbit, which you're not, any image connected with Kathryn wouldn't be remote viewing, it would come to you through telepathy. We can't always tell the difference—a good deal of what is thought to be remote viewing is actually telepathy; in other words, the images are unconsciously picked up from someone's mind rather than directly from physical reality. There's no way to be sure. Only because it's possible to see things no one else has ever seen do we know that direct perception is a true capability."

They began with photographs. "This used to be done

with prints in sealed envelopes," Corwin said. "But that way, even if the monitor has not personally seen what's in the envelope, telepathy can't be ruled out, because he may be perceiving its content and communicating it on an unconscious level. Letting the computer choose the photos from among thousands reduces that chance; still it's not completely foolproof. In most cases that doesn't matter—telepathic perception in itself is a big achievement for most people, and if the goal is to get information, where it comes from is not important. But you are already a telepath, and you need to practice direct perception. So we'll get around the problem by using only mentors as your instructors; we've learned to close our minds so that not even unconscious input can be obtained from them."

They moved to a table in a compartment separate from the one where neurofeedback equipment had been installed. "Just relax for a few minutes," Corwin said, "and then simply let things happen. This works like the other skills you've been taught—willpower is counterproductive. If you *try* to see, you'll fail. The images will come from your unconscious mind; you must allow them to rise, just as you allow your heartbeat to slow or speed up instead of trying to force it."

To his surprise, Terry was given paper and asked to record his impressions with a pen instead of an electronic stylus. "It may seem anachronistic," Corwin said, "but you needn't write out whole sentences, after all, and it won't matter if your writing isn't legible to anyone else. Just put down key words and rough sketches of shapes you perceive."

He couldn't possibly have any idea at all of the chosen photograph, Terry thought. The procedure seemed vague, almost silly. Nevertheless, when the green light signaled that the computer was displaying a particular photo on a monitor hidden from them, he found himself thinking of a row of towers, shafts rising higher than he could see without raising his eyes, with no distinguishing features he could make out other than an impression that they were not identical. He wrote "tall, straight" and sketched vertical lines with a jagged horizontal line above them, more a diagram than a picture.

After a few minutes Corwin took the paper from him and removed the cover from the monitor. Terry gasped. It was a scene from ancient Earth: tall skyscrapers of varying height, unlike anything that existed on the colony worlds, and clearly the inspiration for the pattern of lines he had drawn.

They tried several more. A few of his impressions were far off, others accurate in some respects, but none had the striking resemblance shown in his first sketch. "That's normal," Corwin told him. "Even after long practice, you'll have misses as well as hits. But overall, your rate of accuracy will be well above chance."

Aldren, too, had said not all viewings were true—and that when there was no way of checking, you couldn't know whether a perception was true or not. Or whether you were seeing in real time or a scene from the future. . . . *He had a vision of my face,* Terry recalled, *something to do with an extraordinary destiny. . . .*

He became aware that Corwin was looking at him strangely. Evidently Aldren had not mentioned that vision in his message to the mentors. To cover his embarrassment Terry said quickly, "I guess I haven't thanked you for asking Commander Chiang not to hunt for me last night." There was no reason not to speak of it when even the captain seemed to feel it had been a good thing.

Corwin smiled and said "I'm glad that it worked out for you—and for Kathryn. Do you understand what happened when you were together, Terry? Besides the joy of love, I mean."

"I know we became stronger telepaths, and not just with each other," he said. "And I guess I know why you wanted her to gain more psi capability. But I don't really see why sharing our minds carries over."

"Everyone is to some degree telepathic on an unconscious level," Corwin reminded him. "During an intense experience when you are focused on feelings rather than the rational thought that usually dominates your mind, telepathically sensed thoughts can rise to consciousness. The barriers that ordinarily suppress them come down, provided you're emotionally receptive to the idea of psi and feel no fear of it. And once this has occurred, those barriers are weakened, so you become conscious of telepathic input much more easily than before. Extreme stress can cause this, as you found at the start of your training. Sex does it even better."

What would have happened if Kathryn and I hadn't met? He couldn't help wondering, though he didn't really want to know.

It wasn't accidental. Jessica knew you were with the landing party, and that you were able to communicate telepathically. We made sure she'd be at the cookout.

You planned it? But why—

"Kathryn was in a unique position, and not just because of her wish to qualify for the Ritual," Corwin said aloud. "It's not usual on Maclairn for people to be without partners. As you know, marriage isn't defined by law, here—"

Terry nodded. That had been explained in the initial briefing. Maclairnans considered it none of the government's business who was living with whom and considered it wrong to make any legal distinction between singles and people with partners. Moreover, in the founding generation there had been more women than men and all of them had borne children, by IVF if too old to conceive naturally, so such a distinction would have been impractical.

"Nevertheless," Corwin went on, "most couples have made long-term commitments and consider themselves lifemates. The others form temporary relationships that because of the mind-sharing involved are never merely casual. Without lovemaking we would feel isolated and incomplete. Kathryn wasn't attracted to any of the men near her age who aren't permanently bonded, and because of her background she wouldn't have wanted a non-exclusive relationship in any case. We were saddened to think of her remaining alone."

Isolated and incomplete . . . that's how I always felt, Terry thought, *and then as soon as I saw her. . . .*

Yes. Love at first sight isn't just a fairy tale; among telepaths it often happens. If I hadn't believed you were feeling more than physical attraction to each other, I wouldn't have done what I did.

"There was another reason why we took action," Corwin continued after a pause. "I wouldn't want you to get the idea that that it was a matter of expediency, either in Kathryn's case or in yours. But actually, enhancement of your psi capabilities, too, is important to us."

"Why?" Terry asked, puzzled.

Soberly Corwin said, "Aldren has told us that you welcome your psi gift, that you're not merely unafraid of it, but eager to pursue further training. Is that still true?"

"Yes, it's—it's like a world that's always been just out of range, something I was searching for that I couldn't define . . . even before I met Kathryn. . . ." It was hard to find words to express it. He hoped the mentor was sensing the feelings the question stirred.

"Constant psi sensitivity can be a burden," Corwin warned, "particularly for a person who hasn't grown up in a society where it's considered normal. Once you've developed the ability to maintain it during your regular activities, it can be hard to turn off. And it can interfere with those activities if you let it take over too much of your mind."

Terry was silent. Corwin went on, "As you get in deeper, powers can emerge that are more difficult to deal

with when you're among outsiders. Aldren mentioned healing, didn't he? He noted that he'd introduced you to self-
healing, which ordinarily wouldn't be done this early in
your training."

"Yes." *He said I might someday be able to heal others, that keeping it secret wouldn't be easy. . . .*

"And you've seen what happened to *Picard*'s
hyperdrive controls." *I think you know what that implies,
though it wouldn't occur to many newcomers.*

It . . . bothered me, when I first heard about Ivana,
Terry confessed silently.

"So are you willing to explore your psi capability, knowing that once you do, you'll be stuck with it for as long as
you live?"

"I don't have much choice, do I? It's part of me. It's
the reason I always felt different, as if I didn't fit anywhere except when I was flying. Now that I'm aware of it,
I can't turn away."

"You're wise, if you already know that," Corwin declared. "Okay. I hadn't planned to speak of this so soon,
but since you're better prepared than I expected there's
no point in holding off. We—the mentors who discussed
the protection of Maclairn before Aldren left—had an idea,
a very tentative idea that may come to nothing but which
Jessica felt should be pursued. We suspect that if a ship
were to approach this planet, we might sense it. We know
that remote viewers among the first settlers got some
information about the colony's site from low orbit. And
we know that both Peter and Jesse's wife made telepathic
contact with him while he was aboard *Picard*. Since then
we've become far more accustomed to using psi than they
were, and I've been briefly in touch with a friend on the
surface."

"But Fleet won't let an intruder get as far as low orbit," Terry said.

"Theoretically, psi is not affected by distance. We don't
believe it can be used across interstellar space, but there

were reports of its having worked within Earth's solar system. So there is a remote chance that a patrol near one of the outer planets might sense the presence of an intruder sooner than electronics could—even, perhaps, precognitively."

"The odds aren't very large. The solar system is a big place."

"Yet you're planning to put sensors on those planets in the belief that intruders might visit them. Our first thought, when Admiral Derham told us that *Picard* might be salvaged, was that mentors should travel with the crew. But he pointed out that the chances of contact weren't great enough to justify taking people with no technical skills along on every trip for years to come. Then Aldren suggested that he might be able to send us at least one Fleet officer capable of distant sensing."

Terry drew breath. "He sent . . . me? He thought I could do this?"

"That's our hope. Assuming that you can be given sufficient training—maybe not before your first flight, but there won't be an intruder soon in any case, despite Jessica's worries. You would have to devote a part of your life to developing your psi skill on a long-term basis, and it would probably contribute nothing. You must want to do this for its own sake, not just gamble on a long shot."

"I do want to," Terry declared, "whatever it takes."

"So Aldren thought. And everything I've perceived in you bears it out."

"Does Captain Vargas know?"

"Yes. He screened explorer pilots' records for Aldren to choose from. He'll see to it that your schedule permits extra training. One more thing, Terry—telepathy is instantaneous. Whether you directly sensed an intruder or picked up a sensor signal, you might be able to warn Maclairn without the delay long-range radio transmission involves."

It was a dizzying prospect. After everything else that had happened since yesterday, it was almost too much to take in.

19

IT WAS DECIDED that while *Picard* was being overhauled, Terry would go down to the surface to be taught remote viewing skills that could not be learned from pictures. After only one night aboard *Shepard*, he found himself on the lake boat, heading toward the capital—and Kathryn.

She met him at the marina near the dam and they walked across the bridge that spanned it to the funicular that would take them to the level below. It was a rough dam made of boulders and fused rocks, as if some natural disaster had formed it rather than any human plan. "What happened?" he asked. "We were told the lake wasn't here during the settlement's first years."

"Jesse blasted the canyon walls from space," Kathryn told him, "just before he sent the failing starship away. He channeled the last of its power into the beam because otherwise it would have been wasted, and they needed a way to conserve water."

"He was either experienced with beam weapons or very lucky," Terry declared. "I thought he'd been a freighter pilot when he was in Fleet."

"A freighter *captain*. He'd been prepared to defend his ship against pirates. But it's been said that unconscious remote viewing may have played some part in targeting for the dam."

Terry frowned. "That means it might go on all the time beneath consciousness, even among outsiders." He had already, he noticed, begun to think of people not in on the secret by the Maclairnan term.

"Certainly," Kathryn agreed, "just like telepathy. All training does is make us more fully human."

Put that way, it was not quite as overwhelmingly awesome as it had seemed to him during the night, when he'd begun to wonder what he was letting himself in for. He had been frozen inside so long that except when he was with Kathryn, there were moments when he felt as if his new mind powers were a mere dream state from which he might wake. He had been glad that Corwin had tested his pain control because it reminded him how real and down-to-earth those powers were—which, he perceived, was why Corwin had done it. Now, with Kathryn beside him talking matter-of-factly about what he was soon to learn, Terry's usual self-confidence had returned.

At the bottom of the funicular they boarded a railcar that took them the short distance to the center of Petersville. It wasn't the biggest town on Maclairn, but it was the oldest and in Kathryn's opinion, the most attractive. The public and commercial buildings were of natural yellow brick roofed with flat tiles, all surrounded by the slender, fast-growing trees that seemed to dominate settled areas on the planet in contrast to the barrenness of the rest of it. Most of the private homes had stone foundations rising halfway up the walls, with wood siding above. They were large, as it was customary for several generations to live together, but closely spaced. Many had small garden plots filled entirely with brilliant yellow sunflowers.

"Sunflowers were the only flower seeds the founding starship carried," Kathryn explained. "We grow them for oil, seeds to eat, and chickenfeed as well as for brightening residential areas—you'll see large fields of them. Alternating with green crops, they're spectacular."

There was a park by the river, she said, with shade trees. The river was currently dry, as the dammed lake above it was not quite full. "If it doesn't rain soon, the mentors will take action," said Kathryn, "and we'll be cut off from the Old Settlement for a few days when the lake is too high and turbulent for boats."

Action? Terry inquired, but she did not tell him more and he realized that she did not know the details. With awe, he grasped her suspicion that some sort of paranormal rainmaking was involved.

He was to be a guest in Jessica's house, where Kathryn was living, but she did not take him there immediately. "Jessica will want to welcome you, and she won't be home until dinnertime. So let's do your shopping first," she suggested. Fleet personnel were to wear civvies while on leave or on duty in the settlements; League money was of course worthless on Maclairn, but arrangements had been made for them to receive an allowance in local credits.

To his surprise, he found that all clothes in the shops were handmade. The very limited manufacturing capability developed by the colony had been devoted to production of the robotic machines essential for the heavy work of building and large-scale agriculture required by an expanding population, plus the electronic devices necessary for communication and for continuing access to the electronic knowledgebase brought by the founding starship. That knowledgebase had provided the data needed to establish advanced technology. But there had never been an intermediate industrial stage. There were no factories for production of consumer goods other than very basic ones such as thread and woven cloth. The people took pride in handcrafts, Kathryn explained—there was little other work for those who weren't high-tech specialists. Except for the ones employed in agriculture or food services, most did not have jobs; they created and personally sold such things as clothing, jewelry, and home furnishings.

Terry bought chino pants, several brightly-colored shirts, swim trunks, and sandals, which Kathryn assured him would meet all his needs; his flight jacket would serve when he went outdoors after dark. There wouldn't be much else for him to spend money on, she said. Community events were free and most other recreation was centered on gatherings in people's homes or outdoors.

Jessica's house was a spacious one, located near the town's center and reached by one of the broad stone-paved paths radiating from it. There were no streets on Maclairn, and no vehicles except the robocarts used for deliveries. They were not needed, since for generations the colonists had been used to walking. "What about the disabled and elderly?" Terry inquired.

"There aren't any. Remember, everyone stays healthy—when necessary with the help of psi-gifted healers—and people who have used their mind-training since youth don't deteriorate in old age."

Though he was by now used to adjusting his temperature to the heat, Terry was glad to reach the cool interior of the stone-walled house. In the center of its huge great room was a circular stone fireplace with a hammered-copper hood, surrounded by large stuffed floor cushions. "The Council meets in this room," Kathryn said. "It was patterned after the lodge on Undine where Ian Maclairn formed the Group. Peter was still alive when the house was built, you see, and the time he'd spent at the lodge was his most cherished memory."

Jessica was waiting for them. Terry had met her briefly at the cookout, but had not had a chance to talk with her. Now he was impressed by what a vital, energetic woman she was. Dressed in the informal pants and colorful shirt that everyone wore, she looked no different from people he had seen in the shops. It was hard to believe she was, as Kathryn had told him, a hundred and twenty-one years old—but then, he still wasn't used to the fact that Aldren was over a hundred.

"Welcome, Terry," Jessica said with warmth. "We're happy to have you with us." There was an odd intensity in her voice—no, not her voice; he was merely sensing emotion that seemed greater than the occasion warranted.

"I'm glad to be here, ma'am," he told her, realizing too late that although she was the top leader of the planet, it probably wasn't appropriate to address her as he would a Fleet commander. Despite the somewhat mysterious feelings underlying her greeting, he had the same immediate sense of connection with her as he'd had with Aldren, Roanna, and Corwin—and from what Kathryn had said about her, he suspected that she had even greater psi powers than they did.

"You'll have just time to change before dinner," she said. "We're having some other guests." She ushered them to the east wing of the house, where he found it was taken for granted that he would share Kathryn's room.

While he put on the unfamiliar new clothes, Kathryn enlightened him about the dinner guests. "Most of them will be mentors; the idea is to find out which one you hit it off with. They'll be couples, but only the men are eligible—someone of the same sex is always appointed because the emotional relationship between mentor and trainee becomes very close. If they were of opposite sexes there'd be danger of it getting romantic."

"I didn't realize it was a long-term arrangement."

"Oh yes, some Maclairnans have the same mentor from the time they're thirteen until middle age. You'd have liked it to last with Aldren, wouldn't you?"

Yes, he would have; Aldren was the closest friend he'd ever had. He'd liked Corwin, too, during their brief meeting, but Corwin would soon be leaving for Earth. Now, apparently, he was to choose someone he would be working with for as long as he was with *Shepard*—and he hoped that would be a long time. How would he know in a few hours which stranger he liked best?

You'll know. You'll choose each other, telepathically, just as you and I did before we became lovers. Mental compatibility doesn't depend on physical attraction.

Dinner was served in the great room at a long low table around which people sat on cushions, as they had done in Japan on ancient Earth. It was set with elaborately-decorated glazed pottery dishes and strikingly beautiful glassware that Kathryn said was hand-blown. The food was simple: roast chicken again, accompanied this time by baked potatoes, fresh vegetables, and iced herbal tea. As only chicken and fish embryos had been brought by the founding starship, the Maclairnans had never tasted red meat, but then neither had he until he joined Fleet and visited large agricultural colonies; on Earth few could afford such luxuries. Here, however, synthetics were also unavailable, as were dairy products and fruits. Kathryn had missed variety at first, she'd told him, but she didn't notice anymore.

Terry didn't notice what he was eating, either; he was absorbed in getting acquainted with his companions. There were three couples, one or both members of which were mentors, plus Jessica's daughter and son-in-law, who lived in another wing of the house along with several younger generations who weren't present. All were warm and friendly; he was more comfortable with them than he had ever been with crewmates—was that because mentors were chosen for an ability to put people at ease, or because he himself had changed?

After the meal they gathered around the fireplace, lounging on the floor cushions, and talked for several hours. Terry was aware that they were drawing him out, not so much to evaluate him as because they had never before met anyone who had seen other worlds. All their knowledge of Earth and its customs had been gained from the knowledgebase brought by the colony's founders and thus was two hundred years out of date. "It's even worse there now," he said, "as I guess Kathryn has told you. Government regulations are so restrictive that nobody bothers to achieve anything—and if they earned enough money to save any, thieves and rioters would take whatever was left after taxes. And of course, there's no room left for building homes. So most of the planet looks like the slums in the pictures you've seen. The wealthy live in enclaves, and conditions everywhere else slide downhill—

people don't know how things used to be. I do only because as a kid I liked poking around the Net, seeing stuff
that hasn't been accessed for years."

"Someone who wants to help the less fortunate doesn't
get very far," Kathryn added. "I tried, as an attorney, but
there was so much red tape in the way that I couldn't
accomplish anything."

She seemed embarrassed, as if there were some reason she should have done more. Terry realized that he
knew little about her background; she seemed not to want
to talk about it, and she didn't allow it to surface when
their minds merged.

"We don't have any hope of changing conditions on
Earth," Jessica said, "only of teaching individual people
ways to cope with them—and of gradually influencing the
collective unconscious so that in time, human capabilities
will increase. It will never be possible to create a better
society on Earth itself. The future lies in the colonies
those with psi powers will found."

"Collective unconscious?" Terry asked. "What's that?"

"The undercurrent of unconscious telepathy through
which the people of a world come to share similar ideas
and attitudes," said one of the mentors. "It has shaped
history, which we've been studying in that light since Ian
Maclairn's time. It doesn't extend beyond a single planet,
which is why each colony's culture, including ours, is somewhat different from the rest."

"And why we believe we can spread acceptance of psi
to more people than we actually contact," someone added.
"When a critical number of individuals who believe in it is
reached on a given world, recognition of new mind powers as natural phenomena will be extended without action on anyone's part—and will reduce the fear that causes
resistance. That's far in the future, of course. We are
merely setting the process in motion."

"How can you teach a critical number of people if
they're afraid?' Terry protested.

"We won't be teaching psi skills directly," Jessica explained. "We will simply teach control of pain and of health by volition, just as Aldren did on Titan. But as you know, Terry, that's done through unconscious telepathy, so trainees gain experience with psi whether they're aware of it or not. In most of them consciousness of it will emerge more slowly than it did with you; yet in the meantime underlying knowledge that it exists will be unconsciously passed on to all their close contacts—in other words, introduced into the collective unconscious. In effect that knowledge will be contagious."

"Historically, on Earth, this happened often," added someone else. "In primitive cultures where psi was viewed as real, and even where it wasn't, mass hysteria sometimes arose by this means with disastrous effects—for example, the persecution of witches, some of whom had real psi powers. Society wasn't yet ready to deal with the innate fear of such capabilities."

"There's no denying that the promotion of psi can be dangerous," Jessica said. "When the time is ripe for it, as it is now, it's a step forward, but the people who act as catalysts need to be very careful. We've spent two hundred years preparing for that role, and we believe we can avoid the pitfalls. For one thing, public demonstrations of psi that could draw antagonism will be avoided."

"We'll be doing the opposite of what evil manipulators did," Kathryn pointed out. "Our training is designed to help individuals gain confidence in their own volition, not to make them conform. Lack of trust in volition is the root of the fear of psi—people aren't sure that they could control psi powers if they had them. So the mind training we provide has direct bearing on overcoming that fear besides enabling trainees to maintain their health."

The conversation turned to Terry's experiences in the colonies. By the time the evening was over he perceived that the mentors were absorbing his impressions telepathically as well as from his words, but that didn't disturb him; it seemed natural to share with them. Especially with the gray-bearded one named Tristan. It was a while before he realized that he had exchanged more thoughts with Tristan than with the others, both aloud and silently. But when he did, he knew they had formed a friendship that would last.

It was near midnight when they rose to go. Tristan took him aside as the rest were saying goodnight to Jessica. "I'll be your mentor, if you agree, Terry," he said, smiling. This was a formality, Terry knew; it was already silently understood between them. He nodded, feeling no hesitation.

"I'll see you in the morning, then, at the neurofeedback center," Tristan said, and then added, "I believe what Aldren told us about you is true."

Later, in Kathryn's room, she said, "I'm glad you chose Tristan. He reminds me of my grandfather, though he doesn't look anything like him."

"I'd like to meet your grandfather. Will he ever come here, do you think?"

"Perhaps, if he can, but he has—responsibilities. Besides the Maclairn Foundation, I mean." As if sorry she had raised the subject, she quickly changed it. "Did you always plan to leave Earth, Terry?"

"I can't remember a time when I didn't want to fly in space. The dreariness of Earth didn't bother me much because I never doubted that I could get into Fleet—by hacking the academy entrance exam results, if it came to that. But of course it didn't; I scored high all the way through training. I thought I had everything I could ever want when I got my commission." *But,* he added as he embraced Kathryn, *I never guessed what it would be like to have you.*

Terry knew, when they joined in love, that he had lived his entire life until now without any idea of how it felt to be happy.

20

AT BREAKFAST, JESSICA seemed tired and somewhat un-easy. "I didn't sleep well," she confessed. "I lay awake a long time, and then used my mind training to drop off—but I had dreams again that I don't remember."

"Her dreams bother me," Kathryn said as she and Terry walked to the neurofeedback center. "The other mentors think she's unreasonably worried about the possibility of Maclairn being discovered. That's not really likely to happen soon, after all. It would be too much of a coincidence for a ship to come upon this system a few months after we got here, since it's been nearly two hundred years since *Picard* did. And there's no chance of the secret getting out until a lot of people on other worlds have been trained. Yet she was in a great hurry to get the contract signed and the arrangements made for Fleet to come. Look at the way she appointed me ambassador when I'd just arrived and hadn't yet had mind training, and knew very little about Maclairn."

"I did wonder, when you're so young," Terry said. Kathryn had practiced law for several years on Earth so she must be older than he was, but not by much.

"She sent Aldren and Roanna to Earth without giving them time to learn anything about the League, too—they went back with the original expedition, to prove that the people here have psi powers, instead of waiting for a delegation to be sent. And when it did come, she made a lot of detailed plans with Admiral Derham before there was any official discussion of protection by Fleet. I got the feeling that she may have used telepathic persuasion to influence him, and that's not ethical when a person's too inexperienced to recognize it."

"Well, she's the leader. I guess she feels responsible for Maclairn's safety, even if there's no immediate danger."

"Terry . . . I think it may be more than that. I've wondered if she may have had *precognitive* dreams. Ian Maclairn did—he dreamed about his people coming here, with Jesse as Captain. He saw Jesse's face in a dream before he'd even met him."

Terry drew breath. *Aldren saw my face in a dream, though he wasn't sure it was precognitive . . . he said he'd sensed that I may have some extraordinary destiny. . . .*

He did? Oh, Terry! Aloud she asked, "Does Jessica know? Because if she does, it would explain why she was so eager for me to meet you, and arranged that cookout . . . and why she told Corwin to—"

"Jessica told him to speak to Commander Chiang?"

"To judge our feelings for each other, and take action if he believed they were deeper than physical attraction. She didn't inform me till afterward, of course."

"I don't know whether Aldren sent her a private message. There was nothing about his dream in the one the other mentors heard, because I could tell Corwin was surprised when he sensed me thinking about it. And Kathryn, why would it make Jessica think I can protect Maclairn from danger? If I can, which isn't likely, that wouldn't be an extraordinary destiny. It's what I was sent here for, the job *Shepard* has been given."

"This whole plan for training you to sense intruders through remote viewing is extraordinary," Kathryn said. "The mentors are doubtful that it can be done; most of them think Jessica is grasping at straws. And I don't like the idea of her exploiting you."

"I'm not being exploited," Terry assured her. "I want to learn whether I ever sense an incoming ship or not. And it's giving me a chance to be here with you for a while, isn't it?"

"There's that," Kathryn said, her frown fading. "We should just be happy she talked your captain into it, I guess. Still . . . I hope 'extraordinary destiny' means a pleasant destiny."

Chilled, he quieted a suddenly-queasy stomach. It had not occurred to him that it might not be pleasant.

The neurofeedback center was a brick building containing many small compartments equipped with dual setups where young people came for mind training. There were many instructors, Kathryn explained, only a few of whom were mentors—although only mentors could conduct the stressful sessions, most later ones were handled by less skilled teachers. She herself was now working with an instructor named Elbra, who had become a close friend and who was teaching her to close her mind when necessary to keep important secrets from being unconsciously leaked. After telling him where to find Tristan, she went to keep her appointment.

Tristan's office, like Aldren's, had comfortable floor seating, but there was also a small table and bench at which Terry sat, with paper and pen before him, during his remote viewing sessions. He found he was able to quickly enter the necessary stage of consciousness simply by recalling the appropriate mind-pattern. "Our neurofeedback training makes this much easier than it was on Earth for people without it," Tristan said. "They had to spend a lot of time learning to alter consciousness by more traditional techniques that were hard for most people to master. Here, we progress directly to viewing, and trainees advance rapidly."

On the first morning, after explaining that remote viewing was simply one form of a psi faculty called clairvoyance, Tristan tested Terry's ability to perceive not only concealed pictures, but nearby hidden objects such as the contents of a cabinet. From then on he was asked to view actual places. Tristan arranged with other mentors to select the targets without telling him where they were, being careful not to reveal them to him telepathically. Terry was not introduced to these assistants, nor, contrary to the training procedure often advocated in old writings from Earth, did they go there on the appointed day.

"According to the books, they went during the viewing session and intentionally focused on what they were seeing—on all their sensory impressions—and attributed the trainee's success in getting a feel for the place to remote viewing," Tristan said, "when actually there were no grounds for thinking it wasn't merely unconscious telepathy. Unknowingly, they went out of their way to encourage telepathy. Here, our assistants will place markers at several locations and let a computer pick which one you will target, giving you only a description of the marker. After your viewing session has been recorded, you and I will be told by the computer the location it chose, and we will go together to see what's there."

In this way, during the course of the next week, Terry saw a good deal of Petersville and its surroundings. Most of his sessions produced at least a vague resemblance to the target, and some were astonishingly accurate. He sketched a circular shape that turned out to be a water tower. He described the inner courtyard of a low stone apartment complex. He wrote "Low roof, no windows, noisy" and was taken to a manufacturing plant that produced robocarts.

Once, he froze up and laid down the pen, suddenly struck by a foreboding he could not explain. For some reason he did not want to sense the target, which Tristan grasped even before he did from the feelings he was broadcasting. "Write something down," he urged, "anything. Don't worry about whether it's related to the target or not." And Terry wrote, "Hot. Melting."

He was reluctant to visit the target and protested that it wasn't necessary since he hadn't seen anything, but Tristan persisted. It proved to be a craftworker's shop where a young woman was making pewter tableware, the molten pewter beside her in a small cauldron. "I don't understand," Terry said. "There isn't anything wrong here—why does it give me the jitters?"

"Don't you know, Terry?" Tristan said quietly. "Relax,

see what impressions you pick up from her mind, not specific thoughts, but her awareness of what she does."

Terry let himself perceive impressions. After a pause he said, "She—she melted that pewter with her *mind*. The way Ivana destroyed *Picard*'s hyperdrive."

"Yes, talented craftworkers sometimes do that. Psychokinesis is also used in a few industrial processes where it's the simplest way to deal with small quantities. In time the idea won't upset you, once you realize your mind won't do anything destructive against your will."

During what free time Terry had, Kathryn showed him more of Maclairn and talked more about the society she had enthusiastically adopted as her own. Its goal from the beginning, she said, had been to create an example of what human civilization might someday become. There was no sickness, since everyone had mind training in how to prevent it and there were healers to deal with such serious conditions as did arise. There was no poverty because anyone who lacked income could do work for the community and receive credits—one credit per hour regardless of the job's nature, a tradition begun in the early days when everyone worked together to survive. There was no crime, for telepaths empathized with each other and in any case, criminal intent would be impossible to conceal.

"The key to making it applicable to humankind's future," she told him, "is that we've integrated our focus on inner development with high technology. No society on Earth ever did that. Believers in enhanced human potential blamed technology for the world's problems and wanted to revert to an earlier stage of evolution instead of moving ahead. That would have been fatal, of course. Resources would have run out with no way to replenish them and the people still alive would have fought over what remained. Fortunately, instinct assured that technology kept progressing to the point where we could establish interstellar colonies, even though it resulted in other aspects of human evolution being ignored. But now, for civilization to survive, we need balance."

He and Kathryn traveled by rail to other nearby towns, passing through green farmland and sometimes through vast fields of the tall sunflowers grown for oil and seeds, fields that from the shuttle he had seen as brilliant patches of yellow against the duller gold of native vegetation. There were also forests of the fast-growing genetically engineered trees planted regularly and systematically harvested as soon as they were large enough to provide lumber. The trains were crowded with agricultural workers who commuted from the towns to supervise the robotic machines that did the actual labor; all of them seemed cheerful and content.

This was true everywhere. Terry soon grasped the secret of Maclairn's society, the foundation of its superiority to all others: everyone was free! The government didn't tell anyone what they could or could not do. People didn't tell each other, either—they had diverse lifestyles and did not frown on those who chose differently from themselves. Some liked high-tech living, others preferred simplicity. Common sense prevailed; anyone too lazy to do even a minimal amount of work went hungry when his or her credits ran out, which didn't last for more than a day or two since there was always work to be done. Those who worked long hours and got rich were respected but not envied. Above all, people helped each other, not just in case of misfortune, but routinely. No one organized this; it just happened.

"It seems like utopia," he protested, "and there's no such thing. Even I know enough about human history to realize that. So what's the catch?"

"There's no catch," Kathryn said, "though of course people suffer as they would anywhere from things like disappointment and grief. And occasionally deranged people become cruel or violent, which the mentors are trained to deal with; in rare cases where they couldn't, where psychopathic uses of psi threatened serious harm to others, there have even been executions. Evil can't be completely eliminated. What makes this different from previous societies is the fact that everyone is psi-capable. There's no misunderstanding or indifference to others' feelings, much less hidden hostility, among people who are telepathically aware of each others' emotions. And that's why the spreading of our capabilities is so important."

As the days passed Terry's liking for Maclairn grew. He and Kathryn swam at a beach near the marina, a favorite gathering place for young and old alike. In the evenings they went to her friends' homes, or sometimes to a ballgame or concert, and once to a dance. He had never before enjoyed himself with people. Now he was welcomed warmly as if he had known them all his life. They were aware of his feelings and he of theirs, even when there was no conscious telepathic communication, and everyone was interested in hearing about the other worlds he had traveled to. The mood on these occasions was relaxed and happy, and eager though he was to fly *Picard,* he found himself sorry that his training period on the surface would soon be over.

21

ON THE LAST day before Terry was scheduled to return to *Shepard,* Tristan targeted for remote viewing a place on Maclairn where no one had ever been, a spot on the map chosen arbitrarily by coordinates. It was too far away to reach by land; there was a shuttle on the ground because some crew members were on weekend leave in Petersville, and Terry received permission to use it for the day. Kathryn and Tristan's lifemate Merelda came along for the ride.

Terry's remote viewing impression had been of

water, but the satellite map, when examined, showed no sign of a sea or river visible from orbit. He also had mentioned a feeling of being closed in, as if in a very narrow canyon; but when they neared the specified coordinates there was no canyon to be seen. He hovered the ship over a flat valley and set down as close as he could get to the outcroppings of rock that covered the actual site, which they would have to walk to reach.

"It doesn't look familiar," he said as they clambered over them. "Could I have been seeing something at a different location?"

"It's possible," Tristan told him, "but more likely it was simply an ordinary miss."

"What bad luck, the one time we came all this way," Kathryn said.

"It doesn't depend on luck," said Tristan. "We don't know what it does depend on, but it's not just chance."

"I don't *feel* as if I missed," Terry declared. "I don't see anything I recognize, but I sense . . . something, some resonance I can't define."

"Maybe you saw the future," Merelda suggested.

"It would have to be a long way in the future for water to be anywhere among these rocks, unless it was just rain I saw." Troubled, he stared at the rough wall of the cliff they had come to. There was nothing confining about it; with his back to it, he could look out at the whole valley. Yet he knew inside that he had been near this place before. . . .

"Déjà vu?" Kathryn questioned. "That's common, after all."

"This is more than that, not just a flash. I know I'm close to where I went this morning, where my mind went, anyway."

"Déjà vu may be a psi phenomenon, perhaps related to past unconscious precognition," Tristan said. "You may have had precognitive knowledge that you would be here now, rather than a remote viewing of what's here."

"God, Tristan, if psi capabilities are that complicated, how can we trust what we learn through them?"

"We can't. Viewings are mere signposts, not roadmaps, and after two hundred years—even longer, counting Ian's research on Undine—we still don't understand how they work. We know telepathy does work because other forms of communication can verify it. We know precognition is possible because events are sometimes accurately predicted. And we know remote viewing exists apart from telepathy because we have records of places described before any living being had been to them. But in the majority of cases, we can't tell which capabilities are operative."

"I've been told that Ian saw this planet as it looks from space and showed it to Jesse in a dream," Kathryn said reflectively. "Did he see remotely across interstellar distance, or was it a precognitive telepathic perception of the colonists' first sight of it?"

"That's something we've always wondered. Actually we can't be sure he hadn't seen the original discoverers' photo of it in the Net database, though the emotion he projected with it doesn't fit that explanation."

They sat at the foot of the cliff to eat the lunch they had brought, hard-boiled eggs and chunks of bread full of crunchy sunflower seeds. The view of the valley was beautiful despite the dryness of the land; low native shrubs, a golden blanket, stretched toward the jagged mountains beyond.

"In some ways I envy you, Terry," Merelda said. "I've always wondered how it would feel to travel. We've seen vids in the knowledgebase, but when no one here has ever been offworld . . ."

That made this planet unique, Terry thought. Nowhere else in the galaxy was there an inhabited planet whose people had no access to space. It would, he thought, be intolerable. "I've landed on quite a few worlds," he told her. "But most of the ones explorers visit don't have breathable atmospheres, you know. We have to wear spacesuits or stay inside sealed rovers, even when the temperature isn't too extreme. I've only seen one or two that were potentially habitable."

"And yet you love exploring," Kathryn said.

"Well, it's not what we find, though that's fascinating sometimes. It's what we *might* find. Something ... different, something that means more than rich resources and primitive forms of life for the exobiologists to study." Tristan knows, he thought. Tristan had absorbed it from his mind and shared the feeling. Close as he was to Kathryn, she had not.

"For a few moments, when the first expedition arrived and saw signs of habitation, we thought this world had been colonized by an alien race," she said.

"Did you really? I thought that was a story you made up to explain what you'd been doing with a privately-owned starship."

"We made up the story that we'd been *hunting* for aliens—though I think our captain half-believed it. He hadn't been told the real reason why he was ordered to take us to a planet charted as worthless. But when we saw buildings and planted fields where none were supposed to be, we were scared, Terry. Not so much for ourselves as for humankind, because it would mean a terrible shakeup even if they were friendly. Earth's civilization would collapse."

"Culture shock, the theorists call it," Tristan said. "There's been speculation about it for centuries; not all believers in advanced aliens were crackpots. For a while, before interstellar travel began, many scientists expected them to be found through radio astronomy if not through physical contact."

"And before that, from the late seventeenth century till the turn of the twentieth, nearly all educated people believed the planets of other stars were inhabited," added Merelda. Terry frowned. She was a historian, so she should know; but he had never heard that. In any case, since long before he was born, belief in the existence of extra-terrestrials had been ridiculed.

Did you *think it was ridiculous, Terry?* Tristan inquired silently.

To be honest, he hadn't. "I don't expect to ever find any ETs," he said. "If they existed, we'd have come across them by now, considering how many solar systems we've explored. And yet it just doesn't seem reasonable. We've found higher forms of life on plenty of worlds—even primatoids on a few. How is it possible that evolution went no further except on Earth?"

"That's one of the great mysteries," Tristan agreed.

"As I once told Aldren, I think the search for aliens was a sort of symbol," Terry said. "And maybe it's not good that humankind has lost it. Most people, even most star pilots, don't have any real interest in exploring, and I've read that they used to—that scientists once believed it was a basic human impulse."

"Historically, it certainly was," Merelda said. "It still was, to some extent, two centuries ago, according to what the knowledgebase tells us. Are you saying that's no longer true?"

"Nobody I know is looking for anything more than mineral deposits that will make them rich. And nothing's written about hoping for more. All the settled worlds are pretty much the same, and nobody *cares*. They don't even care much that civilization's said to be declining in the colonies as well as on Earth. They just assume there's nowhere left to go."

"Life on Earth's been getting worse since long before we were born," Kathryn said ruefully. "I hated it, as who doesn't? I thought Colonial League law might give me a chance to emigrate—and now that I'm here, in a happier world, I'm not looking for anything else."

Troubled, Terry probed, *Don't you wonder about the rest of the universe? I'm happy too on Maclairn, happier than I've ever been, but I couldn't ever stop wanting to see more.* . . . She didn't respond. For the first time it occurred to him that there might be basic things about which they disagreed. It was a thought he didn't want to pursue.

He got up and walked restlessly along the cliff wall, which was not sheer until higher up; at its foot there were piles of boulders. Noticing a wide crevice between them, he investigated and found that it went deep into the cliff, leaving a low opening though which it might be possible to crawl. "Hey, I think there may be a cave back here," he called out. "Bring a flashlight from the shuttle."

By the time the others reached him, Terry was already part way through. He could sense clearly now that there was water somewhere underground. He *had* seen it remotely! His inner sight wasn't an illusion, it had shown him an actual place—and that excited him more than any of the other powers he had gained, except for the joy of sharing thoughts with Kathryn.

She followed him through the opening on hands and knees, aiming the flashlight beam ahead of them. A short tunnel led to a small cavern with a roof high enough for them to stand under. Water trickled through a crack in the opposite wall into a pool little more than an arm's length across; as they shone the light into it, they couldn't see the bottom.

"There must be an underground outlet," Kathryn said. "Most of the water on Maclairn is ground water; the wells have to be dug deep. It doesn't rain often, but when it does it rains hard, and sinks in through cracks in the rocky areas. Ponds on the surface soon evaporate."

Terry stared at the pool, still marveling at the accuracy of his vision. Water . . . a feeling of confinement. . . .

Behind them, there was a sudden sound of falling rock. He turned and saw, in horror, that the entrance passage had been filled by an avalanche of stones, blocking the only exit.

22

"OH, GOD," KATHRYN said. "What if it's filled the whole tunnel?"

It undoubtedly had, Terry knew. He'd had enough experience surveying new worlds to know better than to crawl into an unknown cave. No explorer team would have done such a thing. He had been so absorbed in verifying his remote viewing, and had felt so at home on Maclairn, that he hadn't thought of its wilderness as hazardous.

The stones that had fallen were not too large to be moved, but there were a lot of them, and more were likely to settle into any opening they managed to make. To try might do more harm than good, even if they had the strength to keep working.

Terry? Are you okay? Tristan's thought surged into Terry's mind, driven by urgency, and he realized with relief that though conversational telepathy was generally limited to people within sight of each other, the strong bond between them, enhanced by stress, had made it possible.

We're not hurt. But there's no way out of here.

Show me! Tristan commanded. *Look around you and at the rock slide, and concentrate on what you see. Shine the light on the walls and roof of the cave.*

Terry did so, knowing that however clear a picture he could project to Tristan, it wouldn't reveal any means of escape. "At least we've got water," he said to Kathryn. "We're not going to die from thirst."

What is *going to happen to us?* It wasn't a question to ask aloud.

I don't know, he admitted. "Tristan can't clear that passage. He'll contact Petersville on the shuttle's comm, but there's no way anyone can get here soon. They'll have to send another shuttle down from *Shepard*. They may have to bring heavy equipment and cut another opening."

"Terry . . . how long is the air in here going to last?"

Not long enough, probably, as the rock overhead was too solid to permit any ventilation; but there was no point in saying so. Nor was there any need to tell Kathryn how sorry he was for having put her in harm's way. He squeezed her hand, and their thoughts were wordlessly shared.

She was putting a brave face on it, but he could feel her claustrophobic agony at the tightness of the walls surrounding them. That aspect of it didn't bother him, accustomed as he was to long confinement in small spaceships with a finite supply of oxygen. But on a ship you knew how long the oxygen would last and expected to replenish it. And the carbon dioxide you exhaled was being removed. Here, they would die of carbon dioxide poisoning before their oxygen was gone.

Merelda's gone to the shuttle to call for a rescue team, Tristan told him. *I'll stick with you, and I'm going to try to clear an air hole.*

How could he? Terry thought. The shuttle contained no tools, and even if he managed to pull out some stones without dislodging more, he couldn't reach far enough in to make an opening. *Should I work at it from this side?* he asked. *I'm not sure what good it will do—the distance is too long for us to connect.*

Maybe later you can help. But till we're sure it can be done, you should exert yourself as little as possible, to conserve oxygen.

That was true, he knew. Every extra movement lessened the supply. *We mustn't even speak aloud,* he warned Kathryn. *Sit down, and relax as much as you can.* They sat on a low slab of stone and pressed close together for warmth; the cave hadn't absorbed much of the outdoor heat and they couldn't afford to waste energy in shivering.

Terry, came Tristan's insistent thought, *relaxing isn't enough. Your life and Kathryn's will depend on using the*

*mind training you've had. To start with, slow your heart
and lower your blood pressure. . . .*

Of course—why hadn't they done so immediately, as
native Maclairnans would have? What they had learned
about volitional control was meant for practical use in a
crisis, though neither of them was experienced enough
for it to be automatic.

It's possible to consciously lower your metabolism,
Tristan went on. *I can't teach you the specific skill with-
out neurofeedback, but I'll give you as much awareness as
I can of what you need to do. You'll have to pass it on to
Kathryn; she and I aren't close enough for her to get it
directly from me.*

Silently Terry assented. *Don't lie down,* Tristan
warned. *The carbon dioxide in the air will sink. Get into
a position where you can lean against something, then
relax your muscles totally and don't move again. It may
be uncomfortable, even painful after a while, but that's
okay—you know how to prevent suffering from pain, and
doing so will keep you in the right state of consciousness
for controlling your body's functions.*

Terry braced himself with his back against the rough
rock wall, already feeling it scrape through his thin shirt.
He put his arm around Kathryn so that she was leaning
against him. *I'm okay,* she told him. *Remember the
neurofeedback patterns, Terry . . . focus on the colors. . . .*

He tried not to think beyond the moment. Tristan
was still communicating to him, he realized; the knowledge came to him wordlessly. They must let go of all fear,
all worry about what was to come, because the body is
programmed to respond to fear by priming for action—it
speeds not only heart rate but metabolism in general,
and produces all sorts of biological effects that take energy. And using energy consumes oxygen. . . .

*In the Ritual the Stewards of the Flame pledge to live
without fear,* Kathryn mused, *and I never understood why
until now. I thought it was just a symbolic thing, because*

nobody can help being afraid sometimes. But it refers to a physical *state—not allowing your body to react to fear, It's why their bodies don't wear out.*

With some irony, Terry replied, *Well, we're getting plenty of valuable practice.*

That's true, Tristan agreed. *We won't have to arrange an artificial emergency for you, as we often do in advanced training so people can learn to deal with legitimate fear.*

It was unlikely that they'd live long enough to enter advanced training, Terry reflected grimly, but he immediately cut off the thought, hoping Kathryn hadn't picked it up. He couldn't tell what she was feeling, which dismayed him until he recalled that she had been taught how to close her mind for privacy—she probably didn't want him to know how scared she was. He tightened his arm around her, aware that he could protect her best by not intruding on her withdrawal.

You can't force yourself into an altered state of consciousness, he remembered. Aldren had said that brain functioning can't be changed by force of will, that willpower is actually counterproductive. You have to decide what you intend and then just *let go* and allow it to happen. He had grasped how to do that when subjected to pain, and had been able to apply the skill to other controls over his body. What use had all that been, if he could not do it now? Determinedly he visualized the mind-patterns he had learned, the symbolic representations of his brain's functioning; and gradually, breathing very slowly, he lost contact with his surroundings.

Hours passed. At one point he became conscious of pain in his motionless, cramped limbs and made the mental adjustment to not be bothered by it, not rousing enough to affect his lowered metabolism. Underneath, he had a sense that Kathryn was all right, though the telepathic communication between them was no longer at the conscious level. If anything were *not* all right with her, he would know.

It had all been so good, he thought dreamily. Aldren, the training, his fantastic ability to end pain . . . Maclairn . . . Kathryn . . . *Picard* . . . Too good to be true. Perhaps it wasn't true, but was just something that he'd imagined while dying. Such happiness couldn't last forever. . . .

He had no idea how long it had been when he became aware of Tristan calling, *Terry! Terry, come alert now, but don't disturb Kathryn. Make your way to the tunnel, slowly. . . .*

Rousing himself, Terry obeyed, willing Kathryn to remain in her semi-conscious state when he withdrew his arm from her shoulders. It was a effort to move. Vaguely he realized that oxygen deficiency was already beginning to affect him; at the Fleet academy they gave you experience with that, so if it ever happened again you would know you weren't thinking clearly. You were supposed to change your oxygen tank—there were some in every shuttle for emergency use. If you weren't wearing a mask you should put one on. Why couldn't he find his mask? He was dazed, confused; but he couldn't ignore Tristan's call. . . .

Pull out a stone at about the level of your waist, Tristan commanded. *Then if nothing falls into the space, take out another from further in.*

This was senseless, Terry thought, but he did as he was told. *The tunnel roof is solid*, Tristan assured him. *It's a firmly-lodged boulder. We are taking the top layer of stones from the slide beneath it. We're almost through now—you just need to remove the ones on your side.*

He wondered if Tristan's psychic viewing power was failing him. Perhaps he could see inside the tunnel clairvoyantly, but he could not be estimating the distance accurately. No matter how many stones he and Merelda had gotten out, they could not have reached beyond the length of their arms, and the tunnel was more than twice arm's

length. Was it wise to use extra oxygen in the effort of lifting heavy stones when it couldn't possibly do any good?

No matter, Terry decided. The air wasn't going to stay
breathable much longer anyway; if a rescue team wasn't
already close—which Tristan would have told him, if it
were—running out a little sooner wasn't going to make a
significant difference. He went to work on the stones,
heedless of the damage to his hands, which were soon
bruised and raw.

When he freed the stone at the limit of his reach, he
saw daylight.

He must be hallucinating, he decided. The light was a
long way off. Tristan obviously couldn't have touched
stones in the tunnel's center. Instinctively, he pressed
his face against the opening, gasping at the sudden breath
of fresh air. But only for a moment; then he staggered
back to Kathryn and carried her to the hole, holding her
face close to it.

We've got the oxygen tanks from the shuttle, Tristan
was telling him. *We're going to send one through; grasp it
as soon as you can reach it.*

The daylight was abruptly blocked again and Terry
almost panicked. Then he saw the end of the tank moving toward him. He reached, and as he grasped it, he felt
it move in his hands. What was pushing it? Tristan must
have found a long pole of some kind, yet the area was
bare; there were no trees in the wilderness on
Maclairn. . . .

His hands trembled as he fumbled with the valve and
regulator. The mask had been taped to the tank; he helped
Kathryn put it on. Already somewhat revived by the air
flow from the hole, she drew a few deep breaths and then
held it out to him. *We'll take turns with it*, she insisted.

*Okay, for now. Tristan is sending another, though I
don't see how he propelled the first one, or even how he
made so long an opening.*

Terry, there's only one way he could have. He's a

mentor, after all. A lot of the mentors have strong enough psychokinetic power to move stones. It's no more incredible than melting metal, is it?

You mean he pulled out those unreachable stones with his mind?

He must have. But no wonder it took hours, moving so many is far more exhausting psi work than I've heard of anyone doing. It's a miracle if it didn't kill him.

Appalled, Terry burst out, *Oh, my God! Tristan? Tristan, are you there?*

There was no response. But a second tank was now blocking the air hole; had Tristan pushed it, and then collapsed? Had he risked himself to save them? If Tristan had been harmed he would never forgive himself, Terry knew. His remorse over Kathryn's peril had been tempered by the fact that he would share her fate, but to live on at the cost of Tristan's life. . . .

He pulled the tank free and put on the mask, belatedly realizing that they were still not out of danger; the oxygen wouldn't last forever and he mustn't expend energy on emotional turmoil. Calming his body again, he embraced Kathryn and they sat down to wait. Well before the tanks were empty, the unmistakable sound of a shuttle told them that rescue was near.

The team had been delayed because the only shuttle currently aboard *Shepard* was down for maintenance due to a problem on its last flight; they'd had to recall and recharge one of those engaged in deploying surveillance satellites. Once on site they were able to clear the stone slide using robotic equipment and shore up the tunnel securely enough for Terry and Kathryn to crawl out. Merelda was sitting on the ground beside Tristan, who lay motionless with his head between her hands. Terry rushed to them, his inner anguish requiring no vocal expression.

He'll be all right, Merelda assured him. "He's depleted. He needs time to recuperate, maybe a long time—

the kind of psi he used, prolonged over hours, demands more energy than could be summoned by anything short of an extreme crisis. But he won't be permanently harmed by it. The mind is resilient, Terry, especially for someone with a mentor's skills."

She was very pale, and looked near exhaustion herself. "Did you use psi on the stones, too?" he asked in dismay.

"No, I haven't that talent. But I'm a trained healer, and right now I'm giving some of my energy to Tristan." She smiled. "Don't worry, I'll recover."

"It was all my fault," Terry mumbled. He turned away and reluctantly submitted to examination by the rescue team's medical officer, who proceeded to bandage his lacerated hands. He had not attempted to heal them himself, though Aldren had shown him it was possible. He was not sure, now, that he wanted anything to do with the psi powers that had led him into that cave.

23

TERRY WAS TAKEN directly to *Shepard* since he had been scheduled to return there the next morning. He had no chance to say goodbye to Kathryn, who went with Tristan and Merelda in the other shuttle. Several Maclairnan healers came to the Old Settlement to meet them, and were to stay with them in one of the prefabs until Tristan was strong enough to walk down to the boat landing. There was, of, course, no possibility of communicating with him; Terry could only hope that Merelda would convey how sorry he was.

After debriefing by Captain Vargas, who showed no sign of blaming him for the near-disaster, he felt a little better. Corwin was harder to face, for he knew the mentor would sense the doubts he now felt about pursuing remote viewing. He had vowed that he wanted to develop his psi capabilities when Corwin had warned that it might not always be pleasant. How could he admit that his inner certainty had been shaken?

"It's not that I'm afraid of facing danger again," he said, "but how can I trust my own perceptions? How can I know they won't mislead me?"

"Sometimes they will, Terry. If you're thinking they'll make you omniscient, you're expecting too much."

"Corwin . . . did I see remotely that there was water there and walls of some kind, or did I see the future precognitively?"

"That's something we never know for sure. There isn't any positive way to distinguish the two. I think, though, that if it were precognition you would have had some sense of foreboding. And you didn't; you felt nothing but happy excitement at discovering your viewing was accurate."

"Yes, that's just it. I didn't suspect anything could go wrong."

"In other words, you *want* viewing to be precognition. You didn't see the tunnel remotely, after all. When you saw it with your eyes, it was up to you to evaluate it, just as much as if you had never done any remote viewing of the site."

"Oh." It was true, Terry realized; he *had* felt that remote viewing ought to suggest the import of what was viewed, he had since the accident anyway. "You're saying that I'm trying to pin the blame for my own stupidity on my psi powers."

Corwin nodded. "The viewing you've done so far has involved nothing that should trouble you. But Terry, psi can get much more complicated, because precognitive viewings do happen, and you'll rarely have any means of judging how to interpret them. Even in true ones you will see probabilities, not certainties. Precognition isn't predestination—what you do, and what others do, will affect the outcome. If that weren't so, free will couldn't exist."

"You mean I could alter the future by how I respond to what I see?"

"Of course. Who can't, through any kind of sight? There's no denying that viewing potential futures is a heavy responsibility, but I'm sure you'll be able to handle it."

Terry was too tired to argue, and when Corwin suggested that they schedule another remote viewing session for the next day, he shrank from the idea. He was on the verge of refusal when it occurred to him that this was another instance of what Aldren had described as getting back on a horse. "It's important," Corwin agreed. "because if you let yourself start thinking that you'd rather not do this, you'll become psi-blind; impressions of what you're trying to view simply won't rise from your unconscious mind." And so in the morning, with one of the other mentors aboard choosing targets elsewhere in the ship, he correctly described two out of three.

The rest of the day was devoted to planning *Picard*'s mission, for it had been certified as ready to fly. That evening Terry briefed the three lieutenants assigned to its crew: his roommate Drew Larssen as engineer and Mikaela Orlov as copilot—presumably the XO had not been blind to their attraction to each other—plus Zuri Kifeda as comm specialist. The first time Drew addressed him as Captain he was so startled that for a moment he didn't respond.

A normal explorer team on a mission to catalog previously-undiscovered worlds would have included people knowledgeable about geology and exobiology. This had not been thought necessary, since there were experts aboard *Shepard* who could be brought back later if anything worth investigating was found. Some of the planets—and certainly the asteroids—might have resources that were valuable, Terry knew. When the solar system had been charted several hundred years ago, only potentially habitable worlds were considered. Now extraction equipment was so much more advanced that smugglers in a small ship could mine enough of scarce minerals to be worth carrying. So unlikely as it seemed that anyone would check out this system within the next few years, it wasn't beyond the realm of possibility.

The chances of their encountering an intruder on this or any trip in *Picard* were, of course, infinitesimal. Their main mission was to deploy sensor stations on the other planets of the solar system, as well as on the major asteroids most likely to attract prospectors. Satellites, some launched by AI from the cruiser and others deployed from shuttles, had already been placed in high orbit above Maclairn; these more distant ground-based stations would relay to them. That would be mere spot coverage; a jump ship could emerge from hyperspace anywhere. But it would head for a large asteroid or a planet, so sooner or later the sensitive instruments on one of the stations, if not the orbiting satellites, would pick it up. The ideal was for patrollers to reach it before it got close enough to observe that Maclairn was inhabited. They would establish contact and warn it away, saying that Fleet was conducting secret maneuvers in the area, a plausible enough story.

If an intruder wasn't detected until after its crew had already seen signs of habitation it could not be allowed to leave the solar system. Since the crew would have no reason to suspect this, they probably wouldn't resist capture; but if by any chance they did, the patroller would use the weapons with which it was equipped. Whether or not force proved necessary, they would be taken aboard *Shepard* and their ship's hyperdrive would be disabled, resulting—unless they were Fleet explorer officers who proved qualified to share the secret—in their permanent confinement to Maclairn. Which would not, Terry thought, be an unfair outcome. If they were smugglers, they would get far better than they would if caught within the League.

"If *Picard* ever does meet an intruder," Terry pointed

out, "we'll be far enough from Maclairn for a mere warning to be all that's needed.

"Isn't it possible that that the excuse of Fleet maneuvers won't be believed, sir?" Drew inquired. "Patrollers couldn't have come from anywhere but a cruiser, since they can't land—but *Picard* might be suspected of smuggling."

That was true, Terry realized. If the other ship was a legitimate Fleet explorer its crew wouldn't attempt an arrest; explorers carried only sidearms. A civilian ship, however, might be more heavily armed. It might assume that *Picard* was a rival for whatever rich resources the solar system proved to offer.

"It's too remote a possibility to worry about, at least not until far enough in the future for arrival of intruders to be more likely," he said. "Still, if we were qualified to use beam weapons it might be a good idea to make some provision for defense." Unlike a freighter officer he had not been trained in the use of any space-based weapons but those mounted on patrollers, nor, he assumed, had the members of his crew. Fleet was not a fighting force; its need for arms was limited to occasional police actions.

"Captain, I'm qualified," Drew declared. "I once served on a freighter and we all had to learn fire control, though we never met any pirates."

So, after discussion with the XO, Terry decided to have a laser cannon installed on *Picard,* and departure was delayed while this was done. Meanwhile, Drew took a refresher course in a simulator. By that time Terry was familiar with the crew members' backgrounds. Drew was an excellent engineer who after his brief freighter experience had been permanently assigned to troubleshooting at Centauri Ops Center, and he had assisted Commander Linley with the overhaul of *Picard*. Mikaela Orlov, as a better-than-average shuttle pilot and flight instructor, was eager to learn to pilot interplanetary ships; and Zuri Kifeda was an experienced comm technician who had spent the past week readying the sensor stations they were going to deploy. None of them besides himself were trained explorers, though they had learned survival skills during basic Fleet training. Hopefully, the need for more advanced preparation wouldn't arise.

24

THERE WERE FIVE planets besides Maclairn in the system, none of which had been explored or even named. The Maclairnans, of course, had had no time to visit them while their starship was available and no means of doing so after it was gone. *Picard* had not investigated them when it approached the colony two hundred years ago, although its instruments had recorded basic information about their nature, as had those aboard *Shepard*. Since arrival, *Shepard*'s AI had also been tracking the largest asteroids, starting with those closest to Maclairn.

It was with eager anticipation that the team set out for the nearest planet, known as Three since it was the third nearest the sun—Maclairn itself being the second. The plan was to stop at several asteroids on the way, those currently in a position to be intercepted. Others would be visited on later trips. The astrogation data was fed to *Picard*'s AI before departure; no piloting would be needed until it came time to land.

Terry had not often landed on asteroids; interstellar explorer teams generally concentrated on planets. But during flight training he'd gotten some experience with those near Earth, taking supplies to mining companies, and there was no reason to expect these would be different. It took less than eight hours to reach the first of them—a jagged chunk of rock about five kilometers across, with rough crags bristling from its surface. For some reason the sight of it chilled him, as if some deeply-buried memory were threatening to emerge. But it was, he knew, just the sort of place prospectors would head for, and therefore an ideal place for a sensor station.

Landing was going to be tricky, as there wasn't much level area. Ordinarily that was the kind of challenge he looked forward to. Now, however, he was on edge for other reasons. It was a strange feeling to be in full charge of the mission—he had not quite realized how much in the past he had relied on the captain to handle any emergencies that arose. Captain Vargas had remarked that he would have less trouble adjusting to command than most young officers because he'd never done much socializing with his peers and so wouldn't have to go out of his way to discourage inappropriate familiarity. For once, maybe that wasn't a disadvantage, Terry thought grimly. But he was set apart in a different way now. His teammates' lives depended on his decisions. They were millions of miles away from any other source of support.

He commanded the AI to establish a low parking orbit and turned his attention to the shuttle, in which the equipment to be deployed had been loaded before departure from *Shepard*. He, Drew, and Zuri suited up for the short flight to the asteroid's surface. One member of an explorer crew must stay aboard the ship when a team landed—in this case Mikaela, to whom he'd given basic orientation to *Picard*'s control console. Having been the junior pilot on his previous explorer missions, Terry sympathized with the disappointment he sensed in her mind; but as captain he didn't let it show—although, as Corwin had also mentioned, unconscious telepathy worked two ways and his inner feelings would be hard to conceal even in situations where he needed to display total confidence.

The moment he was at the shuttle's controls, however, he lost all trace of doubt—as always, flying elated him. He connected smoothly with the asteroid's surface, easily avoiding the crags, and they climbed out. It took a few minutes to adjust to the low, almost zero, gravity and the strange sight of the nearby curved horizon. Terry examined the terrain and gave the order to place the sensor station in the spot that seemed most stable and most noticeable. Presumably, if any prospectors failed to pick up its warning broadcast before landing, they would heed the "off limits" notice prominently fixed to it and depart from the solar system before interceptors could reach them. He and Drew carried it from the shuttle and secured it to solid rock, moving somewhat awkwardly since it had been a long time since either of them had worked in zero g. They then took photos and some rock samples while Zuri verified its functioning through communication with Mikaela aboard *Picard*.

By the time they were back in the shuttle Terry was trembling with exhaustion and the strain of responsibility. The liftoff went smoothly and everyone was in an exuberant mood he found difficult to share, though he made sure that no one noticed. That night he slept badly. A sense of some threat just outside his consciousness intruded on his dreams; several times he woke and had to convince himself that all was well with both ship and crew.

And then, suddenly, he was wide awake, sure that there was *something* demanding his attention. Not in the ship. Far away, but real and alive. Another ship, perhaps. . . .

This was crazy. Of course there couldn't be another ship already in the system the very first time they patrolled it. The odds against that were too extreme for the thought to be taken seriously. But his heart was beating fast; he had to use his mind training to calm it. The conviction that he had really sensed something didn't fade, and he lay awake the rest of the night.

In the morning, his common sense told him that because he was being trained in remote viewing with the hope that he might sense intruders, it wasn't surprising that he'd imagined that he was doing so. It had been merely the power of suggestion, enhanced by the stress of his first command. But all day the thought nagged him: what if it had been a true viewing? What if his perception had been real?

Within the next few days they placed sensor stations on several similar asteroids, Mikaela and Drew taking turns at remaining in orbit. When at last *Picard* reached Three everyone crowded around the viewscreen on the bridge, eager to see a real new world rather than a mere rock ball. But was a small, dead world, even smaller than Earth's moon, and if there was anything different there from the landscape of the asteroids, it wasn't apparent from space. Terry, whose heart had been lifted by the excitement he always felt on approaching an unknown planet, was used to the letdown that often followed. But the others had been expecting more from their first planetfall, and were discouraged by the anticlimax. As it was not their job to do a detailed survey, the stay on Three was short.

"Captain, since we're first on this planet it's your right to name it," Drew reminded him after the sensor station had been placed.

Terry hesitated. The supply of names from the ancient mythologies of Earth had long ago run out and planets were now generally named after outstanding historical figures. Any tentative name he suggested would have to be checked against the knowledgebase to be sure it hadn't been used, and in any case he couldn't think of anyone other than obvious choices that he wished to honor. It would be better to name it after a Maclairnan, he felt, but no one still living was eligible and the Maclairnans had given the names of their past leaders to towns. "I think I should consult Jessica about that," he told Drew. "We'll go on calling it Three for now."

Like all explorers, *Picard* had four small single staterooms used as doubles only when needed; on long expeditions members of small crews needed privacy. On the morning after departure from Three, Terry left his just as Drew emerged from Mikaela's. The look on Drew's face was comical. "Captain!" he exclaimed. "Sir, we were just—"

"You needn't be embarrassed, Lieutenant," Terry said, hiding a smile. "On explorers it's acceptable to share rooms from time to time—and it's more than acceptable on Maclairn. You can stay in that one if you're welcome there."

It was just as well, he thought, for them to become consciously telepathic, which sleeping together was sure to trigger now that their mind training had awakened the potential for it. That would strengthen the unity of the crew. Already they got along with each other better than any other he had shipped with, for they all knew what the rest were feeling without discussion and there wasn't the irritability that was apt to develop after a few days of being cooped up in a small ship. That they would support each other in case of trouble did not need saying; it was simply taken for granted.

This, more than the specific mind skills that would be useful in an emergency, was the greatest benefit of the mind training to Fleet—and to humankind as a whole, Terry realized. The harmony so evident among the Maclairnans didn't require being born to it; acquired telepathic sensitivity was enough. And that made the mentors' plan for extending mind powers beyond Maclairn more than an idealistic dream. It was a real, practical goal worth whatever it cost to achieve.

That day *Picard* broke orbit and headed further out to the planet called Four. It proved to be less rugged than Three, mostly flat and thus not a promising location for minerals of value. Landing appeared routine and Terry let Mikaela pilot the shuttle alone while he himself stayed aboard *Picard*. The crew placed the sensor station without incident, then headed back to Maclairn. There hadn't been room in the cargo bay for more stations, so they would wait until the next trip to deploy one on Five—or rather, on one of its frozen moons, for it was a gas giant far from the sun.

Terry had feared that his sleep would be interrupted again by imaginary perceptions, but during the days it took to get to Four and back it didn't happen. On the night they were closest to Maclairn, however, he felt a vague uneasiness, undoubtedly a mere recollection of what he had felt before at that distance, but nevertheless hard to deny. He couldn't shake the suspicion that *something*, something that didn't belong, was out there.

25

ONCE BACK ABOARD *Shepard* Terry found that Kathryn had left for Earth, and the fact that he had expected this didn't lessen his disappointment. He was due for his first leave and he had no choice but to make the best of it. When he got to Petersville Jessica greeted him warmly and invited him to stay in Kathryn's room; for the time being all officers on leave were being hosted in private homes, though a lodging for them was under construction. He wasn't sure if it would be better or worse if he were not sleeping in the bed they had shared.

As soon as he was settled he went to see Tristan, who was by this time fully recovered and back at work in the neurofeedback center. The moment they met he sensed that no discussion of the cave incident was necessary. Tristan took it for granted that the remote viewing sessions would continue, and between those and further neurofeedback training, his days were fully occupied. In the evening there was usually something to which Fleet personnel were invited—a sports event, concert, or cookout—as well as informal gatherings in homes and in taverns. Terry was welcomed and it was great to be with people with whom he could connect, including some of his fellow-officers who had become aware of their emerging psi powers. But he would have enjoyed himself more if Kathryn had been with him. As it was, he spent much of his spare time accessing the knowledgebase, absorbed in reading up on centuries of research and speculation about the paranormal.

Kathryn, Tristan said, had been through the Ritual and was now a Steward of the Flame. "There will be a small corner of her mind closed to you, even during sex," he warned. "It can't be avoided in your case, though normally couples who are committed to each other beforehand are initiated at the same time."

"Is keeping the ceremony secret really so important?" Terry protested. "I mean, if I found out I wouldn't tell anybody—"

"It's not that you wouldn't be trusted with it. The problem is that it has to be kept from *you*, because knowing in advance would make it virtually impossible for you to get through the Ritual if you ever want to."

"Could I? Would an outsider be qualified?" There was nothing he wouldn't do, Terry thought, to be close to Kathryn.

"Well," Tristan told him, "if you went through the Ritual you'd no longer be an outsider. You would be committed to our goals. It's a matter of deep dedication and willingness to make whatever sacrifices are necessary, not mere liking for Maclairn or desire to share a partner's secrets. Still, if you truly wished it, it wouldn't be incompatible with your League citizenship or your present duties in Fleet."

But what if Fleet sent him back to exploring? Terry asked himself. He could never give it up; it had been the core of the future he'd pictured since boyhood. In the back of his mind he'd hoped Kathryn might come with him if he ever moved on. Yet she did not have the longing for new discoveries that he did . . . and she was now irrevocably bound to Maclairn.

Most of his advanced mind training didn't require the presence of a mentor and was done under the guidance of another instructor, usually Elbra. When he mentioned that he was familiar with the neurofeedback software, she allowed him to operate the computer during the practice sessions of the teenage trainees and eventually to supervise them. Terry found that he enjoyed it; his old obsession with computers began to come back, with the added fascination of watching people interact with the displayed mind-patterns, and he realized that he would be good at the job if he had any spare time to fill between space flights. Mind training for crew members was continuing aboard *Shepard*; maybe the instructors there could use some assistance.

Near the end of his leave, Tristan decided it was time for him to learn more about healing. "It was highly unusual for Aldren to introduce you to it so soon," he said, "though we do eventually teach everyone to control bleeding and heal minor cuts or burns. He evidently felt you have the ability to go further—perhaps to heal other people."

"He mentioned it," Terry admitted. "I—I'm not sure I want to." Telepathy was one thing, and even remote viewing was merely a matter of developing capabilities latent in everyone. But to be a healer was something else. After a lifetime of feeling different when in contact with people he had at last begun to relate to them; he did not want to be set apart as someone they revered.

"Certainly you wouldn't want to make it your profession," Tristan agreed. "and it's unlikely that you possess the gift for repairing internal damage that a full-fledged healer has. But in an emergency, the ability to aid the injured might prove useful."

That was undeniable; as an explorer captain he was responsible for the welfare of his crew and after all, the original stated purpose of the mind training was to learn if it was practical for use in Fleet. So after demonstrating that with neurofeedback he could indeed heal self-inflicted cuts, he found himself watching as Tristan took the knife and proceeded to slash his own arm. Terry was appalled, though he knew Tristan wasn't suffering and could heal himself if necessary. He sat frozen, staring, while the blood gushed from the wound and dripped onto the floor. *You must act, Terry,* Tristan commanded. *I'll help, but not before you take the initiative.*

In desperation, he matched the mind-pattern on the wall, which remained from his self-healing, and reached out to connect with Tristan's mind, instinctively projecting the visualization. The flow of blood slowed, and finally stopped.

"You have aptitude," Tristan said. "I completed the healing; you are not experienced enough to sustain the necessary state of mind. But you grasped the concept. You sensed that it's not something you do *to* a person; you help him, through telepathy that for him may be unconscious, to do it himself. All healing is self-healing; the human body has that capability, though we believe unconscious psychokinesis is sometimes involved. The healer merely shows the way."

"I didn't know what I was doing," Terry confessed. "I couldn't even have tried if there'd been time to think about it."

"No. That's why a novice has to be shocked into action. But you have had practice in letting things happen without trying to force them, and another time, you will know."

"Tristan . . . will I learn to use more psychokinesis?"

"Probably not. It usually appears in childhood—many children born here can move small objects around, and there are poltergeist incidents among adolescents—but no one here has learned later in life except Peter, who was exceptionally psi-gifted and who had a strong need for it because he was confined to a chair. Historically, adults on Earth occasionally developed PK, but there's no compelling reason for you to do so. As for the more spectacular things, few people other than mentors have that power, and we don't encourage it unless it emerges spontaneously."

With inner relief, Terry nodded. The idea of bringing about physical effects with his mind still disturbed
him. As he acknowledged this, Tristan sensed it, and
said, "On second thought, there is one other form of
PK that may someday prove useful to you—and may be
useful right now for overcoming any negative feelings
you may have."

"What's that?" Terry inquired apprehensively.

"The control of fire."

"Oh, Tristan, I'm not sure—"

"Which is precisely why it would be a good thing for
you to learn. I don't mean anything major like melting
metal. Just lighting candles and more importantly, putting them out."

"Okay," Terry agreed, realizing that there was nothing else he could say.

Tristan took a candle from the cabinet beneath his
desk and as Terry watched, it seemingly lighted itself.
Putting his neurofeedback helmet back on, Tristan said,
"Match the mind-pattern."

Their minds connected, and a feeling of confidence
came over Terry, as it always did when working with an
instructor. The candle went out. "It's simply an exagger-
ated form of temperature control," Tristan said. "I could
not light it with my mind if there were no wick; I simply
made the wick get hot, and then cool, using the same
kind of volition we use for everything else. There's no
magic involved, no chance of a raging conflagration en-
gulfing you unless you're foolish enough to set something
afire that would be unsafe to light with a match. Now
I'll relight it, and we'll put it out together."

Before long Terry had mastered the technique for both
extinguishing fires and starting them, and the
neurofeedback pattern was indelibly impressed on his
mind. Flame was an apt symbol for mind powers, he reflected. There was a sense of being in control that he
hadn't had with the other skills, which produced less well-

defined results. There was great power in it and he grasped how easily it could be misused, yet he felt in no more danger of misusing it himself than of becoming a traditional arsonist. His underlying fear—like that of psi's deniers—had been groundless.

On his last day with Tristan, Terry hesitantly raised the subject of his illusory perception of something lurking in space. "I know it can't be real," he said. "Even if there were a ship out there, which there can't be, it's just too incredible that I could be taught a little about remote viewing and go right out there and succeed at it. But Tristan, how will I know if there ever *is* an intruder, if I'm going to keep imagining one when there's not?"

Tristan frowned. "It's a bit unusual for someone to simply imagine having remotely viewed some discrete object, like a ship," he said slowly. "Are you sure you weren't seeking to see, as you do in a normal viewing session?"

"I know I wasn't—I was asleep and it woke me, but it didn't feel like a dream. I didn't *want* to sense anything; I tried to shake it off."

"Well, as you said, your nerves were on edge because of your new responsibility. Once you get used to that, you won't be so sensitized to the thought of unseen dangers." As Terry stood to go, Tristan added, "Terry—don't mention this to Jessica. She's already troubled by her own imaginings; if she gets the idea that you share them, she'll view it as confirmation."

"I knew she's more worried than anyone else about intruders coming soon," Terry said. "But surely she doesn't think she's sensed one?"

"Jessica is a hundred and twenty-one, and for most of her life she's been burdened with the knowledge that she has greater psi capabilities than anyone else—and that she was fated to become our leader because of it. It's not really surprising if in her old age, she feels she may be perceiving something the rest of us don't."

"I suppose not. But there couldn't have been a ship nearby even as long as the days between the times I imagined it, let alone since she began worrying. It would have either appeared by now or left the solar system."

"She knows that. Nevertheless, it was Jessica who insisted that you be immediately trained in remote viewing, and if she were given cause to think that precaution has led somewhere—"

"Well, I certainly won't tell her, or anyone else except maybe Kathryn." He hoped that he could forget the whole thing . . . and yet. . . .

Something had been nagging at Terry, and though he wanted to push it aside, he knew suddenly that it was the reason he had consulted Tristan about an event he'd vowed he would ignore. "Tristan . . . is it possible that with both of us it could be precognition?"

Tristan paused a long time before answering. Finally he said, "That thought did occur to me when you told me how real it seemed. I'd be lying if I said it hasn't occurred to Jessica; it's the main reason why hearing of your experience would upset her. But Terry, if it *was* a viewing of the future, there is absolutely nothing you can do about it beyond what is already being done. Fleet is taking every possible measure to detect the approach of an unauthorized ship. You have to let go of it, and take things as they come."

"That's not true," Terry said, acknowledging the thing he had not wanted to admit to himself. "Fleet can't do anything more, but me—I can't just dismiss what I sense. I have to stay alert all the time and try to judge whether the future has arrived, just as Jessica does."

Tristan nodded. *I did not want to lay that on you, but since you see it yourself. . . .*

It could be years! Terry thought. An intruder might come tomorrow or not until he was an old man, and he would never be able to relax his vigilance.

26

SETTING OUT FOR planet Five, Terry was both more confident and less so than on *Picard*'s first mission—more sure of himself because he'd had some experience with command, yet at the same time worried because conditions would be a great deal harsher than on Three and Four and landing might prove difficult if not impossible. Five was a gas giant with many moons about which little was known. The strong gravitational forces surrounding it would make navigation tricky; the AI was programmed to handle it and he had flown near such planets on previous exploration missions, as well as near Saturn during his training tour on Titan . . . but you never knew just what to expect in that sort of situation.

Unlike Three and Four, the moons of Five were not potential landing sites for prospectors. They were covered with ice several kilometers thick, and it would take a major expedition with heavy equipment to reach whatever valuable minerals they contained. They were, however, of interest to science, as it was likely that at least some of them had liquid oceans—and possibly primitive forms of life—beneath their icy crusts. That had proved to be the case in many other solar systems. So any ship that approached one of them would be a Fleet explorer and its captain would obey an off-limits notice picked up from orbit. It was important to place the transmitter in the optimum location for local reception as well as for warning *Shepard*.

Picard spent several days in the vicinity of Five gathering information about its moons—their gravity, composition, temperature, atmosphere, and so forth— a routine task for explorer missions in which Terry had considerable experience. All this data could have been obtained remotely, of course, if there had been a base installation within the solar system; but explorers, by definition, went to solar systems not previously surveyed, so *Picard* was equipped to gather it directly and through the use of small unmanned probes controlled by its AI. The captain's job was to evaluate it and judge which moon was the most likely candidate for closer investigation.

Many of the moons were too small to be worth considering; others were too distant from Five to have enough tidal heat for liquid water to exist. Two were actively volcanic, which meant not only extreme peril on the surface but a real possibility that a sensor station would be engulfed by lava in the not-too-distant future. Of the few good possibilities, Terry chose the third most distant moon from the planet, designated Five-C. It had a noticeable small but level plateau sheltered by mountain ridges; a station placed there, surrounded by colored markers, would be sure to attract the attention of any explorer team that orbited it.

On the fifth morning, ship's time, after their arrival at Five, he moved *Picard* into low orbit above Five-C and checked out the shuttle for landing. Everyone wanted to go to the surface; both Mikaela and Drew had had turns at staying behind and neither wanted to be left this time. Zuri had to go, since she was the only member of the team capable of testing the transmitter after it was placed. Terry was torn. It would be a dangerous surface expedition and he felt it was his place to lead it, but on the other hand, what if some problem arose aboard *Picard*? Their lives depended on its presence, and orbiting a world near a massive giant like Five was not as routine as orbiting small isolated planets like Three and Four. If the AI failed to maintain a stable orbit only he would be able to correct it, whereas Mikaela was an expert shuttle pilot. Balancing the risks, he decided to stay aboard himself and let her make the landing.

Nevertheless, it was with some misgivings that he watched the shuttle depart. As captain he was, after all, responsible for whatever happened during the mission whether he was present or not, and that was more unsettling to think about when he was merely supervising than when he was in personal control. He was hooked into the crew's comm link, of course; he would be aware of everything that happened and could give orders as necessary. But from orbit he could not actually see what was going on.

He decided to report to *Shepard* an hour ahead of schedule so as not to miss anything on the local comm while he was transmitting. As on previous trips, he had been making routine status reports four times a day. Because of the long time delay in radio communication at this distance from Maclairn, conversation was impossible; he expected no reply beyond the simple "Roger, *Picard*, your status acknowledged," from the comm technician on duty, which would arrive over an hour later. But he knew Captain Vargas was following the reports closely. "I am now orbiting the third moon of Planet Five," he stated. "Lieutenants Orlov, Larssen, and Kifeda are enroute to the surface. Expect a supplemental report when the sensor station has been placed."

Zuri reported to him continuously on the shuttle's progress and the view of Five-C from above. "There's so much glare from the ice that we can't see details," she said. Although this far out from the sun its light was dim, reflected light from Five added to it; they would have to adjust their helmets to filter it once they stepped onto the surface. "We're over the landing site now . . . there's a good level spot near a tall ridge, with no visible fissures. . . ."

Terry held his breath. "Altitude five hundred feet . . . two hundred . . . touchdown! Not even a jolt, Captain."

"Congratulations to Lieutenant Orlov on a smooth landing," Terry replied. He'd had no doubts about Mikaela's skill, but anything could happen on a world as unlike habitable planets as this one.

The placing of the sensor station went well, the only difference from previous deployments being the use of deep spikes to keep it from slipping on the ice. He verified reception of its transmission once Zuri had activated it, while Drew sprayed orange markers in a wide circle, the color penetrating deep into the ice. Mikaela reported that she was heading back to the shuttle to begin the checklist for liftoff.

"Everything checks out fine, sir," said Zuri finally. "We're done here—" Abruptly, to Terry's dismay, her words were cut off by an ear-splitting roar—not mere static, but surely a sign of something very, very wrong.

"Zuri!" he cried out, knowing as he did so that she might not have survived whatever had made such a sound. "Drew! Mikaela! What the hell is going on down there? Talk to me!"

For several minutes there was silence. Then Drew's voice came over the comm, so unsteady that it was hard to make out the words. "Oh God, an earthquake . . . the earthquake set off an avalanche, the most god-awful sound—"

"Report your status, Lieutenant!" Terry ordered, realizing that this was not a time to slip into informality. An earthquake? It was certainly possible; the gravity of Five could easily create seismic activity on its moons, though he had seen no sign that quakes were frequent on this one.

"Captain, there's been a violent quake," Drew stated, his voice still shaky. "We were thrown to the ground, and then there was an avalanche, a huge mass of ice came off the ridge nearest us onto the shuttle—"

"The shuttle?" Terry froze. "Was it damaged?"

"I don't know, sir. It's covered by the icefall."

"Can you clear away enough for it to lift off?" They *had* to, Terry knew, yet without shovels or any other tools. . . . "The heat from the engine ought to melt enough ice for it to free itself," he said, hoping this was true.

"You don't understand, sir—it's buried, buried deep. There's no way we can get to it. And Mikaela's inside."

27

"OH, MY GOD." He shouldn't have sent his crew to the surface without him, Terry thought in despair. It was intolerable that they were facing death while he was safe in orbit. . . .

And then in the next moment he realized that it was by miraculous good fortune that he was the one aboard *Picard*. Because he might be able to land it. As far as he knew no ship as large as this had ever been landed on ice, but it shouldn't be impossible. The ice shell was more than a kilometer thick; the danger lay in slipping, not breaking through. And there was no time to waste, because the oxygen supply in their tanks was limited and they couldn't reach the spares. He didn't let himself think about Mikaela.

"Is Lieutenant Kifeda all right?" he asked Drew.

"I'm here, sir," Zuri replied. "I'm trying to restabilize the sensor station—it was dislodged by the quake but not damaged."

"Why hasn't Lieutenant Orlov reported? Comm transmission wouldn't be affected by the ice cover, would it?"

"The shuttle's tipped over. She's out of her spacesuit so she hasn't got her helmet comm, and I guess she can't reach the main board."

"Well, sit tight, lieutenants," Terry said. "I'm coming down to get you."

There was another silence. Finally Drew said, "You mustn't do that, sir. It's too risky—even if you can manage to land that big ship, there may be aftershocks."

"I suppose there may be," Terry agreed, "but there's no alternative."

"The alternative is for you to head back to Maclairn

without us, Captain. The ship is needed; Fleet can't afford to lose it. And *you* are needed. We're not—Zuri and I are agreed on that, and Mikaela . . . we're not even sure she's alive."

"That's not an option," Terry declared. Surely they knew that a captain didn't desert his crew—not ever, under any circumstances. "I'm coming for you. But it will take another orbit to get low enough to land. You've got to do exactly what I tell you to make your oxygen last."

"I don't see that there's much we can do to use less of it, sir," Drew protested.

"Yes, there is. I was trapped in a cave on Maclairn and my mentor taught me how." He wasn't sure how much mind training the crew had had beyond managing pain and controlling their temperature; had he been successful in lowering his metabolism only because he was psi-gifted? Certainly that had helped him absorb Tristan's instruction.

The cold should help. Their suits would keep them warm enough to survive, but they should maintain as low a body temperature as possible short of hypothermia; they did know how to do that. But the trick of directly controlling metabolism—that had been shown to him telepathically, and for them, telepathy didn't yet work on a conscious level. And besides, he hadn't enough psi experience to communicate from orbit.

While pondering this, he was simultaneously commanding the AI to descend. There was, thank God, no atmosphere to create friction; it wouldn't have to be done as gradually as on the planet where he had previously landed an explorer. But it was nevertheless necessary to lose momentum—far more difficult with a big bulky ship like *Picard* than with a shuttle. And he would have to lose the last of it at the exact point where his crew was waiting. To achieve this he would have to take manual control.

"Drew, Zuri," Terry said, with effort maintaining a calm tone. "Spread the tarp the sensor station was wrapped in and sit down on it. Then don't move your muscles and don't talk. Relax as you did for mind training—remember what Aldren showed you about pain, how it felt to let go when you knew more pain was coming. Remember the mind-pattern on the wall, visualize the colors, how they blended, how they moved. . . . With all the power he could muster he silently projected the image from his own memory, and the memory of what he'd received from Tristan and passed to Kathryn. . . . Telepathy worked better for concepts than for conversation over distance, Corwin had said; maybe not for him, but he had to try.

"Lower your body temperature," he ordered aloud, "and slow your heart. This is what we were trained for, the reason they taught us mind skills to use in dealing with emergencies. This is part of what Maclairn is doing for the rest of humankind—giving people control over their own minds and bodies. And teaching them how to help each other by sharing minds, as we've all been starting to do. If we can make contact, I'll show you. . . ."

"Mikaela and I shared our minds," Drew burst out, "And now she's . . . oh God, Terry—"

They had slept together, Terry recalled—perhaps more than once. That would have enhanced their telepathic ability not only with each other, but with everyone; possibly they were no longer merely latent telepaths. "Reach out, Drew!" he commanded. "If she's still alive she needs you—you can reach her if you relax completely and call to her silently. . . ."

It might be mere wishful thinking, but he sensed that Drew had grasped this. Terry's tension was lessening as he gained control of his feelings and attempted to follow his own advice. "I'll be in comm blackout in a minute or two, around on the back side of the moon," he warned. "Don't panic and stay very still. Just keep on relaxing, so your body won't use too much oxygen."

On the second orbit, by this time on powered descent, Terry spotted the bright orange markers they had placed around the sensor station, which fortunately had been out of the path of the avalanche. Drawing a deep breath, he switched to manual control and felt *Picard* begin to drop. There would be no second attempt if it missed the target area; unlike a shuttle, this ship was too heavy to reverse direction so close to the ground and he was now committed to either a soft landing or a crash. What if he came too close to where they were sitting? The ice gleamed in the weak sunlight and he shuddered at the thought of setting down on a slippery surface from which he might or might not able to lift off again. Even the liftoff from Maclairn had been iffy. . . .

But this was *his* ship. He had restored it to life and had been given command of it; surely it wasn't his fate to lose it now.

"I'm about to land," he told Drew and Zuri. "Stay where you are unless it looks like you're going to be hit— you probably haven't enough oxygen left for any exertion. I will bring tanks to you."

Putting on more power, he maneuvered over a small ridge and let *Picard* settle. Plumes of steam rose around it as its thrusters touched ice, blinding the camera that fed his viewscreen; he realized that he would see nothing until it was too late to make any adjustments in the angle at which the ship came to ground. At the last minute he became aware that he had not been relying on sight in any case; his inner sense, the same sense he used for remote viewing, had shown him where to set down. There was a brief jar, and then no more movement than the reactive shaking of his hands.

He recalled, vividly, the image that had occurred to him his first morning on Maclairn when the sight of *Picard* on the ground had made him think of a beached whale.

The ship seemed solidly grounded; there was no trembling of the deck as he struggled into his spacesuit and ice boots. He got two oxygen tanks out of the storage locker and went through the airlock onto the frozen surface of Five-C.

The gravity was slightly higher than one g, which was helpful in keeping his footing on the slick ice. Drew and Zuri were some distance away; he was closer to the avalanche than to them. The shuttle was indeed buried beneath it, tipped onto its side; he could make out the shape. And as he walked, he got an idea.

"She's alive!" Drew called as he approached. "I—I tried to reach Mikaela in my mind like you said, sir," he added as Terry helped Zuri change her oxygen tank. "And I know she's there, I don't know how I know, but I'm sure. Only she'll die! We can't just leave, and let her die."

"No," Terry agreed. "How accurate are you with that laser cannon we installed, Lieutenant?"

"I did all right in the simulator, sir. Why?"

"I'm thinking that with it set on low power, we might blast some of the ice off the shuttle."

"We can't see it well enough," Drew protested. "There's nothing to aim for; we'd never locate the hatch. We could destroy the ship."

"That's a possibility. But it's the only chance we have of getting Mikaela out."

"I might kill her," Drew whispered in horror. "If I estimated wrong, I might literally shoot her with it."

"Yes. But as you said, she will die for sure if we do nothing."

They made their way back to *Picard*, which was fortunately positioned so that the beam could be directed toward the shuttle. "I'd do this myself," Terry said gently, "but I've had no training at all in fire control. It has to be you, Lieutenant Larssen."

Drew nodded. Terry powered up the ship and channeled power into the beam. Taking the controls, Drew aimed, hesitated for a moment, and then fired. The blue glare of the laser reflected by the ice nearly blinded them;

when it faded, they could see that a small section of the shuttle's hull was exposed. It was not near the hatch, however. "Try again," Terry ordered. "We know its orientation now."

"I've got to be careful not to fuse the hatch," Drew stated grimly.

"Aim high. The ice above it will melt and fall away in chunks,"

Drew complied. On the third try the hatch, now near the top of the hull rather than on the side, appeared to be accessible. They rushed toward it; nearly stumbling as they ran. Only one person at a time could enter the airlock, and Terry commanded the others to wait while he climbed down into it; he did not want Drew to find Mikaela's body if the oxygen inside had run out.

She was sprawled on the wall that had become the deck, not suffocating, but injured—her leg had been broken when she fell during the quake. With a sinking heart, he saw that it was a compound fracture; she had lost some blood. How were they going to get her into a spacesuit for the transfer back to *Picard*?

She was trying to speak; Terry pulled off his helmet so that he could hear. "I'm sorry, Captain," she whispered. "I guess my landing wasn't stable enough—the ship fell over after I got back in it, and I must have hit my head—there was a roaring noise and I blacked out."

"Your landing was fine," he assured her. "There was an earthquake."

"Earthquake? The others—"

"They're okay. We'll be taking off in *Picard*." Sensing her anguish he asked quickly, "You're not in pain, are you? You remember how to stop suffering from pain?"

"I—I tried to, but it doesn't seem to work like it did with Aldren." It wasn't working at all; she was in agony. Terry recalled that Aldren had said it would not work with a semi-conscious person or one too sick to judge danger. He would have to do it for her. It was like healing, he perceived—you didn't do it *to* someone, you just showed the way. . . .

Shutting out all thought of their situation, he relaxed and reached out to Mikaela's mind. As the link was made he was suddenly struck by fierce pain in his own leg; he almost fell. Desperately he shifted into altered consciousness, letting the pain envelop him and then cease to hurt. *Follow me, Mikaela! Mesh your mind with mine, and it won't hurt any more. . . .*

He knew from her face that he had succeeded. "Captain . . . you—you did what Aldren did, I felt it! How—? I'm all right now. Only—I can't get to *Picard*, you know. You'll have to leave me behind."

"We won't do that." At the moment he did not see how to avoid it, but there must be some way.

Suddenly the ship began to sway again, first gently and then with a lurch that threw Terry down beside Mikaela. He seized his helmet and managed to get it back on just as a sharp jolt hit, rocking the ship violently; everything not already dislodged slid toward them. The airlock burst open and Drew, who had just finished cycling it, fell through, landing on top of Terry. The shaking continued for a long time.

This was not an aftershock, Terry realized. It was the main quake; the earlier one had been merely a foreshock. God only knew how much havoc was occurring outside.

As he thought this, Zuri's scream came over his helmet comm. And then, "Captain, the ice just *cracked*! A crevasse opened up and *Picard* . . . fell into it."

28

TERRY FELT THE blood drain from his face. Oh, God— *Picard* . . . Dizzily he scrambled up to the airlock, grasping the seats anchored to what had been the deck, and waited the interminable time it took to cycle it. When he climbed out there was no escaping the worst of his fears; Picard was only half visible, its upper portion sticking out at an angle from a wide crevasse that not been there before. The engine section was undoubtedly crushed beyond repair.

His ship. He had lost his ship. That was all he thought of in the first few seconds, before it dawned on him that without the ship they were all going to die.

"Zuri, get into the shuttle," he commanded. "Fast, so I can go back in myself." It was a miracle that the airlock still functioned; if it had been damaged they would have only minutes of life remaining. As it was, they might have hours. No longer than that, for the shuttle didn't carry many extra tanks. The main supply was aboard *Picard*, and even if those tanks were intact, it would probably be impossible to retrieve them.

When he reentered the shuttle he found Drew down beside Mikaela, holding her leg with his hands. "It's still bleeding," he said despairingly. "I don't dare put a tourniquet on for fear of what that might do to the bone."

The bleeding wasn't severe enough to require a tourniquet, Terry decided; she wasn't losing a significant amount of blood, and strong pressure on the leg might cause the bone to splinter and do worse damage. But it couldn't be allowed to continue, and Drew could not staunch it indefinitely. Tristan's words came back to him: *In an emergency, the ability to aid the injured might prove useful . . . you must act, Terry.* He had been shown how to do it. The last thing he wanted in the middle of this other crisis was to become a healer . . . but a crisis, after all, was what it took to enhance latent psi power.

He knelt next to Mikaela and laid his hand gently over Drew's. Closing his mind to everything else, he visualized the healing pattern, the mind-pattern he had seen in sessions both with Aldren and with Tristan. *If you ever need to call on the skill, you'll have an underlying memory of the state of consciousness it demands*, Aldren had told him.

Mikaela, listen to me, listen in your mind! Terry urged. *You don't need to go on bleeding, you can stop it, just like we did with the pain.* . . . As vividly as he could, he imagined the flow stopping. . . .

"Take your hand away now," he told Drew. "She's not bleeding anymore."

"I don't understand—she was just a minute ago, and I didn't press hard—" Drew broke off, staring at Terry. Zuri and Mikaela, too, were staring at him. They had enough telepathic sensitivity to know it hadn't stopped by chance.

He realized that he would have to say something. "You know the Maclairnans have capabilities people don't usually have," he explained, "and we're being trained in some of them. The pace is different for different people, but it doesn't stop with physical skills like those we've all gained so far. I've been given extra training on Maclairn because the mentors want me to take on special duties. Eventually, you too may learn to use mind powers you haven't been shown yet."

They were silent, regarding him with awe. Finally Drew said, "What you told us over the comm about using less oxygen—you said a mentor had taught you that. And what you said about sharing minds, about reaching Mikaela . . . that wasn't just talk. You meant it literally."

"It worked, didn't it, Drew? Everybody has latent telepathic ability. Aldren told me some people find that idea frightening, that's why he doesn't mention it until there's good reason to. But it's how we learned what we did from him—didn't you wonder how merely looking at patterns could have enabled you to acquire mind skills?"

Drew nodded slowly, and his eyes met Mikaela's. Terry added, "Stress brings it out in people. And so does love."

Zuri burst out, "It's not fair that we're gaining these powers only when we're going to die!"

"If we die, it's for a good cause," Terry declared, "because protecting Maclairn is the only way to help spread them to other worlds—someday to everyone. But I'm not ready to say we won't live through this. *Shepard* will come for us when they realize we're in trouble."

"Will they?" Zuri questioned. "Will Fleet move a cruiser out of orbit on the long chance that a few officers might have survived whatever caused their comm to stop transmitting?"

Terry wondered. He had reported the earthquake, stating that he was about to land *Picard* to pick up the shuttle crew. When they didn't hear from him again they would naturally assume he had crashed, because if he hadn't he could have sent another report from the ground. And they knew the shuttle hadn't enough oxygen to last until they could reach Five. Moving *Shepard* away from Maclairn would be a major step and a rescue would require risking at least one more shuttle and its pilot. They would not do it merely out of curiosity about his fate. They would need a reason to think there were survivors.

"I don't know," he lied, "but we can't just give up. We've got to try to salvage some oxygen tanks." They were so impressed by his psi powers that they thought he could do anything he attempted, Terry saw, and it would be better to act as if they could save themselves than to sit still and wait for death. "Zuri, stay with Mikaela," he ordered. "Try to get her to eat something; she needs to keep up her strength. Drew, follow me out as soon as the airlock's free—and bring a rope." He himself took a laser gun, thankful that he had followed standard explorer ops procedure and seen to it that the shuttle was stocked with basic emergency equipment.

Terry and Drew quickly ate some protein bars, then went outside, taking flashlights. The sun, at this distance little larger than a bright star, was setting; though the dim eerie light of Five was enough to illuminate the terrain, if they got into *Picard* they would need them. The vast expanse of blue ice was more unnerving in semi-darkness than it had been earlier. Knowing themselves unlikely to see daylight again, they were more chilled by it than by the thought that the temperature outside their spacesuits was at least two hundred degrees below freezing, or by the occasional mild aftershocks that were still occurring. Ongoing comm contact with Zuri and Mikaela helped; still, by the time they had made their way to the crevasse that had swallowed *Picard* they were trembling from more than fatigue.

The cracks in the ice near the ship were too wide to stride across and there was no way to anchor the rope; they had no choice but to leap, despite the all-too-real possibility that the ground would shake before they could land. The rope, however, proved essential in gaining access to the tilted *Picard*. It took many tries to lasso a handhold designed for EVA use in space, but once the line was firmly attached Terry was able to climb up and open the outer hatch. As he expected, there was no power for cycling the lock. "I'll have to drill and release the air pressure," he called. Loss of the ability to pressurize the ship wouldn't matter, since it couldn't fly and they couldn't get Mikaela into it anyway. All the same, as he triggered the laser gun, he felt the pain of destroying any part of the ship he had cherished.

Once inside, he lowered a ladder for Drew. He didn't bother to visit the bridge, as with the ship unpowered there would be no means of transmitting a distress signal; instead he managed to clamber into the compartment containing the stored oxygen tanks. Enough had been filled to last three people through five more eight-hour surface expeditions, and without power there was no way to fill any more—nor were empty tanks available. That would give them little more than a standard day of oxygen beyond what the shuttle now contained. *Shepard* could get here in a day, if it started soon; it was a much faster ship than *Picard*. The likelihood of its coming was small, Terry thought; but a day of life was better than nothing.

Handing thirty oxygen tanks down the ladder to Drew, one at a time, took nearly an hour. They were forced to rest before attempting to get them across the ice cracks, which they did in batches, wrapped in tarps from the ship, with the aid of more ropes. It was impossible to drag more than half of them back to the shuttle; they would have to return later for the rest. First, Terry knew, they would need sleep; there was a limit to how much energy could be mustered even through the control of internal biochemistry on which they'd been relying.

The sight of the orange marking surrounding the sensor station was welcome, for it meant they were almost there. The station, surprisingly, had been spared by the quake; it was erect and probably still functioning. At least they had accomplished what they had come here for; Maclairn would know if any intruding ships passed this way. . . .

Suddenly, with a thrill of hope, Terry realized what that meant.

The transmitter was sending a periodic all clear signal to *Shepard*. But if it could be made to send the alert signal, Captain Vargas would understand that this couldn't be coincidence. The chance of an intruder appearing near Five at the same time as *Picard*'s landing was incalculably small. He would realize that if the signal had changed, someone had survived to change it.

"Lieutenant Kifeda," Terry asked quickly on the comm link, "Can you force the sensor station to switch to alert mode?"

"Yes, Captain," Zuri replied, "I can, though I can't test it without *Picard*'s receiver."

"Then get out here fast and do it," Terry said. "If *Shepard* picks up an alert they'll know we're still alive."

The signal wouldn't reach *Shepard* for more than half an hour, of course, and no reply could be received. They would have to wait while their oxygen supply lessened, not knowing if rescue was on the way. But there was a chance. It would be worth the ordeal of intentionally lowering their metabolism, not moving, eating or even speaking, because help might arrive if they could hold out long enough.

Except for the trip to get the remaining oxygen tanks, they lay quietly in silence, doing their best to ignore slight aftershocks that sent shudders through the ship. With a mixture of awe and dismay Terry realized that only his crew's trust in him, and the telepathic projection through which he kept them calm, made this possible. The stress of their peril heightened the latent sensitivity that had been awakened by their initial training; and toward the end he felt that Drew and Mikaela, at least, were beginning to exchange thoughts knowingly.

Though he knew it was pointless to keep track of the time left, he couldn't help calculating in his mind. There were barely two hours remaining when the shuttle's comm came alive: "*Picard*, this is *Shepard*. We are in orbit and we see your marker. Do you read us? Over."

Terry, who had lain down with the remote mike in his hand, replied quickly, "Roger, *Shepard*, we read you. This is Captain Terry Radnor. *Picard* cannot be salvaged but we are all alive. We need immediate pickup as our oxygen is almost gone. There are still aftershocks from the quake, so be careful. Over."

"Captain Radnor, can you come to the point marked by the orange circle?"

"Negative, *Shepard*. Lieutenant Orlov is injured and will require an enclosed stretcher. We will meet you at the marker to carry it; no emergency medical care is needed." He hoped they would know better than to risk a stretcher bearer's or medic's life in addition to the pilot's; Mikaela's leg could be healed soon enough by the mentors on board the cruiser.

"Roger, Captain. A shuttle will be on its way ASAP.

We will keep you informed of its progress. Out."

Less than two hours later they were aboard *Shepard*. Terry was too relieved by the crew's safety to look back, but as the cruiser broke orbit he could not help feeling a pang of sorrow at knowing he had seen the last of *Picard*.

Part Three: Promise

29

ONCE *SHEPARD* WAS back in orbit above Maclairn, Terry was ordered to report to Captain Vargas for a more thorough debriefing than the one immediately following the rescue from Five-C. He dreaded it. He wasn't used to failure; he had experienced self-blame only during the brief hours when Aldren had forced him to confront his inability to display superhuman endurance. Now he had lost his ship, and a captain who had lost his ship, no matter what the extenuating circumstances, was never viewed in quite the same way by Fleet as one who had not.

They went over the details of the mission, but for Terry it came down to that one point. "I lost my ship, sir," he said finally, realizing that the captain had made no direct reference to the fact that it was unsalvageable. "And we need that ship. I'm responsible for whatever problems are caused by our not having it." *Not to mention what the mentors have hoped I might achieve by remote viewing while I'm traveling around this solar system*, he added silently.

The CO regarded him thoughtfully. "You lost your ship, but you saved your crew," he said. "Do you think I'd rather have it the other way around?"

"Of course not, sir. But if I'd picked a different moon to land on in the first place—"

"It was the same one I'd have picked. That quake couldn't have been foreseen, Lieutenant, not on a world with no signs of recent seismic activity. Your willingness to accept responsibility is commendable, but save it for a time when you've really made a mistake."

What now? Terry wondered. He would become a patrol leader as originally planned, he supposed. But there were already enough patrol leaders, and that job seemed even less appealing than it had before he'd served as an explorer captain.

Captain Vargas went on, "I have talked to the members of your crew. They all feel you deserve a medal for risking your life to keep them alive, and I agree. I will recommend you for it in my next dispatch."

Terry was so astonished that he said nothing. Vargas continued, "You'll be happy to know that Maclairn's ambassador returned from Earth while you were gone."

"Yes, sir, that's good news." He hadn't been sure whether Kathryn would be back by now. Perhaps, he thought, if he wasn't needed right away he'd be given longer leave than a weekend, even though he'd recently had one.

"She brought dispatches from Fleet headquarters. I have been informed that the captain of the Maclairn Foundation's ship *Promise* wants to retire, and they don't think it would be wise to let another hired crew in on the secret. Therefore, they have asked Fleet to crew it, which would have the additional advantage of allowing it to be armed—there's probably no need, but the civilian passengers have expressed some concern about pirates. Since there are no officers at headquarters who have had mind training, the request has been passed on to me. My first thought was that we have no one qualified to pilot a jump ship apart from commanders who are needed here. But now that you are free, I've reconsidered. Would such an assignment interest you?"

"Copilot of *Promise*? Oh yes, sir!" It would mean that

he would travel with Kathryn; they would never have to be separated. It was too good to be true.

"Well, copilot was not exactly what I had in mind, Lieutenant," Vargas said, smiling. "It's my intention to make you captain."

Stunned, Terry burst out, "Captain? Of a passenger ship? But sir—" He couldn't have heard right; no mere lieutenant could command a passenger ship, let alone one carrying an ambassador and high-ranking civilians.

"I think we can rely on you to make the safety of the passengers your top priority," Captain Vargas declared. "But if you're thinking that your present rank disqualifies you, you are right. You will be promoted to lieutenant commander, effective on the day you take command—"

This was incredible! He had thought it would be at least two more years before he was eligible for promotion.

"—which will be soon," Vargas continued, "because you will need to make a test flight with the retiring captain, and since he is a civilian he cannot be given authority over Fleet officers."

In a daze, Terry expressed his thanks for the trust placed in him and went to phone Kathryn. Perhaps, he thought, she'd had something to do with this; the Maclairnans had a great deal of influence with Captain Vargas and he would be unlikely to disregard the ambassador's wishes. Jessica, too, might have had a hand in it. Nevertheless, his telepathic sensitivity had told him that the CO's approval had been genuine.

After a joyous reunion with Kathryn during a five-day leave, he inspected *Promise*, which was in an orbit lower than *Shepard*'s. It was a somewhat larger ship than *Picard*, designed to carry twelve people including the crew, the legal maximum for civilian starships; but otherwise it was similar. There was little new for him to learn as far as piloting it was concerned. And the customary protocol for day-to-day living with passengers, far more formal than when only Fleet personnel were aboard, he could learn from Kathryn.

His promotion and new appointment were announced at dinner in the wardroom that night. Terry, unused to being the center of attention, accepted the congratulations of his fellow officers with as much dignity as he could muster, startled and touched by the warmth with which they offered them. When Captain Vargas pinned the silver sunburst of a lieutenant commander to his lapel he was nearly overwhelmed by the telepathic current in the room. How much of it was due to the others' developing psi ability and how much to his own new awareness of connection with people, he couldn't tell.

His first duty as captain was to select a crew. He chose Drew Larssen as engineer and told him to become thoroughly familiar with the design of the ship as well as to assist with the maintenance check that was already underway. Also, he ordered him to oversee the installation of a laser cannon like the one that had proved useful aboard *Picard*. Now that *Promise* was becoming known in Earth's solar system as a private ship that carried passengers, there was a small chance that pirates might try to seize them for ransom; and whereas his untrained crew would be no match for pirates if it came to a fight, they would be less likely to pursue an armed ship than an unarmed one.

The choice of a copilot was more difficult. Mikaela would not be fully recovered from her injury in time for the next trip, and in any case it would have to be a man since she and Drew were not committed to a permanent relationship and the two officers must share a stateroom. Terry wasn't well acquainted with the other pilots, many of whom were members of couples and therefore ineligible. Whoever he chose would have to be trained enroute since none of them had any experience piloting starships. Though the copilot's main job would be to fly the shuttle, he must be able to take charge of *Promise* while it was orbiting a planet.

Word had gotten around, and to Terry's surprise everyone wanted the job—not just because it offered a chance to handle a jump ship, but because his own reputation had spread. He could scarcely believe this until, embarrassed, he was informed by Drew that since the Five-C ordeal *Picard's* crew had virtually revered him. It wasn't only that he had risked his life for them, Drew said. They had been deeply impressed by his advanced psi powers. "None of us knew Fleet people were gaining the abilities the Maclairnans have, aside from managing our physical reactions," he admitted. "You—well, I can't believe you're the guy I've been rooming with all this time. There's not a lieutenant on this ship who wouldn't jump at the chance to serve under you."

With dismay, Terry realized that it was starting—the thing he had feared when he'd told Tristan that he wasn't sure he wanted the ability to heal others. He had no wish to be viewed as a hero, much less be credited with special powers. Yet how could it have been avoided? He could not have let Mikaela suffer from pain or go on bleeding when he was able to prevent it. He could not have let anyone die from lack of oxygen when he knew how to help them lower their metabolism. God, he thought, what will they think when they find out what I'm learning remote viewing for?

It was just as well, perhaps, that *Promise* wouldn't be spending much flight time in Maclairn's solar system. Yet wasn't that a cop-out? Wasn't an important part in protecting Maclairn what he wanted most?

He went to see Tristan the next time he was free to go down to the surface. They talked a long time. "You are a forerunner, not a superman, just as many of us on Maclairn are," Tristan said, "and forerunners are always set apart from their contemporaries by their capabilities. The answer isn't to hide those capabilities—it's to work toward making them more widely available. That's why from the beginning, we've considered ourselves stewards here rather than superiors worthy of being admired by people who lack what we've gained."

Terry nodded, seeing for the first time what the term Stewards of the Flame really meant. He had not understood it before; he'd assumed it was just a mystical-sounding phrase chosen for ceremonial purposes. Was he, perhaps, like those formally pledged even though he wasn't one of them?

There was another question that had been haunting him. "Tristan—was going into that cave more than just stupidity on my part? Did I have some sort of unconscious foreknowledge that I could someday save others by what I learned there?"

"That's too big a question for any of us to answer," Tristan replied slowly. "There might have been precognition involved, but on the other hand it might have been synchronicity, which is something that has never been understood. All we can be sure of is that such connections are not just random chance. To say that they are, as the majority of scientists try to, is to ignore the mathematics of probability that they claim to respect."

"How can they ignore mathematical fact?"

"How can they ignore statistical proof of the existence of psi? Scientists have always swept facts that don't fit current theories under the rug, because to accept them would be to leave themselves stranded without the firm ground of a theory to stand on. And that's a state only a very exceptional scientist can tolerate. Wait and see, Terry—as captain of *Promise*, you will meet the mentors who have been working on Earth, and you will begin to grasp what we're up against."

After consultation with the XO, Terry chose Lt. Amir Khalil as copilot of *Promise* on the basis of skill as a shuttle pilot and his expressed interest in interstellar astrogation, as well as his strong support of Maclairn's goals. Once Commander Linley had signed off on the maintenance

work he and his new crew took the ship on a six-day test
cruise with the former civilian captain as advisor. It went
smoothly, but of course it was bound to, within the solar
system. The real test of his piloting ability would come
with his first jump.

They went out as far as Three and orbited it before
coming back. Terry felt increasingly uncomfortable as they
neared it, not because of anything to do with *Promise* but
because a vague sense of unease nagged at him whenever
he wasn't busy with his work. Finally, in the night, he
realized what had brought it on. It was the memory of
the strange experience he'd had twice before at this distance from Maclairn, the sense that there was another
ship somewhere in the vicinity. Or was it just memory?
Tristan had acknowledged that what he'd felt before could
have been precognition. But why would precognition come
to him here and nowhere else, when that form of psi wasn't
related to distance?

He had not sensed it during the swift return from
Five-C aboard *Shepard*, but he had been exhausted then
and had slept soundly. Now, he found he could not sleep.
There was *something* just beyond the edge of consciousness that he couldn't push aside. Not until they approached Maclairn on the return trip did he feel free to
take joy in having become a starship captain.

30

THE CURRENT OBSERVERS that Kathryn had brought to
Maclairn were not scheduled to leave for another ten
days and Terry was able to spend many of them with
her, exulting in the fact that they wouldn't be parted when
it was time for *Promise* to go. They looked happily forward to the trip, sharing in the planning; she, after all,
represented the ship's owner and was responsible for
all details other than those connected with the ship's

maintenance and operation, though he would be in full command while in flight.

Four days before departure, when he was back aboard *Shepard* supervising the dispatch of *Promise*'s cargo and consumables, Terry was called to report to Captain Vargas. "It's come to my attention, Commander, that Kathryn expects that *Promise* can carry more passengers from now on because she won't be using up a stateroom," the CO said.

Terry reddened. Of the six double staterooms aboard she had previously occupied one alone and the captain another, leaving one for the other officers and only three for passengers; if she shared his, there would be four. "Well, yes," he said. "I guess we did assume—"

"I realize you have been lodged together in Jessica's home. It's entirely acceptable under Maclairnan custom, and on a trip involving just Fleet personnel, or one carrying only mentors, we wouldn't object either. But future civilian passengers will come from many cultures, some of them very conservative, and you will socialize with them as an official representative of Fleet. I'm sorry, but we can't have it made obvious that the relationship between the two of you is in any way inappropriate."

Frowning, Terry considered this. It was a long-term problem, and the restriction would undoubtedly extend to whatever hotels they stayed in on Earth. They couldn't make trip after trip without ever sharing a bed, and he did not like the idea of sneaking. If they were caught at it, the repercussions would be worse than if they lived together openly. Besides, it was a waste of much-needed passenger space.

"Sir, there's another possibility," he declared. "We're committed to each other, which is the equivalent of marriage under Maclairn's law. If we were also married under League law, no one could object. As captain of a deployed cruiser, aren't you authorized to perform weddings?"

Captain Vargas looked thoughtful. "Yes, I'm licensed to do that," he said after a pause. "But if I marry a couple I'm obliged to offer counseling. And you must think very carefully before you enter into a legal marriage, Terry. There's more to it than having an exclusive sexual relationship."

"It's not just sex with us," Terry protested. "I thought you knew that."

"Yes, of course—I know you care deeply for each other and wish to share your lives. But think: what about the future? You are an outstanding officer and you have it in you to reach the top—perhaps to command a colonizer someday. Kathryn appears dedicated to her career as legal advocate for Maclairn. Can you ask her to choose between abandoning it and the long separations your expeditions may require?"

This was the question that had tormented Terry from the moment he'd first realized the depth of his love for Kathryn. He would not ask her to choose—she was a Steward of the Flame and pledged to work for Maclairn's cause. The choice would have to be his, and it would apply as much to exploring as to possible higher command. Either he must give that up to stay on Maclairn, or they would have to be parted someday. He had put off thinking about it, hoping that as long as he was based here the issue would not arise. But it was true that it would be settled if he married her. Though few modern marriages lasted a lifetime, he could not see himself ending his for the sake of career advancement; he would not do that to Kathryn even if he wanted to.

And yet, wouldn't that be what he was doing if he decided he couldn't marry legally? If he told her that they must sleep apart aboard *Promise* because he'd been advised not to bind himself?

"It's too late for either of us to choose," he said. "We're already bonded; a ceremony won't make any difference."

Captain Vargas sighed. "So I thought," he admitted.

"Aldren explained to me that with telepaths the bond can become unbreakable after very short acquaintance. All the same I had to speak because I wasn't sure you knew the extent of the opportunities that may open up for you. I suspect that if Kathryn truly loves you, she will not let you reject them, and that there are painful separations ahead. But it would not be any less painful if you held back now."

That afternoon he went down to the surface on special leave to formally propose. Kathryn agreed with enthusiasm, but then she said hesitantly, "There's something you don't know about me, Terry—something I've put off telling you."

"I know everything I need to know," he assured her, smiling, "Our minds merge every time we have sex."

"That reveals current thoughts, not past history. You don't even know my surname."

"I thought you dropped it when you became a citizen of Maclairn."

"I did, but we're going to Earth, and if I'm your wife it's going to come up. I'm a Bramfield." At his blank look, she asked, "Haven't you ever heard of Arthur Bramfield?"

He shook his head. "I left Earth as soon as I got out of school, and at the Fleet academy we didn't pay a whole lot of attention to the news. If he's a notorious criminal or something, don't worry about it—I don't care who your relatives are."

"Arthur Bramfield is the CEO of the Maclairn Foundation. He's my grandfather."

"You told me your granddad was the head of it when we first met," he said, puzzled.

"But I didn't tell you that he's one of the richest people on Earth apart from that. He's a billionaire in his own right, Terry, and my parents died when I was little—that makes me an heiress. It's something I've never wanted, but I'm stuck with it."

Stunned, Terry could only gape.

"I love Granddad very much—he and Gram raised me, and he's a wonderful person," she went on. "And I don't mind his having money; he supports many charities and has put a lot into the Foundation, which is what pays for keeping *Promise* operational. But I never got a chance to live like other girls. And when I finally met someone I thought I might marry . . . well, as I told you, he dumped me when I asked him to come to Maclairn. It wasn't only that he was scared off by my interest in psi. My inheritance won't be of any use on Maclairn, you see, and it turned out that it was all he really cared about."

Troubled, Terry said, "You—you didn't fall in love with me just *because* I didn't know, did you?"

"That was what attracted me so fast," she admitted. "No man had ever wanted me for myself before. But after that, nothing mattered except being with you—I'd have loved you even if you did want my money. On Earth, though, there'll be people who won't believe that you didn't marry me for it; behind your back they'll call you a fortune hunter."

"Will your grandparents think that?"

"No. They'll recognize you for what you are, and they'll be happy for me."

"Then do we care what other people think?"

She frowned. "I don't if you don't, but I had to warn you. Some, even in Fleet, may assume you got command of *Promise* only through Granddad's influence. Being rich and famous gives him power; that was why the Foundation was able to make contact with League officials in the first place, and why they were willing to negotiate a contract."

Terry had wondered how that came about; an ordinary group of people claiming to have found a world where ESP was widespread would be dismissed as crackpots. "Does Captain Vargas know who you are?" he asked, suddenly worried that it might indeed have been the cause of his unexpected promotion.

"No. Admiral Derham does, because I went back to Earth with his group, but he promised me he wouldn't tell anybody. No one here knows except Jessica. And let's leave it that way."

The wedding was held two days later aboard *Shepard*, not only because it had to be performed in League territory, but because most of the crew wanted to attend. The captain, after talking with Kathryn by phone, decided that there was no need for him to counsel her face to face; so she didn't come aboard until a few hours before the ceremony. She brought with her only her close friend Elbra as an attendant; the Maclairnans would celebrate afterward with the wedding feast customary among them when couples declared themselves lifemates.

There being no such thing as a wedding gown on Maclairn, there had been some question about what Kathryn was to wear. Terry, Drew as best man, and the official honor guard—composed of both men and women—would be wearing their dress uniforms, and she had not brought any formal attire from Earth. White was considered inappropriate because on Maclairn it was reserved for the Ritual. In the end she wore a pale gold-colored dress, exquisitely hand-sewn like all Maclairnan clothes, with a small sunflower in her blond hair. Terry thought she had never looked more beautiful.

The rings they exchanged were of copper, fashioned for them by Tristan through same psychokinetic process used by mentors to create the Stewards' flame pins. It was traditional, he'd said, for jewelry of special significance to be made in this way, to symbolize the blessing of the community as a whole on whatever pledges its members made to each other.

"I, Terry, take you, Kathryn, to be my wife, to have and to hold from this day forward, for better or for worse, for richer, for poorer, in sickness and in health, to love and to cherish until we are parted by death." That was the traditional commitment he declared aloud; but underneath, telepathically, he added, *The words we say aren't needed, for we are already one and nothing can ever part us. Whatever happens in the future, we have that to hold to, and it will always be the touchstone of my life.*

After the ceremony there was a reception in the wardroom complete with toasts, followed by dancing and merriment on the mess deck that promised to go on for a long time. But Terry and Kathryn, along with members of the wedding party, soon left aboard a shuttle and were met at the Old Settlement by a crowd of well-wishers who accompanied them to the boat landing. It was lit with torches, as it had been on the night when they first saw each other. As they boarded the boat Terry thought of how much his life had changed since then. He had more than he had ever dreamed of having—it seemed almost too good to be true. For a moment, he felt a chill, which surely couldn't be precognition. . . .

He had not believed Captain Vargas's warning about separations ahead; he would not allow himself to contemplate it. And yet, suddenly recalling Aldren's prediction about an extraordinary destiny, he was struck by fear of what that might mean. Around him celebration had begun; a fleet of small boats accompanied the large one down the lake, with everyone calling back and forth and sometimes singing. Still he shivered from the cold night air despite the cloak that had been provided to cover his dress uniform—or was it the cold, when controlling his body temperature was second nature to him now? In their seat on the boat's top deck he held Kathryn close, repeating to himself, *nothing can ever part us. Whatever happens in the future, we have that to hold to. . . .*

In Jessica's house there was a roaring fire in the great room's huge central fireplace; there had been no economizing on wood, scarce though it was on Maclairn. The feast was laid out buffet style—decorated cakes and other baked goods, with the ubiquitous chicken ground into a pastry filling. People helped themselves, then sat as always on mattresses and floor cushions, many of which had been brought in for the occasion. There was more warm laughter, more singing. With his arm around Kathryn and a mug of ale in his other hand, Terry forgot the shadow that had briefly come over him, and soon he was too busy receiving the congratulations of Jessica, Tristan and other friends to give any thought to the distant future.

The festivities lasted till dawn. Since nothing had been said about a honeymoon retreat, Terry assumed they would sleep in Kathryn's bedroom, as usual. But as the sun was rising, after the last of the guests had left and Jessica had gone to her own wing of the house, Kathryn lingered by the dying fire in the great room. "There's an old tradition," she said, "that began on the founders' birthworld. Couples formalized their commitment by making love by the lodge fireplace, which had symbolic meaning there because it was the center of the Group's fellowship and the place where the Ritual was held—it was a reminder that they shared a special bond beyond what legally-defined marriage meant to outsiders. Of course nowadays only a few people have opportunity to spend the night in this room, the one patterned after the lodge on Undine where the idea for Maclairn began. But since we do—well, when Jessica told me about it, it seemed sort of romantic, Terry."

It's very romantic, he agreed, pulling one of the floor mattresses close to the hearth. It was more than that. Like the rings, it meant that their love for each other and for Maclairn were intertwined, that the linking of their minds during lovemaking was in some way a symbol of the mind powers that would be offered to the rest of humankind. They did not need to put this into words. They simply knew that it was the bedrock of their marriage, far more than the League paperwork they had signed.

Silently they took off their wedding clothes. Seeing

Kathryn's familiar body in the firelight, Terry felt as if he were looking upon it for the first time. There had never been anything furtive in their union, but now, as husband and wife—lifemates—they came together in a different way, not with the excitement of mounting feelings, but with the comfort of love that was stable and lasting. He joined his own body and mind to hers, knowing as they merged that there could never be a better time for them than this.

31

PROMISE BROKE ORBIT two days after the wedding with two returning observer couples and a mentor couple aboard, plus the former civilian copilot and engineer, who had to be transported back to Earth as passengers. The captain had decided to stay on Maclairn, for which Terry was glad; he didn't want there to be any doubt in their minds about who was in command.

Since Maclairn was relatively close to its sun, more than a day was required to get far enough out to jump. Terry looked forward to the climactic moment with a mixture of eagerness and trepidation. He had never had full responsibility for a jump before, though as copilot on his previous explorer missions he had programmed the hyperdrive many times under supervision. This was, of course, the sole difference between a starship and a mere interplanetary ship, and *Picard*, since its resurrection from grounding on Maclairn, had operated only as the latter. Little action was involved in piloting either ship, since the AI handled most maneuvers; but the command to jump was too critical to be entrusted to anyone but the captain.

The Maclairn-to-Earth jumps had been made three times, and *Promise* retained those calculations in its memory. Nevertheless, with the lives of eleven people in his hands, Terry spent a good share of the hours of passage to his chosen jump point going over and over them, as if he had to program from scratch. Even the best astrogators sometimes miscalculated, he knew, and it did not help to recall that even Maclairn's founding hero Jesse had done so, resulting in the founders' ship emerging so far out from the sun that they'd had to go into stasis to make their life support last. Jesse, to be sure, had been forced to jump too hurriedly because the ship was being pursued. But it could also happen through carelessness. Too far from the destination sun was better than coming too close and falling into that sun, though running out of life support would be equally disastrous on modern ships, where no stasis facilities were available. And of course, a seriously miscalculated jump could mean the ship might end up in some entirely different solar system, or even in empty space far from any sun, with no known stars as reference points, making it impossible to get back. Starships did occasionally disappear.

Kathryn, who had taken the jumps during her previous trips aboard *Promise* for granted, was somewhat dismayed when she sensed these concerns in Terry's mind, and in reassuring her, he managed to calm himself. But as zero hour approached he began to get nervous again. He had given the instructions to the AI well in advance; he would merely have to speak the command to execute. Much as he wanted her presence for support he knew that the bridge was always off-limits to passengers during a jump, and so he sent her away.

The AI, which was programmed to recognize his voice, began the countdown: "Forty seconds until jump . . . thirty . . . please authorize, Captain Radnor."

He drew a deep breath. "Proceed."

"Twenty seconds . . . ten . . . five, four, three, two, one, executing."

There was the usual moment of disorientation, as if the compartment were whirling around him, though actually it was not. "Report our position!" he commanded.

"We are approximately 1.2 billion klicks out from New Tahiti, ETA 87 hours."

He had done it. His calculations had been on target and the hyperdrive had functioned. The most time-consuming part of this leg of the trip was yet to come, as it would have been unwise to jump in any closer to the sun; but the flight to the planet itself would be routine. Feeling shaky from released tension, he went to tell the passengers that they were now more than sixty light-years away from where they had been ten minutes ago.

The stopover in New Tahiti's solar system was necessary because on reaching Earth they'd be unable to get through customs without evidence of where they had come from. New Tahiti was a tourist colony that asked no questions of arriving passengers, whereas overcrowded Earth demanded documented records of a ship's point of origin. Though everyone aboard *Promise* had Terran citizenship—except the mentors, for whom false identity details had to be provided in any case—they would be suspected of smuggling if they admitted to having visited unnamed, unopened worlds; the first expedition's claim of having searched for aliens would not work a second time.

And so Terry and Kathryn looked forward to a few days of honeymooning at the most expensive vacation spot in the galaxy. Along with the passengers, they would sleep aboard *Promise*; Maclairn Foundation funds would cover the landing fees but would not stretch to resort hotels. The scenic unspoiled wilderness and white sand beaches of New Tahiti, however, could be enjoyed without cost by anyone with the means to get there. Not enough people could afford interstellar passage for it to become overcrowded.

Nearly four days were spent on the way. In ships too small to carry service personnel it was customary for the passengers to take turns preparing meals, but since Kathryn was officially hosting the observers she felt it

was her place to do it. On the first night Terry started to
help, as on explorer missions this duty was shared by the
entire crew; but he quickly realized that for the captain
of a passenger ship it would be inappropriate. His job,
she informed him, was to make conversation. Meals were
formal, as on a liner; it was a way to pass the time, and
civilians liked to sit with an officer in a classy uniform.
There were two round tables that seated six in the mess
room, which doubled as a lounge. He headed one with
Kathryn, one of the observer couples—who would rotate—
and the mentors; a somewhat reluctant Drew and Amir
were assigned to alternately head the second while the
other stood watch on the bridge.

The observers were full of enthusiasm for what they
had seen on Maclairn, where they had been lodged in the
homes of Council members. They had all gone through
the first phase of mind training while there, as had the
former crew members during their layovers, so it was
permissible to talk about it. No secrets were kept from
observers except the identity and astrogational position
of Maclairn's star. That was known to no one, apart from
a few Foundation and League officials, except Admiral
Derham, Captain Vargas, the original captain of *Promise*,
and now Terry.

There had been ten observers before these: six on the
first trip—Admiral Derham and his wife as representa-
tives of Fleet, a couple representing the League, and
Kathryn's aunt and uncle representing the Foundation—
plus four on the trip from which she had recently returned. They had been carefully selected by her grandfather, Arthur Bramfield, from among people he personally knew and trusted. Most of them were doctors
or psychologists, and their role would be to run the
health clubs that would be established in various cities
as fronts for the mentors' work. The mentors now
aboard were headed for Los Angeles, which was the
current observers' home.

"You aren't going to like it," Dr. Schroeder warned. "Los Angeles is one of the worst places on Earth to live—compared to Maclairn, it's pure hell. But it serves our purpose. Nobody in Los Angeles will question or even notice one more health club that promotes wacky ideas. You can even discuss psychic phenomena openly—though of course it would be professional suicide for me to acknowledge any awareness that you're doing so."

His wife Dr. Lewis, who for many years had studied what was known of parapsychology on Earth, agreed. "It was unpopular to take such ideas seriously two hundred years ago, as you know from the knowledgebase that's been available to you," she said. "But now it's not just that they're ridiculed; there's even stronger antagonism than the reaction that set in after the successful psi experiments of the twenty-first century. No respectable publication will touch the subject anymore, not even from a historical standpoint. In some places the opposition gets ugly."

Terry frowned. "People keep telling me that, but I still don't understand it."

"Well, Captain Radnor, I've heard that you are both a deep space explorer and psi-gifted, so it's not surprising that the narrow-mindedness of the average scientist is incomprehensible to you. To someone whose whole life—whose very identity—has been founded on a materialistic picture of how the universe works, any suggestion that this picture might be wrong is threatening, and the brighter such people are, the greater their fear, because their very intelligence leads to an underlying suspicion that there might be some truth in it. That's why actual evidence of psi makes most scientists less, rather than more, willing to grant the possibility of its existence, and why some feel impelled not merely to deny but to destroy the evidence."

Fyodor, one of the mentors, said quietly, "Lucine and I don't expect finding converts to be easy. But there will be individuals who are drawn to psi, those who don't have professional reputations to lose."

"Of course," Dr. Schroeder agreed. "And we will back you all the way in reaching out to them. We must be very careful, though, even in Los Angeles, or the authorities will find some pretext to shut us down. There's more regimentation and less tolerance of unorthodox opinion than there used to be before the overcrowding of Earth got bad enough to make everyone edgy."

"Yes, that's a major factor," added Dr. Lewis. "There's more to the opposition than the innate fear psi often arouses. You see, Captain Radnor, to believe in psi is to acknowledge the power of the individual human mind— the primacy of mind over mere physical bodies. And that's something the authorities of a regimented society don't want to see acknowledged."

Kathryn stared at her. "I hadn't thought of it that way," she said. "But in the meetings with League officials about the contract, I could tell that some of them weren't happy about the discovery of Maclairn. They wanted to keep it secret not just because the public would demand access, but because they wished it hadn't happened. Are you saying the government has a hidden agenda?"

"Undoubtedly," Dr. Schroeder declared. "I would be very much surprised if either your grandfather or Jessica is unaware of that. Probably Ian Maclairn was aware of it two hundred years ago when he made his plan to keep the colony isolated while it gained strength."

Fyodor nodded. "Why else would our supporters have pushed for a Fleet cruiser to protect Maclairn? Admiral Derham certainly knows, and Captain Vargas, as well as all the mentors. But there are no specific accusations that can be made, so nothing was said to you; it was felt that as ambassador you should be left free to form your own unbiased conclusions."

Oh, my God, thought Terry. The chance of stray

explorers or smugglers wandering into Maclairn's solar system in the near future had always seemed too small to justify the expense and risk of deploying such an extensive early warning system. If there was another worry—if there might be danger of covert action by people who *knew* the secret—the captain, as an official representative of the League, could scarcely have informed *Shepard*'s crew.

But Vargas must have realized that aboard *Promise* he, Terry, would hear about it sooner or later. Had he wanted to alert him to what guarding Maclairn might involve? He and Jessica might have planned it together; they might even have had more reasons for encouraging the development of his psi capabilities than the vague hope that he could remote-view an intruding ship.

They might have sent him to League headquarters as a spy.

32

THE INTERLUDE ON New Tahiti was idyllic, though brief. They stayed several days, long enough to give the guest couples, who had told friends they'd won the trip in a sweepstakes, sufficient familiarity with the place to explain their absence when they got home. Terry could not go down to the surface every day, of course, since one pilot had to stay with the ship. But while there he and Kathryn enjoyed the glorious views of forested mountains, lounged on the uncrowded sandy beaches, and swam in a sea so calm and clear that it was hard to believe that it hadn't been constructed by terraforming. This world alone, of all that had been discovered, was blessed with a climate and natural features reminiscent of how tropical areas of Earth had looked four centuries ago. It was like going back in time.

Since the stopover would be included in every outbound trip, leaving wasn't difficult, and Terry's thoughts quickly turned to the challenges ahead. The jump to Earth's solar system went smoothly, as did the remaining days of travel, which he spent teaching Amir and Drew how to maintain *Promise* in orbit while he was absent. Arrival at the customs station near Earth's moon, would, he knew, be his first test of imperturbability. He had often hidden his activities during his hacking days, but never before had he put across outright lies.

"Terran Control, this is civilian hyperdrive spacecraft HS *Promise*, inbound from New Tahiti, requesting permission to approach, over."

"*Promise*, state your business and persons on board, over."

"This is Lieutenant Commander Terry Radnor in command. I am carrying two more Fleet officers, a civilian attorney, and eight returning tourists, all citizens of Earth." Kathryn, of course, was not an official ambassador with diplomatic privileges since she did not represent a known world.

"Have any of these persons landed on any world other than New Tahiti since leaving Earth?"

"Negative," replied Terry firmly.

"Roger, *Promise*. Establish lunar holding orbit at 50 km and prepare for boarding."

In due course two officers in a small shuttle docked, ran their wand over the passengers' identity chips—which in the case of the mentors had been implanted aboard *Shepard,* showing a false birthplace and residence address as authorized under the secret contract—and inspected the ship thoroughly for persons or cargo unaccounted for. Terry held his breath, fearing that they might check the content of personal data bracelets, as he and Kathryn carried coded dispatches for Fleet headquarters and for the Foundation. In what he hoped was a casual tone he affirmed again that his ship had not visited any undeclared planets, whereupon, after long delays, *Promise* was given a certified trip transponder and cleared to proceed to Earth.

He had been to Earth fairly recently, during his leave before reporting to Titan. Nevertheless, after Maclairn, he was struck anew by its teeming cities and its decadence. Earth had once been beautiful, he knew. There had been stretches of unpopulated land other than the parks in which he had occasionally—by hacking the reservation system—been able to obtain camping permits. But rural areas had been history since long before he was born. The vast agricultural complexes that had taken over bore no resemblance to farms, and in the endless suburbs too many people were crowded into too few square meters per head. Violence on the streets was rampant. The wealthy lived in high-rise apartments, isolated from the squalor below; there was little need to descend below the interconnecting bridges when most contacts were electronic anyway. Terry's family had not been wealthy. He had grown up in a typical middle-class neighborhood of Greater Denver, where there might have been a view of the mountains on the rare occasions when the air was clear had not mile after mile of run-down town houses stood in the way.

Kathryn, on the other hand, had lived in the affluent New England enclave where her grandparents owned property. "When I was in college I was uncomfortable about being so privileged," she'd told Terry. "I didn't want to stand out as a privately-paid student in law school—I was planning to work my way through like my friends— so Granddad arranged an anonymous scholarship. It was funded by the Foundation, though I didn't know it at the time; all along he was preparing me to represent Maclairn when the time came for its discovery. I would have chosen to work pro bono in some urban area if he hadn't insisted that I specialize in Colonial League law. As it was, I picked the weakest colonies to defend against League bureaucracy during the three years I practiced, but I didn't feel I was really achieving anything."

Terry stayed aboard *Promise* while Kathryn went to Los Angeles to find living quarters for the mentors, get them settled, and establish bank accounts for them, which gave Amir and Drew a week of shore leave. Then he left them in charge of the ship and joined her for a visit to her grandparents. She had not revealed that she was married when she called them after landing, for it would have raised too many questions that could not be answered on an unsecured phone.

They went to the Bramfield penthouse, which was not only in an area where there were still trees, but had a sweeping view of the ocean. Going up in the elevator, Terry was suddenly shy. Since joining Fleet he had met few civilians, not counting the Maclairnans, and the prospect of being judged by a billionaire CEO was somewhat intimidating. But when Arthur Bramfield held out his hand, he was immediately at ease. He sensed that this was an upstanding, warmhearted man despite his riches, and that he had deep love for Kathryn.

"You must be the new captain of *Promise*," Bramfield said, observing Terry's uniform. "Kathryn said she was bringing home a guest, but I hadn't realized that my request for a Fleet crew could be fulfilled so soon. I'm tremendously glad to know it has been."

"Terry's more than our captain," Kathryn announced. "He's an official member of the family."

"You're married? Under League law, not just on Maclairn?"

"Well, Fleet wouldn't let me share the captain's stateroom unless we were," Kathryn said, smiling. "But we didn't put up any arguments."

"So you're Terry," her grandmother said, hugging him. "We heard about little else from Kathryn the last time she was here, and we're delighted to welcome you. I wish we could have been at the wedding."

They had pictures of the ceremony aboard *Shepard* and the wedding feast on Maclairn stored in their data bracelets for transfer to the big screen. Afterward they enjoyed a celebration dinner of steak, broccoli potatoes with butter, and a fresh fruit salad, topped off by ice cream—Kathryn's grandmother knew what would be most craved when returning from a world that lacked meat or dairy products, and could afford gourmet food such as real beef. It was a happy evening, and the guest bedroom to which they retired was more luxurious than any accommodations Terry had ever seen. He began to feel that perhaps Earth was not such a bad place after all.

But the next day, after Arthur Bramfield had listened to the letter from Jessica downloaded from Kathryn's data bracelet, the conversation turned serious. "Jessica has a great deal to say about you," he said to Terry, "and I see that besides the joy you have brought to my granddaughter, we're fortunate to have you in command of *Promise*. More than that, you can't know how relieved I am to have someone to whom I can speak freely going to and from League headquarters with Kathryn. You may be in a position to hear things that she does not, and—from what Jessica tells me—to sense more of what is going on in officials' minds."

"I can't read thoughts people don't want to communicate to me," Terry protested.

"But they will want to, not knowing that you can detect their feelings. Those who hate the idea of a psi-based culture will broadcast their hatred. They will say one thing when they mean another."

Terry frowned. "Do you think there's real danger from such people?"

"Yes. I have spent my life awaiting the discovery of the colony established by Ian Maclairn and making plans for fulfilling the dream he expressed to my ancestors. Year by year I've watched opposition to such aims grow, and it's been instigated in many cases by calculated propaganda."

"The passengers aboard *Promise* said the authorities don't want the power of individual minds to become known."

"That's true. It threatens not only their personal stability, but the basis of their control over the public—people aware of how much they can control with their own minds don't like having the government tell them what they should want. As long as it was all just speculation, rejection and ridicule were the only weapons needed to suppress the evidence for it, but now . . ."

"Now there's proof. And people committed to showing others the proof."

"Which from the government's standpoint, is bad news. As Kathryn must have told you, some on the committee opposed the contract at first. When they realized that word would get out unless they enforced secrecy, they switched in order to keep track of the situation. I suspect that a few of them hope to eliminate the proof, one way or another."

"Surely they can't attack Maclairn! If they planned to, why would they have sent a cruiser?"

"Like us, they want to keep intruding ships from revealing Maclairn's existence. The cruiser is no problem for them since they can't attack in a military sense anyway—there are enough who support us to prevent anything like a major strike. Admiral Frazer, the commander-in-chief of Fleet, is a strong supporter, and it would take a coup to circumvent his authority. They will use more subtle methods. They can't take overt action against us, but they will do all they can to hurt our cause."

"Send small ships to Maclairn disguised as pirates maybe, thinking we'll be intimidated if they can do enough damage?"

"Possibly. We don't know what they'll try. All we can

do is stay alert, and identify which officials aren't to be trusted so we can watch them."

"I'll do my best," Terry vowed. "If only I hadn't lost *Picard*, which I now see more than ever that we need—I suppose Jessica told you about it?"

"She told me that you lost it through an act of heroism that you have no cause to regret. However, it's true that an interplanetary patrol in Maclairn's system would be useful, if only to make plain that we are on guard. You should continue that, Terry. *Promise* will be at Maclairn for thirty days between trips, and there's no reason why you should keep it in a holding orbit all that time—though presumably you'll want to spend part of each layover with my granddaughter."

"Can we use *Promise*?" Terry exclaimed in surprise. "Captain Vargas never suggested that we could,"

"He wouldn't have, since *Promise* is owned by the Foundation. Hand me your bracelet and I'll give you authorization here and now."

"Thank you, sir," Terry said, torn between eagerness for the added responsibility and a touch of apprehension. This meant that he'd be in a position to sense the presence he had before, the thing he couldn't define. *Could* a ship be lurking in Maclairn's system, a disguised government ship maybe, that was conducting ongoing surveillance? If so he should do something about it. Yet he was not sure enough of his perception to warn Fleet, or even to mention it to Arthur Bramfield.

33

THAT EVENING TERRY and Kathryn visited Corwin and Kamila at the health club that had been established for them to work in—the first of many that were being financed by Bramfield from his personal fortune, ostensibly as a legitimate business investment. It was located in a low nondescript building like so many others that cluttered Earth, but on the inside it was luxurious, with a pool, hot tubs and saunas, exercise facilities, and a number of private rooms with neurofeedback equipment. As on Titan, neurofeedback was offered to everyone as a stress-reduction therapy, and no one noticed that some clients were offered other forms of training for which they were not charged. Kathryn's aunt and uncle, who had previously returned from Maclairn, served as managers, and they arranged staff scheduling so that the mentors were on night shifts when few others were around.

"It's risky," Kathryn said, "because it all depends on people referring friends they trust, and the wider the circle spreads, the more danger there is that someone will invite the wrong person. They don't know about Maclairn, of course—they're told only as much as you were on Titan. And they aren't informed about the psi aspect unless they develop conscious awareness that they're acquiring such capabilities. Some meetings are held on the side, though, to attract the minority interested in speculating about the paranormal."

Corwin greeted Terry and Kathryn warmly, surprised and pleased to learn that Terry had become captain of *Promise* and that they were married. "Things have worked out better than we could have hoped," he said. "Arthur didn't wholly trust the former captain's discretion; that was why he encouraged him to retire. Having the two of you handle all communication with Maclairn will take a load off his mind."

"You look tired," Kathryn said, noticing the change in Corwin. "Are you happy here?"

"As happy as can be expected, considering that we're watching a civilization on the verge of self-destruction. Kamila and I were appalled at first by what we saw. We knew in theory what Earth is like, but to be surrounded by crowds of people—billions, if you count the population of the whole planet—most of whom have no real connection with each other and no notion of their own capabilities, or any interest in humanity's future ... and who take out their lack of fulfillment in rage against the rest of society. We're used to sensing people's feelings, after all, and here we have to avoid it to keep from being totally overwhelmed." He sighed, adding, "Just being among so many weighs us down."

"This isn't a very good neighborhood," Terry said, frowning. "I'm wondering if it's safe."

"What neighborhood is?" Kathryn said. "Short of locating in a secured high-rise where too many questions would be asked about late-night clients, any place Granddad chose would have been just as vulnerable. We have to be able to reach a wide range of supporters."

"And we're reaching them," Corwin declared. "I don't mean to sound discouraged. Our trainees are enthusiastic, and they're gaining more inner freedom than the average citizen of Earth has ever imagined. What's more they're beginning to sense others' feelings and getting together in homes to talk about things they can't discuss in the public club. In time the new view of human relations will spread. That won't happen overnight, or even within our lifetime. But we're accomplishing what we came here for."

"We're taking positive steps toward reversing the trends that are leading Earth to ruin," Kathryn agreed.

"Reversing them for humankind, yes. But as Jessica has recognized all along, it's too late for Earth. The people we train and their descendants will go to the colonies, and eventually found new ones of their own. It has to start here to achieve a widespread transformation. The society of Earth itself, though, won't recover. There's no way we can influence a large enough percentage of the population to have a significant impact on this world's collective unconscious."

"Oh, Corwin." Terry sensed the mentor's sorrow.

"We've always known this, Terry—Ian knew from the

beginning. But we're achieving something vital to future generations. I grieve for Earth's civilization only because of the present frustration and the centuries of past tradition that are dying out."

Kathryn downloaded Corwin's letters from Jessica and his friends from her data bracelet, then went to talk with Kamila, who was just finishing a session with a trainee, and deliver hers. Terry remained, raising a question that had been troubling him. "Corwin," he said, "things have been happening to me so fast, I don't know what to think. . . . When I was promoted and made captain, it was a direct result of my having lost *Picard*, which only happened because my crew was endangered—and I felt guilty because I'd benefited from those things. But now Arthur Bramfield feels what I'm doing on *Promise* is more important to Maclairn than staying with *Picard* would have been. So what I'm wondering is, why did it happen—landing just where there was about to be an earthquake, I mean? Did some sort of unconscious precognition influence where I chose to land? And did it tell me that the crew would survive, or did I risk their lives to get where I am now?"

Corwin shook his head. "You can't answer questions like that, Terry. You'll go insane if you even ask them. Why does fate ever work out the way it does? If you want me to tell you precognition plays no part in it, I won't, because I don't know and neither does anyone else. But I can say that you have nothing to feel guilty about. You did not consciously choose to expose your crew to undue risk, and conscious choices are the only ones for which we're morally responsible."

"That's all very well in theory. But I need to know what part precognition plays in my choices because I keep sensing something strange near Maclairn, as if there's a ship where reason says there couldn't be, and Tristan agreed that I can't just ignore it."

Slowly Corwin said, "I think that if a time comes when

you should take action, you will know. Don't shut your perceptions out, but don't worry about them, either. We can't live our lives on the basis of vague feelings that might or might not be precognition—just about any feeling could be put in that category. To be consciously psi-gifted means to live with uncertainty, which is one reason why most people fear it so deeply."

"Oh." He had not seen it in that light, Terry realized. He had not understood that he too was subject to such fears. "You did warn me," he recalled, "when you told me psi sensitivity could be a burden."

"There's got to be a balance between rationality and psychic intuition. That's what we've been aiming for on Maclairn—it's necessary to have a culture based on combining psi with technology as a base from which to spread new capabilities. In the past, when only isolated individuals developed them, they often failed to integrate them with ordinary living. Sometimes they lost touch with reality. That's not going to happen to you because you have an active life as a Fleet officer and pilot that there's no danger of your rejecting."

"Are you saying not everyone can handle such capabilities?"

"I'm careful who I train here, yes. Even control over unconscious physical functions is not safe for everyone who has grown up on a planet where a supporting collective unconscious hasn't developed. Which is the underlying reason why nothing we can do will save this world."

Terry thought about this when, several days later, he looked back at Earth from *Promise,* shining blue and white—there were few traces of green left on it—with no hint of the ruination of its once-thriving civilization. He had been born there, and despite his departure for Fleet and his new love for Maclairn, he did not like to think that its living conditions would continue to get worse. His mother was there—he hadn't contacted her to tell her about his marriage because she believed him to be away on a long cruiser mission and he couldn't say otherwise without revealing the existence of a secret. He supposed that things wouldn't change much within her lifetime—the mentors took a very long-range view. Still, he felt sadness.

34

HIS MOOD DIDN'T improve when they reached League headquarters on the moon. He had known Kathryn wouldn't be treated like an ambassador when her status was secret, but the coldness of their reception dismayed him. They were kept waiting for a long time in the office she visited under the guise of legal consultation about New Tahitian affairs, but when she was finally shown in it didn't take long to conclude her business. The commissioners had accepted the dispatch from Jessica she carried, she said, but had showed little interest in it. Terry could sense their hostility even through the wall of the waiting room. They did not want to be reminded that Maclairn existed.

He had promised Arthur Bramfield that he would try to identify officials who couldn't be trusted, and it seemed to him they couldn't be sure of any of them. Not that they would all be willing to use underhanded methods to weaken Maclairn or discourage the sending of mentors, but they wouldn't support it, either, according to Kathryn's impressions. And he did not see how he would ever have opportunity to judge them individually. "It's just a matter of staying alert," she'd told him, "alert to anything we sense or overhear that might suggest trouble." Then, as they were leaving, the possibility of trouble became all too clear.

Kathryn came out of the office with a short, stout man who looked like a typical bureaucrat, the sort who in Fleet would have stayed behind a desk telling active officers how to do a job they knew much more about than he did. Terry rose to meet them. "Commissioner Hiller, may I present Lieutenant Commander Terry Radnor, captain of our ship *Promise*," she said.

"Oh yes, Admiral Frazer authorized a Fleet crew for that ship," said the official. "But that's awkward when it's privately owned. I'm thinking that it should be transferred to Fleet."

My God, thought Terry, *if they do that they'll assign the crew through Fleet's bureaucracy and I'll be removed. What's worse, the Foundation will lose control of it. They'll be able to cut back the number of trips.*

Legally, they can't seize private property, Kathryn assured him. *And they can't pass some kind of special law that would let them without revealing why we're special.*

"Fleet ships don't go to New Tahiti, Commissioner," she pointed out,

"Fleet charters go wherever they're contracted to go, just as the crew does. It would be cheaper than maintaining a private ship."

"But wouldn't the tour operators consider it competition, considering how heavily they're taxed? Besides, the people who take trips to New Tahiti view a private ship as a status symbol; we'd lose business." *I hope he's bright enough to figure out what I'm saying*, she told Terry silently. *I can't spell it out in front of his office staff, but surely he knows that we're keeping Maclairn secret only by masquerading as a luxury tour.*

"Uh, perhaps," the official admitted. "On the other hand, there's been some worry about pirates, and a Fleet ship would have the advantage of arms."

"We are armed, sir," Terry declared.

"You are? Well, yes, I suppose a Fleet crew would be. If you want to take the chance of carrying civilians in a ship that doesn't look as if it's armed, I guess we can leave it that way. I'd be careful if I were you, Captain. It may not be safe." He turned and went back into his office.

"Why would he make a suggestion like that at this stage?" Kathryn wondered, as they left the Headquarters dome and headed toward the Luna City passenger terminal to meet their new group of observers. "If Fleet wanted the ship, they'd have said so earlier when they agreed to the crew."

Terry had been thinking, and the idea that occurred to him he did not like. "They don't want the ship," he said. "If they took it over the secret would have to be revealed to more Fleet personnel. That conversation was a warning, Kathryn. A warning that the observers and mentors we carry are in danger of being attacked."

"Well, all ships are in some danger, but it's not very large. And our League contacts haven't shown much interest in our ability to attract passengers; they'd be happy if we had fewer."

"If the ship were attacked by pirates," Terry said grimly, "we might lose both the ship and passengers, and not be able to make any trips. Even if we escaped, it would discourage future observers. Which would please the authorities who want no more civilian contact with Maclairn."

"Then why would he warn you to take precautions? Anyway, it's so unlikely—"

"He was telling me that it is not unlikely, if we keep making frequent trips."

"Does he think he knows more about pirates than a Fleet captain?"

"I'm afraid he does know more," Terry told her. "I could sense his feelings, and they didn't involve concern for our welfare. It was less a real warning than a threat."

"Oh, my God. You think they would actually sic pirates on us?"

"Not outlaws. Mercenaries in a ship provided through the underworld, with a guarantee of immunity from prosecution. This is in line with what your granddad said to me, what he asked me to watch out for. They can't move against us openly, but who could tie it to them if it looked like piracy?"

Kathryn stared at him in horror. "You installed the laser cannon just because pirates wouldn't bother with an armed ship. You said that in a fight we couldn't win."

"No. We couldn't. Not with a single laser cannon and only one crew member who knows how to use it."

"Then what are we going to do? We can't just let the passengers embark."

"It won't happen on this trip, or even the next one," Terry said. "They want to scare us and convince us to change our plans without being forced to. But we've got to tell your granddad. Is there any way you can communicate with him in code?"

"Not about a threat like pirates."

"He'll probably get the message if we send it in clear; he knows I wouldn't be suddenly afraid of encountering real pirates. Still, I'd hate to have it go through a regular phone center. How about if I buy a new data bracelet and send it to him as a gift for his hospitality?"

The shopping mall in Luna City offered a wide variety of decorative data bracelets; Terry deliberately chose one identical to the one Arthur Bramfield already owned, thinking this would be a clue to its hidden purpose. "Mr. Bramfield," he recorded, "I'm honored by your welcome to me as a member of your family, and I'm sending you this small gift, as it looks like the sort of thing you might want to add to your collection. Kathryn and I had an informative meeting with League officials about the New Tahiti cruises, and I feel you should know that Commissioner Hiller warned me that the danger from pirates is greater than we have realized, especially if we make frequent trips on that run. You may want to discuss this with whatever passengers you sign up in the future. Kathryn sends you her love. Respectfully, Terry Radnor, Captain, HS *Promise*."

"Surnames? Respectfully?" Kathryn exclaimed. "It

sounds stuffy—you and Granddad were on a first-name basis five minutes after you met."

"Exactly. He'll know right off that it's not what it seems."

After mailing the package at the exorbitant interworld cargo rate, fortunately covered by Kathryn's Earthside credit, they visited Fleet headquarters to deliver Captain Vargas's dispatch to Admiral Frazer, the one officer there in on the secret. "Your promotion is confirmed, Commander," the admiral told him when he picked up the reply after dinner. "I can't recommend you for a medal since I can't document what it's for, but I agree with your CO that you should have it. I wish you the best of luck— your present command will not be an easy one."

He doesn't know the half of it, Terry thought. Or does he? The man's support of Maclairn came through clearly; he was unquestionably trustworthy. "Sir," he asked, "have you heard anything about an unusually big problem with pirates in the New Tahiti system? Commissioner Hiller warned me to take precautions."

"Did he? That's very interesting," Admiral Frazer said. "I wasn't aware of that, and I thank you for mentioning it. You may be sure that I'll see to it that our ships in that system are on the lookout for pirates."

It was plain from the telepathic undercurrent that they understood each other.

35

ON THE RETURN trip, *Promise* made a stop at Titan to take messages to Aldren and Roanna sent by Corwin and Kamila as well as by their friends on Maclairn. Terry also carried a message from Admiral Frazer to Admiral Derham, as Fleet's normal channels of communication weren't considered secure enough for any specific mention of Maclairn. He didn't announce himself by name when they arrived; he simply said, "Titan base, this is HS *Prom-ise*. The captain wishes to present his compliments to the base commander and requests permission to land." Derham, not having heard about the change in crew, was expecting the civilian captain and was surprised and pleased to see Terry. "Lieutenant Radnor! Or, I see, it's now Lieutenant Commander—I had a feeling you wouldn't be a lieutenant for long. Tell me, were you able to get that old explorer into space?"

So Terry had to tell about the sad end of *Picard* and all that had happened since. Admiral Derham knew Kathryn, of course, having traveled back to Earth with her as a member of the first group of observers. He and his wife invited them both to dinner in his quarters along with Aldren and Roanna, and they had a long talk. Aldren seemed deeply worried about the threat of violence against *Promise*. As they were leaving he embraced Terry and said, "I've known there was trouble brewing. I hoped we might be spared until the presence on Earth was better established, but if it must come now, I know of no one I'd trust more to deal with it than you." Silently he added, *I have always felt that you have a significant role to play in Maclairn's venture, and the fact that you've been appointed captain of* Promise *so soon bears that out. Godspeed, Terry.*

The rest of the trip was uneventful. Kathryn spent her time providing orientation to the incoming observers, three couples from Houston who had come to the moon by commercial shuttle to be met by the shuttle from *Promise*. As on all inbound trips, one stateroom was unoccupied to leave room for the mentors who would go with them when they left.

Terry felt that it was only fair to warn Drew and Amir about the unexpected danger they were likely to face. He asked them to remain on the bridge after the jump and explained the situation, which took a while since the idea of hostility to psi on the part of the League's government was new and puzzling to them. "You don't have to stay on the crew after this trip," he assured them. "It's become hazardous enough to call for volunteers."

"Well, then, I volunteer," said Drew. "Do you think I'd want to back out?"

"Not really, but I'm obliged to give you the chance," Terry said. Amir, too, expressed willingness to stay with the ship, and for the rest of the trip Terry accelerated his effort to teach him to pilot interplanetary ships. He also gave Drew some basic instruction in astrogation. "You've both got to be able to handle anything but a jump," he said, "because if we ran into trouble something might happen to me, and you'd have to get the passengers to safety."

He discussed it with Captain Vargas after they got home. "I don't think there's a chance that either the Foundation or Admiral Frazer will want to reduce the number of trips, sir," he said. "And anyhow, there's no way to know their decision until we're on Earth again. So I don't see any need to alter our plans except for getting more weapons training."

Vargas agreed, so during the layover both Drew and Terry spent many hours in the simulator practicing with a laser cannon, and all three members of the crew got a refresher course in handling sidearms—something they'd learned as cadets but had never had occasion to use. In addition, accompanied by Zuri Kifeda, they took *Promise* as far as Three and Four as authorized by Arthur Bramfield to patrol and inspect the existing sensor stations and place more on asteroids. Thus Terry's time in Petersville was short, but since he and Kathryn would be together during the trips to Earth, that wasn't a major hardship.

The disconcerting sense of a lurking ship didn't come again while they were patrolling, except for one night when Terry was able to convince himself that it was just memory of what he'd experienced before. He hoped that whatever had caused it was over with. He had too many responsibilities as captain of *Promise* to worry over not having reported a potential problem.

During the weeks that followed, two more trips to Earth were made. No pirates appeared and Terry received no more threats at League Headquarters; but he could sense growing hostility on the part of several officials he met there. Once the weapons training was finished except for regular target practice, he had more time free when on Maclairn, and week by week his love for the place increased, magnified by his exposure to the ever more depressing conditions on Earth.

It wasn't just that the physical surroundings were less crowded and dingy than on Earth and the pace of living less frantic. People on Maclairn knew how to genuinely enjoy themselves instead of rushing around to glittering bars, parties, and conferences where no real communication occurred during long hours of noisy, meaningless talk. As his telepathic sensitivity continued to grow, he became more aware of how much psi increased trust and understanding among them, in contract to the suspicion and lack of caring that was prevalent elsewhere.

He and Kathryn continued to live in Jessica's house; it wasn't worthwhile to get a place of their own when they were away so much of the time. In any case small homes were rare on Maclairn; generations ordinarily lived together until there were enough young children to require more space. It was almost unheard of for a woman Kathryn's age not to have children, whether or not she had a lifemate. For some years after the colony's founding increasing the population had been essential, and though families were smaller now, the tie between mother and child was still viewed as supremely important.

This, Kathryn had explained, was because of the unconscious telepathic bonding of unborn babies with their mothers, which Maclairnans, unlike people elsewhere, were aware of and considered the primary factor in a child's development—far more significant than genetic parentage. For this reason, and because in the first generation even women without male partners or too old to conceive naturally had borne babies via IVF, under the colony's law children belonged exclusively to their birth-mother. Neither the genetic mother nor the father had any legal responsibility for them; if the father was living with the birth-mother he normally had the same relationship with the children as he would elsewhere, but if a couple split up he had no right to custody. Nor did he have any financial obligation. All children, being vital to the colony's survival, were supported by taxes and free childcare assistance was provided by the community.

One night, as they cuddled among cushions piled on the thick floor mattress that dominated their room, Kathryn said, "Terry . . . what would you think about starting a family?"

"Do you want kids?" he asked. "Wouldn't it interfere with the trips we've got to make?"

"Not really. We're here half the time, and friends would look after them while we're gone—Maclairnan kids, even babies, are usually raised by more people than their parents. I might have to miss a few trips at the beginning, but my aunt would be willing to take my place. She loved Maclairn when she was here. We'd be short a stateroom, so we'd have to go back to carrying just two observer couples on those trips, but I don't think Granddad would mind."

A family. It was something he'd never considered, but the more he thought about it the more he liked the idea. It would mean truly belonging to Maclairn, putting down roots. He was getting further and further away from his dream of exploring distant stars, he knew, but that dimmed beside the contentment he felt in his marriage and his command of *Promise*. He had everything he had ever wanted except a chance to discover new worlds; one more commitment would simply add to his happiness. "I'd like that, if you're sure you want to take it on," he told her.

The next day they had their contraceptive implants

removed by a Maclairnan healer, a simple process since they didn't suffer from the pain of surgery and the scars of the incisions quickly faded. "I always expected to have children someday," Kathryn admitted. "It's a way of showing faith in the future, isn't it? And the future is what our work here is all about."

Several more trips followed. There were now mentors in London and Tokyo in addition to those in Greater Boston, Los Angeles, Houston, Chicago, and New York; Kathryn's duty as courier between them and Maclairn required constant travel. Terry accompanied her, but they realized that as the number of locations grew, they would need to split the job. When it became impossible to visit all the mentors on every trip, there would have to be collection points for hand-carried data bracelets.

By this time Terry had stopped worrying about the pirate attack that hadn't come. Apparently the opponents of Maclairn were not unscrupulous enough to resort to actual violence, or perhaps they had realized that it would be useless when the threat of it hadn't worked. Arthur and all the couples he had recruited were firm in their determination not to be put off by danger. "What we're trying to achieve is worth sacrifice," he declared. "No advance in human capability, from the discovery of fire onward, has been made without it. People have always been willing to accept risk as the price of progress."

When the danger did materialize, it wasn't the armed attack they had expected. They had just emerged after the jump from New Tahiti and were three days out from Earth, near the orbit of Jupiter but on the opposite side of the sun, when the long-range comm speaker came alive. "Mayday, mayday! Any ship in range, this is HS *Starhawk*, inbound from Centauri. We are disabled and request aid, over."

Amir was alone on the bridge when the call came in,

and he paged Terry. "Shall I respond?" he asked. "A Fleet ship would be better equipped to help them, but there may not be one around."

Terry frowned. "We're legally required to respond whether or not we can help," he said. "But we've got to be careful. A fake distress call is the oldest pirate trick in the book."

"I thought the pirates would attack us in the New Tahiti system."

"So did I. Here, there's a greater risk of a Fleet ship reaching them first, unless they have inside information about ops scheduling. It's likely that they do, and that they've been tracking us so they could jump almost simultaneously and emerge nearby."

He picked up the mike. "*Starhawk*, this is HS *Promise*. What is the nature of your emergency?"

"*Promise*, thank God you're in range! Our pilot has had a heart attack and is unconscious. We had no one aboard who could set our course as we came out of hyperspace. We need astrogation and medical assistance." It was a woman's voice.

"*Starhawk*, what is your present position?"

The woman stated it, and it was close. "Too close for coincidence," Amir said in a low voice. "Can't we just outrun them? They won't fire on us from a distance; a pirate wants to seize, not to destroy."

"We have no real evidence that they're not what they say they are, and if they're really in trouble we'd lose our license if we failed to go to their aid," Terry said. "That may even be part of the plan—if the Foundation was denied a starship license, it would end contact with Maclairn. I wouldn't put it past them to fake a medical emergency with drugs." To *Starhawk* he said, "How many persons have you aboard?"

"Three men besides the pilot and myself. We can rendezvous," the woman added. "I am a qualified shuttle pilot though I haven't flown interplanetary ships." It wasn't an unlikely story; Amir had been in the same position until a short while ago.

"I'll bet they've got plenty of rendezvous experience," muttered Drew.

"*Starhawk*, this is Captain Terry Radnor of *Promise*. Maintain your present speed and heading. We'll initiate the rendezvous," Terry declared.

"Roger. I will launch our shuttle and be prepared to dock."

"Negative, *Starhawk*. Do not, repeat do not, deploy your shuttle." Terry knew what he would have to do; he had figured out the aggressors' most likely strategy weeks ago. "I will dock with you," he stated.

Drew gasped. "You can't do that, Terry!"

"There's no alternative. We can't allow them to board."

"But they'll capture you when you enter their airlock."

"Probably," he admitted grimly, "but that's better than having them capture our passengers."

36

AS THERE WAS no way to reach the shuttle without leaving the bridge, Terry could not avoid encountering Kathryn. She needed to know anyway, of course, but he wished he could keep her from finding out until it was too late to argue. She came out of the lounge while he was pressurizing the shuttle bay. "What's up?" she asked. "I heard Amir page you; is there a problem with the shuttle?"

"We've picked up a distress call," he said. "I'm going to see if I can help."

"Don't listen to him," said Drew, at his heels. "We don't think it's a real distress call; they're pirates and he's going to confront them alone. I say it's crazy."

Kathryn blanched. "You can't!" she exclaimed. "They'll kill you!"

"No, they won't. They'll seize me for ransom, and your

granddad will pay up if the League refuses to negotiate."

"But if they're what we've expected, they're already being paid. What makes you think they'll hold you instead of getting rid of you on account of what you know?"

"Because it's what real pirates would do, and they've got to keep up the pretense. They don't know I'm aware of the scheme."

"Hiller knows you are, and he might have warned them."

Terry realized uncomfortably that this was true. "Even so," he said, "they won't kill me in cold blood. They may have immunity from prosecution for piracy and assault, but not for murder; there's no way that could be covered up. Besides, if Hiller and his pals wanted me dead they could have arranged an accident long ago on Earth. Their aim is to scare passengers into refusing to travel in a Foundation ship, and this is the only way to prevent that."

"The passengers aren't going to be scared if their captain is captured?"

"Not as scared, or as endangered, as they would be if they were all captured, which is what would happen if we let armed men into *Promise*. And as I've explained to Drew and Amir, we have to allow contact in case it's really a ship in distress."

"I'm going with you," Kathryn said determinedly. "They'll realize that Granddad will pay much more for me than for you alone, and that he's in a position to have them tracked down for revenge if anything happens to me. He is, you know. He's got underworld contacts—he had some sort of hold over the original captain to ensure that he'd keep our secret."

"I didn't know," Terry said, "but that's helpful. It means he can have them tracked down anyway once I've identified them. I'll bet they weren't informed about that little detail, and I'll make sure to mention it in time for them to change their minds about holding me."

I can go, then? Kathryn persisted.

Of course not. You know me better than to think I'd let you. To Drew and Amir he said, "We need a signal in case they force me to tell you it's a medical emergency. If it is, I'll say I wish we had a medic aboard *Promise*. Otherwise, assume they're hostile."

"I can fire a warning with the laser cannon, scare them into letting you go—"

"No! The laser cannon is for defense—to open fire without provocation would get us all killed. If I am not back in an hour and haven't given you the signal, you are to get *Promise* away from here as fast as you can."

"Away from here? You don't think we'd go off and leave you behind, do you? I won't, any more than you left me on Five-C," Drew declared.

"That was different," Terry said. "If there were only Fleet officers on board, you wouldn't abandon me; I know that. But this is a passenger ship. Your prime duty is to them, so you are to go immediately once you're sure I'm being held. That's an order, Lieutenants."

Reluctantly, they nodded. "Yes, sir. Where should we go?" Amir asked.

"Mars is closest, and they'll head for it to demand ransom. Try to get there ahead of them and alert Fleet— you can start reporting piracy on the comm as soon as you pick up a station. But say nothing suggesting they're not ordinary pirates to anyone but Admiral Frazer." Turning to Drew he said, "Lieutenant Larssen, you are senior and you are in command. I count on you to get our passengers to safety."

"Yes, sir." It was not a time for personal farewells between officers.

But Kathryn, Terry took into his arms. "Oh God, Terry," she whispered, "We knew we were in harm's way, but I never imagined anything like this, me not facing it with you. I don't want to be safe when you're not—"

"Your job is to keep up the passengers' morale," he told her firmly, "and of course to contact your granddad, the sooner the better." He drew back, not daring to say more. He must not start off on a mission like this in tears.

In the shuttle, waiting for the bay to depressurize, he did not let himself think ahead. He had had no experience dealing with criminals and was not sure how to talk to them; anything he might say would probably sound like mere bravado. But then, did it really matter? He wasn't aiming to be a hero—they would do as they liked with him, regardless of how he reacted.

Only a short way into the flight the AI told him that *Starhawk* was within range, and he busied himself with the commands for docking. He doubted that they had followed his instruction to maintain their course, unless they had already been approaching *Promise*. From now on there would be no pretense that their pilot was incapacitated; once he was docked, they had no further need to lure him.

As he expected, five people stood waiting for him as he passed through the open airlock and entered the ship. What did you say on such an occasion—"Hello, I'm Captain Radnor?" He decided to say nothing.

"I've got a surprise for you," said the woman, who did not identify herself but was evidently the leader. "Our pilot's not unconscious. All we want from you is your ship."

"That's no surprise," said Terry.

At this, they seemed somewhat taken aback; perhaps they had no suspicion that he knew too much about their employer to be kept alive. "Do I look stupid?' he went on. "Your alleged distress call wasn't very creative. You appeared out of nowhere about the same time as we jumped in ourselves, and that means you'd had a conscious pilot less than ten minutes before. Heart attacks are rarely so conveniently timed."

"If you knew that, you *were* stupid, considering that you came aboard alone."

"Not stupid enough to let you dock with us."

"It hardly matters who docked first," said one of the

men, "since you're going to instruct your crew to open your airlock when we get over there."

"That's where you're mistaken," Terry declared. "They wouldn't obey me if I spoke to them under duress; they've got passengers to think of."

"Then we can blast our way in."

"What for? What good would the ship do you if the passengers were exposed to vacuum? We aren't carrying any cargo but personal baggage."

"One or two of them might survive, and the death of the rest would be on your head."

"But you've already got one," Terry pointed out, "and I'm worth more to you than the others. I'm the grandson-in-law of Arthur Bramfield, who as you may know is one of the richest men in North America. You'd better cut your losses while you have something to bargain with."

This news had an effect; it took them a while to recover. Terry's laser pistol was taken from him, as he had known it would be, and he was pushed roughly into a seat while the mercenaries conferred. They had undoubtedly been promised ransom money on top of what Hiller's intermediary was paying them; if he had not mentioned the identity of the captain, it could only be that he hadn't wanted them to be put off by fear of Bramfield's revenge. Thank God, Terry thought. His greatest worry had been that they might know Kathryn was aboard.

After a few minutes the woman again confronted Terry. "Arthur Bramfield will want you in one piece," she said, "but he'll settle for less if he has to. The only question now is how many pieces will be missing."

A big, burly man who actually looked like a pirate pulled Terry to his feet and propelled him over to the comm board. "Call your ship," he growled, "and tell your crew that Bramfield won't be pleased with them if his grandson-in-law isn't returned intact."

"Like hell I will," Terry replied in what he hoped was a strong voice. Until now he had not been seriously afraid;

it had not occurred to him that he faced anything worse than roughing up. Yet this development was all too logical. The men didn't know why they had been hired to intercept *Promise*, he realized, and they naturally assumed that its crew had no motive for holding out beyond self-interest. They did, apparently, know that incurring the wrath of a powerful billionaire was a less inviting prospect than being held for ransom.

"If you don't, we will," the woman declared, "and they'll let us dock whether or not you've ordered it."

"That's not going to happen. Haven't you grasped the fact that Bramfield owns the ship and would be even less pleased if it were taken?"

"If he cares more about the ship than about you," she observed, "then you're not worth as much to us as you claim."

"Hey," said one of the other men, "maybe this solves the mystery of why we were paid to make this look like ordinary piracy. Maybe Bramfield wants to get rid of this guy without antagonizing his granddaughter."

"In which case, we'd be doing him a favor by finishing him. How about it, Radnor? Relations been cool between you and the old man lately?"

Oh, shit, thought Terry. He had backed himself into a corner.

"He doesn't take you for a weakling, I'll say that for you," the third man said. "More likely he's afraid you'll ditch Fleet and muscle in on his empire."

"We don't know that," the woman pointed out, "and the odds are better if we go with the original plan. Come on, Dobbs, let's get over to the other ship."

When the two had left in their shuttle, the three remaining men tied Terry to the seat in front of the comm vid pickup, binding his left arm, outstretched, to the armrest with his hand hanging over the end. He did not struggle, knowing it would be useless.

"We'll start with a couple of fingers," the big man

announced, "just to show we're serious. If they don't open up when our shuttle arrives, the hand goes next." He drew his laser pistol.

"Urick here amputated a whole arm once," remarked one of the others. "He's almost as good as a surgeon." Terry swallowed and said nothing.

The man named Urick took the mike into his other hand. "*Promise*, this is *Starhawk*," he said, "Turn on your vid screen, please. Your captain wants to speak to you."

God, thought Terry in despair, Kathryn would be on the bridge. He did not think she would be panicked into capitulation, or that Drew would obey her if she did, despite her being the official representative of the ship's owner. But he could not see how he could endure the thought of what she would suffer if she watched.

Kathryn! he cried in agony, hoping that their stress level would enable telepathy to bridge the distance between ships. *Kathryn, this isn't as bad as it will look. I'm immune to pain, remember. I've even learned something about healing. . . .* But of course, he did not have the ability to restore body parts that were gone. Fingers were one thing, but if they proceeded to hands, or arms, or . . . He cut off the thought, not wanting to speculate about what might have been implied by the word "intact."

"*Promise*, this is *Starhawk*," the man repeated. "Respond please, over."

"They're gone," Terry said, praying it was true. "They were under orders to leave if I didn't contact them within an hour, and it's been almost that long now."

"Leave their captain? I don't think so; Fleet doesn't operate that way. But they could have been ordered to maintain comm silence, so we'll assume they're watching. Any comments for them, Radnor?"

"No," said Terry, gritting his teeth.

"Okay then, here goes."

As the targeting beam came on, terror struck him.

What if he couldn't shift into the state for controlling pain? He could just steel himself, maybe—but no, that was what you mustn't do. You were supposed to relax. To make the mind training work, you had stop caring what happened or how you would react to it. . . . He closed his eyes and did his best not to care.

Easily, without awareness of when it happened, he shifted into altered consciousness and scarcely felt the cut. At the last minute he remembered to scream convincingly, hoping Drew and Amir, and especially Kathryn, would understand why. If he didn't react normally to pain the men would conclude that he was psychotic, and might then doubt his claim to a tie with Arthur Bramfield.

The blaze of the laser was bright even through his lids and when he opened his eyes the afterimage was so brilliant that it was a moment before he saw that the two smallest fingers of his left hand were gone. The stumps had been cauterized by searing heat, and his hand and forearm were severely burned. At least, he thought dizzily, he wouldn't have to control bleeding.

"*Promise*, we know you saw," said Urick. "If you want your captain to keep his hand, get into position for docking."

Oh Drew, pleaded Terry to himself, *the hour is up. Please, please obey your orders—you can help me only by being gone when that shuttle gets there.*

In the next moment the woman's voice came over the comm. "*Starhawk*, I'm not picking up any sign of a ship with the sensors. Make Radnor tell you where it's headed."

"It jumped," Terry lied. "It's headed where you can't follow."

Urick stared at him. "*Why*? Why sacrifice yourself just to save contract passengers? We wouldn't have killed them, you know. All we wanted was whatever their relatives would pay."

"You won't kill me, either," Terry said. "I'm all you've

got left to sell, and Bramfield will prefer to receive me in as good shape as possible."

Promise would travel free of threats from now on, he knew. Hiller would not try the same thing again; two pirate attacks on the same ship would raise suspicions. And when the trips continued without pause, Maclairn's opponents would see that there was no point in trying to stop the Foundation from recruiting.

37

AS IT TURNED out, no ransom was ever demanded; *Promise* got to Mars first and Fleet patrollers were waiting for *Starhawk* when it arrived. Terry was taken directly to the medical center in Marsport, but he checked himself out as soon as his hand was bandaged; he wasn't free to explain why he didn't need drugs for the continuing pain of the stumps, and he knew the mentors aboard could heal him faster than physicians could. He returned to the ship for a happy reunion with Kathryn. By the time they reached the moon four days later, his hand and forearm showed no sign of injury except for the missing fingers.

He went down to the moon's surface, letting Kathryn and the passengers take a commercial flight to Earth, because he was ordered to report immediately to Admiral Frazer. After he had given a detailed report of the incident the admiral said, "Once the paperwork is put through you'll receive the medal you've earned twice over, Commander. An encounter with pirates is something I can announce publicly."

"I don't need a medal," Terry protested. "It was my job to protect my ship."

"But you did it heroically without resorting to violence. Media coverage will be a good thing apart from the fact that you deserve recognition—if more captains were willing to stand up to pirates, there wouldn't be so many attacks."

Terry acquiesced; it was true enough that something needed to be done to reduce the seizures of innocent passengers. But he didn't look forward to the attention.

"There's something else I want to discuss with you," Admiral Frazer told him. "We've been testing a new type of interplanetary ship that's as fast as a starship in normal space and can land like a shuttle—in fact it's no larger than a shuttle. I believe such a ship would be of value for patrolling Maclairn's solar system—I know you've been using *Promise* to do that between trips, but if you could train more pilots there would always be at least one ship available. Do you agree, Commander?"

"Yes, sir. It would certainly be extremely useful."

"Well, then, what I want you to do is take the prototype back with you. You can carry it instead of your shuttle, and *Shepard* will loan you a Fleet shuttle until you pick up yours. We can't make extensive test flights in Earth's system because it hasn't been publicly announced yet—it has considerable potential for civilian use and we're not ready to accept bids. Maclairn's system would be an ideal place to try it out under operational conditions."

It was agreed that Terry would remain on the moon to be trained in the capabilities of the new ship while Drew and Amir, who were due for leave, hitched a ride to Earth on a Fleet transport and a caretaker pilot from the admiral's staff stayed with *Promise*. "He's not in on the secret," Frazer said, "but I'll warn him that the ship might be targeted for sabotage."

It seemed strange to be back at Fleet's huge base on the moon. Terry had spent three exciting years at the Academy there, fresh from high school on Earth, and revisiting it after all that had happened since made him feel unreal, as if he were two different people. He was no longer awed by the vast numbers of shuttlecraft arrayed on the lunar plain or the ships that orbited above it, and liftoffs didn't arouse him as they once had; but the memories stirred nostalgia. He was now viewed by the cadets there as a celebrity. Word about the pirate episode had gotten around; to his embarrassment, trainees and instructors alike crowded around him in the general mess, eager to hear the story. Fortunately, though he was temporarily quartered with staff officers, his days were spent with the engineers and test pilots at the research section of the installation.

The prototype ship was beautiful—sleek, for travel through atmospheres, yet efficiently designed for interplanetary operation. And of course, it lacked the worn appearance of the ships he had known; everything about it was brand new. Like *Picard* it had been christened in accord with a long-standing tradition of naming small ships after characters in modern mythology, in this case *Skywalker*—a name that had undoubtedly been used before but under which no ship was currently registered. From the moment Terry saw it, he knew that it was, or would be, connected to him in some special way. Yet great though it was to fly, he felt an odd sense of unease. Not until the day he left did he recognize this as the same sort of feeling he'd suspected might be precognition.

At the end of the week he flew *Skywalker* to *Promise* and took it aboard, then proceeded to Earth to pick up Drew and Amir. As the new ship wasn't supposed to be seen at the spaceport, an Earth-based Fleet shuttle brought them up and took him down to the surface. He met Kathryn, who had just finished settling the new mentors in Vancouver, and they went together to see her grandparents.

Arthur Bramfield had, of course, already been told the details of the pirate encounter; but nothing had been said on the phone to confirm that they hadn't been ordinary pirates. He had needed no one to tell him that. Now, after commending Terry for his handling of the threat and expressing his thankfulness for the escape, he confessed that he was still troubled. "I agree with you, Terry, that they can't use the same tactics against us again," he said. "You ended that once and for all. But I'm afraid they won't stop trying to discourage us."

"Admiral Frazer warned me never to leave the ship or its shuttle unguarded, or to allow maintenance to be done on Earth or New Tahiti by anyone other than Drew," Terry said. "But we've always taken those precautions. All work on our ships has been done on Maclairn, and the shuttle hasn't been on the ground elsewhere any longer than it took to load or unload passengers."

"I know, and I don't see how they could be touched, short of a missile attack, which is not the kind of thing that could be attributed to criminals." He frowned. "This new ship—did its developers know about Maclairn?"

"No. It was built by Fleet's regular research team. Whether the League commissioners aware of Maclairn knew it was being built, I can't say, but Admiral Frazer is on top of the situation. He would have seen to its security, and he hadn't told anyone where he was sending it."

"Who knew it was taken aboard *Promise*?"

"No one but the caretaker pilot, who was a member of Frazer's personal staff."

Arthur sighed. "They're not going to give up, Terry. Sooner or later they'll find some vulnerability we haven't foreseen, and there's no way we can defend against it. Yet we have no choice but to keep right on doing what we're doing."

"Of course we haven't," Kathryn said. "The founders of Maclairn counted on us to continue what they started, no matter what it costs."

The schedule allowed just two days with the family and Terry wanted to see Corwin, so, knowing that he worked a late night shift at the health club, he and Kathryn went there after midnight. "It's a bad neighborhood," he observed again, "but if Corwin and Kamila and their trainees walk through it at night, I suppose it's no worse than anywhere else." Nevertheless, he took his laser pistol. It would be terribly ironic if they had survived a confrontation with pirates only to become victims of muggers.

Corwin was in the process of teaching a new recruit to deal with pain and had just completed the first training session; he was free to talk with them during the necessary interval before the second. "There's no one else here tonight except the security guard," he said, "and Kamila's at home. She'll be sorry to have missed you." Then, observing Terry's mutilated hand, he said, "The training's proven worthwhile in its own right, I see. Sometimes, working with people who haven't grown up among others immune to pain, it's hard for me to be as ruthless with them as I must. We do it for its effect in opening minds to other forms of voluntary control and for awakening telepathic sensitivity; few ever have a need to use it as you did."

"It saved us all from capture, and perhaps from death," Terry said. "I might have cracked if I'd been experiencing what they thought I was."

"I doubt that," Corwin told him. "People with your strength of character usually do better in a crisis than they think they will. But it saved you from unnecessary suffering, and that's good to remember when I think of what my trainee is suffering now."

"Never doubt, Corwin," Kathryn said. "We're all happier and more sure of ourselves than before we had mind training, as well as more connected to each other. It all goes together—we can't separate one capability from the rest."

"Or from our freedom from outside coercion," added Terry. "After all, that's why the enemies of Maclairn want to put a stop to our recruiting. Arthur thinks they'll keep trying. Have you got any idea what they could do to us, now that they know they can't take our ship?"

Corwin was silent. Suddenly foreboding swept over

Terry, nearly swamping him. It wasn't precognition this time, he realized. It was something Corwin was hiding behind a deliberate barrier against telepathic sensing. "If I did," Corwin declared finally, "I wouldn't tell Arthur unless it was something he could prevent. Everybody in the world—in any world—is at risk all the time; we are all going to die someday, and the only question is when."

"That's a fatalistic way of looking at it," Kathryn protested.

"No. It is realistic. We're free only when we accept it, and stop seeking absolute safety that can never exist. What matters is not to be safe, but to be doing something worth doing whether we live or die while doing it."

With difficulty Terry quieted his sensation of alarm. He wasn't in the habit of worrying about his safety any more than Corwin was; he hadn't even worried much when he boarded *Starhawk*. He'd taken all possible steps to make sure *Promise* was safe. There was nothing to be gained by trying to guess what might happen in the future.

They talked for a while longer, then embraced as was customary among Maclairnans and said goodbye. Terry and Kathryn walked as quickly as they could to the parking structure and stood at the entrance, waiting for the automated retrieval of their groundcar.

In the next instant the ground was jarred by the force of a tremendous explosion, and as the sound wave hit, deafening them, they turned to see the entire health club building burst into flame.

38

"OH, MY GOD! Corwin!" Kathryn shrieked, and ran forward. Terry pulled her back, holding her tight in his arms. They clung together, too stunned for tears. Firefighters were already gathering, but there was nothing they could do.

It would be pointless to waste scarce and expensive water on a blaze that could not possibly be put out; they turned their attention to adjacent buildings.

There were few spectators. Violence of all kinds was so common in the suburbs that it attracted little excitement, and it was, after all, the middle of the night, when most people were barricaded in their apartments behind triple-locked doors. Police came and cordoned off the area; they did not bother to search for survivors, since it was obvious that there could be none.

"Was it deliberately torched?" Kathryn asked when she could speak. "Was an arsonist in there when we were?"

"No," said Terry bitterly. "There was a guard at the door, after all. It must have been a time bomb placed earlier in the day and set to go off when only a few people would be there. The conspirators evidently preferred not to kill any more innocent bystanders than were needed to make their point."

"Conspirators—you mean terrorists? But the health clubs steer clear of politics."

"Not ordinary terrorists, any more than the pirates were ordinary pirates." Seeing that she had not grasped the nature of the attack, he added, "Arthur and I were so hung up on trying to predict what might be done to the ship that we overlooked the obvious alternative."

"Oh," Kathryn said in a small voice. They stood there, mute, as the building collapsed into a pile of fiery rubble. *Terry, I thought I knew what we were getting into . . . I said over and over that it was dangerous, remember? But I didn't picture our mentors being murdered.*

You mean you didn't let yourself picture it. You're not naïve, Kathryn, any more than the mentors themselves are.

"Do you think Corwin knew it could happen?" she asked aloud.

"Of course he did, and he knew it could happen soon. That was what he was trying to tell us. I sensed something but he wouldn't let me draw any specifics from his mind—he just wanted us to realize, if it did happen, that he'd accepted the risk knowingly."

"Then they *all* know. Even before they get here."

"I guess they do. They've studied Earth, and they don't grow up with the insulation we have to develop here as kids, the shell that keeps us believing we're unlikely to get killed." Or was it more than that? Terry wondered. Corwin was psi-gifted; had it been precognition after all?

"We've got to go," Kathryn said, gathering herself together. "We should be there in case the police call."

"To tell Arthur," he agreed. "Since he owned the building they'll contact him right away."

"Yes, but first we have to tell Kamila."

"Oh, my God. Of course." The police probably didn't know who had died, but if they had records of who worked there they would call the whole list. And it would be even worse if they didn't—if he and Kathryn hadn't been here, Kamila would have waited in vain for Corwin to come home.

When they got to the apartment where the mentors had lived, Kamila met them with frozen calm, despite the agony he sensed beneath the surface. No one had contacted her—she had sensed her lifemate's death when it happened, as psi-gifted people often did. All they had to tell her were the grim details.

They took her back to the Bramfield penthouse with them, where Kathryn's grandmother made her as comfortable as possible in one of the guest rooms. "Thank God *Promise* is on Earth," Kathryn said to her. "We have a stateroom free, and we'll delay departure a few days so you can pack your things."

"I am not going back to Maclairn," Kamila said quietly. "My work is here."

"But you'll want to be with your family—" Corwin and Kamila, like virtually all older Maclairnans, had children, grandchildren, and great-grandchildren.

"Don't you see, Kathryn—if I left, our enemies would win. They would have driven me out, and Corwin would have died for nothing."

That was true, Terry realized. The only thing to do was rebuild the health club and keep going; they would bring in more mentors so that Kamila wouldn't be alone, but there must be no other changes. The whole plan would fall apart if scare tactics had any effect on it.

Arthur Bramfield was crushed, but he too knew that there must be no delay in rebuilding. The only concession to intimidation would be to tighten security; like all buildings open to the public the club had had a security guard at the door, but one was evidently not enough.

"Are the others in danger—I mean right now?" Kathryn asked miserably. "Is this only the beginning of a long series of bombings?"

"No," Arthur said. "So far, it will look to the public like random violence; what's one bomb more or less these days? But if they destroyed more than one Bramfield Club, especially after an attack on a ship I own, it would be seen as a vendetta against me. There would be an investigation, which is the last thing our opponents want. They are just as concerned about keeping our activities secret as we are, remember, and they have no control over the official League authorities."

"You might think about getting a bodyguard for yourself, though," Terry said, "and for Kathryn when's she's here. What scared me most about the pirates was the thought of the hold they'd have over you if Kathryn were taken. And of course if *you* died, who would keep the Foundation going?'

"I'd inherit not only Granddad's personal funds, but the Foundation chairmanship," Kathryn said, "and after me, my children, or my aunt if I'm childless. Any wealthy person has that all set forth in legal paperwork."

"But I'm changing my will," Arthur said, "to put you in line after Kathryn, though God willing, it will never come to that. There's no one I'd rather trust with the responsibility."

God, thought Terry, he means for the money! Someday when we're old, Kathryn and I will inherit billions! He hadn't taken it in before. He knew little of money, having never had any apart from his Fleet pay, and the idea of it awed him. Yet contact between Earth and Maclairn depended on money to operate *Promise,* support the mentors, and maintain the health clubs, and that would always be true. . . .

He felt a chill as a new thought came to him. "Arthur," he said, "could Hiller's next strategy be financial, like manipulating the stock market or stealing funds electronically? Something you may not know about me is that as a kid I used to be a hacker. I never stole any money, but I've seen how it's done."

Arthur nodded. "That hadn't occurred to me, but you're right. I trust my financial managers, but their standard security measures may not be adequate against a targeted attack by government insiders."

"You need to hire an independent hacker to keep watch, sir. I could handle it, but I won't be here."

"I'll do that. God, how else are we vulnerable? I didn't expect things would get this bad so soon."

"Well, we seem to have covered all the bases," Terry said. "But if we're guarding everything on Earth, that's all the more reason why it's important to be vigilant on Maclairn. It's a good thing I'm on my way back, because the danger there is greater than Captain Vargas yet knows."

Alone in their bedroom, Terry and Kathryn held each other and gave way to the tears they had been holding back. "Kamila and Corwin were bonded for nearly fifty years, from the time they were teens," Kathryn said, "and she has at least another fifty years to live. Can you imagine what it will be like for her? All Maclairnans know they may be separated in extreme old age if one partner dies before the other, but usually the survivor doesn't live long.

The light goes out, they say, and their bodies just close down. Kamila isn't old enough for that, she's only a little past sixty."

"I can imagine what it would be like for me, if I lost you," Terry whispered. "And yet when they come here, they know what might happen."

The bond between mentors and their students was strong, too, he realized. He'd had deep feeling for Corwin, almost as deep as his feeling for Aldren and Tristan. They had had telepathic contact under stress as well as friendship. "And it was Corwin who brought us together," he said sadly to Kathryn. His heart ached at the memory of that first magical night that they owed to Corwin's intervention.

"All the others he's trained over the years will grieve, too," Kathryn said. "Early death is virtually unheard of on Maclairn—"

"Others . . . God, Kathryn, what about tonight's new trainee? He died too, died right after facing unbearable pain, without the second session that would have shown him how to lessen it. Is it right to take the risks we do if people like that can get hurt?"

"Either what we're doing is worth risk or it isn't," Kathryn declared. "Corwin thought it is, and if he was wrong then his death was meaningless, which implies that everything anyone has suffered in connection with developing new powers, in training or later—"

"I haven't committed myself the same way you have," Terry said slowly. "I'm sure as hell not going to be pressured into quitting, but I'm a Fleet officer, after all. I know the Stewards of the Flame have secrets you can't tell me, but do they . . . help? Do they explain why Corwin and the other mentors make the sacrifices they do for a future they can't live to see?"

"Being a Steward is just a symbol, Terry. The secret part is purely symbolic—it doesn't tell you anything about life you don't already know. But sharing symbols does help. We'll hold the Ritual in Corwin's memory, and our grief won't hurt quite so much while our minds are joined." She nestled in his arms and added, "The Stewards have a saying—but I can't tell you that. It's how Maclairn's founders were able to face the hardships and dangers they did, and how the mentors do, I guess."

The colonists had believed humankind could move forward, which was more than anyone on Earth had cared about for a long time. Commitment was just another word for caring, Terry realized, and he too cared—as much, perhaps, as Corwin had.

39

DURING THE TRIP back to Maclairn with a new group of observers, everyone was subdued. The three couples had of course been recruited long before; hearing of the bombing didn't reduce their enthusiasm, although they were warned of the increased risk they might face at the health club they were to establish in Berlin when they got home. But the dark mood of Kathryn and the crew put a damper on conversation.

Since Maclairn received no news from the League worlds except via *Promise*, there was a great deal to be told when they arrived. To Kathryn fell the painful task of informing Jessica of Corwin's death, which she did by phone before escorting the observers to the surface. Terry briefly summarized developments to Captain Vargas, making plain that they would need to have a long talk later to reassess the risks Maclairn was facing. He said little about the pirate encounter and was somewhat irritated when Drew spread the details among *Shepard*'s crew, resulting in a hero's welcome for him and the revelation of Kathryn's status as an heiress.

The one bright spot in the days after their return was the arrival of *Skywalker*. Everyone admired it and all the pilots wanted to fly it; Terry busied himself with taking them out one at a time as copilots. His intention was to train Mikaela Orlov, who was by now fully recovered, more intensively with the idea of making her its acting captain during his next trip to Earth. But he held off because Drew and Mikaela moved into a stateroom together and it appeared that Drew wouldn't want to go to Earth again without her, which would mean giving command of *Skywalker* to Amir.

All of Maclairn went into mourning for Corwin. Memorial services were held in every town; but attendance at the main one, the symbolic burial of his body in the lake, was limited to mentors, his personal friends, and his former trainees because there wasn't room for more people on the beach and the terraces immediately above it. For several hours boats came back and forth, bringing them. Torches were lit not only by the water, but on every terrace, making a spectacular display of lights as seen from the lake. As he stepped off the dock Terry was nearly swamped by the emotion he perceived, the combined telepathic projection of the assembly's sorrow.

Because they'd been the last to see Corwin, Terry and Kathryn, like others close to him, had been asked to say something in remembrance. Kathryn recounted what he had said to them shortly before they parted: "'What matters is not to be safe, but to be doing something worth doing whether we live or die while doing it.' I think it would make a good epitaph," she declared.

Terry, who had talked to Jessica beforehand to get approval of the announcement he planned, spoke last. Taking the wireless mike from her he said, "Not long ago I led an expedition to the other planets of this solar system, and I was told that as captain of the first ship to land on the one we've called Three, it was my right to name it. I didn't do so at that time because I felt it should be named after a Maclairnan—planets cannot be named after living persons and I was not familiar enough with

Maclairn's history to choose someone who had died. Now surely there can be no more appropriate name for a neighboring world than that of the first person to die for the cause of spreading the capabilities developed here to all humankind. I therefore name the third planet from this sun Corwin, and I will submit that name to Fleet to be recorded in its official atlas of the galaxy when the need for secrecy is past."

There was a murmur of approval from the gathered people, and the service moved on to its climax: the placing of floating candles from the boat that would have borne the body if there had been one. The emotion produced by the telepathic union of several hundred mourners intensified. Voices carried over the water in the traditional funeral song, reverberating from the canyon walls:

> *May the radiance of candles we light now amidst*
> *   our tears*
> *Fuel the rising flame within us to be passed on*
> *   through the years.*

"It was sung at Ian Maclairn's funeral on Undine," Kathryn whispered to him, "and at every one since then. I've seen a vid of the first one held by the lake—that was for Ivana's birth-mother Kira, who was the first person to die of old age on this world. This time is just the same."

As the candles on the water flickered and went out, the dock light flashed three times. Reluctantly Terry let go of Kathryn's hand and went toward it; this was the signal he had been told to watch for. He and the few others present who were not Stewards of the Flame must leave now, for the Ritual they must not see was about to begin. Looking back at the array of torches that grew dimmer as the boat took him away, he realized that he did not want to go. It wasn't just that he hated to be separated from Kathryn or break his telepathic tie with the assemblage of caring people. He wanted to share what they had, the conviction that what Maclairn aimed to do truly mattered, that he could make a difference to the future by taking part in it.

What made him feel he wasn't totally committed? he wondered. He was irrevocably committed to Kathryn, to the family they hoped to have, to Maclairn as the world that would always seem like home to him. He had vowed to defend it, and he wasn't going to let the strong-arm tactics of its enemies scare him off. He believed whole-heartedly in the cause of giving new capabilities to humans everywhere. So what was holding him back from the full dedication the Ritual was supposed to symbolize?

He knew in his heart what it was. He still imagined himself as an explorer of distant stars. What if Fleet promoted him again someday? What if they eventually transferred him to a major discovery or settlement team, or offered him command of a colonizer? Would he be willing to resign his commission rather than abandon Maclairn, even if Kathryn agreed to go with him? He had been told that being a Steward of the Flame would not mean he must stay on Maclairn forever; he would be free to make trips, even long-term ones. But its welfare and its cause would have to remain his top priority. He could not declare allegiance to some other world.

Yet he had already given his allegiance, hadn't he? As with his marriage to Kathryn, his choice had been made without conscious deliberation, and a ceremony wouldn't make any difference.

The next day he went to see Tristan. "You said once I might be allowed to be a Steward of the Flame," he said.

Tristan regarded him soberly. "Yes, if you truly desire it. It's not a decision to be made lightly."

"My decision was made unconsciously, Tristan, and I couldn't change it if I wanted to."

"That's how it often happens. Okay, we'll start preparing. As you know the Ritual involves some very advanced psi. I believe you're up to it, but we need to practice some of what you've done in the past."

They had daily neurofeedback sessions throughout the next week, during which Terry's skill in control over his body's reactions and in pain management were confirmed along with his psi capabilities and his ability to self-heal. Various new stressors were added, until he demonstrated that he could maintain a mind-pattern, or even switch to a new one, regardless of shock or emotional turmoil.

Tristan asked for the details about what had happened to his hand and examined it closely to verify that it was completely healed. When Terry mentioned that it had been badly burned in addition to the amputation of the fingers, Tristan was pleased to hear that this hadn't unduly upset him. "If you were able to handle it without suffering from pain, that's a good thing, because it's closer to real-life situations than having fingers cut off. We can skip some of the more grueling lessons that are normally given during advanced training because you've already proven that your mind skills can protect you in an emergency."

At the end of the week Terry left for the first operational test of *Skywalker*, taking both Mikaela and Amir along with Drew and Zuri Kifeda. The new ship was great; being able to land it instead of having to leave it in orbit while using a shuttle simplified the job of checking sensor stations immensely. They visited Corwin and Four, but did not go as far as Five; nobody wanted to see Five-C again, and Captain Vargas had decided that the risks of placing stations on Five's moons were unwarranted.

Their last night out, Terry woke again with an undeniable sense of a nearby presence. God, he thought, this couldn't be mere precognition—it was too insistent! There was no visual component to the perception, but unless there were weird space monsters around, it had to be a ship. He tried to laugh it off, telling himself he must have had some silly nightmare about space monsters that carried over into consciousness. But he was not prone to nightmares, and in any case a new and ominous thought had come to him—what if their League enemies had had a spy ship in the system all along? All their speculation about the unlikelihood of random explorers or smugglers arriving, and the impossibility of a ship staying in the vicinity instead of approaching Maclairn, were invalid if it was being intentionally spied on with the aim of detecting some vulnerability in Fleet's warning system.

Once back on Maclairn, he mentioned this thought to Tristan. "I don't know what to say," Tristan answered. "But unless you have real evidence, I wouldn't alarm Captain Vargas. Psi impressions can be false, and there isn't anything you can do about an invisible ship anyway if it stays clear of the sensors that have been deployed."

The Ritual was scheduled for three days later. On the morning of the event Tristan told him something about what was coming. "Only five people will take an active part," he said, "Jessica as presiding mentor, me as her backup, Kathryn as your sponsor, you, and a torchbearer. But the others present will be more than onlookers—they will be there to support you. What you will be asked to do would be impossible without the telepathic backing of the whole group."

"All my life I felt cut off from people," Terry said slowly, "until the day Aldren told me I was telepathic. From then on everything changed for me. It's fitting, I guess, for telepathy to be an important part of what Kathryn says will be another transformation."

"The point of the Ritual is connection with people," Tristan agreed. "It's a way of confirming not only that you're sincere in your commitment, but that you have absolute trust in others with like aims—that you can rely on them and they on you. That's one of the pledges you'll make: to support them unconditionally, as they are already pledged to support every person who joins us. And it's vital that you do trust them, Terry. You will face an ordeal that you cannot get through without drawing on their psi power as well as your own."

"What sort of an ordeal?" He had not realized that he would be formally tested.

"We don't tell you that ahead of time, except that it involves proving that mind powers can protect you from physical trauma and pain. In your case you've already proven it in tolerating the mutilation of your hand. But we will ask you to prove it again, even more dramatically."

"Will it be painful, then?"

"Not unless you panic and lose the volitional control you've developed. If you do, you could get seriously hurt— but that won't happen, because Jessica will probe your mind and she won't proceed if she senses you're vulnerable."

Terry frowned. Previously he had gotten the impression that it would be a wholly joyous occasion.

Perceiving this thought, Tristan went on, "The Ritual *is* joyous, because you discover powers within yourself that you didn't know you had, awesome powers that give you confidence in your own strength as well as your ability to connect with others. So as a full participant you'll be both frightened and elated at the same time."

It hadn't occurred to him to be frightened. What, he wondered, had he gotten himself into? Kathryn had come through it all right. . . .

"Fear is a good thing," Tristan said, "because like all primal emotion it increases psi power. That's why we deliberately arouse it in preparation for the Ritual as well as in early mind training. So don't be down on yourself if you feel it—you're supposed to." Smiling, he added, "But it's not the only way to enhance telepathic sensitivity, so go spend the afternoon with Kathryn."

That he had been serious about the implication of this advice became apparent when Kathryn suggested spending the late afternoon in bed. After they made love, they remained there until it was time to dress for the Ritual, which was to be held early in the evening and followed by a celebration feast.

"Terry," Kathryn said, turning on her side to face him, "there's a change in the plan for tonight. I was supposed to be your sponsor, but I can't be—I've got to be torch-bearer instead."

"Why?" he asked in astonishment. He'd been given to understand that the person closest to the initiate was always the sponsor. He'd counted on having her beside him.

"Because no pregnant woman can be a full participant," she said. "The stress might endanger the child."

It took him a moment to grasp what she was saying. "Pregnant woman? Kathryn, you're—"

"Yes," she told him happily. "I've suspected it for several days, but we don't have biochemical pregnancy tests here, you know, and I wasn't going to mention it yet. Then this morning I remembered the rule about the Ritual, so I went to Jessica and she confirmed that I'm pregnant with a boy."

"Oh, Kathryn, that's wonderful!" Terry said, hugging her. Then he asked, "What makes her think it's a boy? Surely it's too soon to tell."

"Jessica is a gifted healer," Kathryn informed him, "and a healer's perception reveals the sex of a child long before tests could. So we know I'm carrying our son Radnor."

"You've named him already?"

"The founders' dropped surnames were given to their children or their close friends' children. If we have a second son we'll call him Bram, but Radnor comes first—I wouldn't think of naming him anything else, Terry."

A son. On the very day he was committing himself to a permanent tie with Maclairn. It was confirmation that he was doing the right thing, and his spirits soared.

40

THE RITUAL WAS held in the great room of Jessica's home, the one where the Council met and where Terry and Kathryn had slept on their wedding night. "That's where it was held on Undine," she said, "in the lodge this room is patterned after. Large gatherings like memorials are exceptions; a pledging involves far fewer people, different ones each time since a lot of young people are pledged every year. Only a few happen here in this room, of course—just those over which Jessica personally presides."

They showered and dressed in crisp white short-sleeved shirts—the color worn for the Ritual and only then—and joined the gathering. About fifty people had assembled, mostly mentors. Tristan and Merelda greeted Terry warmly and introduced those of the others whom he didn't already know.

"I'll be your sponsor, since Kathryn can't," Tristan said. "Martin will take my place as Jessica's backup."

"Martin's a member of the Council, the one in charge of psi development," Kathryn said. "You'll be better off with him taking part, because I'm not nearly as strong a telepath."

"You're totally telepathic with me," Terry pointed out.

"Yes, but I've only been a full participant once, and Martin has long experience. And I'll be right there, after all, holding the torch."

The difference between this and full participation was a mystery to Terry, but he supposed he would soon be enlightened. The people circled around the central fireplace, standing where the floor cushions normally were and leaving a gap on the side opposite the windows. He and Tristan joined Jessica and Martin, forming a semicircle in the empty space. Kathryn, carrying an unlighted torch nearly as tall as her shoulder, stood in its center between Martin and Tristan, with Terry at one end facing Jessica at the other.

Someone turned down both the music and the lights, and as the room hushed, Jessica embraced Terry. "Welcome to our circle, Terry," she said softly, "and may God be with you in your pledging." She stepped back and spoke to the group.

"We're gathered tonight as witnesses to Terry's commitment to the cause of Maclairn," Jessica said. "In the Ritual of his pledging we will renew our own commitment, remembering the time when we too faced the fire and for the first time felt its power to inspire our lives."

Was her reference to the fire literal or symbolic? Terry wondered. He recalled what Kathryn had said about it symbolizing something larger than their personal union, which made more sense than assuming that the particular fire beside which they stood was in any way inspiring. It seemed a bit odd that they were burning scarce wood when it was too early in the evening to need warmth.

Jessica went on, summarizing the precepts on which the culture of Maclairn was based: primacy of mind over body; living free of fear; development of paranormal skills; telepathically-enhanced communication; and commitment to extending new capabilities throughout the worlds of humankind. "Although," she said, "our hope of spreading our abilities through action is not the essence of our commitment. From the beginning, it has been said among us that simply being who we are—proving that it is possible for individuals to develop the full potential of the mind, and to make use of it in our lives—is in itself of immense value, whether or not any overt social action is possible. This is our prime responsibility.

"The wording of the Ritual has been the same since the time of the founders, who were united by opposition to the tyrannical medical laws of Undine," she continued. "Since then we have been less focused on resistance to external pressure than they were, for we have not been facing danger or hardship. We have never changed it, for there is value in continuity with those who came before us. And now it seems that we who become stewards of the powers we know to be attainable by human minds again risk harm by hostile outsiders. You are the first in modern times to pledge under such conditions, Terry. That you do so in full knowledge of what confronts you is a reminder to us all of what our fellowship truly means."

She paused briefly, then pronounced the formal invocation: "In silence, let us commend ourselves to whatever Power we hold highest, each of us in our own way."

Terry was not an adherent of any formal religion, but he recognized this as a call for what by anyone's definition might be called prayer. Were they all to face some sort of challenge? Suddenly apprehensive, he prayed that he would prove able to meet whatever was coming with composure.

When the assembly stirred he raised his head just as Kathryn lifted the torch higher and, to his astonishment, it burst into flame. No one had lighted it—it was simply, apparently miraculously, blazing. In the next moment it dawned on him that Jessica had done this with psi, just as he and Tristan had once lighted candles. And then the candles held by the onlookers suddenly and simultaneously glowed with life, and he knew that this was the ultimate manifestation of the flame symbol that signified mind power.

To Tristan, Jessica said, "Do you wish to sponsor Terry in his commitment to our cause, sharing the peril of his pledging, and do you believe him qualified to undertake this commitment safely?"

Tristan answered, "Yes, I do."

Jessica turned to Terry. "Do you accept Tristan as your sponsor?"

"I'm happy to accept him," Terry answered. If there

was peril, would Kathryn have shared it? No doubt she would, since she'd said there would be risk to her unborn child. It was just as well that it had turned out that she needn't take part.

"Terry, do you confirm the pledge you have made to keep everything you know or may learn of Maclairn, and of the Stewards of the Flame, secret from all but those to whom you are authorized to reveal it, now and forever, at whatever cost to yourself?"

"I do," Terry replied.

"Do you by your own free choice commit yourself to live by the precepts of the Stewards of the Flame, as I have stated them?"

"Yes, I do." There was nothing in them he had reservations about.

"Will you support fellow Stewards in all ways, even at the risk of your personal safety?'

"I will do so gladly."

"Do you believe that your mind has power over the well-being of your body, and that it can protect or heal you from sickness, injury and pain?"

"I do," he affirmed steadily. There seemed to be special emphasis on this point and he could tell from the emotions of the others that it was leading somewhere.

"Terry, are you willing to confirm your commitment by proving your trust in that power?"

"Yes, I am." His heart began to race and as he had been taught to do, he quieted it.

For a moment Jessica was silent, motionless, but he felt her mind touch his, drawing from it no less fully than Kathryn did during lovemaking. All that he was, all that he had dreamed of being, was open to her evaluation; but he felt no desire to shrink from it. The awareness that she knew him, cared about him, was strengthening, for he now perceived that Jessica was far more than the distinguished elderly woman in whose home he was living. She had not become leader of Maclairn through seniority alone, he saw; she was truly psi-gifted beyond any other mentor he had encountered.

It did not matter what they did to test him, Terry realized. He was protected both by his own strength, which Jessica had just acknowledged, and by the overwhelming supportive presence of the group. She was channeling their psi power, holding it in focus as an anchor for him to hold to. He looked out at the candlelit faces surrounding him and felt his mind mesh with theirs, not as an indistinguishable part, but as an independent node of a network with access to whatever resources he might need. Whatever fear he might otherwise have felt vanished as the link was established.

Kathryn lowered the torch she bore, holding it horizontally with the flame at waist level half way between Jessica and Terry. He could feel tension mounting among the onlookers. In the formal words she had said were traditional, Jessica continued:

"Unfaced fear is the destroyer. We will acknowledge fear and accept it, we will go past it and live free.

"We will trust the power of the mind over all restrictions, whether imposed from within or by the world outside.

"We will act always through volition, allowing neither internal nor external pressures to enslave us.

"We will support one another unfailingly in fulfilling this pledge.

"We believe that we are stewards of a flame that will illuminate future generations.

"And we now seal our commitment with the symbol of the mind's power, which is fire."

The blaze of the torch between them dazzled him so that he could not see her expression; he knew only that he trusted her and through her, all the others, not only those present but those who, like him, would overcome whatever obstacles they must to pass Maclairn's heritage on. He was proud and happy to be a part of it. It was so timeless a feeling that for a moment, when Jessica's left hand reached for his, he did not grasp what was happening in the here and now.

His own hand was halfway to hers before he became aware that hers was in the flame, and was not burned.

"Put your left hand on mine, Terry," Jessica commanded softly.

Incredulous, he froze with the hand still outstretched. But Kathryn's silent command came instantly: *Don't hesitate, Terry! You can do it if you don't stop to think about it—I did.*

Tristan, too, was urging him: *You must, Terry. Now, before you lose your nerve.*

Terry thrust his hand forward into the flame, knowing that to draw back would be a repudiation not only of the pledges he had just made, but of the power within himself that was now an inseparable part of his identity. It would be a rejection of the connection with other minds that had come to mean everything to him. And it would mean alienation from Kathryn, not in a literal sense but in terms of the goal they shared. He did not reason this out in the few seconds it took to do it. He did not even remind himself that if he was burned, it would hurt no more than when the hand had been burned and mutilated before, for pain would not have mattered to him in the light of the things that did matter.

Immediately he was high, floating somewhere in space, detached from his surroundings but inwardly aware of the psi support of others: Tristan and Martin, whose hands were now on his, and the many onlookers who were touching the flames of their candles, thereby magnifying their psychic potency. It was like his first volitional shift of consciousness, with Aldren, but far better; and the memory of it would be with him forever.

Standing somewhere outside time, he would not have thought to withdraw his hand if the three others, removing theirs from the fire, had not silently told him to. Less than twenty seconds had elapsed. As he dropped back into reality he stared in awe at his unburned fingers and wondered if what seemed to have occurred had really happened.

Again Jessica embraced Terry; then she pinned a small copper flame, insignia of the Stewards, to the lapel of his shirt. Kathryn laid the torch in the fireplace and threw her arms around him, exulting in the dissolution of the last barrier to full merging of their thoughts. The others clustered around and they too hugged him, first Tristan and then the rest. He felt as never before that he truly belonged among them, that they were his family.

It was not his miraculous immunity to fire that had brought this about, he knew. It was his inner willingness to commit himself totally to the vision of the future Maclairnans shared, even to the extent of an irrational gamble on its validity. As the words of the Ritual said, the fire was only a symbol. "Oh God, Kathryn," he said to her as they settled on the cushions now brought back to the hearth, "I never understood what's happening here till now—"

"We're defying the idea that prevails everywhere else, the belief that humankind is not progressing and never will. That belief seems reasonable if you look at what's happening on Earth, and even in most of the colonies. To see that it's false you have to believe in the impossible . . . and if you let yourself do that, it becomes possible after all."

Still awestricken, Terry said slowly, "I'm not sure I really did what I did tonight, that it wasn't some sort of fantastic illusion. But even if it was, I don't question what it stands for. Corwin—I wondered how he could go on with his job so calmly when he knew he was a sitting duck—"

"You asked me," Kathryn recalled, "And I told you there was a saying among the Stewards that I couldn't reveal then. 'It's like touching flame,' they say. 'We just *do* it—and to be able to do it, we have to know we could be burned, and be willing.'"

Would the destiny Aldren had foreseen for him work like that? he wondered. He was now sure that his destiny was linked to Maclairn's, but that in itself couldn't be called extraordinary. Did the vague, persistent sense of an intruding starship he'd experienced have something to do with it? Was that why it had disturbed him—had there been precognition not just as to the intruder's presence, but in connection with whatever challenge was ahead of him?

The people around him were soon celebrating as they had at the wedding feast, and the solemnity faded. But for Terry, the preternatural psi power aroused by the Ritual lingered, and he felt he would burst if he could not somehow make the most of it.

41

IT WAS VERY late when they finally got to bed. They made love again, joyously as always but with the added elation produced by the Ritual's lingering effects, Afterward Kathryn dropped off, exhausted from the day's two portentous experiences.

Terry remained too excited to sleep. All his faculties were sharpened; he felt in touch with the entire universe, as if he could reach out and perceive the most distant stars. . . . Then, gradually but unmistakably, he began to sense the presence that had haunted him in space: the perception of an unseen ship lurking somewhere within range of Maclairn. And he knew it was there not in the indefinite future, but *now*.

Whether or not it had been precognition before, there was no longer any doubt of the ship's reality. His remote vision, heightened by the increased telepathic sensitivity that had enabled him to touch flame unharmed, was revealing it to him; a vague picture was forming in his mind. It wasn't shaped like a ship, or in fact shaped at all, but was merely a perception of some artificial object made of metal. Something that couldn't be a normal feature of any solar system. It couldn't actually be close, the satellite ring would have picked it up—but Jessica had sensed it at a distance repeatedly. She had lacked a means of pursuing what she sensed, but he did not. He was through with denying the power he'd feared to acknowledge in himself! He might be able to locate the ship, and if so he must do so before the enhanced psi capability given him by the Ritual wore off.

Terry got up and put on his clothes—his Fleet uniform, because if he met the intruder he would need to give an official warning on the comm vid. He was not going to consult his superiors aboard *Shepard*; there wasn't time for that, for which he was glad because they might not share his confidence and in any case they would insist that he take a crew along. For some reason he felt that would be unfair—he was now committed to the defense of Maclairn, no matter what the risk, in a way the other officers were not; and inner awareness as well as logic told him that if its enemies indeed had a spy ship in the system, the risk was very great. More precognition? he wondered. It hardly mattered, since on this particular morning circumstances, whether by luck or something else, had converged to provide an opportunity that wouldn't come again. He was empowered by the Ritual— and *Skywalker*, with a far greater range than any shuttle or patroller, was still on the ground instead of on the cruiser where it would be by nightfall if he returned to duty as scheduled.

Kathryn slept peacefully, her face half-hidden by the pillow. He longed to kiss her goodbye, but now that she was pregnant she needed her rest and anyway, he didn't want her to protest. No matter what he said, she would grasp everything in his mind and would be bound to feel that his compulsion to go into danger alone was not rational. In fear that unconscious telepathy would wake her, he left quickly, scrawling a brief note saying he was returning early to *Shepard*. They wouldn't be parted for long, after all. He would either sight the intruder and warn Fleet by comm, or return before she had time to be seriously worried by his absence. It would actually be safest for him to go alone and unarmed; even if the ship was crewed by hired outlaws they would be unlikely to kill a single challenger in cold blood, whereas if confronted by a team they would expect a fight.

It was still dark as he hurried to the rail station, but by the time he got to the lake dawn was reddening the sky, striping the ripples on the water. This early there were no boatmen around; he pounded on the door of the marina office and offered the one on duty a larger-than-normal fare to take him to the Old Settlement, sorry that he had not learned to handle a boat himself. On the way up the lake he thought of how beautiful it was despite the barrenness of the rocky canyon walls that rose on either side, so close at most points that the water looked yellow instead of blue. It reminded him of some of the isolated places where he had camped on Earth—but there, he had never had the feeling of attachment to his surroundings that he had come to feel on this world.

It was very calm; only the soft hum of the motor broke the silence. His heart, in contrast, felt close to bursting—with love for Maclairn, for Kathryn sleeping back in Jessica's house, and already for the son she carried. His son! Radnor . . . he would be father to a native Maclairnan. For his son's sake even more because of the pledge he had made, he must do all he could to protect Maclairn's secret.

The lieutenant on watch at Fleet's ground base was surprised to see him, but did not question a superior officer's need to fly when he saw fit. Terry ordered her to top off *Skywalker*'s water tank and replenish its supply of emergency rations. His spacesuit, fortunately, was stored aboard. After completing his preflight check, he paced impatiently while the intake pump and liquefier raised the ship's stored air supply to maximum. Then, without further preparation, he took off.

He had no idea where he was going; he would let his psi faculties guide him. Commanding the AI to set a course toward Corwin, he sat back and waited for the call that was bound to come once the surveillance satellites picked him up.

The comm came alive. "*Skywalker*, this is *Shepard*. What's your destination? Over."

"*Shepard*, this is Lieutenant Commander Radnor," Terry replied calmly. "On my last flight down I noticed an anomaly in the instrument readings. I'm just checking it out. Over.

After a pause the watch officer came on. "You didn't report any anomaly, Commander."

"No, sir. I didn't want to cause concern until I was sure. Since I'm the only pilot experienced with this ship, I had to evaluate it personally."

"Very well, *Skywalker*, but keep your comm channel open and report every ten minutes. You should have advised us before lifting."

"I'm sorry, sir," he lied. "I'll check in as soon as I'm past the satellite ring. Out." In ten minutes he would be a long way past, and he had no intention of checking in until he was beyond the range of patrollers. He would be in big trouble when he got back, of course, unless he had something really significant to report such as the sighting of the intruder he felt ever more certain would appear. If he was wrong, it might end his career—but after last night, he was in a mood to sacrifice anything demanded as the price of living up to what he had pledged.

The mentors aboard would support him, Terry realized, and would inform Jessica, who had always hoped that he would sense something and who had a great deal of influence with the captain. Mentors found the culture of Fleet, based on unfailing obedience to orders, strange and unnatural; he knew that inwardly they disapproved of it. And after all, *Promise* belonged to the Maclairn Foundation, whose arrangement with Fleet was subject to renegotiation. If he had to resign his commission Arthur Bramfield would cancel the contract and hire him as civilian captain.

The response to his call to *Shepard*, when he finally made it after ignoring repeated demands to respond, was predictably furious; they had scrambled patrollers to search for him, as he had known they would. "Sir, I was trained in remote viewing for the specific purpose of sensing unauthorized ships," he told Captain Vargas. "I have sensed one. Seeing that I'm the only pilot checked out on *Skywalker* and no other ship of ours has enough range, I felt I had no choice—if I'd waited for permission to pursue the intruder it might elude me. Stay on alert, because either I'll verify its presence or it will be picked up by the satellite ring. I will report my status hourly. Out." He turned off the comm without waiting for the inevitable outraged reply.

For Kathryn's sake more than Fleet's, he made the brief hourly reports. Apart from this, time passed in silence while Terry, though always aware of the nagging sense that his was not the only ship in the vicinity, recalled the joy of the Ritual—the firelight, the mind-touch of his gathered friends, the strengthening link with Kathryn in the knowledge that she carried his child, the solemnity of the pledges that had become the defining center of his life—and above all, his transformation in the moment when his mind merged with Jessica's and Tristan's as their hands touched in flame. He knew that had not been an illusion. Undamaged though his hand looked now, *it had happened*. Nothing could ever take that from him. No matter what the future held, he was forever one with Maclairn and what it symbolized. He fingered the copper flame now pinned to the lapel of his uniform; whether this was against regulations he did not know, nor, at the moment, did he care. In a conflict between two loyalties, there was no longer any doubt as to which was primary.

42

EVENTUALLY, TERRY REALIZED that he must sleep soon. He debated between setting an alarm to wake him once an hour and prerecording a status report; but Fleet would recognize the latter as automated and Kathryn would worry, so he decided on the alarm. He was afraid in any case of missing what he was seeking. Having come this far, it would be a terrible irony to be asleep when closest, though *Skywalker*'s AI was programmed to alert him if its sensors picked up any sort of signal.

Underneath, he was aware that there was no good reason to assume he had chosen the right course to intercept the intruder. There wasn't even any reason to think the time was right, for if what had come to him these past weeks had been precognition, it still could be, despite his strong conviction that it wasn't. And why had he supposed the ship would be found in the direction of Corwin, which was by now elsewhere in its orbit, merely because he had first sensed it on the way there? Why, he wondered, had he felt compelled to defy logic and caution in a sudden impulse to fly in this particular direction?

But the sense of *something there* was stronger than ever, overwhelming, so that his head swam and he began to sweat. Unaccountably, he felt a sudden desire to be back on Maclairn where he belonged. He was blurry-eyed from fatigue—this was still the day of the Ritual in terms of when he'd last waked—and perhaps, after all, he was hallucinating. . . .

And then, abruptly, a starship loomed in front of him—huge, filling his viewscreen, an ominously strange shape unlike any ship he had ever seen.

Incredibly, he had intercepted it precisely, despite having had no way of predicting the direction in which to fly. Was he dreaming this, Terry wondered, or had unconscious remote viewing led him to it . . . or, perhaps, had the other ship been simultaneously seeking *him*? It was much larger than *Skywalker,* larger even than *Promise,* and undoubtedly faster. Its sensors could have tracked his trajectory. The crew, whatever their mission, probably wouldn't want their presence to become known.

He had not expected anything like this. No one had thought there could ever be an intruder significantly bigger than an explorer, for the mere existence of a privately-owned starship large enough to hold more than twelve people was in itself illegal. In the years since formation of the League, Fleet had not needed to enforce its monopoly. An illegally-sized ship would have been detected during construction, or at the very least if it tried to unload cargo anywhere, so nobody had attempted to build one—and of course, undercover League conspirators could not use a Fleet ship. How had the owners of this monster managed to conceal it?

Steadying himself, Terry decided to proceed with his original plan for warning them off; it wasn't his job to deal with prior violations of League law. Setting the comm to broadcast on all frequencies, he declared, "Unidentified ship, this is FIS *Skywalker*. This entire system has been placed off-limits by Fleet, as maneuvers are underway here. You are required to jump at your earliest opportunity. Over."

There was no response, though it was impossible that they hadn't heard. Terry turned on the comm's vid so that they could see him and repeated the hail: "Unidentified ship, this is Lieutenant Commander Terry Radnor, captain of FIS *Skywalker*. You are in off-limits territory and you must depart immediately. Know that there is a cruiser present in this system that will enforce compliance. Please acknowledge, over." They had no choice but to obey; even a ship of this size would be no match for an armed cruiser.

The comm remained silent, its vid screen blank; but the ship moved closer, almost as if they planned to rendezvous. Terry had no intention of doing so; while they surely would not blast him out of the sky without provocation, they might well take him prisoner if they could induce him to board—and he had had enough of being held captive by outlaws. What their ostensible aim might be in coming to this outlying solar system was hard to imagine; they couldn't claim to be pirates here, nor could they masquerade as smugglers since they couldn't show themselves to sell any resources they might acquire—unless perhaps they planned to transfer cargo to smaller starships instead of approaching inhabited planets. Terry turned cold, for that made sense, now that he thought of it. A really large smuggling ring, controlled by the underworld, might be able to function that way. But in that case . . . maybe they *would* blast *Skywalker*. They would have a credible reason for getting rid of a pilot who knew more than their underworld bosses wanted known.

And if by chance they hadn't been warned about the cruiser, now that he'd revealed its presence they would investigate all the planets of the system, hoping to take it by surprise. While they couldn't win in an open fight, they could do a good deal of damage by a sneak attack. Expecting no trouble, the officers aboard *Shepard* would not be armed; the satellite alert wouldn't reveal the size of the intruder—they would send patrollers to meet it assuming that it would be easy to capture. If it carried high-yield weapons. . . .

Oh, God, Terry thought. Why had he again let the excitement of remote viewing override his common sense?

Just as he had ignored normal caution when he entered the cave, he had rushed blindly into a situation in which he might be trapped. And yet ... the cave experience had proved fortunate in the long run. Tristan had seemed to feel he had been guided by some mysterious inner impulse that had meaning. Might such an impulse account for his rashness this time, too? He alone now knew what *Shepard* could not foresee. Had precognition led him here to warn them? He must call even before learning the ship's identity; switching the comm to Fleet's frequency he started to do so ... only to find that the comm panel was dead.

Dead! No power seemed to be reaching it. This could hardly be a coincidence, but what technology of theirs could kill just one power circuit within his ship? An EMP would have taken out everything.

The starship was still approaching, and it was even larger than he had thought because he had first seen it at a greater distance than he'd realized. It seemed headed to collide with *Skywalker*—maybe they meant to ram him! Frantically Terry reached for the AI console, attempting to change course. The override switch had no effect, and in horror he perceived that the other ship wasn't moving after all; *Skywalker* was being inexorably drawn toward it. A tractor beam? Such things existed in fiction, but not, as far as he knew, in real life. His instruments showed that the AI was fully operative; it was executing maneuvers leading not to a collision, but to a normal docking. Somehow they had taken remote control of his ship.

Where would anyone have obtained technology that could do that? If it was available, pirates would be using it, and he'd heard no reports in Fleet that any were. For a moment he wondered if Fleet was testing some secret new development, just as they were testing *Skywalker*, which would also account for the unprecedented design of the starship. But since it involved a crew other than *Shepard*'s they wouldn't have picked Maclairn's solar system to do it in, not when there was a bigger secret here to protect. And in any case Admiral Frazer, knowing of his plan for patrolling, would have told him.

He sat helplessly watching the viewscreen as, directly in front of him, a port opened in the starship and *Skywalker* was drawn through. There was no prospect of escape, now or ever, with his ship in their hands—the conspirators could not demand ransom for him without saying where and how he had been captured.

"Commander Radnor, please forgive our presumption in bringing you aboard in this way," said a voice on the now-reanimated comm. It had an unusual pitch and he could not tell whether it was a man's or a woman's; perhaps it was synthesized. "You and your crew will be escorted to a place where you will be made comfortable."

The inner hatch opened without action on Terry's part; they were evidently in control of his airlock. A suited figure appeared, motioning him to put on his own suit and helmet; the docking bay must be unpressurized. He was led through the other ship's main airlock and then, astonishingly, through a second airlock into a compartment furnished with an odd-looking couch and two circular chairs. Nothing more was said to him; his guard, still wearing a helmet, soon left him alone.

Terry got out of his spacesuit, thankful that he had worn his uniform, rumpled though it now was. He hoped he could manage to maintain some dignity, despite the humiliation of having been taken without opportunity to resist.

43

THE ROOM'S AIRLOCK cycled and a different, shorter guard entered, wearing clothes that completely covered him—or her, for again Terry could not tell whether it was a man or a woman. Loose-fitting tunic, trousers, and long gloves, all white, plus a headscarf and face mask that revealed only the eyes. That was a good sign; if they took the trouble to make themselves unrecognizable it might mean they planned to let him go.

"Good evening, Commander Radnor," his captor said in the same peculiar voice he had heard over the comm. "My name is Laesara, and while aboard you will communicate only with me. I see you wear a Fleet uniform and that puzzles me, as your ship is not one of Fleet's."

It sounded like a feminine name so he decided this was a woman. "I am a Lieutenant Commander in Fleet," he stated. "My ship is a new model recently carried in for testing."

To his surprise he sensed dismay in her, almost as if she had made some terrible blunder. With even greater surprise he realized that she was telepathic, though she was intentionally concealing most of her mind. She spoke slowly and rather formally; Anglo did not appear to be her native language, and he was perceiving some of what she said before he heard her words.

"What were you doing here alone, such a long way out from Maclairn?

Terry's heart lurched. They knew about Maclairn! That confirmed that they were hired spies, since its name had been revealed only to the Foundation observers and a few high League officials—but how could opponents of Maclairn have hired a telepath? Where could they have found one? Mustering as much composure as he could, he declared, "I was patrolling to warn ships away. Fleet has placed this solar system off-limits because of the tests we are conducting here. You should have left while you had the chance; since you're already aware of Maclairn you will be taken into custody." Thank God they had ignored his warning—since they might have contacts who knew less than they did, they couldn't be allowed to leave. He must think of some tactic to stall them until he could find a way to contact *Shepard*.

"There has been a mistake," Laesara said, seeming genuinely regretful. "We do not show ourselves to the Fleet ships."

"I imagine not," said Terry dryly, "considering that yours is illegal."

She regarded him thoughtfully. "I can tell that you are psi-gifted, Terry Radnor," she said, "and that you have had training. It can hardly be by chance that you were patrolling so close to us. Yet we had not thought anyone in Fleet was as capable of remote viewing as Maclairn's natives."

"There's a lot about me that you don't know," he declared, dismayed by the confirmation that they were aware not only of Maclairn's existence, but of its people's psi powers.

"So it seems," she agreed. "But it would be to your advantage for us to know it, Terry, if you are what you say you are." Incredibly, she continued, "We have no wish to treat an innocent person as we would someone who meant harm to Maclairn."

"I have nothing to hide on that score. My job is to guard it from harm."

"Will you allow me to probe your mind, then? I am unwilling to do so by force, which would be unethical. But I am not sure just what we should do with you, and it will help if I can evaluate your background."

Terry saw no reason to refuse. She appeared to have more psi ability than he did and could probably sense much of what he was thinking in any case; he had not yet been taught how to conceal thoughts that were backed by emotion. As to Maclairn's secret, she evidently already knew enough to make resistance pointless, regardless of how she had obtained it.

"Sit down, Terry," Laesara instructed, "and relax as you would for mind training. I will not hurt you, but it may be frightening; the mentors use less powerful techniques than mine."

He did not like to think how the people aboard this ship had gained knowledge of mentors' techniques. Had some of those on Earth been seized in the short time since he and Kathryn had left? They would have died rather than submit to examination by outsiders not already aware of their capabilities—had they been forced by captors with greater powers than their own, captors less concerned about ethics than this strange woman who he sensed was sincere? Despairingly he sat back in one of the circular chairs, thinking that if the secret was out, if it had gone beyond the small group of opponents who were as eager to keep it from the public as Maclairn was, then all that had been accomplished toward gradual acceptance of psi had been futile.

And then Laesara's mind touched his and it was like Jessica's probe in the Ritual, but even more overwhelming. All that he had ever thought, or done, or hoped for was being drawn from him; his whole life surged into memory, from his childhood on Earth to his hacking days, his training in Fleet, the years of exploring space . . . Aldren . . . Tristan . . . *Promise* . . . Jessica's fears . . . and above all, Kathryn. Kathryn, and his unborn son. God, she would know soon that he was missing—she would be frantic . . . he had left without saying goodbye. He was not sure how or when he could get back to her, and he did not know how he could ever keep the pledges he had made as a Steward of the Flame. He saw the flame before him now, as it had been last night, but now it was about to consume him. He cried out in agony, not physical pain, but the anguish of finding himself engulfed by more emotion than he could bear. . . .

"Terry!" Laesara grasped his hand, and he knew she had perceived his entire life history, up to and including the Ritual . . . oh God, the secret of the Ritual that he had sworn never to reveal . . .

"I am sorry, Terry," she said gently. "You are more fully aware of telepathy than I expected you to be—with most of your people the probe would have remained beneath the level of consciousness." And silently, reflectively: *I am sorry for more than that, because you have acted bravely in defense of Maclairn and you do not deserve the fate in store for you.*

He was too dazed to respond. "Rest now," she said. "You have had two major shocks since you last slept, and more are ahead. I must consult my colleagues about what is to be done."

Alone again, Terry gradually regained control of himself. Somehow he must devise a way to let Maclairn know of the threat. His inner compulsion to come here *had* been purposeful—he had to believe that, or what good had all the mind training and preparation done?

These people were not spies or smugglers. Now that he had time to think, he realized that there was just one thing they could be: members of another secret group with psi capability. It was not improbable that there had been a second, independent discovery of the mind powers Ian Maclairn had developed; after all, if they were indeed the next step in human evolution, they might well have been discovered simultaneously on more than one world. The League had not known about Maclairn until recently, and still wouldn't know about any similar groups that might exist elsewhere.

But this group had technology far in advance of Maclairn's. It could not be just a small settlement on an isolated world. One way or another it had acquired enough power to build and operate a gigantic starship without being detected, and had learned not merely that Maclairn existed, but its location—something neither the League officials nor the mentors on Earth knew in terms of star charts. What were its people doing, lurking near Maclairn? Were they hoping to make peaceful contact without being turned back by Fleet—or were they planning an attack? There was no reason to think their motives were as benevolent as those of the Maclairnans, who were making great sacrifices to offer new capabilities to humankind. They might well want to maintain a monopoly on psi and use it to dominate the League.

He *must* contact Fleet, or else the mentors. There was no chance he would get anywhere near the comm room of this ship, much less of his own, considering that he was confined in the compartment not merely by a door, but by an airlock. Was there a remote chance that telepathy could reach far enough? Corwin had said it might. Jessica had long sensed that something was out here, something she'd hoped he could find, and if she was aware that he was missing she'd be alert to any sign of his whereabouts. Terry closed his eyes and threw all the force he could muster into a desperate call. *Jessica . . . Jessica . . . hear me! You were right! There's a huge starship, Fleet must be warned. . . .* Over and over, until he was dizzy and exhausted—*Jessica! Jessica . . . Tristan . . . Kathryn. . . .* Surely Kathryn could sense his mind-touch— their bond was unbreakable, even though she wasn't especially psi-gifted. *Oh, God, Kathryn . . . hear me, please hear even if you can't answer. . . .*

The airlock cycled again. He looked up and Laesara was standing near him, the grey eyes in her masked face displaying evident sympathy. "They cannot hear you," she said. "Their psi power is not yet sufficient to cross that distance, nor is yours."

Since there was no denying that, he didn't answer.

"Fate has taken a tragic turn," she said sadly, sitting down in the chair beside his. "We both had the same aim— to warn intruders away from Maclairn. What you and Jessica sensed in the past was not precognition; we have been here all along. You sought us because you believed us to be an interloper, and when our instruments detected your unknown ship, we believed the same of you and pursued you. If we had known you were from Fleet we would not have shown ourselves. We did so thinking it was safe— an explorer or smuggler would have assumed our starship belonged to Fleet and would have heeded any warning we issued. By the time we heard your hail and knew you would not, it was too late. You had seen us."

"Did you expect we would never see you until you invaded us?" Terry demanded. "When you say you aim to warn away intruders, I assume you mean ships that might interfere with your taking over Maclairn. So you are not all-powerful. If you should succeed in defeating *Shepard*, other ships will come."

"Oh, Terry. We mean no harm to *Shepard*, any more than to Maclairn itself. We are not going to take it over. Our existence must never be known. But since there is a remote chance that Fleet might fail to keep all other ships away, we are stationed here as backup, to guard it with superior technology, because Maclairn is far more important in the scheme of things than you know."

"I don't understand," he protested. "If you're our allies, why conceal yourselves from us?"

She hesitated. "We have decided to tell you the truth, Terry Radnor. It might be better not to, since it will put you in the extraordinary position of knowing a secret with which no one else among your people has ever been burdened. Yet having judged you, I believe you would prefer that to facing your fate in ignorance."

An extraordinary position ... an extraordinary destiny, then? Terry's heart beat faster. Aldren's precognition had been real. . . .

Laesara had picked up the thought. *Aldren foresaw that your life would be extraordinary? Oh, they are as advanced as we have hoped they would be, the mentors ... but you have misinterpreted his vision, and I must now set you straight, painful though it will be for us both.*

"There is no way to say this but the direct way," she told him. "We are not what you think we are. You are the first of your race to experience what millions have longed to experience throughout many centuries of the past, for you are in open contact with people you would call aliens."

44

"ALIENS? EXTRATERRESTRIAL ALIENS, you mean? Come on, you don't expect me to believe that," Terry protested. "It won't wash—it's been known for a long time now that there aren't any."

"I realize you may need convincing," Laesara agreed, "since you are the first person to be shown that there are."

"That doesn't make sense—lots of people used to claim they were shown. What does make sense is that you probed my mind and found it was an old fantasy of mine, something I wished were true even though I knew it wasn't. I'm not that easily fooled, Laesara."

"Why do you think this room has an airlock, Terry? Didn't it strike you as surprising that the air pressure in a room would be different from that in the rest of the ship?"

"You might put poisonous chemicals in here sometimes. Or biohazards."

"We might, but since there are none in here now we would leave the lock open. In fact, it is in use because the atmosphere in the rest of the ship is unbreathable for some species, including yours and mine. Many of our compartments have airlocks because we are not all of the same ancestry."

For the first time it occurred to Terry that there might possibly be some truth is this. But . . . abducted by aliens! That surely couldn't be happening to him. Being abducted by aliens had been dismissed as a joke for more than a hundred years, much longer than that by scientists.

"You're not planning to invade Earth, are you?" he asked, not meaning the question to be taken seriously.

But he sensed when Laesara replied that she was deadly serious. "Our goal is to protect Earth and its colonies, which requires that we protect Maclairn—for it is the key to your people's future. If Maclairn's mission fails, your race will lose the place among us that has awaited you for millennia, and eventually it will die out. The stakes are high, Terry. High enough to justify sacrifices."

He regarded her with astonishment. "As you now know, I'm pledged to protect Maclairn and its goals. If what you say is true I'm certainly not going to argue with it."

"You may, when you find out what is ahead of you."

"I guess that means it's something I won't like," Terry said, regaining his balance. "And so I've got no reason to believe you're not just feeding me a nice story to make me go along. If you were really alien you wouldn't be so—human, or speak our language so well."

"If you need more proof," Laesara said, "I will remove my mask."

He had assumed that she wore the mask and voluminous clothing so that he would be unable to identify her if the ship's crew was ever arrested. The idea that she might be truly alien, with alien features, was somehow shocking, for she did seem human. It chilled him to think that perhaps she was not.

Slowly, Laesara pulled off first the mask and then her headscarf and gloves. "I am not green," she said, smiling, "but as you can see, I am not of any race originally from Earth. And as you may have suspected, my voice is synthesized. My vocal chords are not like yours, and my eyes, in which I am wearing contact lenses, are gold."

Terry gasped. Her skin too was golden—not golden brown, but a light, translucent gold that almost glowed. Her features were unmistakably inhuman, with a small flat nose, wide mouth, and receding chin. Her hair was sparse, white, and fuzzy, with gold scalp showing through. And she had seven fingers on each hand.

"I will not introduce you to the others aboard," she said, "for I do not think you would wish to see them. Their resemblance to your species is less than mine. On the other hand, our team does include people who can pass as Earthborn. They live on your worlds as our agents, from whom we learn about your customs and your progress."

"Agents on our worlds? For how long?" Terry demanded.

"Since the dawn of your history, Terry, from time to time. Not continuously until the twentieth century, when you first entered space."

"The UFO reports were true, then."

"Not literally—we shield our landers from sight. And certainly there were no abductees. But the truth became established in the collective unconscious of your race through latent psi, and metaphorical conceptions of us spread by means of unconscious telepathy."

"I once told Aldren that the search for aliens in itself was a metaphor," Terry recalled.

"And you were right, as far as specific ideas of us were concerned. Nevertheless, humans have always sensed that there is sapient life throughout the universe, because there *is*. Just as in remote viewing you perceive reality, even when the details are obscure and sometimes misleading."

"Do your people have a name?" he inquired.

"You can refer to us as the Elders, for that is what we are. We are a federation of many races older than yours that evolved on different planets."

"But we've explored thousands of solar systems, and we've never found any inhabited planets," Terry protested.

"No, because our technology shields them from sight, shields whole solar systems so that your instruments cannot detect them—not only ours, but those of younger races."

"Why? Why do you hide from us? Are you afraid we'd attack you?"

"Your technology is not sufficiently advanced to be a threat—and in any case we have been hiding from you since prehistoric times. Fear is not the reason." Laesara's voice was soft, but her eyes penetrated him. "Now we reach the crux of the matter, Terry. We hide because it is essential to your welfare that our existence not be known to you. Those of us who visit immature civilizations—yours, and those younger than yours—swear to die rather than reveal it. Were a young race to learn how far behind it is, it would never evolve as it should; it would make no independent progress and would have nothing to contribute to the Federation when old enough to join. Its people would not develop the qualities they need to hold their own among older races; they would be like retarded children."

"Scientists used to believe older civilizations could teach us."

"So we too once thought, long ago. But it does not work like contact between different cultures of a single human species." Laesara's feelings became very intense. "It is important—tremendously important—that you understand this. Are you absorbing it?"

Terry nodded. With awe, he was absorbing more than she was saying aloud. Telepathically, she was projecting her conviction that revelation of the Elders' existence would bring about the extinction of humankind.

"There are worlds where civilization has died or is dying because we made ourselves known to them too soon," she went on. "It is the heaviest burden on our conscience and it must never happen again. We never interfere with the progress of a young race; we only observe. We take no action unless its actual survival is threatened by some external force, and then only subtly, so its people never know we did so."

"Yet you say you're guarding Maclairn."

"Yes. You see, Terry, we observe younger worlds throughout their people's evolution and never provide any assistance, because that would do more harm than good. But obviously, for each human species there comes a time when it is mature—when it is ready to join the Federation on equal terms. And for Earth that time is not far off."

"You're about to—contact us?" Excitement rose in Terry. Was he the first real contactee? Had fate chosen him to serve as their ambassador, as Kathryn had become ambassador to the League?

"Soon, as we reckon time," Laesara said, "though it is still several of your generations away. The final criterion has not yet been met anywhere but on Maclairn."

"Our mind powers? Psi?" That was understandable; the public wouldn't be able to deal with the existence of the Maclairnans, let alone of Elders with even greater powers. Besides, until the majority became telepathic enough to sense the feelings of aliens, they couldn't be trusted to mingle peacefully with them.

"Without those powers you would be viewed as dangerously deficient by the citizens of our worlds," Laesara agreed. "What Maclairn is doing by spreading acceptance of psi is essential. Yet as you know, there is opposition that means danger both to the Maclairnans and to the plan. If that plan fails, your people's evolution will be set back for centuries, and may even be permanently halted, because Earth's civilization is now dying and the colonies are not strong enough to forge ahead alone. In many, their desire to progress has been lost."

Puzzled, Terry protested, "How can you know anything about Maclairn? You can't have an agent in place; it wasn't discovered until a short time ago and you couldn't have guessed what was going on there any sooner. And the colonists have known each other for generations; they would recognize a stranger even if one could have been gotten in."

Laesara explained, "We investigate odd occurrences, such as the crew of a private starship claiming it has been hunting for aliens. We traced *Promise* to the Maclairn Foundation and our agent at League headquarters probed the returnees from the first expedition, posing as a psychiatrist verifying their report of what they had seen. He also observed Aldren and Roanna, though it would have been too risky to let himself be noticed by them; and later he monitored the contract negotiations."

"Did Kathryn—our ambassador—meet him?" Terry asked in surprise.

"Yes, but neither she nor anyone else suspected that he was not what he seemed. That you are Kathryn's lifemate and captain of *Promise* came as a shock to me when I probed you—it makes what I must do even more painful for me than it would have been otherwise. But I am sworn to put the best interests of Earth and its colonies above all personal considerations."

Terry frowned. Several times she had implied that some mysterious ordeal awaited him, and by now he realized that she was not threatening him, but trying to soften the blow. Quickly, wanting to learn as much as possible about the Elders' interest in Maclairn, he asked, "Aren't there any people elsewhere with psi powers?"

"Yes, but they are scattered, as they have been throughout history. Only Maclairn has a psi-based culture at Earth's technological level that can thrive and lead. A major step in evolution must start somewhere, and for your people it has started there. Ian Maclairn's vision was on target. The Stewards of the Flame are indeed stewards of the key—the determining factor in Earth's eligibility to join us and claim its rightful heritage."

"You know even about the Stewards of the Flame?"

"Our agent saw records of the starship that Maclairn's founders hijacked, so we know it was originally chartered to transport a group by that name from Undine. We did not know the name is still used until I drew it from your mind." Soberly she added, "I sensed then that you are worthy of it, both by Maclairn's standards and by ours."

God, Terry thought, Aldren had been right about his

extraordinary destiny, if it was his role to be the go-be-tween. How excited the mentors were going to be. . . .

Laesara, grasping his thought, looked at him sorrow-fully. "You have not understood what I've been telling you, Terry. The mentors must not know. No one must know, the mentors least of all since it would affect their actions and thus constitute interference on our part."

Reluctantly Terry conceded, "I guess I do see. I won't tell them yet, if it would do harm."

"But they would draw it from your mind sooner or later, however hard you tried to conceal it. This would be true if you knew no more of us than the existence of our ship, else I would not have burdened you with additional knowledge."

"I don't think they'd believe me anyway if I said I'd been in contact with aliens."

"They know you, and know you are not mentally ill, and unconscious telepathy would reveal that what they sensed in your mind was authentic. Nor could you keep it from Kathryn, and she too would be unable to hide it from the mentors. Even our agents dare not interact with them."

"What can I do, then? I don't want to upset the process you say is necessary."

There were tears in Laesara's eyes. "The problem is what you *cannot* do, Terry Radnor," she said sadly. "You cannot be allowed to go back to Maclairn, ever again."

45

STUNNED, TERRY STARED at her. Laesara had seemed so gentle, so concerned with ethics, that he had stopped fear-ing for his life. If the future of humankind depended on sacrificing it he supposed he'd be willing, but he couldn't see that it did. "Are you just going to kill me in cold blood?" he demanded incredulously.

"Kill you? Of course not," Laesara said, obviously horrified. "We do not kill, except when it can save innocent lives that are clearly endangered."

"Well, you'll have to," Terry declared, "if you want to stop me from going back to Maclairn. It's my world now, the place where I belong. I'm pledged twice over to defend it. Kathryn is there, and she's carrying my child."

"I know," Laesara said unhappily. "That is why the irony of our seeking each other was so tragic. But you have no choice—you have had none since you sighted our ship, nor have we. I do not expect you to renounce your life on Maclairn willingly, but it is not up to you."

"You can't confine me in this sealed compartment forever." Privately, he wondered. The ship was large enough to contain many compartments; they could easily spare one, and with a poisonous atmosphere outside, he could not escape from it. His suit and helmet had been removed.

"We can't," she agreed. "You will be taken to another world."

"One of yours?"

"No, we have an inviolable policy against that, for your own good. Great though your psi powers are in comparison to the majority of your people, they are not yet sufficiently developed. You would be viewed as handicapped."

"Where, then? You can't keep me on a human world in anything short of a hidden high-security prison. Fleet has a presence everywhere, and I can prove my identity."

"Your identity will be changed, Terry—physically, even to the level of your DNA. And the world to which you go will not offer you a chance to leave it."

Angrily Terry protested, "You can't do this! You said you were going to consult your colleagues about what to do, which means there were alternatives. I'll bet not everyone agreed that I can't keep a secret from the mentors. I believe I can, and what's more, I believe *they* could— I don't think it would create any sort of disaster if they knew about you Elders—"

"Oh, it would, Terry—absolutely, it would. It would influence all their decisions, and they would lose heart, knowing that other races surpass them. They would lose the will to work as hard as they must to move humankind ahead. Our opinion is unanimous on that, because it has been proven by past experience on worlds that didn't make it."

Terry was uncomfortably aware that Kathryn had speculated that the arrival of aliens would cause Earth's civilization to collapse, and Tristan had said early theorists had thought so. It might be true of open contact, but surely not if it was secret from all but a few trustworthy people. And yet . . . what would Fleet do if they knew the Elders were guarding Maclairn with technology superior to its own? Would the crew of *Shepard* be as vigilant as they were now, or would it seem like pointless effort? Might not the mentors react in the same way?

Perhaps so. Yet he could not give up everything he had ever cared about when the risk was so uncertain. There had to be another answer. "What alternatives were considered for disposing of me?" he asked.

"A few people thought your memory of us should be erased."

"If it's the only option besides leaving Maclairn, I guess I'd pick that."

"But it is not an option, except in the eyes of those who would countenance depriving you of all that means most to you. We can wipe memories, but not selectively— you would lose the personal ones you value, including your love for Kathryn and for Maclairn itself. To choose it would be self-defeating."

Terry nodded miserably. "Can't you create some sort of hypnotic compulsion to keep me from thinking about you, then?"

"Not without destroying your mind. If it was made deep enough to work, you would end up insane. And in any case, to take away your free will would be worse than killing."

He couldn't contest that. Laesara continued, "My colleagues and I met to decide where you will be sent. The other issue was whether you should be informed about us. I maintained that you should be, because otherwise you would have found yourself forcibly transported to another world without knowing why and would think you were the victim of pointless cruelty. And also, Terry, because I believe you have a right to know the end your misfortune serves. It may be some small compensation to be aware of what lies ahead for humankind, and realize that its struggle to progress is not futile, as too many of your people suppose in view of Earth's problems."

"I'd rather know than not know," Terry agreed. "But I can't pretend I believe what you're doing to me is unavoidable, or that it's fair."

"It is not a matter of fairness. Countless people over the ages have suffered greater losses than yours to get humankind this far, both your own people and ours. Some of our agents have sacrificed their lives to prevent the disclosure you think would be harmless—there was a woman several centuries back, for example, who allowed herself to be burned as a witch rather than reveal that she was alien. In the light of what is past, we cannot afford to take chances now."

Terry was silent for a long time, coming to terms with defeat. Finally he said, "I can't accept exile, Laesara. You can take me away from Maclairn—there's no way I can physically resist. But as long as I'm alive, I'll search for a way to get back. And someday, one way or another, I'll find one."

"You will try," she agreed. "You are not the sort of man who would give up, which is why we must take care to eliminate all avenues of escape. But someday you will find new meaning in your life, Terry. I have talked to members of many races on hundreds of worlds, and I know an achiever when I see one. I wish you well."

She meant it, Terry knew. He sensed telepathically

that she grieved for him. Ruefully, he recalled having stated that he would not argue if asked to make sacrifices for Maclairn's sake. But he had imagined doing something spectacularly heroic, or becoming a martyr like Corwin. To let both Fleet and the mentors think he'd failed them—to simply disappear, when it was so *unnecessary*. . . .

Not until later, when the Elders brought a gurney sealed against the alien atmosphere and prepared to take him for physical alteration, did he really believe it was happening.

The ship was well equipped for modifying bodies since they had altered some of their own agents who were almost but not quite human. Nothing of his former life was to remain with him—not his skin color, his facial structure, or even his voice—and certainly not any of his possessions. Anticipating this, just before they came for him Terry took the tiny flame pin from his uniform's lapel, carefully reclosed its clasp, and swallowed it.

46

LYING FLAT IN the gurney, its airtight bubble feeling more like a coffin lid than a shield against the poisonous air outside it, he felt terror beyond anything he had ever imagined. They were about to kill him—not his entire body, to be sure, but everything physical that made him who he was. They had sworn that they would not alter his mind, but how could he be sure that it would remain intact after such a drastic change to his self-image? After he had lost all tangible evidence of once having had a career, friends, a home world, a lifemate?

The worst part was not the prospect of surgery; Terry knew, after all, that he would not suffer even if it involved pain. Nor was it the idea of exile from Maclairn, to which he was determined to make his way back even if it took a lifetime. The true agony was picturing Kathryn, left to mourn, not knowing what had become of him . . . bearing their child alone, a child who would grow up without a dad. Never to see her again, never to hold her in his arms and merge his mind and body with hers . . . he did not think he could bear that! He thought he would go mad.

"Is there no way you could get a message to her?" he had asked Laesara. "I know you couldn't tell her what's really happened to me, but just to let her know I still love her, and that I'm all right—"

"That would not be kind, Terry. It is better for her to believe you are dead, as she will when your ship fails to return. How could it be otherwise unless you had deserted her? And she must be free to love again someday. You would not want her to be alone forever."

But she would be, Terry thought in anguish—just as he would. They were committed to each other, bonded. Surely Laesara, as a telepath, must understand that. She had condemned them both to loneliness for the rest of their lives. *Oh, God, Kathryn . . . Kathryn. . . .* It was his last thought as he went under the anesthetic, knowing he would wake in different form.

When he regained consciousness he sensed that time had passed; he could not tell whether it had been a short time or a long one. He looked at his arms and they were an even paler white than the normal untanned skin tone maintained during a life spent mostly in space and under domes—almost as if he were an albino. Amazingly, his missing fingers had been restored. He feared he would scarcely recognize his face in a mirror, though they assured him that only minor things had been done to it. More drastic had been the surgery to his vocal chords to prevent voice recognition. There were, he was told, slight changes in his DNA, for skin color and to change his dark brown hair to light blond. They had also changed his fingerprints and hand-veins but had been unable to do anything about his iris or retinal pattern; even if he were to obtain an eye scan, however, the other alterations would preclude its acceptance as proof of his original identity.

There were no remaining scars of any kind, and he realized that they must be even more skilled in psychic healing than the mentors. Nevertheless, he felt vague pain all over his body. He couldn't seem to turn it off, and feared they had taken even his mind-control capability until it dawned on him that the pain stemmed from his emotions rather than from physical damage. He was offered food, the first since coming aboard, but could not keep it down.

No matter, they informed him silently. *You have been given intravenous nourishment that will provide you with energy for several more days.* Terry thought, with sadness, that if his bodily functions had been working normally the flame pin he had hoped to retrieve might be gone by now. He had so wanted to keep some small trace of Maclairn. . . .

Laesara was waiting for him in the compartment with the airlock, which he supposed must be the front room of her private quarters. The viewscreen, previously dark, was now on, and he looked out at a cloud-covered world, a featureless off-white streaked with gray.

"This is the planet Ciencia," she told him. "You will not like it, for we necessarily chose an unpleasant world, one to which neither mentors nor Fleet will ever come. In this colony there is an embargo on all offworld commerce— its people do not wish their culture to be contaminated with ideas of which they disapprove. They are devoted to science, which is why they gave their world a name that means "science" in one of Earth's ancient languages. They believe that non-scientific speculation—including religion, mythology, and metaphysics, as well as most art and literature—has retarded human progress and is the source of Earth's problems. This is nonsense, as I'm sure you know; but for centuries there have been people who felt that way and once interstellar colonization became possible they were able to create a society from which all references to such ideas have been systematically excluded."

"How could they?" Terry protested. "The knowledgebase includes everything important ever written on those topics."

"Not their version—it is heavily censored. Their Net is monitored in case anybody develops thoughts that are frowned upon. Their only ansible is restricted to government use. As far we can tell, they have succeeded in wiping out half of Earth's heritage."

He recoiled in dismay. He had read widely in the standard knowledgebase during his spare time on various worlds and aboard *Shepard*; the thought of censoring it seemed like sacrilege. Though he had not been raised to believe in any of Earth's ancient religions, he respected them—and certainly he admired imaginative literature. "The whole knowledgebase is available on incoming ships," he pointed out.

"Starships are not allowed to approach; officially there are only local ships for mining nearby asteroids, though there are, of course, smugglers."

"It's against League law to turn away Fleet starships," Terry declared, "and Fleet has bases on all colonized worlds."

"Not if they forgo its protection," Laesara said. "Fleet keeps an eye on Ciencia to make sure it is not building up a military force capable of attacking other colonies, but it does not land there or even orbit."

On the verge of asking why out of all the colonies in the League he was being sent to such a repressive society, Terry choked back the words. It was obvious why. If no starships ever came, there was no way he could ever leave. Without either a Fleet base or access to an ansible, he could not report his situation. And if all ideas considered unscientific were excluded, the mere idea of psi would be anathema to these people—he would never be able to connect with anyone. . . .

Laesara met his eyes. "I see you understand," she said. "But Terry, there could be more reasons why we have chosen to send you to a world like this. Think about it. You have plenty of time ahead for thinking."

He sensed that there was something she wished to tell him, but could not say, could not even let him perceive telepathically. Some mitigating factor in what seemed like the worst possible situation. Did she *want* him to escape? Or was this just a strategy to avoid leaving him without hope?

"Your name is now Terry Rivera," she continued. "An identity has been created for you in the League database, which of course is accessed by the government here through its one ansible, and your implanted ID chip now matches it, showing you to be a native citizen of Ciencia. The biometric characteristics it lists are those we have given you. By profession you are a computer programmer, but at present you are unemployed. You have enough credits banked to live on until you find a job."

"Do I just appear out of nowhere?" he inquired bitterly.

"You will be left in a deserted forest area, an environment with which I believe you can cope since you have had wilderness camping experience. Your story is that you have camped for some time near an outlying settlement, but are now almost out of funds and need to find work in the city again."

"It looks like wet weather for camping," he said, inspecting the world on the viewscreen more carefully. "I don't see any breaks in those clouds."

"There are no breaks," Laesara agreed. "Ciencia has one hundred percent cloud cover."

"All the time? What keeps it warm enough to be habitable?"

"Most of it isn't. Long-term terraforming is underway, and meanwhile high technology makes living in the region of the colony possible, if not comfortable."

"Oh, my God," Terry whispered, stricken not by the prospect of being cold, but by the agonizing realization that once down there, he would never again see the stars.

"You will be provided with a smartphone that will direct you to the city," Laesara continued. "You have wit and courage enough to make a life for yourself, Terry. I do not say it will be an easy life, but I believe that ultimately you will find it tolerable."

That, Terry thought, was impossible. How could it be anything but torment when his career, his lifemate, his identity, and even the sight of the stars had been taken from him?

"You are still yourself," Laesara assured him. "Physical characteristics are superficial; your true identity is in your mind, and that, we have not touched. I will not see you again, but I will always remember you. Godspeed, Terry Rivera."

He did his best not to respond telepathically, not wanting her to sense how scared he was. So far, anger had carried him through. If he let himself accept her sympathy, he might give way to grief and fear.

Part Four: Ciencia

47

IT COULD NOT be true, Terry thought as he watched the Elders' lander lift, hover barely higher than the trees, and then simply disappear. Yesterday in terms of waking awareness—though it might have been longer while he was unconscious—he had had everything: captaincy of a starship, a promising career, friends he could connect with, a newly-adopted home world, a wife to whom he was irrevocably bonded, an unborn son . . . and a purpose, a cause that had become central to his life. Now he had nothing, not even his own full name.

He surveyed his surroundings with growing dismay. He had been abandoned in a frigid wilderness, with nothing in sight but an endless forest of tall, dark evergreens—genetically engineered, no doubt, as they could not be native to a world like this, nor could any normal tree withstand perpetual sunless cold. Presumably they were grown for lumber and he was in the middle of a closely-planted stand. There was no undergrowth; the ground was covered with a thin layer of dry snow. Automatically, he adjusted his body temperature, realizing that without the mind training he would have had no chance to survive in such a place.

The sky, of course, was obscured by clouds—low, uniform clouds of dull gray. Neither sun nor stars would ever be visible here. He doubted that he would get used to it.

He was wearing appropriate clothes for the climate: pants, a thick shirt and a heavy hooded jacket, all made of top quality thermal synthetics, as were his socks and gloves. They had been given to him just before he boarded the lander, and at first he had wondered how the Elders happened to have human clothing of this sort aboard their starship. Then he'd remembered that they had recently observed Ciencia. These must be the clothes their agent had worn; that man must have come by the same route, for the pilot had informed him telepathically that they could land no closer to the city. Their ships were shielded through some unimaginable technology that made them invisible both in space and in the atmosphere, but it could not be used close to the ground.

He had been provided with a pack that held a tarp and sleeping bag, also of the most advanced lightweight materials; a canteen; and a small supply of concentrated food. He was not hungry. Perhaps the intravenous nourishment he had received was not yet depleted, but on the other hand, he was too deeply stricken by the horror of his situation to have any desire for food. He wanted only to crawl into the sleeping bag and sleep, perhaps forever, shutting out the sight of this dismal world and the knowledge that he could never leave it. . . .

At least he had been told he could never leave it. But that was unacceptable. He wanted to live, and he could not live with the belief that everything that had ever mattered to him was lost forever. He was pledged to Maclairn. Someday, somehow, he would get back to Maclairn, Terry vowed. Only that goal would give him the strength to get through one day at a time.

Taking out the smartphone he had been given, he consulted the map it displayed. He couldn't use the phone to call for help in an emergency since it would be unwise to attract attention to himself, but its GPS could guide him to the nearest road. The city was, he estimated, about a three-day hike from where he was now, assuming days not much shorter than he was used to. Hopefully the effort of getting there would enable him to shut out all other thoughts.

For about five hours, according to the smartphone's clock which might or might not show hours somewhere near Earth-standard in length, it worked. He allowed himself to be aware only of the snow-covered terrain immediately before him, putting one foot in front of another in unbroken rhythm, slowing his pace when his energy lagged but never pausing to rest. If he rested he would remember where he was, and why; and if he did that, he might be tempted to rest too long. It was too cold for much rest, despite his ability to control body temperature; and so he kept going, glad that the increasing pain of his muscles required him to focus on banishing the physical aspect of his suffering.

But the time came when he noticed that it was almost dark. Though there was no visible sunset on Ciencia, the fading of the already-dim light reminded him that the planet rotated like any other. At night he would have to sleep, or at least try to get some sleep, which he knew would be difficult despite his longing for it. He would also have to refill the canteen. Reluctantly he stopped and hollowed out a place in the snow, lining it with the tarp. There was no wood for a fire; the sparse-limbed trees had no low branches. But his pack proved to contain a battery-powered pot that enabled him to melt snow for drinking water.

Not daring to think about the future, he could no longer avoid looking back. God, Terry thought, the last time he had slept, as distinguished from being sedated, was the night before the Ritual! The highest point of his life . . .followed almost immediately by the lowest. The memory of his hand touching Jessica's in flame, the elation he had believed would always remain with him, was now a searing torment. He had been willing to be burned if it came to that; he would have died for Maclairn, as he had known underneath that he might when he pursued the intruder in *Skywalker*—but not this. Not this half-death to which the well-intentioned pursuit had led him. None of them had conceived of a price this high for attempting to defend Maclairn.

What would they think when he didn't return? They would blame his ship, Terry thought miserably. *Skywalker* was experimental, and he had falsely reported a problem with its instruments; they would assume it had killed him and would not send another. That beautiful ship, so well suited to Maclairn's needs—the Elders couldn't use it, they might even destroy it. . . . His eyes filled with tears, and then suddenly he was crying. He could not cry for Kathryn, not yet; his feelings about her went too deep. He would lose control once he let himself weep for her. Yet his emotions surged to the point where he could not keep them in, and so he wept for *Skywalker*.

48

HE SLEPT THE dreamless sleep of sheer exhaustion, rousing several times during the night but using his mind training to calm his body's startled reaction to the remembrance of where he was. When he came fully awake he thought it must be close to dawn, or what passed for dawn under the heavy cloud cover. He lay in the insulated sleeping bag for a long time, waiting for the sky to lighten further—and then he realized that it never would. Whether the sun was dimmer than Earth's or the clouds thicker, he did not know, but he wasn't going see what he thought of as full daylight.

Terry forced himself to eat something—and then was sorry, because having been empty for some time while he was intravenously nourished, his stomach rebelled. The local water to which he wasn't yet accustomed also caused trouble; during the next few hours cramps forced him to stop several times. Dull pain remained afterward; he was able to manage it, of course, but ending the physical discomfort didn't help with his emotional anguish.

It began to snow. Except when bodily needs required stopping, he kept moving in the direction indicated by the smartphone's GPS. It would have been impossible to find his way on this world otherwise, with no stars to steer by and probably no magnetic pole. But, he recalled, it was not considered a habitable planet apart from the technology its colonists employed. Though that was true of quite a few colonized worlds, it seemed more incongruous on one with a breathable atmosphere than on those where people lived under domes.

He had no internal sense of the passage of time; there was no indication of midday and to him the day was just one long blur in any case. But when the sky seemed to be growing dimmer again he checked the smartphone clock and found that it was indeed shorter than a day on Earth—twenty-one hours, into which he judged it was divided, as in most colonies, so as to make the hours as close as possible to standard length. Whether the astronomical year was given significance in the local calendar he did not know. On Maclairn it wasn't, since there were no appreciable seasons and it was convenient to use Earth years for calculating ages and a historical timeline. It was unlikely, he thought, that there were seasons here, since he'd been told that it never got warm and if it were any colder everything would be frozen solid.

Toward nightfall he reached the road. He saw to his surprise that there were no trees on the other side of it; then he realized that it was a logging road and the area on that side had been clear cut, leaving a vast expanse of debris and stumps barely softened by the snow. There was no traffic, and there might not be any until the trees on his side were mature enough to harvest. It would be some distance yet before he encountered people, so there was no reason to push forward any farther before making camp for the night.

The absence of people ought not to be bothering him, Terry reflected. He had gone camping alone in the past and had enjoyed it. But that was before he had known what it was like to communicate telepathically. Now, he realized, he would be lonely whether or not in the company of others, for they wouldn't be telepathic; even those who were potentially psi-gifted wouldn't know how to connect. How could he endure going back to the isolation he had felt before meeting Aldren?

Aldren. Oh, God, whatever destiny Aldren had foreseen for him could scarcely have been this. *Why?* he thought in despair. If he had been meant to play some extraordinary part in furthering Maclairn's cause, why had fate taken away the opportunity? He hadn't retreated from it—on the contrary, he had committed himself irrevocably and risked his life to pursue what had appeared to be a threat to that cause, only to find that doing so had deprived him of the power to contribute to it in the future. Precognition wasn't predestination, Corwin had said, so Aldren's vision might not have been true; still he had assumed his own actions would have some positive effect on the outcome. He hadn't thought it would be better not to act.

After spreading out his tarp and boiling more water, he again attempted to eat, for he had been expending stored energy through volitional control of his metabolism, and he knew this would not be possible for much longer. He found that volitional control could also manage intestinal functions, which he had not thought to try earlier; Tristan had once said this was a form of advanced training he would be wise to go through. Necessity forced him to learn on his own, and by morning he was able to absorb enough nourishment to get through the coming day.

Until now he had given no thought to what awaited

him in the city, but before setting out along the road, he took time to investigate some of the information about it on the local Net. It was not promising. The city was large and starkly modern. He would be able to find his way around and to buy food, but where would he get shelter? He had no idea what the colony's custom was, but few allowed camping on public streets and it would be too cold to lie down without the sleeping bag. Presumably, the funds with which he had been provided could be accessed in the normal way, via his identity chip; if not, Laesara would have warned him. But it would be nearly dark before he arrived, and were there any hostels for vagrants? The people of most colonial cities, unlike those of Earth, were well settled in permanent quarters.

There was no use worrying, he decided, as he trudged along the deserted road. Why worry about anything, ever again? The worst had already happened to him. Assuming that they didn't shoot strangers, he had nothing left to lose.

Late in the day he came to the city's outskirts, where there was a crossroads with a few scattered small buildings. The other road must lead to the settlement from which he had supposedly come; it would be well to know something about what sort of place it was, so he zoomed out the map until he saw it, a mere dot labeled "Sawmill." There was only one city in the colony, which shared the name Ciencia with the planet, a fairly common arrangement among those he had visited that didn't yet have large populations. Outlying settlements often bore the names of their functions. so he judged that this one included not only the lumber mill to which the harvested logs were taken, but the homes of the people who worked there and the small businesses that served them. It would of course have a large power station to serve mill operations and wood-drying kilns, so there was no reason to think living conditions there would be primitive.

Nevertheless, the bleakness of the land around him made him think of it as a cold, desolate place.

As he was about to click away from the map he caught a glimpse of another dot on the opposite side of the large patch representing the city. Terry heart jumped as he saw that it was labeled "Spaceport."

Of course the planet had a spaceport; he had known that. As no starships were allowed to approach, there would be no shuttles; but Laesara had said that there was mining activity within the solar system. Even if its other planets weren't used, the asteroids would be mined, and in fact that would be more efficient than trying to extract scarce minerals from an inhospitable world such as this. If there was extensive asteroid mining, there would be a need for pilots—and he had plenty of skill in landing on asteroids.

Why, he wondered, had she overlooked this fact, letting him believe he would be forever confined to Ciencia's surface? To be sure, he could not escape from its solar system if there were no starships. He could not regain any of what he had lost. But he could at least be in space, doing work he had always liked, and the stars would be visible if not attainable.

The realization gave him a burst of energy, and he suddenly found he was hungry. The concentrated food was nearly gone—most of it wasted through sickness—and noticing a brightly-colored sign on one of the buildings he passed, he decided to test his credit. He went in and ordered a sandwich and soda, holding out his forearm confidently for his chip to be swiped. To his relief, the transaction went through.

After that, the hike into the city took less than two hours. Though it was nearly dark when he left the restaurant, the sky got brighter and brighter as he approached the urban area until it was illuminated by a reddish glow. The air, too, seemed warmer than it had further out. Skyglow, he realized: caused by the brilliant lighting of the streets and buildings, intensified by reflection from the low cloud cover and the snow at the city's perimeter. On Earth skyglow was considered pollution and efforts, not always successful, were made to reduce it; but here on this dark, cold world it was evidently embraced as comforting. They did not skimp on power.

He wondered what the colony's power source was. Not solar, obviously, nor could it be wind. Possibly hydro-electric or geothermal; but more likely they used fusion power. There were certainly plenty of uninhabited areas where they could put nuclear power plants, and they had no aversion to reliance on high technology.

Now sure of his credit, he was ready to seek lodging, but the smartphone had no listings for anything like a hotel. Since there were no other cities on the planet and no starships came, there would be no travelers. The streets were clean and uncluttered; there was plenty of groundcar traffic but no sign of pedestrians. He was conspicuous, he realized, and that was not good—he must find shelter soon. All the buildings were tall, not skyscrapers, but with enough stories for effective conservation of heat; there appeared to be no single-family residential district. Light sparkled on their many-windowed walls, which must be of some synthetic material providing better insulation than glass. Understandably, the builders had wanted to let in as much light as possible.

Terry hesitated. The information on the Net revealed that Ciencia had no slum district, and therefore no flop-houses—which was the case in virtually all colonies, he knew; the knowledge of cities he had formed on Earth was not applicable here. Finally he looked under "rent-als." He found he could check his credit balance through the smartphone, but comparing it with the amount deducted for the sandwich he had eaten, he could see that his funds would not cover many weeks of rent, not even the required minimum down payment.

Where did the asteroid miners stay when onworld?

he wondered. They wouldn't rent permanent quarters; there must be temporary ones at the spaceport. And there must be a late bus from the city, because spacers on shore leave always took full advantage of local nightlife. The spaceport was where he wanted to go in any case, so that the first thing in the morning he could start seeking employment. He took the first bus he saw marked "Terminal" and from there, after a three-hour wait, had no trouble getting onto the one headed for the port. His clothes and pack attracted some strange looks from the other passengers, who were a rougher lot than the Fleet crews he'd known and some of whom were drunk; but he was past caring. By tomorrow night he would be a pilot again, and at least part of the nightmare would be over.

49

THE CLERK AT the spaceport hotel asked no questions, payment in advance being the only requirement for admission. Terry had thought he could never take pleasure in anything again, but his expectations had been lowered to the point where a hot shower and a real bed were cause for rejoicing. He went to sleep almost immediately, and slept soundly.

But in the morning, while eating an exorbitantly-priced breakfast in the hotel's cafeteria, he began giving thought to reality. How was he going to prove that he was a qualified pilot? He didn't have a local license. He'd been informed that his identity record listed him as a computer programmer, and it certainly wouldn't say anything about piloting experience. He could not mention that he'd been a Fleet officer; they would check on that and be told he was lying. Moreover, he was identified as a native citizen of Ciencia who had never left the planet.

Maybe he was in too much of a hurry to get it settled. It would be better to wait until he could hack his record, which he was surely capable of doing. But he couldn't do it with a smartphone; he'd need a more powerful computer than that. He could get a high-end tablet—but no, assuming that he had enough credits to buy it, which was unlikely, he wouldn't have any left to rent quarters. The wise course would be to get a programming job and use a company computer; he knew how to cover his traces—but he could not bear the thought of such a long delay.

He sat toying with his food, trying to think of some way around the obstacles. It was not to be borne that a mere identity chip stood between him and the work he was best qualified for! A simple chip, tied to the central records at League headquarters ... oh, God. The identity records, unlike credit accounts, were at Headquarters. Ciencia's government merely accessed them through its one ansible; whatever updates there were would be sent back in message form, not incorporated. The ID database was not on the local Net, and therefore could not be hacked. Altering the local mirror file would not do any good, since it would be frequently refreshed.

Well, Terry decided, he would just have to brazen it out somehow, and hope they wouldn't bother to check his credentials. He had no other choice.

He went out into the gloomy weather and surveyed the spaceport. He had never seen such a collection of dilapidated-looking ships—but of course he had never been to a civilian port other than major commercial ones. Asteroid miners could hardly be expected to keep their ships up to Fleet standards. Presumably they were spaceworthy; if they weren't, a sizeable percentage of them would be newer. As he watched, a large one streaked in, hovered, and settled onto one of the empty pads. Terry's heart raced. In spite of the pain that would always be with him now, the mere sight of a ship in flight excited him.

Around the edges of the port were offices of the mining companies. Under the assumption that a large company would be the most likely to need more pilots, he entered the biggest and most impressive nearby building, Astra Rare Minerals, and approached its reception desk. "Where do I apply for a piloting job?" he asked.

"You don't," stated the woman at the desk flatly. "We're not hiring."

"Will you have any openings soon?"

"You can't know much about mining, or you wouldn't ask. We have a waiting list of flight training applicants years ahead, and you're too old to get on it—you should have signed up when you were fifteen like everybody else who wants to fly."

"I'm not a trainee—I've got a lot of experience landing on asteroids."

She regarded him in amazement. "Crashed your ship, did you? You should know better than to think any company is going to hire you after that. Don't waste my time."

Deflated, Terry turned and stalked out to the field. It was logical, now that he thought about it, for her to assume that an experienced pilot looking for a job must have been fired from his previous one. All the pilots in Ciencia's solar system worked at this spaceport—there was nowhere else an applicant could have come from.

Though he knew he would get the same reaction everywhere, he tried several more mining companies, and then began to notice that there were a lot more ships in evidence than appeared to belong to them. Many were prominently marked with company names, but most of those on the ground were smaller, unmarked, and in worse shape. He walked out to one on which some exterior maintenance was being done and greeted the mechanic.

"Nice ship you've got here," he said. It didn't look at all nice, but it would no doubt perform well enough in flight. "Is one of the pilots around?"

"I'm the pilot," the man replied. "I own it, I fly it. I'd hardly be trusted to work on it if I didn't."

"But you must have a crew."

"Miners, yes. You looking for a job?"

"Doing what?" Terry asked, sensing that to get an offer from the first ship owner he approached would be too good to be true.

"Digging out rock, of course, and loading it. What else would I be hiring for?"

"Actually," Terry said, "I hoped you might need a co-pilot. It's not really safe to fly without one, you know."

The pilot stared at him. "Well, that's an original approach. You suppose maybe I'm rich like the big companies, or the police? You can't have been in the business long if you think that."

"I've got a lot of flight experience."

"But not enough to keep from losing your ship, evidently."

On the verge of a question, Terry saw that it was stupid. The reason everyone assumed he was a failure seemed to be that pilots not employed by the big companies owned their ships. They were freelancers, small operators who couldn't afford to hire anyone but the laborers needed for mining. If a ship was destroyed in an accident its pilot, lacking cash to replace it, might hope to work for someone else—but such opportunities were apparently rare.

"It was a while back," he said, realizing that any recent losses would be common knowledge, "and it wasn't my fault, just a bad break. You know anybody who needs help?"

"As a matter of fact I do," the pilot said. "Renssalaer's relief pilot got injured last week and he's looking for a temporary replacement. He's due in later today, if you want to stick around."

It was better than nothing. Terry spent the interminable wait time taking a closer look at the ships on the ground, assessing the differences from Fleet ships and realizing that he would have quite a lot to get used to. It also dawned on him that asteroid mining was hard physical work and pilots would undoubtedly be expected to do their share of it when not actually flying. It was a step down from being captain of a starship, but at least he would be in space. He couldn't face life on this world without that. If the piloting job didn't last he would sign on as a miner rather than be grounded.

Renssalaer proved happy to see him and showed off his ship proudly, taking note of Terry's obvious familiarity with spacecraft. "I don't want it sitting idle while I'm onworld," he said. "The only way to survive in this business is to keep bringing in ore, but I've got a family and I want some time with them. We'll make a few trips together so I can check you out, and then if I like what I see, you can go out on your own when my next kid's due."

Surprisingly, he had not asked for details about Terry's experience. He seemed willing to dispense with formality, no doubt because it turned out that he couldn't afford to pay him and expected him to work for a share of the profits. As Terry would have been glad to work for food and shelter alone, this was not a problem. As they were signing the agreement, however, Renssalaer said, "I'll just have to swipe your ID for my log, it's the law, you know."

Drawing a deep breath, Terry offered his arm. Maybe the chip wasn't supposed to contain any actual employment history. . . .

"What the hell—" Renssalaer was staring at the screen of his smartphone. "You've got your nerve," he said in a cold voice. "Did you think you could get away with talking your way onto a ship without anybody seeing your record?"

"Look, I know it doesn't say I'm a pilot," Terry said. "I don't have a current license, but I'm as good as anyone who does have. The fact that I'm qualified as a programmer doesn't change that, and I can even do some AI maintenance, which would be an asset to you—"

"It doesn't matter what you can do," Renssalaer said angrily. "No one's going to let you anywhere near a mining ship, which you know perfectly well. Now get off mine, before I call the police and have you arrested for fraud."

"What fraud?" Terry protested. "I never said I was licensed, only that I'm experienced, which is true." But he couldn't prove it was true, he thought in dismay.

"It is fraud to conceal a relevant criminal charge," Renssalaer declared.

"Criminal charge? I don't know what you're talking about."

"Yes, you do. You're too intelligent not to be aware that no mining operator will hire or even carry a man who has stolen cargo, despite the charge having been dropped for lack of enough evidence. If you weren't guilty you'd have invoked your right to a trial."

Terry reached for the smartphone. "Let me see that! There's got to be a mistake."

"No mistake. ID records don't contain mistakes. Take a look."

It was there. "Police record, Planet Ciencia: Theft of platinum from mining ship, case dismissed due to insufficient evidence to convict."

Terry's head swam. It wasn't possible—Laesara would not have given him such a record. She had been sympathetic, had done only what was necessary to keep him from leaving the solar system. It had been made plain that no starship would ever be accessible; why bar him from the sky entirely?

Saying no more, he left the ship and stumbled dizzily back to the hotel, where he managed to reach his room and, in stunned misery, collapse on the bed. He had paid in advance for a second night, which was fortunate because he did not think he could summon the will to leave or even to walk to the lobby. He did not see how he could keep on functioning.

It was worse than before he'd believed he could fly again. At first, the shock of losing everything had virtually paralyzed him; he had done what survival required from mere instinct. He had not let himself think what would happen in the days and years to come. But now, he'd had a plan to salvage at least a little of his former life, to do something that would be tolerable, even though it could in no way compensate for what he could not hope to regain. It was like what he'd read of torture: if the victim was given relief from extreme torment and then faced with a repetition of what he'd been led to believe he'd escaped, he was more likely to crack than if the pressure had been continuous.

Why, *why* had the Elders done this to him? It served no purpose; it was sheer cruelty, and he had not thought them cruel, unfair though he believed their original decision to be. And he was helpless against it. He was barred not merely from flying, but from labor in the asteroid mines. He would never rise above the lowering overcast that hid even the sun.

The thoughts he had so far kept at bay now overwhelmed him. *Promise*, his pride in being captain, a position he'd believed would continue for years . . . Maclairn, where he had been happy, where he'd had real contact with people, where friends would soon be mourning him . . . and Kathryn. His grief over separation from Kathryn would not lessen, he knew; from now on he would be only half a person, cut off from the merging of mind and body that had transformed him from the isolated, unfulfilled youth he once had been into a man capable of commitment. His love for her would remain central to him, and because it would, whatever life he might make for himself on Ciencia would be empty. What use was there in even trying to move ahead?

His tears for Kathryn finally came, overwhelming him as he had known they would. Alone in the small, bare hotel room, he clutched the rough-textured bedcover and sobbed uncontrollably until at last he fell into nightmare-ridden sleep.

50

THE NEXT DAY Terry rode the bus back to the city, checked his smartphone for rentals, and chose the cheapest one on the list. It was a mere cubicle with a bed, shower, toilet, and a few small cooking appliances; as it faced a well, there was no view of any kind from its window. Since he was used to living aboard ships with staterooms no larger, this didn't bother him, and he would not have cared in any case. He dumped his pack on the bed and went out to buy some clothes appropriate for job hunting, spending as little as possible on them.

Never before had he applied for a job—there was no work for teens on Earth and he had entered the Fleet Academy the week after graduating from school. So he was not sure just how to go about it. He looked at job listings, picked the address closest to his room, and held his breath while the receptionist examined his ID, fearing that that his false criminal record might bar him other work as well as from space. As the case had been dismissed and programmers with advanced skills were in demand, it was ignored; he was given an interview, followed by an aptitude test. Programming languages didn't vary from world to world and Terry was familiar with the current ones, so once his test results had been checked he was hired on the spot. It was work far below his skill level—mere coding—but he was told he would have opportunity to advance.

Advancement was the last thing on his mind, insofar as there was anything on it at all. Days went by one by one; he did not bother to take note of them. He got up and dressed like an automaton, relying on the smartphone to tell him when he woke if it was a weekend. At work, he concentrated on the job he was given and was glad for the routine nature of it; it meant he did not have to think. He didn't notice the purpose of the computer programs he worked on. They were unrelated to financial accounting—with a theft charge against him, he would obviously not be entrusted with anything like that—and the data they manipulated, connected in some way with biochemistry, was meaningless to him.

He paid little attention to his surroundings; the city held nothing of interest to him and its gray roof of sky made it perpetually bleak, so that he was glad to get back to the tiny room that at least approximated the shipboard accommodations he was used to. Nor did he notice the people he encountered, other than to observe that except for those naturally dark-skinned, they were as pallid a white as his own skin had been made—the result of having lived their entire lives without exposure to the sun.

During the evenings, when it was too early for the oblivion of sleep, he read. He had always spent a good deal of his spare time exploring the Net and had read widely on many subjects; now he investigated Ciencia's history and found that it was indeed a world focused on science. Considering that it got input from offplanet only through the strictly-controlled government ansible, it was remarkably advanced in all technical fields, especially biochemistry. He also noticed that the Net was as heavily censored in other respects as Laesara had said it was. He could find no trace of any reference to religion, spirituality, metaphysics, or mythology, except by scholars who dismissed them as ancient superstitions or cited them as the cause of war and persecution on Earth. Fantasy, too, was banned. And of course there was no information about "pseudo-sciences" such as parapsychology. People born here, he realized, would never have heard of such concepts.

He did not read fiction. Fantasy novels didn't exist; science fiction, which he had formerly enjoyed, dealt with space and alien worlds, which he couldn't bear to be reminded of; mainstream fiction included love stories, which he couldn't endure either since he would never again be able to love. This would have been true even if he were not faithful to Kathryn, he realized; having once experienced full union with a telepathic partner, no telepath could find a lesser form of sex satisfying.

His telepathic ability had not diminished, although there was no one on Ciencia to connect with. Sometimes he was aware that he might sense feelings, but because he was shutting out all feelings including his own, he did not perceive them consciously. Unconscious telepathy was presumably operative here as elsewhere, and Terry recalled that the collective unconscious did not extend from world to world. That, he assumed, was why people tolerated the suppression of all non-scientific ideas. They didn't draw them from the collective unconscious as they did on Earth because no such ideas had been absorbed into it in the first place. The founders had all been people who weren't inclined to metaphorical thought.

The weather on Ciencia remained uniformly gloomy. Sometimes it snowed; sometimes it didn't. The snow melted quickly from the main streets of the city, which had radiant heat cables under the pavement. It was possible to walk to work without the heavy boots he had arrived in, and Terry reluctantly purchased a pair of shoes. By now he had been paid for six weeks of work and had plenty of credits banked; he was not sure what he was saving them for. But his instinct was not to spend any more than he had to.

Terry did not often think of Maclairn; he generally managed to repress all recollection of it. Then one morning he awoke with questions pushing their way into his head. What had they done about the next trip to Earth? The observers had to be taken home and the next mentor couple placed; they couldn't have abandoned the plan on account of his presumed death. Yet there had been no one aboard *Shepard* who could pilot a jump ship except senior officers needed where they were. The captain who'd retired was on Maclairn, but Captain Vargas had said a civilian couldn't be placed in command over Fleet officers.

Had they appointed Drew captain even though he wasn't a pilot and used the civilian just to calculate the jumps? There wouldn't have been a spare stateroom; they'd have needed a female captain so that Kathryn could continue to share. They might have sent *Shepard*'s XO, Dorene Hastings. Or had Kathryn even gone on the next trip? She'd been grief-stricken, and she was pregnant—maybe she had sent the passengers without an escort and asked her aunt to bring out the next group. . . . Oh, God, Terry thought. It wasn't his job to worry about it anymore, yet here he was speculating about the trip as if he were still captain. As if he could someday be captain again, when that was never going to happen.

Of course Kathryn had gone to Earth! She'd have gone as soon as she could get there, because she wouldn't have given up hope that he was not dead. She would reason that if he had been captured, not killed, by an intruding ship, he might have escaped on Earth or some other world—and if he had, he would contact Arthur Bramfield. A man as prominent as her grandfather could be reached from anywhere in the galaxy.

And he still could be, Terry thought in despair. If he were free he wouldn't need to find a way to reach Maclairn; he could merely get in touch with Arthur, and his physical alteration wouldn't matter because they shared memories through which he could identify himself. The Elders hadn't known that. They had believed no one but Maclairnans would accept his claims. To be sure, the physical changes would be hard to explain. But Arthur would give him the benefit of the doubt, and send him home.

Terry choked back tears as he came fully awake. He had been dreaming; that was why such a fantastic scenario as this had emerged in his mind. There was no way to reach Arthur Bramfield because there was no possibility of reaching a starship. Laesara said no starships ever came to Ciencia except smugglers.

Smugglers! Terry sat straight up in bed, his heart

pounding. Why had he not thought before about the smug-glers' ships? They would hide, of course, from the aster-oid miners; they would probably orbit far from Ciencia itself, maybe even around some other planet in the sys-tem. Their shuttles would have to land secretly. Where? Would they unload their cargo, take it to the city them-selves, or would there be an arrangement for accomplices to pick it up? What were they smuggling, anyway?

That was a puzzle. He knew little about smugglers apart from the fact that Fleet arrested them when pos-sible; but he had always assumed that they smuggled goods into colonies to avoid the tax on imports, or in the case of minerals, the League tax on prospectors' finds. Unscru-pulous Fleet explorers smuggled because legally, what they found on uninhabited planets belonged to Fleet. But there would be no point in smuggling anything to Ciencia, where production of high-tech goods was thriving and which had a surplus of asteroid miners who could get minerals more cheaply by digging than by paying smugglers for them.

He was looking at it backwards, he realized suddenly. Starships would not be bringing illicit cargo to Ciencia—they were smuggling it *out*, circumventing the ban on starship traffic, and then smuggling it into other colonies where it was heavily taxed, or perhaps even selling it legally. Why then couldn't they smuggle a person out?

Perhaps the Elders had thought it wouldn't be worth their while—certainly he could never accumulate enough money to pay for passage. But Arthur Bramfield would pay ransom, just as he would have paid the pirates. It would be sufficiently high to justify any risk a smuggler might incur. . . .

Except that he had no proof that he was related to Bram-field, and no way to contact the smugglers in any case.

As to the proof, all he'd have to do would be convince them to carry a message, and Arthur would pay in ad-vance, for Kathryn's sake if for no other reason. Contact-ing them, and getting to a place where their shuttle could pick him up, would be considerably more difficult. But surely, in time, it could be done. It was something to aim for, and so far he hadn't had an aim. It made all the difference. Now, with grounds for hope, he could begin to live again.

51

NEWLY INTERESTED IN the future and tired of reading long texts on a smartphone, Terry invested in a tablet computer. He had had it for only a few days when he made a major discovery.

The reader software, like that on all tablets, allowed words and phrases to be highlighted for reminders. He wasn't in the habit of doing this, as he was a fast reader and kept the ideas that really mattered to him in memory; it wasn't as if he were studying for exams. But he did try out all the features of any device he owned, and so when in an ebook on Earth's history he came across a statement referring in a thought-provoking way to the alleged "nonsense" that had once distracted people from science, he highlighted it—and was suddenly transported to a new screen.

An easter egg! The term was familiar to any programmer, though its origin was lost in the mist of antiquity. He had created some himself in the past, both as a legitimate software developer and as a hacker. The idea was to hide a joke or a picture or a special feature in such a way as to be found by those "in the know" and to surprise anyone else who stumbled upon it by highlighting, clicking or touching some specific content on a screen. Most were intended for innocent entertainment. But in this case, the text that came up was highly illegal on Ciencia and the programmer, if caught, would undoubtedly be subject to arrest.

It contained an excerpt from the classic fantasy novel *Fellowship of the Ring*.

Fascinated, Terry began highlighting key words on the new page, which brought up other pages filled with forbidden ideas. You had to experiment and get the highlighting just right, sometimes only part of a phrase, other times including adjacent words; and certain combinations would cause a whole chapter to appear. It wasn't something anyone could do accidentally. And of course, the sentence that had originally led him into it would not be highlighted by a person who wasn't attracted by the idea it expressed.

So the censored database wasn't totally censored after all—or rather, material had been added to it after the censoring was done.

He was glad. It had always seemed hard to believe that a world could eliminate all ideas that were deemed unscientific. It was contrary to human nature. Belief in the spiritual and mystical was too universal to be stamped out. So was the enjoyment of myth and fantasy. And it was wrong to suppress knowledge of *any* kind. He hadn't given much thought to that while uninterested in what was going on around him, but it was contrary to the basic goal of Maclairn, the full development of human potential—the cause he had pledged to support.

How were people managing to get around it? It was one thing to insert the easter eggs; rebels could certainly do that, and they could spread information about how to find them by word of mouth. But where had they obtained the texts? Some might have been written on Ciencia, but others were familiar to him—works that had existed for centuries on Earth. If these had been deleted from the knowledgebase by Ciencia's founders, and had not been brought via their personal smartphones and other devices—which according to local history had been checked for contraband—then how had they gotten back in?

Nobody had ever been allowed to immigrate. No information was received except via the government's ansible, which was tightly controlled; scientific reports and news were released only after clearance by the censors. These restrictions had existed for generations, and there was no way they could have been bypassed—except one. Smugglers. Smugglers must have been bringing literature from their starships when they picked up cargo to be smuggled out. And that meant somebody on Ciencia must have been willing to pay for it.

If this was still going on, then people other than mere profit-seekers must be in contact with the smugglers.

From then on he spent his free hours pursuing the clues scattered throughout the Net and found illegally-added material to be plentiful, though far from comprehensive in terms of what he knew from reading elsewhere. Terry picked a text that already contained some and inserted an easter egg of his own—his long hacking experience made it easy to find the necessary tools hidden on the Net and to locate a backdoor. Then he carefully erased all traces of his activity from the tablet's memory, took it back to the store, and exchanged it for the most powerful model available. If he was going to learn who was behind the illicit expansion of the knowledgebase, he would need to use all his computer skills.

It soon became apparent that quite a few people were involved, most of them only as readers. It was like the samizdat system that had existed centuries ago on Earth, whereby dissidents in totalitarian nations had circulated hand-written copies of forbidden texts. There were routes through the maze of surreptitious links through which participants communicated with each other, commenting obliquely on what others had said. Cautiously, Terry began to do this, hoping to uncover some clue as to the source of the material but aware that he would not be trusted with such information until he had posted enough remarks to incriminate him if he was caught.

Ciencia's Net had no link to the outside apart from the government ansible; reception from ships was not fed

into it. If some of these texts were coming from smugglers, they had to be physically carried on an electronic
device of some kind, or perhaps a mere chip. That meant
a shuttle had to bring it down and turn it over to a courier. But he had yet to figure out where the smugglers'
shuttles landed. There had been sporadic landings at the
spaceport all the time he'd been there; it didn't seem it
would ever be deserted enough for an unidentified ship
to pick up a load and lift off again without being noticed,
even supposing that it got past the local satellite sensor
ring. And it couldn't—the government police were continuously on the alert and would intercept any ship that
approached without authorization.

Then one evening, shortly after he posted a comment
on the theories of twentieth-century psychoanalyst Carl
Jung—whose works were on the forbidden list—there was
a knock at his door. Terry had never before had a visitor;
he knew no one on Ciencia except his co-workers, who
were interested in little beyond sports scores and with
whom, as with his Titan crewmates in the old days, he
was not inclined to socialize. He was sure he had never
met this man, who was middle-aged but fit and handsome, with silver-streaked dark hair. Nevertheless, he
felt immediately that he was to be trusted.

"I may have the wrong place," the man said, "I was
looking for Skywalker."

Terry caught his breath in surprise. "You've found
him," he said unhesitatingly. He had used the name of his
ship as a screenname, wondering if anyone on Ciencia
would recognize its origin.

"I'm Elrond," the visitor said. "Can we talk?"

"I'd like that," Terry told him. "Come on in." He offered him the room's one chair and sat down on the bed
himself, trying to contain his excitement. He was familiar
with comments signed "Elrond"—a screenname taken
from *Fellowship of the Ring*—in the secret files.

"You're not careful enough," Elrond said. "You should

have known you could be traced if you always logged on from the same location."

"I knew," Terry said. "I just took a chance that someone would find me before the police did."

"You want to get in deeper, then. You know what the penalty for hacking is?"

"Not really. But I haven't got a lot to lose, you see. I've already lost the things that mattered to me—something happened that I can't speak of. And I care about spreading new ideas around. It has to do with a promise I once made to some people I'll never see again."

"I'll be frank," said Elrond. "Getting in's not just a matter of risk. We have to pay the source, the local captain, and sometimes the courier. We take up a collection."

"I figured that someone was paying. How much do you want?"

"Three hundred?"

It was a week's salary. "Okay," Terry said. "How do I transfer it?"

"From your phone to an anonymous chip. On your account it will show as a personal gambling debt."

That was appropriate, Terry thought, inserting the blank chip handed to him into his smartphone and moving the funds. He was certainly gambling on this stranger's integrity—the man might not be paying the source at all; he could be collecting a protection fee. His telepathic sensitivity told him otherwise.

"You're too trusting," Elrond informed him.

Terry decided to take the plunge. "It's not blind trust," he said. "There are ways of knowing not yet widely disseminated. And the source has a lot more to offer than what's on the Net so far."

Elrond stared at him. "You represent the source?"

"No. As a matter of fact I'm trying to get in touch with the source. But I know a good deal about other worlds."

With obvious dismay Elrond burst out, "How do you know more than the rest of us? What assurance do I have that you're not a government agent?"

"Trust goes two ways, Elrond."

After a pause the man said, "I wasn't expecting this. I assumed I was looking for a typical newbie. But I can tell you're something else, something we haven't encountered before."

"If I could reach the source," Terry said, "I could select a lot of important material very fast. I don't know how much we'd have to pay for it, but there'd be no courier's fee."

"You'd be willing to act as courier? Do you know what you're saying? It's illegal to deal with offworlders even through a go-between—it would mean a prison sentence, not just a fine, if you were caught."

"I suppose it would, so I'd avoid getting caught."

"We're short a courier," Elrond admitted. "You couldn't reach the source; our people only meet the incoming ships. The captains run little risk beyond what they've already taken by carrying cargo, and they have to accommodate us because we're in a position to expose them. But as for selecting material, if you know keywords you could hand over a list for the next trip when you make the pickup."

And he could hand over a message for Arthur Bramfield along with it. He hadn't dared to hope it would be so simple.

"Okay," he said. "When?"

"We never know exactly; it depends on how long they spend at the source. There'll be several people on call, in case the one first in line is at work or unreachable when the signal comes in. You'll be a backup to begin with, and you'll have only an hour's notice. We'll have a groundcar ready for you to use."

Terry frowned. There was something odd here; what did it matter how long the shuttle spent aboard the starship? It would be there continuously except when sent to the surface, which would have to be scheduled so that the cargo would be available when it arrived. And how could that be in the daytime when people were at work, the time when it its descent and liftoff were most likely to be observed? "Maybe I should check the place out beforehand so I won't have trouble finding my way," he said.

"You've never driven to the spaceport? I suppose you're not a space buff like most of us—of course there's no reason you should be, though you mentioned other worlds—

"I've always gone there on the bus," he said quickly, not mentioning that he hadn't driven a groundcar since high school. The public spaceport in the middle of the day, in full view? "How will I recognize the ship?"

"Just by its name. It will be an ordinary mining ship, one of the small ones; we don't know which until its landing request to the spaceport is detected. A lot of the freelance captains deal with the source."

An ordinary mining ship! It had never occurred to him; all the starships he had piloted used shuttles, so he hadn't stopped to think that smugglers might rendezvous with local ships instead. No wonder the Elders had made it impossible for him to fly with the asteroid miners.

52

HE PREPARED HIS message to Arthur Bramfield after long thought, taking care to make sure that it couldn't be viewed as a hoax; nothing was more likely than a smuggler trying to extort money from a wealthy man by presenting a fake note that promised payment for its delivery. There was also the problem of its form. An ordinary voice message would not do, since his voice had been changed, and he could not include a picture or even a DNA sample. He would have to rely on a written message mentioning facts only he could know. But he dared not refer to anyone by name, in case it should fall into the wrong hands.

"Dear Arthur," Terry wrote. "This message will come as a shock to you, as I've had no means of sending it before now. The bracelet in which I'm placing it may remind you of the inlaid one I sent you from the moon as a hospitality gift. The captain who carries it may have had considerable difficulty in reaching you and I have promised him generous payment.

"As I expect you know, I left the home of our aged friend on the morning after my formal commitment to the goal we share. I had become aware of the presence of a ship that might interfere with her plans. I encountered that ship and was captured by its crew, but found that it was not sent by anyone connected with the pirates who held me before. It posed no threat to us. Its crew had strong reasons for secrecy, however, and in order to silence me I was taken to the colony world Ciencia, which has no accessible ansible and allows no starships to approach. I have no way to escape unless you can persuade its government to turn me over to you, as, given your connections, I pray may be possible. I go by the name Terry Rivera; tell them to arrest me if I'm not already in their hands. My deepest love to you and to my wife, who I expect still visits you from New Tahiti."

He knew enough of Ciencia's government by this time to believe it was likely that if a powerful billionaire offered them enough money, they would comply. In any case, he could think of no other way to reach a starship if Arthur sent one.

He bought a data bracelet unique enough not to be accidentally mixed up with some other, yet not valuable enough to tempt a thief. After transferring the text message to it from his tablet, he wore it day and night. When the weekend came he rented a groundcar to refresh his long-unused driving skills and make sure he knew the quickest route to the spaceport; there was no telling how soon he would hear from Elrond, and he wanted to be ready. As time passed the suspense mounted until he found it hard to sleep. He continued to comment on hidden texts, but now he did it from various locations such as restaurants and the library rather than from his room. He no longer had a reason to let his wireless transmissions be traced, and it would be disastrous to be arrested before the bracelet had been dispatched. As for the possibility of later arrest, it didn't worry him. If the message got through and Arthur was able to ransom him, he would have to be picked up anyway—and if it didn't, to be behind actual bars wouldn't be much worse than to be permanently barred from going home.

He was getting ready for bed on the night he was finally called. Grabbing his phone, he stood half undressed while he absorbed the instructions: the location of the car he was to use, the names of the ship and captain, the address to which the delivery was to be made. On the way to the spaceport he breathed a sigh of relief. His worst fear had not been realized—he had been haunted by the thought that it might be Renssalaer, unlikely though it was that a captain who was dealing with smugglers would have considered hiring a copilot he didn't know. To encounter Renssalaer would mean arrest for sure and the end of his hope for rescue.

There were just a few lights around the perimeter of the spaceport and the ships on the ground were illuminated only by their frosting of new snow. But as he watched, the ring of landing beacons around one of the empty pads blazed into life, and the brilliant star that was the incoming ship grew and grew until the whole area was brightened. So many times, on so many worlds, he had seen this, Terry thought, and the ache in his heart became a stabbing pain he was not sure he could bear. For many weeks he had been numb, but that had been wearing off lately and now he was struck anew by the agony of his exile. Never to fly again would be past enduring. . . .

He jerked himself back to the present moment. His job was to meet with the captain who had just landed, accept a data chip, spot-check the content for authenticity, and then send a prearranged signal indicating that money was to be paid into the captain's account. There was no danger that a captain might force him to do so without delivering in order to avoid paying the source, as Elrond was in a position to expose anyone who tried. The smugglers' main concern, he supposed, was making payment to their cargo suppliers without inadvertently paying a government spy. They were therefore wary of being approached by strangers, who might be undercover agents watching for dealers. Terry had been provided with the necessary passwords, but he knew that if he made a wrong move he would be turned over to the police.

Contacts were made in the bar of the spaceport hotel, a rather sleazy establishment, as he knew from having spent his first two nights on Ciencia there. Aware that he must look like an asteroid miner, he had dressed appropriately; it was important to mingle with the patrons without calling attention to himself. Elrond had given him a shirt that would be recognized by the captain. Once he identified himself he would be told the man's room number and expected to make his way there for the actual transaction; it would be unsafe to conduct it in public. With dismay, Terry realized that smuggling transactions were not the only reason a man might be invited to another man's room in the middle of the night and that to avoid suspicion he should let observers misinterpret his purpose. He wondered if the courier for whom he was backup had been a woman.

The miners drifted noisily in from the field, eager for food and drinks before heading to their own rooms. The captain, of course, would be last, after securing his ship; probably he would contrive to come alone. Captain

Darrow, Terry had been told—he was a big, gruff man and would be wearing a dark blue flight jacket and black skullcap. Terry sat at a small table from which he could see the door and waited.

When Darrow appeared he rose and approached him openly. "Captain Darrow of *Bonanza*?" he said. "I've heard you're hiring crew." If only it were true, he thought sadly— but then, no hold he might gain over the captain would compensate for the nature of the alleged charge against him.

"I'm not," said Darrow, "unless you've shipped with someone I know."

"I may have," Terry replied. "Do you know Ernie Dryweather?" It was a fictitious, pre-arranged code name.

"Come along to my room after I've had a drink, and I'll look him up in my log," the captain said. And then in a low voice, "Room 137."

"I'll buy you that drink," Terry said. This was improvisation; it seemed to him that the less furtive he was about it, the less noticeable he would be to observers. And if they went to the room together, their avoidance of companions would be more likely to be misinterpreted.

"You're too cool for an amateur," Darrow said when, after conversation over drinks about asteroid mining, they were behind closed doors. "Perhaps pickups are a sideline—do you by any chance deal in cargo?"

"No," Terry said, wondering what he had gotten into. "Are you looking for someone who does?"

"Maybe. If you ever have any to offer, let me know."

"The only thing I can offer beyond the agreed payment," Terry declared, "is the chance to do an errand for me. It's nothing to do with cargo, and there's no money up front except what I'll give you here and now to split with the starship captain. I want a personal message delivered on Earth."

Darrow's eyes narrowed. "What contact could a man who doesn't deal in cargo have on Earth? Even if you did have one, you'd be subject to arrest for pursuing it."

"I'm subject to arrest for making this pickup," Terry said. As an afterthought he added meaningfully, "Just as you would be, if it were to become known that you're in the cargo business."

"Okay. You've made your point, and I'll ask no questions. What's the message?"

"This bracelet," said Terry, handing it over along with a preloaded credit chip that Darrow plugged into his phone. "It's to be delivered to Arthur Bramfield, who as you may or may not know, is one of Earth's best-known billionaires. He'll be pleased to get it, and whoever hands it to him will be compensated accordingly."

"What proof do you need that I've followed through?"

"Bramfield will provide the proof—I think I can assume that the prospect of a reward from him will motivate you. I'd advise you not to mention his name until the starship captain promises you a share."

They proceeded with the delivery of the expected data chip, which Terry inserted into his own phone and read parts of; it appeared to contain a number of ancient texts with which he was familiar, including portions of *The Power of Myth* by Joseph Campbell, an article about yoga, and a chapter of the Christian Bible.

He then transmitted the arranged signal to the server that had been surreptitiously programmed to transfer funds. They were not stolen funds, he'd been assured. The hacking was necessary only to protect the identities of the parties involved. The transfer having been verified, he handed over his list of requested files for the next delivery and left the room without attempt at concealment, heading for his groundcar with a sigh of relief.

As he made his way across the deserted parking lot, however, he became aware that a woman had followed him out of the hotel. Her tight, skimpy clothes and heavy makeup left little doubt as to why she was pursuing him, unless—oh, God. Could she be an undercover agent? Had he somehow attracted the wrong sort of attention after all? He remembered now that he'd seen her in the bar.

She approached him, smiling provocatively. "Looking for company?" she asked.

"No," he replied shortly, opening the car door. Something about her convinced him that this wasn't her normal persona, and there was only one other thing she could be. To assault an agent would lead to worse trouble than to submit to arrest, but could he lose the data chip somehow before he was searched? He was glad he'd taken the precaution of removing it from his phone and carrying it in the pocket of his flight jacket.

The woman went around the car and unhesitatingly climbed into the passenger seat.

Terry did the only thing he could think of. He reached into the pocket and palmed the data chip, with his other hand punching the wrong code into the car's ignition so as to trigger a starter alarm. He then opened the door, thereby shutting the alarm off, and as he did so he dropped the chip onto the pavement. "Sorry," he said, "but you need to get out."

"You're sure don't want to come to my room?"

"In the local lockup? I think not, at any rate not voluntarily. If you're planning on forcing the issue you may as well show me your badge; I assume you've got a gun to go with it."

She said quietly, "You're cautious, I see. We didn't need to worry about the chip being well protected."

"Chip? Don't waste your time hunting—you won't find one on me, or in the car either."

"Oh my God, Skywalker! You mean you didn't get it after all? Did Darrow try to con us?"

He stared at her, perceiving that her dismay was genuine. She was not a government agent—she knew his screenname and was, strangely enough, on his side. "I ditched it," he said sheepishly, "because I could tell you weren't what you seemed to be. What are you, anyway?"

"I came from Rivendell. Did you think we wouldn't check up on a new courier?"

"You mean I wasn't trusted?"

"We didn't know anything about your background. And we couldn't be sure you were competent. Meaning well isn't enough."

"Did I pass muster?" he asked, trying not to be angry.

"Admirably. I can tell you've had experience."

"Not this kind. But I've—been around." It was too bad, he thought, that he couldn't mention his experience with pirates, which might attest to his ability to handle a crisis. "I don't know anything about your background either," he pointed out. "For all I know, you could have heard about Rivendell and be hoping I'll lead you there."

"I'll give you a location that matches what you were told. If we can retrieve the chip, that is. Where did you put it?"

"I dropped it out the car window. It's lucky you revealed yourself when you did, because the next thing I'd have done was drive off." With sudden apprehension he asked, "I wasn't wired, was I? Through the shirt I was given to wear?" He couldn't guess what they'd do if they knew about his message to Bramfield.

"No. We're not suspicious, we just wanted to be sure you made the contact without being observed. By the way, I'm Arwen."

"Elrond's daughter? Really?" Arwen could be her actual name, as it was in common use; but that would be a strange coincidence.

"No, I'm his cousin. They're screennames, of course, but Elrond uses his all the time with his friends; he doesn't like his given name." She smiled at him. "I see you've read it."

"*Fellowship of the Ring*? Of course; hasn't everyone?" He'd spoken without thinking—of course relatively few people would have stumbled on the easter egg. "Everyone among our friends, I mean."

"It's pretty well hidden; since you haven't been with us long you might not have found it. How do you think it will end?"

"You mean the last part's not posted?"

"They never send a whole ebook at once; they want to keep us paying for more."

He refrained from saying he knew that there were three long books in the story. Arwen appraised him curiously. "Skywalker—I like that. Is it from a book, or did you just pick it because you wish you could reach the sky?"

"There's a book," he said, "but mainly it's from a vid, an old classic on Earth."

"We don't get vids—the files would be too long to hide on the servers."

"Well," he said, "that depends on how skilled the hacker is." He was thinking that it would be a good thing to expose the Ciencians to the idea of the Force, a concept that was undoubtedly foreign to them. Maybe the book adaptation would be better than nothing.

Arwen looked down at her tight clothes, embarrassed. "I don't usually dress like this, you know. I wish I hadn't had to, Skywalker. I don't want you to think of me this way."

"We'll be seeing each other again, won't we? At— Rivendell?"

"Sure we will." She smiled happily. Too late, he sensed what was in her mind, and how she'd interpreted his evident pleasure at the prospect. Oh, God, he thought. He wasn't attracted to her, not that way. He was a married man deeply in love with his wife. But he couldn't say so, and how was he to avoid hurting her feelings if this group of people got together often?

"My real name is Nina," she told him. "Rivendell isn't a place, it's more a frame of mind. But I'll take you to Elrond's apartment after we recover the chip."

53

IN THE WEEKS that followed, Terry visited Elrond's apartment many times. There were usually others there, a variety of men and women who were evidently hungry for more forbidden material to read. They were like children, he thought, totally ignorant of what humans normally absorbed from their earliest years onward. They had never heard of fairy tales; they were astonished by speculation about the supernatural; and they knew nothing of religion beyond having been told that it consisted of superstitions the ancients on Earth had fought over. Even the most experienced conspirators were confused by the bits and pieces of texts hidden on the Net, unable to put them in context.

Terry's biggest problem was discussing these texts without mentioning anything that he obviously could not have learned from them. For the first time, he truly understood what the mentors had meant when they'd said that the collective unconscious of humankind did not extend from world to world. And slowly, he began to see that new ideas could be deliberately put into it. That Maclairn's plan for adding acceptance of psi to the collective unconscious was no mere vague hope, but a definite possibility.

He continued to make pickups of data chips without trouble, sometimes from Captain Darrow, sometimes from other captains. The first time, Darrow told him that his bracelet had been safely delivered to the starship and that its captain had agreed to deliver it. He had no idea how long it would be before the smugglers reached Earth; they might visit other worlds first. He resolved not to worry about it. The message was on its way to Arthur Bramfield. In time, maybe soon, he would be able to go home.

In the meantime, in his requests for texts he included some of the best nonfiction about psi that he'd researched on Maclairn, carefully confining it to evidence and informed speculation as distinguished from sensational claims or literal interpretations of metaphor. "The human mind has a lot of capabilities the government doesn't want us to know about," he said. "The more we can learn about them, the better our chances of someday getting the censorship abolished."

Elrond stared at him. "Abolished? You mean you think unscientific writings could be made legal, not just passed around in secret?"

"If we can spread a desire for them to enough people, why not? The laws are made by the legislature, after all. They can be changed if the voters demand it."

"But that would let in all the illogical thinking that contaminated Earth," someone protested. "It would set history back hundreds of years. It's one thing for us to entertain ourselves with stories, but some people might take them seriously."

"They *are* serious," Terry declared. "Science is just half of human knowledge. There are other ways of knowing."

"You said that to me once before," Elrond recalled. "I couldn't figure out what you meant. But the characters in the stories so often seem to believe in things they have no scientific proof for—do you really think that happens in real life?"

"Of course it does. Why else are you sure old texts are worth acquiring?"

"*You're* sure," Nina observed thoughtfully, "You talk all the time as if you knew facts nobody could possibly know."

He couldn't deny that, but neither could he explain it—and it was not, he realized, just a matter of not being able to explain that he'd been born on Earth. Normal human beings took it for granted that not all knowledge beyond personal experience was derived from science. Some of them believed God spoke to them, or to their forebears. Others were aware that its source was a mystery. He couldn't imagine what it would feel like to grow up without any such knowledge.

By this time it had been recognized that Terry was as good or better at hacking than any of the other conspirators and that it was inefficient for him to pick up data chips to be passed to someone else; he now secreted the texts on the Net himself as soon as he got them. Since this eliminated one potentially-dangerous meeting, he had become the primary courier, with others substituting only when he was at work. He was glad that it occupied his time and his mind. It kept him from having to think about having nothing else to live for unless he was rescued. Although for the others' sake he was careful not to get caught, he personally didn't care one way or the other, and was therefore considered daring, which was embarrassing since he knew he deserved no credit for it.

His official job became increasingly boring. At the beginning he'd welcomed its numbing effect, but now that his programming skills were being used in a more challenging way, he found the routine of it deadly. And so when one day he was casually browsing the Net's computer news he noticed a want ad that stood out, he was for a moment excited by it. "Tech assistant needed for neurofeedback clinic," it said. "Programming experience and ability to maintain electronic equipment required; knowledge of neurofeedback a plus."

He had more knowledge of neurofeedback than anyone else on the planet, Terry realized. Was it possible that they wouldn't ask how he'd acquired it? Was neurofeedback something that a Ciencian might pursue as a hobby? It had many medical applications, he knew, but on Earth some nonprofessionals used it for relaxation and for what they viewed—more accurately than anyone realized—as alteration of consciousness. Of course the software here would not be anywhere near as advanced as that used on Maclairn; over time he might be able to make some improvements. . . .

But of course it would be senseless to take on such a job now. What was he thinking of? He might be rescued by Arthur within weeks or even days. It wouldn't be fair to his employer to disappear shortly after being hired.

Nina managed to be present whenever any of the conspirators met, as they often did—without knowing each others' true identities—to eat and to talk. She was very young, surely no more than twenty in Earth years, though Terry didn't ask her. He couldn't deny that she was pretty, with long auburn hair and a well-proportioned figure; still no woman but Kathryn was ever going to interest him and her evident wish for a relationship was difficult to deal with. He wasn't old enough to be convincing when he tried to treat her as if there were an unbridgeable generation gap, ancient though his life experiences made him feel in comparison to the Ciencians.

It was only a few days after seeing the ad that he was once again driven into despair. He had gone to the apartment after work, only to find that Elrond was at the spaceport making a pickup; Nina was there alone. Before long Elrond stormed into the room, and seeing Terry he confronted him, his face flushed with anger.

"I always suspected you weren't what you said you were," he said. "But I thought you were a decent guy who on the whole had been straight with us. Now I find you're in touch with the source after all. When I made my pickup they handed me merchandise for you, by name, and it was all I could do not to throw it in the captain's face."

Terry stared at him. "What in God's name are you talking about? Merchandise?"

"Here," Elrond said coldly. "I ought not to give it to you, I should put it in the trash where it belongs. But you've done a lot for us, so just this once I'll hand it over. Take it and get out of my apartment."

With shock Terry saw he was holding the bracelet he had sent to Arthur.

He stood and reached for it, the room spinning around him. A reply—he hadn't dared to hope that Arthur could contrive to send a reply, only that he might be able to make a deal with Ciencia's government. Had a starship already come for him, then? Was it in orbit, in contact with the smugglers? In any case, why would Elrond object to his receiving a message?

Totally bewildered, he burst out, "I don't know what you think it is, but it's just something personal. There's no more danger to you in receiving this than the rest of the pickup."

"No danger? I suppose not, though the penalty would be somewhat higher, I think. That's not what I mind. I want no part of the traffic; we've kept our hands clean and they'll stay that way."

"What traffic?"

"There's only one apart from ours, and you've been using us as a cover. Don't think I can't tell what sort of stuff is on that data bracelet."

"Obviously you can't," Terry said, his own temper rising. "It's a private message and nobody could possibly know what it's about."

"A private message from the source? If the merchandise isn't included then it can only be negotiation as to the price."

"For delivering it? But the sender would have paid in advance—"

Elrond frowned. "Don't take me for a fool. Your client's paying the sender, not the other way around, and there's no use pretending I don't know how it works."

Terry was at a loss for words. He clutched the bracelet, wondering if he dared listen to the message in their presence. If he'd be leaving soon it might not do any harm if they found out. . . .

Nina, watching his face, spoke up. "Can't you see he's confused, Elrond? Maybe you're jumping to conclusions."

"There's just one conclusion possible," Elrond declared.

"Nobody can contact the source unless they've got money to offer, and why would he be doing it during our pickups if he wasn't using them to cover for a big time dealer?"

"I thought the dealers took cargo *out*," said Terry. "They wouldn't be paying, they'd be collecting. I did give the starship captain some money to deliver a personal message a while back, and this is the reply."

"He's an innocent," insisted Nina. "Terry—Elrond's assuming you're in the porn business. That's the only kind of digital file brought in besides ours."

"Oh, my God!" Terry exclaimed in astonishment. "I've got nothing to do with that. It didn't occur to me that porn was smuggled. On most worlds it's sold legally unless it involves kids."

"You've been making pickups all this time, and haven't known what you'd be accused of if the police caught you?"

"No. But it's logical; if porn vids are banned I suppose they bring a high price here."

"Don't they everywhere?" Elrond asked, nonplussed. "If you're not procuring them, I apologize, but you must see how it looked." Only half convinced, he went on, "Would it be out of line to ask what you are doing, exchanging messages with the source?"

"I guess you've got a right to. But I have to hear this first—it can't wait."

Terry plugged the bracelet into his smartphone, reaching in his pocket for earphones. It proved not to be a voice message; the opener was merely a brief cover text. His eyes blurred as he read it, unbelieving.

"Since I took your money I owe you a report," the starship captain had written. "I don't know what's in this message so I can't say whether its return will be a blow to you, but when I tried to deliver it I learned that Arthur Bramfield is dead."

54

TERRY'S LEGS FELT weak; he fell back into his chair, not caring what Elrond and the others might think. Oh God, dead—and so was his only hope of ever leaving Ciencia. He would be here for the rest of his life, as he'd originally believed, only now that he'd been expecting to escape, it would be even harder to bear. . . .

They had killed Arthur Bramfield. The enemies of Maclairn had murdered him; he'd been a strong, healthy man and could not have died naturally in the past few months. Maclairn was in even greater danger than before if they'd gotten to Arthur. And he could do nothing in its defense. He had pledged to support its people, yet he could not have the slightest influence on what might happen there.

Nina grasped his hand. "You've gone pale, Terry!" she said. "What was in that thing? Can we do anything to help?"

"I can't tell you," he said despairingly. And then he thought, why couldn't he? Not about Maclairn, of course, but there was no way they could guess anything connected with that, and since his ID showed him to be a native citizen of Ciencia he couldn't be charged with illegal immigration. Even if he could, these friends would never betray him.

He raised his head. "You're entitled to know, and it won't make any difference now. I don't belong here. I'm from offworld, and I've just learned I can never get back to where I came from because the man I tried to contact is dead."

"Offworld? How could you be? No captain could get away with bringing a passenger down from a starship— the miners' IDs are checked when the ship is searched for contraband."

"I've never had contact with the smugglers. I was

brought here against my will by some powerful people who wanted to silence me—I'm not free to tell you why. They preferred not to kill me, so they falsified my ID and made sure I won't ever be allowed to leave."

Elrond frowned. "Please forgive my skepticism, Skywalker, but that sounds like something from one of the fantasy novels we've been reading. If for some reason you can't reveal what the message was about, okay; but don't make up far-fetched stories to get out of telling us."

"I'm not making it up," Terry declared. "It's the truth."

Staring at him, Nina said slowly, "I'd like to believe you. The things you've said about what people can do with their minds . . . I wondered how you could sound so sure. It wasn't just wishing, then? You've been to places where those things are real?"

"Yes, of course, some things. A lot are metaphor—you have to understand the difference between that and literal fact. But psi powers are real, though belief in them isn't generally accepted. Most people say they're imaginary, but underneath they're scared by the idea."

"I don't understand," Nina protested. "You've been risking prison to bring these texts in, yet you'd already read them, on a planet where you could get more like them? Why?"

"Because it's wrong for them to be suppressed. On most worlds people don't tolerate censorship—the League put an end to that centuries ago. I don't like it and so I do what I can to counteract it."

He was in a daze, not fully aware of what he was saying, and suddenly he realized that he wasn't being wholly honest. He hadn't acted merely on principle. "At the beginning," he confessed, "I was just trying to get a message out. You were my only connection to the source."

"You must have gotten it out a long time ago, if you've received a reply from offworld," Elrond said.

"Yes. I sent it the first time I made a pickup."

"Well, then, why did you keep putting yourself in

danger? You didn't have to be at the spaceport to get the answer—you must have been aware that it might be handed to some other courier."

Terry hesitated. "I—don't know," he said, suddenly realizing that this was true.

"But I do," Nina declared. "As you've often said, you believe the government has no right to decide what we can read, and that matters more to you than safety. We don't care if you had other reasons besides that."

"I suppose we don't," Elrond conceded. "If you want so much to see other worlds that you've convinced yourself you came from there, it's not for me to judge you. I've known from the start that you're not quite normal, after all, and it doesn't change the fact that you're willing to take risks."

Stunned, Terry dropped the subject and went home. He had not expected that his friends wouldn't believe what had happened to him, fantastic though it might sound. His isolation from his past was evidently going to be complete.

Later, in his room, he read the news article attached to the captain's note. It had been issued some time after Arthur Bramfield's death. Police were still trying to find the driver of the groundcar that had hit him; they did not believe it had been accidental because he was too prominent for it to be a coincidence, coming less than a year after an attack on one of his ships, the bombing of a building he owned, and the attempted theft of millions from his investment accounts. The Bramfield fortune had been inherited by his granddaughter, the article reported. She was a recluse who rarely appeared in public; no one knew where she lived, although she occasionally traveled from New Tahiti to Earth's moon to conduct some legal business, having apparently given up the rest of her once-thriving law practice. It was rumored that her husband had also died under tragic circumstances, but no details were known. Perhaps it was for this reason that she had dropped out of sight and was donating the bulk of her inheritance to the Maclairn Foundation, an obscure charity that sponsored scholarly research, which had been managed by her grandfather. No mention was made of her pregnancy.

She must be crushed by the grief of her double loss, he thought in misery. No wonder she had refused an active role in the management of the Foundation and had abandoned Earth completely in order to remain on Maclairn. Did she still live in Jessica's house despite her new wealth? If not, perhaps her bereaved grandmother had gone to be with her until the child was born; he hoped so. Intergenerational ties were honored there and he could not bear to think of her being entirely alone.

He too grieved for Arthur, who had devoted his life to the discovery and protection of a world whose influence he would now never see. Arthur, Corwin . . . how many martyrs were there going to be? Many, Terry feared. He had once thought he might be among them. He would have preferred that to a life of senseless, useless exile.

Who was heading the Foundation now, if Kathryn hadn't taken it on? Possibly her aunt and uncle, who had traveled to Maclairn with the first group of observers. He had never met them and would have no way of proving his identity to them even if they could be contacted. Nor could he prove it to Admiral Frazer, and in any case no smuggler captain would be willing to approach Fleet. If it weren't for that, he might just possibly be able to convince Admiral Derham through shared memories, especially since Derham was a telepath. . . .

But any attempt to do so would necessarily involve Aldren. And, Terry realized sadly, he couldn't let Aldren know what had happened. His life had been ruined for the sake of keeping the Elders' existence secret from the mentors. Laesara had convinced him that the future of humankind hinged on this, and he had to believe it, for if it wasn't true then he was suffering for nothing. His confinement to this godforsaken world would be futile. If he ever did get back to Maclairn he must not reveal his identity to the mentors there, for there was no way he could let himself be recognized without explaining what had changed him.

That night he dreamed again of Maclairn, of the beach by the lake where he had met Kathryn, her face illuminated by torchlight; candles floating on the water at Corwin's memorial and perhaps since then at his own; the stone hut where they had first made love; the fireside in Jessica's great room where they had lain on their wedding night; the torch at the Ritual, his hand touching those of Jessica, Tristan and Martin in flame ... their minds meeting others in strength and joy, a bond that would empower them to do anything that needed to be done to bring the human mind's potential to fulfillment....
And Kathryn in his arms, in his bed, knowing she carried their son; leaving her without a farewell in the belief that they wouldn't be parted long enough for it to matter....
As he so often had, he woke with his face wet with tears. He lay motionless, not wanting to face another day under the oppressive, overcast sky.

But after a little while he got up and dressed and emerged into the cold, dreary morning to check out the clinic that was seeking a neurofeedback assistant.

55

THE ADDRESS GIVEN was in one of the smaller and less impressive buildings, off the city's main business street. As Terry entered he saw a plaque on the door on the left: "Alison Willard, Licensed Therapist." The outer office had no receptionist; he pushed the call button and waited. After a moment a woman's voice spoke over the vidcom without turning on the picture at his end. "I don't believe we've met. Would you like to make an appointment?"

"I'm a programmer, I've come about the ad," he said. "My name is Terry Rivera."

"Oh, have a seat, then. I'm just finishing here, I'll be out in a few minutes."

When Alison Willard finally appeared he was immediately impressed by her bearing. She was a young woman about his own age, quietly self-confident though unassuming and rather plain by the usual standards of attractiveness. She wore her brown hair in a chignon that gave her an air of steadiness and dignity.

"Neurofeedback is new to me," she told him, "though for a long time I've wanted to use it in my psychotherapy practice. I've just completed a course in procedures at the medical center, but I have no technical knowledge of the equipment. I want an assistant who can set it up and maintain it as well as adapt the standard software to the individual needs of my clients."

"I could handle that," Terry said. "I've had some experience with neurofeedback—no formal training, but I've studied it as a hobby. I'm knowledgeable about electronics and AI, and I've done a lot more programming than what's required by my present job."

She gave him a searching look. "I'm aware that unlicensed neurofeedback practitioners sometimes make claims the evidence doesn't justify and evade the law by saying it's just a game."

Really? thought Terry. It was understandable on a world where scientific evidence was demanded for everything and academic qualifications proving indoctrination in current dogma were needed by anyone attempting to do professional work. And it was lucky for him, as it could explain his knowledge. "I won't deny that I've played around with it," he said, "but I never took money for that."

"I can't pay very much at first," she warned. "Not until I see how many clients sign up. And you'd have to maintain my database, too."

The pay was the least of his concerns, as long as it

was enough to live on. "Getting away from routine work is more important to me than salary," he told her.

"Okay," Alison said. "I'm a good judge of people, and I can tell you're honest even though there are things you're concealing from me. I'll have to contact your employer, but if what I hear is satisfactory, you can start next week. I've ordered the equipment and it should be here by then."

That afternoon Terry quit his job, which didn't surprise anyone since he'd taken the morning off without asking, and with impatience he finished out the week there. A new start, he thought. Something to make the weeks and years ahead tolerable if not happy. He would never know happiness; there was now no chance of release from the dreary prison to which he had been condemned. But neurofeedback was at least an occupation that interested him.

He liked Alison Willard. He had known few women near his age other than fellow Fleet officers—and of course Kathryn, with whom no one could be compared. Alison proved to be someone he could talk to, insofar as he could talk to anyone without revealing his past. What he'd told Elrond and Nina about it had changed his relationship to them; they now viewed him as an eccentric genius whose idiosyncrasies were forgivable only because of his value as a hacker. Even Nina, who was still emotionally drawn to him and believed he hadn't lied, doubted his sanity. Alison, though aware that he was hiding something, accepted him without questions; and he found that he looked forward to the time he spent working with her.

The neurofeedback equipment proved to be similar to what he was used to except for the lesser complexity of its brain scanning capability; he had no difficulty setting it up and making the software modifications she asked for. The system did not, of course, provide the fine distinctions between states of consciousness dealt with by the mentors. It would probably not accomplish much if it did, he realized, since without telepathic communication from the instructor a person could not learn to switch between them.

Alison was not a psychiatrist and did not work with disturbed clients; her practice was centered on normal people who were troubled by emotional problems caused by stress. Although this was a recognized specialty on Ciencia, Terry soon perceived that her view of it was much less narrow than the official one. "I believe physical illness, too, is often the result of stress," she confided, "though of course I do not claim to cure it. I only help people to relax and feel better, and sometimes their symptoms go away—physical symptoms that drugs were supposed to cure, but didn't. I can't help thinking that state of mind has something to do with it."

"Yes, of course it does," Terry said. That fact was the basis of Maclairn's philosophy, and what he knew of health issues he had learned from the mentors; while he'd been told that conflicting views had prevailed on the world the founders had escaped, he hadn't stopped to think that they would on science-obsessed Ciencia.

"You think so, too?" Alison was obviously surprised and pleased. "According to medical science it's spontaneous remission, but that's just a way of saying they haven't been able to figure out how it happens. They claim that all disease can be cured through our world's advanced biochemistry, yet people still get sick, and some recover in ways science can't explain."

"But it *is* biochemical," Terry protested. "State of mind is what controls the brain's production of the neurotransmitters that produce physical reactions. If they don't know that, it's because they're prejudiced against studying the influence of the mind."

She stared at him. "Where did you read that?"

"I—I don't remember," he said, cornered.

"If you ever do remember, please let me know," Alison said quietly. There was tension between them that hadn't been there before. Was she aware that there was forbidden information about the mind hidden on the Net? he wondered suddenly. He longed to ask her; he was sure she was the kind of person who would value it. But not yet. He was obligated to be cautious, even though he sensed telepathically that she was absolutely trustworthy.

Tentatively, he commented, "Governments don't like people to find out about the power in their minds. It leads them to rebel against what they're told."

Alison's eyes widened. "You're an unusual person, Terry Rivera," she said. "Something tells me you've concealed even more from me than I thought."

He left it at that. But he began to feel that she, more than any of the others he had met, would understand.

56

TERRY CONTINUED TO make frequent data pickups at the spaceport, and the sight of the ships lifting and descending continued to break his heart. All his life he had wanted to fly, expected to keep on flying. Even when he committed himself to Maclairn, it had been in the belief that he would remain captain of *Promise*. He could not say that being grounded was his greatest loss. Losing Kathryn was worse. Losing telepathic contact with other human beings was worse; it was frustrating to be unable to truly connect with anyone. All the same, the longing to sit at the controls of a ship and break through to a clear, star-studded sky often brought him to the verge of tears.

If only ... if only there were some way to persuade one of the captains he now knew to take him along. Yet being a suspected thief was irredeemably damaging. As a courier he was breaking the law and was presumably, like themselves, motivated by self-interest; and they knew him to be smart enough to get away with deception. What reason could he have for wanting to visit a smuggler's starship other than desire to deal himself in? They owned their ships; they wouldn't take any risk that didn't offer a prospect of gain.

They owned their ships. Looking across a layer of dirty snow at the one descending, Terry's head whirled. If he owned a ship, he could fly all he wanted and no one could stop him. . . .

He had no idea how much a local mining ship would cost, but naturally it would be far more than an ordinary individual could afford. How had the captains paid for theirs? Probably they had gotten rich as asteroid miners, a route from which he was barred, or found investors who received shares. Since he had no proof of experience as a pilot, no one would be willing to invest in such a partnership with him. Yet now that he'd thought about it, he knew that somehow, someday, he had to get a ship of his own.

He could probably find a job that would pay more than working for Alison, but it wouldn't be enough more to be worth giving up the one thing that was making his days bearable. Was there any other potential source of income?

Well, he could become a porn dealer, he thought bitterly; there was a lot of money in that for men so inclined.

And then suddenly he asked himself, would it be possible to deal in cargo? Darrow had said to let him know if he ever got into that business. He knew other captains who'd implied the same.

In Fleet, smugglers were thought to be only a notch above pirates. Smuggling was viewed as a crime to be wiped out. He had shared that belief without giving it much thought, but now he wondered. It depended on what was being smuggled, didn't it?

Unscrupulous Fleet explorers smuggled rare minerals to avoid turning them over to Fleet, which legally owned all extraterrestrial resources it retrieved. That was stealing, because Fleet owned the ships, paid the crews, and gave them the share of what they brought in to which they were entitled. But why shouldn't independent asteroid miners sell their finds to whoever they wished? It was against the law because the government claimed the right to tax what was mined in addition to taxing the miners' personal income, which was unfair. More significantly, Terry realized, it was forbidden because Ciencia's government didn't want any starships to come here. He wouldn't hesitate to evade that law—but of course, it applied only to people who already owned ships.

Cargo smuggling, on the other hand, involved exporting goods from Ciencia itself, and depended on go-betweens between producers and captains. He saw nothing objectionable in breaking the Ciencian law against it, nor did he worry about the avoidance of import taxes at the destination. Trading, he felt, should be free of government interference. The only real issue was whether harm was being done to the eventual buyers in other colonies. Ruling out drug smuggling and gunrunning, if any, just what sort of cargo was being sold?

He didn't know. Some form of high technology, he supposed; Ciencia had an abundance of mined materials and skilled technicians, plus advanced scientific knowledge that might well have led to development of products in demand elsewhere. Undoubtedly more could be produced than its small population could consume. There was absolutely no good reason why such products should not be sold to willing buyers.

It would have to be something small enough to load without being observed, something that would fit into boxes that would look like normal supplies. The go-between would have to bring those boxes in an ordinary groundcar unless he could make a deal with a food supplier for space on a truck. And the police would be watching for any load that looked suspicious. But it was done all the time, he knew, so it couldn't be impossible—and because there was high risk, there must be profit.

There was no risk he wouldn't take for a chance at eventually owning a ship.

His heart began to beat fast. He was due to meet with Darrow in a few minutes. Perhaps he could find out. . . .

"You once asked me," he said to Darrow when they had concluded their usual business, "if I could supply cargo. What sort did you have in mind?"

Darrow frowned. "If I asked you that, it was before I knew you, Rivera," he said. "Before I'd read any of what I was delivering to you."

"You've read the files?" Terry asked in astonishment.

"A few of them. I got curious after I got your bracelet back—I didn't try to break the code, but Elrond's face when he picked it up told me it was something he hadn't expected. I don't deal in what he seemed to think it was, and since the files you buy are in clear, I decided I'd better know what kind of stuff I'm carrying. It was a surprise. Some of it's crazy, but there were things that set me to thinking."

"About what?" Terry ventured.

"About how people should use their own minds instead of believing everything they're told. About the mind being more than what's been programmed into it."

"That's true. On other worlds people know it, at least some of them do. The files are public in other colonies."

"And what happens to them here?"

"I'm not authorized to say."

"It would be a good thing if they were made public," Darrow declared.

"For that to happen," Terry pointed out, "the law would have to change."

"There are a lot of laws that should change."

"Like the law against exports? That would dry up your source of income, wouldn't it?"

"Most of my income is from mining. What I get on the side, I'm willing to take because the goddamn government has no right to say my suppliers can't sell it and pay me a reasonable fee for shipping."

"I agree. I'd like to know your suppliers, if they're seeking couriers."

Darrow gave him a long look. "You don't know what you're getting into, Rivera, and I'd feel to blame if it turned out wrong."

"For me? I'm not as naive as I may look. I've done quite a few things the government here doesn't know about."

"Are you aware that except when a scapegoat's needed, the government looks the other way?"

Startled, Terry tried not to show it. He hadn't known that.

"I like you," Darrow stated. "You remind me of the clueless young man I once was. And," he added pointedly, "I know something about you that you don't want spread around."

"I'm not going to repeat anything you say, if that's worrying you."

"Then I'm going to tell you the truth about the smuggling business before you fall into the trap the rest of us did." Slowly Darrow continued, "The government knows all about it. They know who's involved. And they let us alone as long as we toe the line."

"For God's sake, why?"

"Because they want the income. We pay out nearly all of what we get."

"To corrupt police officers, you mean?"

"No. To official collectors. The government's treasury relies on interstellar trade."

"I thought they didn't want any interstellar contact," Terry protested, confused.

"That's what the public is supposed to think. They don't want to let any subversive ideas in—you and your friends are playing with fire, and you're getting away with it only because it hasn't occurred to the government that anyone bothers to smuggle them. But the economy couldn't be sustained if Ciencia wasn't manufacturing stuff to export."

"If it's illegal and you don't profit much, why do it?"

With bitterness Darrow said, "Isn't it obvious? Once we've broken the law, they could arrest us if we ever refused to cooperate. And the penalty for visiting a starship is life in prison."

"Oh, my God," Terry said. "How many of you have been caught?"

"All of us—all the independent ship owners. The big mining companies aren't involved."

"You mean there weren't any captains who didn't start smuggling cargo in the first place?" He himself might be willing to act as a go-between, but he wasn't planning to smuggle with his own ship.

"You don't understand. When someone acquires a ship, he gets a visit from a collector and he's told what's expected of him. He doesn't get a choice."

"But what hold do they have over someone who's hasn't done it yet?"

Darrow sighed. "If you can't guess, you don't want to know."

"Oh." There were plenty of threats they could use, against both the captain and the ship itself, if they didn't have to worry about sticking to legal tactics.

Terry thought about it. If the law against smuggling wasn't enforced, it would be just like ordinary commerce, wouldn't it? There might not be much profit in it, but what he wanted was to fly; he'd be willing to carry cargo for free if necessary. And it would mean contact with a starship, possibly even a chance to bargain for passage on a starship—he might yet escape from Ciencia!

"I guess there's no reason to refuse," he said, "if the illegality of it's just a technicality."

"That depends," Darrow told him grimly, "on how good a price you get for what you sell. You have to do your own negotiating. And if you don't bring in enough, they'll switch you to a more lucrative product."

"Like what?"

"Like psychoactive drugs. The government labs produce drugs and other stuff developed by the advanced biochemistry here, nasty stuff that's not manufactured on any other world. Not all the starship captains will deal in it; if they're approached they give us a wide berth in the future. But those that do pay ten times what they'll pay for anything else, and very little of it goes to the dealer—which is okay by me because it's dirty money. Some of that stuff is suitable only for warfare."

"The *government* is in the drug business?" Terry gasped. Whatever illusions he had had about Ciencia being merely an unpleasant place to live evaporated. "Nobody," he said firmly, "could make me carry harmful drugs. And if you all agreed to refuse, they'd have no ships available to carry anything."

"You couldn't refuse if you were addicted," Darrow said, "and you would be, after a few weeks in their prison. Effectively, ship owners are slaves."

57

TERRY DID NOT sleep that night. The precarious balance he had developed on Ciencia had been thoroughly shaken; in addition to his personal hatred of his confinement here, he now found the evils of its society impossible to ignore. For some time his indignation over the suppression of ideas had been growing. He would not have been surprised to learn that its government was corrupt as well as misguided. But the revelation that it manufactured damaging biochemicals for distribution to other worlds was more horrifying than anything he had imagined.

Had the Elders known? he wondered. They'd had an agent here, and they appeared to be incredibly skilled in ferreting out information. Had they chosen this world as his prison in the knowledge that there was a final, insurmountable barrier to his ever owning a ship? Laesara had suggested that the obvious reasons for sending him here were not the only ones—"Think about it," she'd advised—but that hadn't seemed to be a warning of something even worse than the deprivations he expected. What if he hadn't met a friendly captain to clue him in?

He had believed that he would do anything necessary to obtain his own ship, however illegal it might be. But there were limits. He would not sell hard-core porn; he would not commit murder; and he certainly wouldn't risk being forced into drug dealing.

Ironically, he had learned that ships were relatively cheap. Darrow had told him that when one became available through the death or illness of its owner, it was put up for auction. No informed pilot would want it, so the only bidders were young ones employed by the mining companies, who didn't have much money, and winning bids were therefore low. After a few years' work as a cargo courier he could probably swing it.

Couriers were not required to deal in biochemicals, as they were not involved in cargo price negotiations beyond carrying messages and government agents in disguise delivered the drug shipments. So long as he didn't have a ship there would be little if any danger in becoming a go-between. But why should he bother, if he couldn't buy one with his profits?

Why bother with anything? he thought in despair. Every time he believed he could break free of this world's dreary surface, his hope was dashed—and each time it was worse than if he had never hoped at all. Yet how could he live year after year without any prospect of escape? He was only twenty-six. He might well live to be ninety-six—another seventy years! He could never go home, and Ciencia would never seem like home to him. He would never be able to fly, never even see the sun or the stars....

And he wasn't making use of his mind training. What had it all been for, all he'd gone through and all he'd achieved, if he couldn't do anything important with it? It was useful in minor ways, such as protecting his body from the freezing climate and, he supposed, maintaining his general health. He wouldn't have to worry about physical pain. But there was no opportunity here for psi. He could sense emotions telepathically but not connect with anyone, and there was nothing on the planet worth remote viewing. He could provide reading material about the paranormal but to offer any sort of demonstration would merely get him treated as a fraud or a madman.

When he got to work the next morning he was unable to put on a brave enough face to keep Alison from seeing his depression. "You're often sad, Terry," she said hesitantly, "and I've never asked why. But if there's anything I can do to help—"

"There's nothing anyone can do," he replied evenly. "Something happened to me that I can't tell you about, and I've got to live with it, that's all."

"Do you have a family?"

"No," he said. "Not anymore."

"Oh, Terry." Evidently she assumed his family had died, for she said, "Grief is normal—I can't tell you you'll get over it right away. Sometimes, though, it does help to talk."

He felt the wave of her sympathy, almost as if she too were telepathic, and suddenly he knew that to talk about it *would* help, at least temporarily. But she probably wouldn't believe him, any more than Elrond and Nina had. She was a psychotherapist; she would think he was delusional. And even if she did believe, there was no way she could change his situation.

Day by day he went on with his work, and there was some satisfaction in that, for neurofeedback did interest him and, seeing that it did, Alison began allowing him to operate the computer during her sessions with clients. He had modified the software so that its screen displays were larger and more colorful than the original version, closer to what he was used to despite their lesser complexity. "It's an improvement over what we used in the university course," Alison said, "and I think people respond to it faster. I didn't realize when I bought the system that I'd be getting an advanced version."

"I changed the standard displays," Terry admitted. "I hope you don't mind; it just seemed—more effective."

She was obviously impressed. "Have you ever used neurofeedback with anybody, besides just trying it out yourself, I mean?"

"No," he lied. There was no way he could explain where.

"I'd like to experience it personally with the new displays," she said. "Do you think you could conduct a session with me as subject?"

He did so during her lunch break, regretting the limitations of the scalp sensors that couldn't reveal much detail about state of consciousness. But Alison was profoundly affected. "I never felt so—*good* after it before," she said. "I wouldn't have thought visual effects could make that much difference."

They hadn't, Terry perceived with surprise. Unconsciously he had communicated the state shift telepathically, as he would have with the young trainees he'd worked with on Maclairn, and Alison had picked it up.

That wasn't really strange, he realized. He had known since Aldren's first explanation that everyone was capable of telepathy on an unconscious level. If Alison were to experience extreme stress under the direction of a mentor, the ability to use it consciously might be awakened in her, as it had been in some members of *Shepard*'s crew. If only that were possible here. . . .

But at least there could be communication of emotion between them. He would not be as totally isolated as he'd been so far. That might, he thought, become his lifeline to sanity.

It was barely two weeks later that, coming abruptly into Alison's office, he caught a glimpse of her tablet's screen before she realized he was there. She had found one of the easter eggs.

He sensed her dismay at his having seen, and decided that there was no reason why he shouldn't reassure her. "It's okay," he told her quickly. "I read those, too."

"Really? I should have known, you're so good with computers. How many are there?"

"A lot. You have to follow a trail. I'll show you, if you want."

He did not reveal that he put them there, but bit by bit over the next few weeks he led her to excerpts from some of the most important books dealing with the mind's effect on the body. She took to it with enthusiasm and an avid desire to keep reading; she was discovering many of the same ideas that she herself had secretly believed.

"Where did all this come from?" she asked in awe, not really expecting him to know. "It contradicts everything we've been taught. How could there be so many people who've thought it through on their own?"

"The texts come from other worlds, Alison. From Earth, mostly."

"But how could they? No ships come near except the ones that buy from criminals."

"Exactly. They buy, but they also sell, which of course is illegal, too."

"But then the people who put the texts on the Net are breaking the law."

"Yes. That's why the pages are so carefully hidden."

"Why do they risk getting caught? What do they gain?"

"They care what the rest of us gain. They believe ideas shouldn't be suppressed the way they are here. On other worlds all this knowledge is public."

Alison looked at him, confused. "You must have read a lot more than you've shown me, if you've learned that."

"Quite a lot," he agreed. "I fool around with it in my spare time."

He was continuing, of course, to make pickups and request specific ebooks; so when a few days later Alison mentioned one she'd seen referred to, he got it for her and pointed out that the reference was now hotlinked. "But how strange," she said. "It wasn't, last week. What a coincidence that the people who buy the texts happened to get the particular ebook I asked about—" She broke off, appraising him with awe. "*Oh*. Oh, Terry. Are you in touch with them personally?"

"I'm not free to answer that," he said gravely. She deserved to be told and he was sure she was trustworthy, but he would have to clear it with Elrond.

"Then I know the answer," she said. "I've always felt you were hiding something, and I won't ask you about it again. But I'll help, if there's ever a way I can."

Between working with Alison, picking up deliveries and hacking the Net, Terry kept busy enough to fill his time. The days went by with nothing to distinguish one from another, and he was glad not to have to think about the future.

Then late one night as he was about to go to bed there was a loud knock at his door. Startled, he opened it to Nina. She had evidently been to the spaceport, for she was disguised in her hooker's outfit. It was just as well, he thought, in case anyone saw her enter his room at this hour; he was wary of someday implicating people known to be his friends.

"Terry," she said tensely, "I came to warn you. Elrond has been arrested."

58

SHAKEN, TERRY GOT her to sit down and offered her a hot drink. "Tell me how it happened," he commanded.

"He was making a pickup—I waited for him in the parking lot. I saw the police go into the hotel, and then Elrond didn't come out. So I changed clothes in the back of the car and went in. Everybody was talking about it; they said a smuggler and his cargo courier had been taken."

"A smuggler? Do you know who?" *Not Darrow*, he was pleading inwardly.

"Elrond was supposed to meet Captain Guroff."

Thank God, Terry thought. Guroff didn't know him, but more than that, Darrow had become a friend he cared about. "We can't find out any more tonight," he said, "but the man I'm meeting tomorrow morning may know the details."

"You can't go out there tomorrow! They could be watching you."

"That's exactly why I do have to go. They know I always meet Captain Darrow's ship. If I don't show up, they'll make a connection with the arrest."

"They *know* you meet it?" Nina was horrified.

"We're all watched, Nina. They may think Darrow and I are lovers, or they may assume I'm a cargo courier; either way is okay. But it wouldn't be okay if they read Elrond's chip and connected me with him."

"How could it be okay if they assume you're a cargo courier?" she demanded.

He decided she had to know the reason, so he summarized, warning her not to repeat it and leaving out the part about the drugs. "It's why we've gotten away with buying data this long," he explained. "They don't want to stop cargo smuggling. But if they've arrested Elrond, it may mean they've found out what else is going on. Hopefully they'll think it's just a fluke, that nobody else is involved. Captain Darrow may know."

Terry remembered what texts were scheduled to be in the pickup from Guroff and spent the night with his tablet, carefully removing from the Net all easter eggs to which investigation of their subject matter might lead. That would be some protection if the authorities suspected that the content of Elrond's chip was destined to be posted on the Net. He prayed they would think it was just private reading material. Everything already on the cloud servers would remain safe even if they suspected conspiracy; as the cloud contained all the stored data for the whole planet, it was far too large for anyone to examine, even apart from the fact that he had distributed fragmented files. But if he had to remove the easter eggs related to all subjects, public access would end—and with rising anger Terry resolved that he could not let that happen. It was no longer a game.

Darrow, when they met the next day, thought there was no immediate danger. "They were watching Guroff, not Elrond," he said. "They suspected he was holding back part of his profits, which may have been true; Guroff isn't too sharp. So they're making an example of him. Elrond was caught in the net and if they know he wasn't dealing in cargo they won't admit it, because his presence is part of the evidence against Guroff."

"But it's not evidence. He didn't have any money with him, and the credit transaction, if it was made at all, is in the wrong direction."

"They'll manufacture what they need," Darrow said grimly. "Your people aren't the only ones in the world who know how to hack. There'll be a backdated transfer from Guroff to Elrond in the bank records by tomorrow morning."

Appalled, Terry protested, "He'll go to prison for something he didn't even do!"

"Would he rather go for what he did do? This way at

least the rest of you are out of it, and even if the police have read the chip there's a chance they won't bother to investigate."

Terry felt a sudden chill. He hadn't fully taken it in before—what was happening to Elrond could just as easily have happened to *him*. It still could happen at any time; Darrow was too smart to invite arrest as Guroff had, but he wasn't sure about the other captains he dealt with.

"Though whether they look into it depends on the content," Darrow added. "Some of your stuff might be called subversive."

"This was mostly fiction," Terry said, "and part of a twentieth-century book on ESP."

"Then you're probably safe."

"Elrond's not safe. And what if they try to make him name associates?" Elrond had no mind training, Terry thought miserably. He would suffer terribly if they used harsh methods. "I've got to get him out," he declared. "How do I contact a good lawyer?"

"You don't," Darrow said. "There are no lawyers who'll take on a smuggling case. If it were murder you could find one. Murder suspects are sometimes acquitted. With smugglers it's all for show, and they do their time."

"But he's entitled to a jury trial—that's League law."

"League law means nothing here, though there'll be a sham trial for publicity. I wonder about you sometimes, Rivera. You're bright and you're bold, but you're not always in touch with the real world. You read too much about others."

Terry was tempted to tell the truth. He couldn't keep it to himself forever, he thought, and Darrow was a good friend. But would he believe? He didn't want to risk losing the captain's respect.

"I'm in close enough touch to know I need your help," he stated. "They may not investigate the texts on Elrond's chip, but if they were to find another like it, they surely would. I once told you I might want to get into the cargo business, and you talked me out of it. I'd thought I might use the text pickups as a cover—but now it's the other way around. If I'm caught I'll need evidence of involvement with cargo smuggling to distract attention from my other activities. So give me a contact with your suppliers, and let them know I'm to be trusted."

"By God, you're a tough one," Darrow said. "You're going right on with what you've been doing when Elrond's gone, knowing they may trap you the same way?"

"I'm sure as hell not going to stop," Terry said firmly.

"In that case," Darrow said thoughtfully, "I'll set you up with a supplier who's honest, and I'll buy what you bring me—the more cargo I handle, the safer I am from the government. But there's something I want in return."

"If I can get it for you, I will."

"The stuff on the chips goes someplace where people can read it," Darrow declared, "and since you and your people are risking yourselves to put it there, I'll wager the rest of it's as interesting as what I've seen. Well, I don't want money for bringing it in anymore, beyond what you're paying the source. I do want access."

Terry nodded. With excitement he grasped what this meant. If Darrow, a practical man more knowledgeable about illicit cargo trading than forbidden literature, was personally interested in the texts, it was possible that wider readership might have political impact. It might ultimately lead to a change in Ciencia's policies.

"You said once you'd need authorization to tell me more, I assume from Elrond. Can you put me in touch with whoever's giving it now?"

"That would be me," Terry replied, realizing it was true. He was a more skilled hacker than Elrond and had been doing nearly all that work for weeks, as well as most of the pickups. No one would question it, despite his reputation for being somewhat eccentric. He was now the leader of the conspiracy.

59

WHEN HE GOT to work the next morning, Alison met him with a troubled frown. "Some of the links don't work anymore," she said. "I highlight them and nothing happens."

"I know. They're too dangerous right now to activate." If he was the leader, then he was free to tell Alison, Terry realized. He wanted to tell her; he sensed that she would share his commitment to it, and it had been a long time since he'd been able to share such feelings with anyone.

"You once said you'd like to help spread these ideas," he said. "Did you mean you'd be willing to get involved in something risky?"

"Yes. It's important for people to see that science doesn't know everything. That there's a whole realm of thought that's been withheld from us. Do you really have contact with whoever's putting these texts on the Net?"

"Well, you see, I'm the guy who's been doing it," he confessed. "One of them—and the other one has just been arrested, so I guess I'm in charge from now on."

She was not as surprised as he'd expected her to be, once she got over the first shock; she knew he had exceptional computer skills. What disturbed her more was the revelation that he himself picked up texts from the ship captains. He downplayed the risk of arrest, but Alison was not fooled. "It's not that I don't think it's worth it," she said, "and I admire you, Terry. But I don't know if I can get used to your being in danger."

"It's something we'll have to get used to, if we care about making a difference in the world," he said. "I'm mad, Alison! I was only half awake for a long time, shutting out something that hurt too much to think about; but now I'm worked up over what's going on here. I have to do more than just make information available. We've got to have a goal, a plan for getting enough people involved to change the laws."

"Is that possible?"

"In principle, yes. Darrow said most of the elected officials aren't corrupt—it's the bureaucrats who're running the smuggling racket and it's in their interests to prevent public contact with the outside. We'd need to convince the voters to demand reform."

"Most people wouldn't stand for censorship if they knew so much is being kept from them," Alison agreed. "It's contrary to human nature."

With rising confidence, Terry realized that this was true. The colony's founders had been fanatic about eliminating unscientific ideas and had not objected to the suppression of them. Later generations had had no say in it and had not known what was missing. But according to what he had read, individual human beings vary in the balance they prefer between rational and metaphorical forms of thought—so as the population increased, the proportion who were less one-sided than the founders must have grown.

"Right now we have no idea how many people are reading secretly," he pointed out. "We have to unify them and attract more. I don't know how yet, but there's got to be a way."

During the next few weeks he waited, tense with worry, to see if there were any repercussions from the discovery of the chip Elrond had carried. There were none. Either its content hadn't raised suspicion of more extensive violations, or Elrond had managed to dispose of it somehow.

Miserably, Terry realized that Elrond, who according to Nina didn't know about the government's involvement in smuggling, would assume that he was the one who had inserted the evidence against him in the bank records. What else could he think? It would have been an obvious way to save himself from suspicion, and he was the only person in the group capable of hacking at that level. Elrond had never fully trusted him in any case. But Nina did, so

he asked her to intercede when she visited Elrond in jail.
"You can't explain what really happened if the guards are
listening," he said. "Just tell him I didn't betray him. And
tell him to ask Guroff why he smuggles."

The authorities wasted no time in putting Guroff on
trial. Elrond refused to testify against him despite his
knowledge that he was indeed a smuggler; the man had
been obliging in his dealings with him, and in any case it
wouldn't be wise to risk revenge on the other couriers or
make the rest of the captains think they couldn't trust
them. He told Nina that he had been offered a plea bargain and had turned it down. The outcome of his own
trial was therefore a foregone conclusion, and he was sentenced to five years. Guroff, who had visited a starship—
in itself a serious crime even apart from the smuggling of
cargo—got life in prison.

Darrow greeted the news with grim resignation, aware
that the same could happen to him if he failed to earn
enough from smuggling to satisfy the bureaucrats who
were supervising him—either that or be forced to deal in
drugs, which Guroff had evidently been thought incapable
of getting a sufficient price for. Guroff had been a
hardworking asteroid miner when, with pride in having
saved up the money, he bought his ship, Darrow said. He
hadn't wanted to be a smuggler and had pursued it half-
heartedly, with tragic results. Terry, who by this time
had made contact with a supplier of electronic parts and
was delivering them to Darrow when he made pickups of
text chips, tried not to think about the agents he knew
were watching them both.

He had restored the easter eggs he'd deactivated the
night of the arrest and had been trying to devise a way to
spread awareness of the illicit net's existence without
endangering the people who used it. The reading material available wasn't organized; there was simply a maze
of hidden links that could be followed haphazardly by anyone interested in where they led. That wouldn't do if he

wanted to form a political movement. Trusted individuals would need access to longer texts than could be found by mere surfers, which meant authorizing it on an individual basis and maintaining an encrypted password file. It was becoming a much larger and more perilous undertaking than he had envisioned when he first started to hack—and far riskier than when he'd hacked during his high school days. Then, he could have quit if things had gotten too hot. Now he could not quit. Now other people were involved whose safety depended on his expertise.

He did not know the people who had hung out with Elrond and Nina well. Elrond had thought it wisest to keep their true identities confidential, as his own had been kept from them; and because he was viewed as an oddball none of them had tried to get close. Now he had to contact them personally and make them aware of his plans. This he could do only through Nina, and for his frequent contacts with her to seem natural, it had to look as if they were dating. Nina was only too glad to go along with this but Terry deeply regretted it, for it was obvious that she wanted something he was not prepared to give. He liked her well enough, but after Kathryn he was never going to be attracted to anyone else. Since he couldn't explain this, she was puzzled and evidently hurt; but she kept hoping.

It was more comfortable to be with Alison, with whom he could relax. She was becoming the closest friend Terry had ever had—not counting Kathryn or the mentors, of course. They saw eye to eye on things. They shared thoughts about contraband ebooks that they both enjoyed. Moreover, she had a deep interest in the universe and was fascinated by what she read of other worlds in the official knowledgebase, which did, of course, contain astronomical information and basic facts about Earth and its colonies. He longed to tell her what it was like to visit them and to explore new planets, for he knew she would understand his pain at being barred from space. She too

would like to travel between the stars, he thought ruefully, though it had not yet occurred to her that Ciencia's
isolationist laws should be challenged.

They continued to work together with neurofeedback
clients, Terry taking on some sessions alone while Alison
conducted psychotherapy in her office. He had a gift for
it, she said, as of course he did; his telepathic powers
were active on the unconscious level not only with her,
but with the clients. Someday, he thought, he would explain this to her. But the time was not yet right.

Since Alison didn't mind his taking time off unexpect-
edly, he decided to phase out the rest of the data couriers except for rarely-needed backup. The fewer people
who had even indirect contact with the starships, the safer
everyone would be. Most of the data was now brought by
Darrow, who wasn't charging anything for carrying it, and
soon it all would be, though Terry had not dared to drop
the other captains immediately in case the lack of meetings with them was seen to be connected with Elrond's
arrest. Only when he delivered cargo did he meet Darrow
at the spaceport, for he now openly socialized with him at
other locations in the city.

Picking up cargo from the supplier was a chore, but
not especially dangerous. He was, after all, performing a
service needed by the government racketeers, and as long
as they thought it was his only illegal activity, he wouldn't
be discouraged from it. He had found it necessary to buy
a groundcar with his savings, but the income from sale to
Darrow—who paid well because he knew his records were
examined—soon made up for it. "If I underpaid you the
examiners would smell a rat," he explained. "They'd assume I was keeping the difference instead of adding it to
their percentage. And anyway, I'd rather the money was
in your hands than theirs."

Terry lived frugally and saved nearly all his income,
he was not sure why. Used mining ships did sometimes
come up for auction, and whereas reason told him that he

did not want to be enslaved by owning one, in the back of his mind was the thought that his hope of changing the law might be realized before he got too old to fly.

His friendship with Darrow had, of course, made him think that an opportunity to get off the ground had arrived; on realizing that the captain wouldn't doubt that he was innocent of the theft charge, he had spent three nights in happy excitement. But when *Bonanza* next landed and he sounded Darrow out about it, he was brought down to earth with painful finality. "We can't take the chance," Darrow had pointed out. "I couldn't be sure of hiding you—we're watched, and I can't trust all the miners I carry. If you were caught visiting a starship you'd go to prison, and then what would happen to your scheme for spreading the word?"

"But if I went just to the asteroids, not the starship? I'd be willing to work as a miner for a while."

"What for? You're too important where you are to think like a spacestruck kid. I know how it feels—I was like that myself. Anything to get above the clouds and see what the sky looks like! But you're grown up now. And besides," he added, "if I hired you as a miner I'd have to scan your ID for the log and register your real name."

Darrow, of course, did not know that he was a pilot and had once been a starship captain who now ached at the thought that the freedom of space was behind him. Yet that was all the more reason why he couldn't endanger himself merely for his own pleasure, he thought sadly. Not if he was serious about wanting to further the conspiracy and keep its members safe.

Since Terry was doing all the hacking, the sole function of members would be recruiting newcomers to recruit still more. After giving considerable thought to the problem of secrecy, he decided on a modified clandestine cell structure to replace Elrond's informal arrangement. The people entrusted with distributing passwords to newcomers would in some cases be acquainted, as some of the existing members already were, but would not know the identities or screennames of each other's recruits. None of them would know his identity, or he theirs, except those with whom he had had personal contact. The exposure of any given individual would thus be limited, but by no means eliminated. If someone he didn't know was caught reading forbidden material, the secret of where it had come from and how it was stored would be protected. As far as those he did know were concerned, he would have to rely on their ability to resist pressure—but that had always been true.

There remained the question of who was going to collect the money to pay the source. "I'm not going to coerce anybody to contribute," Terry said. "We'll have a treasurer, but membership isn't going to depend on donations."

"Who are you to decide that?" protested one of Elrond's friends. "We all contributed before."

"Yes, but we're going to grow, and we need support more than we need funds. If we excluded those who can't or won't pay, we couldn't spread our ideas far enough."

"What need is there to give the privilege of reading more than can be found through the easter eggs to people who haven't paid for it? It's not fair to those of us who have."

"Well," said Terry, "that depends on what you're paying for. It's not just for your own benefit. It's to work toward a time when the laws of this world can be changed."

"This is the first I've heard of it. You make it sound like a political cause."

"That's exactly what it is," Terry declared. "If you don't want to take part, it's up to you, but personally that's why I'm risking my neck. And unless someone else wants to take over the hacking, that's how we're going to operate."

It wasn't until he sensed the surprise in their minds that he realized he'd been expecting them to say "Yes, sir," as if he were their captain—and that he'd risen out of his long depression to the extent of acting as if he were.

60

SINCE CIENCIA HAD no contact with other worlds except through the government, it had no public chronometer showing standard Earth time and its days were, of course, out of phase with days on Maclairn; so Terry could not have kept track of the passage of time there if he hadn't found an atomic clock on the Net. As it was, he knew the week when his son was due to be born. Oh, God, he thought, he could never be sure that Kathryn and the child were all right . . . if only telepathy could reach that far. . . .

It did reach Alison, who knew immediately that he was more troubled than usual. They were sensitive to each others' moods now, and he knew that she was hurt by his failure to confide in her. "Terry, if something's gone wrong and we're in danger, I have the right to know," she insisted.

"It's not like that. Just something from . . . the past. Something I shouldn't worry about because it's not my concern anymore, but I can't help remembering."

"I wish you'd tell me about your past. It's a mistake to hold pain in, talking can lessen it—"

"You know nothing about pain!" he burst out, and then, at her look, he was overcome by remorse. She was a psychotherapist, and it was her business to help people who were hurting. "I'm sorry, Alison," he said. "I know I'm not the only person who's lost a lot. Right now is a bad time for me, that's all. I'll be okay as soon as I put my mind on working."

"We have a new client coming this morning," Alison said, resigned for the time being to his reticence.

"Marcia Jordan was injured in an accident some time ago. She's had good medical care, but the pain in her back hasn't gone away. I think neurofeedback may help her, though of course it can't do anything more than teach her to relax. Since this is her first session I'll supervise, but I'll let you conduct it; you seem to get better results."

The moment Marcia came into the neurofeedback room Terry sensed her agony. As a full telepath he felt it literally in his own body. Quickly, trying not to let it throw him, he settled her in the chair and attached the scalp sensors. He began guiding her into the usual process of relaxation, encouraged by her response to the feedback display. But there was more wrong than tenseness; he could feel nerve pain—there had been damage the doctors couldn't repair. He was ashamed at having complained about emotional pain when there were people who had physical pain that wouldn't end ... yet it could be ended by anyone fortunate enough to be taught by a mentor. It was intolerable to think mentors could never come here!

Though in most ways Terry's past was behind him, he still had the mind skills he'd learned from Aldren. He would never suffer in the way this woman was suffering; there was no need to be sharing it even now. . . . Recalling how it felt to shift into a different state of consciousness, he told himself firmly, *It needn't be like this, you don't have to suffer, just relax and the pain will stop.* . . . The familiar shift occurred and he was free of the shared suffering almost instantly. Terry turned back to Marcia, thinking he shouldn't have let his attention drift.

She was smiling. Incredulous, she said, "It just— stopped! It doesn't hurt anymore! I didn't think just watching the screen would act so fast."

Only then did he remember that he had stopped Mikaela Orlov's pain telepathically in the same way.

Mikaela had had training. But the mentors could heal people who hadn't . . . and both Aldren and Tristan had said that someday he too might be able to do so.

Alison was staring at Marcia, aware that something inexplicable had happened but unable to imagine what had caused it. Terry knew he had to take charge of the situation. "It does act fast sometimes," he said. "It's not permanent, of course; it's just a way of training your mind. In between sessions, remember how you felt just before the pain stopped, and let it happen again. Don't try to force it. Sometimes it may lessen and other times it won't. But now you know it *can* happen. With practice, it may happen often."

God, he thought, what had he done? He had enough responsibility with managing the conspiracy, with hacking, with retrieving data from Darrow. He had just managed to gain respect as an underground leader, and being viewed as a miraculous healer was not at all compatible. Yet Marcia would come again and he couldn't refuse to help her. Alison knew, and so he couldn't refuse to help other clients, either. . . .

When they were alone she said, "Okay, Terry. You can't keep this from me any longer. I have to know what you're doing with the neurofeedback and how you learned to do it."

He didn't know how to begin—or how far he would have to go. But he was suddenly aware that he trusted Alison not only with the conspiracy's secrets but with his inner self; if she could not believe what he said, then he could not rely on his own ability to sense people's trustworthiness. His psi-giftedness was the core of who he was, the underlying reason for his commitment to spread acceptance of mind power. He could not refuse to let it guide him.

"What you've read about telepathy is true," he told her, "and more is known than is in the ebooks. Everyone is unconsciously telepathic, including you. I happen to have a gift for using it consciously. I reach the minds of the clients and they respond. I can't pick up their thoughts, though—only their feelings. To exchange thoughts, both people must be aware of what they're communicating."

She wasn't in a position to doubt him; there was no other explanation for what had been going on. But it didn't satisfy her. "How could you know more than is in the books? How could you even know what's in the ones you haven't read yet? The ebooks come from Earth."

Terry drew a deep breath. "So did I, Alison."

She stared at him. "That's not possible."

"I told Elrond once, and he thought I was literally crazy, that I was deluding myself with a story I wanted to think was true. So I've never told anyone else. I—I don't want you to think I'm delusional. I care too much about what you think."

"I could never doubt your sanity. But I don't understand how what you're saying can be true."

He told her, then—not all of it, of course, not about Maclairn or the Elders. But he did say that he had been in Fleet before he was captured. That he had been a starship captain and still longed to fly. That he had a wife he loved and a son who was now, perhaps today, being born.

"I can't explain what I was mixed up in that led to my being dumped here," he said. "I've sworn twice over never to reveal it, and I won't break that oath even though there's no way it could ever be known that I did. But it wasn't anything I regret. I knew I was putting myself at risk, even though I didn't imagine having to live out my life in exile."

She pressed his hand, and he knew that inside she was grieving for him. "Why here, out of all the colonies in the galaxy?"

"Because this is the only one from which there's no way to escape."

He went on to tell her what Aldren had taught him, including only as much as he'd known while on Titan. This was technically a violation of the ESA he had signed there, which he had been warned was binding for life; but since he was sure she would never repeat what was said to her in confidence and there was no chance that she would have contact with anyone beyond this isolated world, he did not think Admiral Frazer would mind.

"Aldren used neurofeedback much more advanced than what we've got," he said. "I've tried to improve ours, but our sensors don't provide enough data—and there's a secret part of the procedure he used that I promised not to reveal. I wouldn't be capable of handling that part myself anyway, and without it a client couldn't learn to turn off pain personally, or control as many physical responses as I do. But I guess I can provide help during sessions. I guess I have to."

Alison said thoughtfully, "Terry—if you're doing it telepathically instead of teaching people to reduce pain by themselves, it doesn't really depend on the neurofeedback, does it?"

"No," he admitted, "though the feedback helps make them receptive. I did it once for a young woman who'd been injured in a crash. I—I stopped her bleeding, too. But we mustn't let anyone find out that I can. I don't want to be pursued as a healer. The powers of the mind are in everyone, and what's important is to get people to believe in their own potential."

"By reading about it?"

"Yes, since that's the first step. That's why I'm working to spread the idea. But on Earth people can read freely and they still don't believe in what the mind can do. A group of us who knew Aldren were trying to promote acceptance of psi, but there was opposition even there. And here we're so far behind that I'm not sure how much good I can do."

"You're doing a lot of good," Alison declared. "I'm proud

to know you, Terry. I'd do anything to help you escape if it were possible, but since it's not, your loss is Ciencia's gain."

61

AS TIME WORE on, Terry threw all his thought and energy into his work, driving himself so as not to fall back into thinking of the past. Alison's clinic was thriving and she made him a partner; they had a long waiting list and gave priority to applicants with physical pain that medical science had not cured. He conducted all the neurofeedback sessions, while Alison followed up with psychotherapy aiming to reinforce her clients' belief in the power of their minds to help them.

He had not wanted to become a healer, yet it would be wrong, he decided, not to use his psi gift, and there was no other opportunity to do so on Ciencia. He found that during sessions, at least, his satisfaction in relieving suffering overrode his general unhappiness, despite the fact that he had to literally share it each time before shifting into the state of freedom from it. To his surprise, in some cases people he helped did gradually learn to reduce pain on their own, despite the fact that he wasn't a mentor and the neurofeedback wasn't as sophisticated as that used on Maclairn—evidently telepathy alone was giving them experience that carried over. Then too, the clinic's clients were developing skepticism about the scientific dogma they'd been taught, and any means that could be used to encourage public interest in heretical ideas was worth pursuing. Perhaps it was worth the risk of being idolized as the word spread, abhorrent as that would be to him.

Now that the shock of his exile was lessening, he did think sometimes about the Elders, and the irony of how his youthful wish to meet aliens had turned sour. It would have been such a thrill once to know of their existence. The idea of finding them had epitomized the discoveries he had wanted so desperately to make as an explorer. But knowing had proved to be a burden, as Laesara had warned that it would be, even apart from the loss of all the personal things he cared about. Though the confirmation that humankind was destined to join with other civilizations in the future was reassuring, it made wondering about such civilizations all the harder. He alone among humans had knowledge that the wisest men and women for centuries would have given anything to possess—but only enough to tantalize. Only enough to make speculation about ETs more frustrating than it had been when it could be classed as fantasy. It *would* do harm for others to have this knowledge! The more he pondered it, the more Terry realized that for the Elders to hide themselves was right. Until such time as humankind was ready for full partnership with them, it was better for people not to be aware of what lay beyond comprehension. So he no longer felt bitterness about their stern policy, and cursed not them but fate for ruining his life.

He had learned not to dwell on this. His days were full; often he worked after hours in order to accept as many clinic clients as possible. At the same time, he devoted evenings to delivering cargo or meeting with conspirators, leaving only the nights for hacking. He got very little sleep.

Membership in the conspiracy grew rapidly. Alison started her own cell; Terry did not know which of their clients she recruited, just as he did not know Darrow's recruits or those of Elrond's friends. But he knew how fast the password database was growing. And these were just the people given access to reading material that couldn't be found through easter eggs. The total number of people influenced was much larger, and before long, he began to sense—perhaps through contact with the collective unconscious—that the public's mood was changing.

It occurred to him the very fact that reading about unscientific ideas was forbidden might be increasing people's appetite for it. On Earth, where such ideas were freely available, those not presented through religious metaphors were generally scorned; or when not scorned, were met with widespread indifference. But people don't scorn what they search for in a game, much less what they take risks to acquire. Perhaps the most effective way to spread such ideas was to ban them. On the other hand, suppression was *wrong*, and his hope was to see it brought to an end.

The government censors did not catch on to what was happening under their noses. It simply didn't occur to them that interest in the unscientific might be an organized underground movement; what amateur writing they found in plain sight they attributed to crackpots. Occasionally Terry posted some badly-written fantasy and speculation openly though anonymously to see what would happen, and received stern email warnings in return. This he did to keep the censors busy so that they wouldn't bother to look any further. If security experts had searched, they could have found evidence of clandestine activity even if not who was behind it; there was no way to prevent that. So he took preemptive action to make them think experts would be wasting their time.

The people he knew, except for Alison and Darrow, continued to consider him rather odd and standoffish; and having spent his youth as a loner, Terry reverted to behaving like one. Remembering what Captain Vargas had once told him about command, he didn't encourage familiarity. An underground movement could not be run like a democracy. Either he was in charge or he wasn't, and he knew that if he wasn't it would fall apart.

Nevertheless, he had to prepare for the possibility that he might someday be caught. He therefore devoted considerable time and effort to training two backups to take over the hacking if necessary, and asked them each to train a successor. He hated the idea of letting these four people in on the location of the files and the methods he used to hide them, yet there was no reasonable alternative.

He no longer saw Nina often, to her great disappointment; though she dated others she had not become attached to anyone. She was a strange girl, tough on the surface and capable of risky action, yet obsessed with a fantasy world centered mainly on *Lord of the Rings*, the remaining books of which he had long ago obtained for her. A number of Elrond's original group had taken their screennames from the story, as she had; and she felt Terry should have done the same. "I don't know who Skywalker was," she said, "but you share our goal and you're our leader, so you should be one of us."

He smiled. "Do you think of me as Frodo, then?"

"Oh, no," Nina said. "You are Aragorn. You are destined to be king."

"I'm not aiming to head the government," he protested. "I'm only trying to bring about some changes in its policy." He recalled wryly that Aragorn was also destined to marry Arwen.

"To bring about change someone has to run for office," she pointed out, "and that will be you."

He had never thought of such a thing. On the verge of reminding her that Ciencia was not his world, he recalled that she hadn't really believed that any more than Elrond had; she had simply been more tolerant of his alleged delusion. "I couldn't be a political candidate," he protested. "I have to stay undercover."

"But you wouldn't need to after you won. And before that, who would know?"

Journalists would be sure to find out, he thought. If there was any sure way to get investigated, it was to seek office. And no candidate who challenged science could possibly win. Change, if it happened, would be brought about by public demand rather than by any single political leader. What was needed was a symbol around which their secret supporters could rally, to make them feel that what they were doing might accomplish something once the novelty of reading forbidden texts wore off. Then, perhaps, a grassroots movement would flourish.

It was too soon for that, much too soon. But not too soon to start searching for a symbol. As the thought emerged, a strange feeling came over him like the precognition that he'd once believed might be among his gifts. "I'll use one of Aragorn's many names," he told Nina, "but not openly. It may not even turn out to be me. When the time is right, I'll write of Estel—which means "hope"— but only to say that someday Estel will transform this world."

Hope for whom? he wondered. Not for him—he had long ago given up all hope of fulfilling the pledge to defend Maclairn that had meant so much to him. But if there was a chance that he could have some impact on Ciencia, his life might not be entirely wasted.

One year went by like another. He counted them by his son's birthdays. Radnor was a year old, then two, then three . . . was Kathryn still alone? He could not expect her not to enter another relationship; as far as she knew, she was a widow. He told himself that he wanted her to find happiness, as he himself never could. In any case he didn't have time to brood over it. He took on more work to make sure he didn't have time.

Shortly before Radnor's fifth birthday, Elrond was released from prison.

Terry wasn't sure what he was going to do with Elrond. No one but Nina, his cousin, had been allowed to visit him in prison, which Darrow felt was because of a fear that one of the captains might tell him why he was there. The authorities weren't aware that Nina knew. Nobody was supposed to know about the racket except the captains themselves, who were instructed not to talk on pain of exposure and arrest; Terry had learned belatedly of the risk Darrow had taken in informing him.

Nina's visits had been brief and monitored, so she had told Elrond nothing about the status of the conspiracy. He might well believe it had been dormant, awaiting his return. He certainly wouldn't be expecting a structured underground with Terry, who he thought was at least partly out of his mind, at the head of it. And he would naturally feel it was his right to assume leadership again. Yet a risky undertaking could have only one person in charge, just as a ship could have only one captain. Terry's Fleet experience told him that there was no place for someone who thought he was captain, but wasn't.

He drove Nina to the prison to pick Elrond up, intending to wait in the car while she greeted him and explained what he needed to know. The guard, however, insisted that not even brief parking was permitted; the groundcar must be put on autocontrol and taken into the stack. Exasperated, Terry complied. He hadn't wanted to be present when Elrond heard the news of his promotion. As he had feared, a subtle announcement wasn't effective—Elrond thanked him warmly for taking over in his absence and, while they waited for the autovalet to retrieve the car, he expressed eagerness to assume the responsibility again. "Though I may not be able to make pickups." he added, "since they'll be watching me now. I still don't know how they caught me, or who planted the false evidence—but I believed Nina when she said it wasn't you."

"Didn't Guroff tell you?" Terry inquired, starting the car and taking back manual control.

"I didn't see Guroff—the lifers are isolated from everyone else. Anyway, how would he know?"

"Elrond," Terry began, "they only wanted you for evidence against Guroff—"

At that moment, as he pushed the Proceed switch, the car blew up.

62

ELROND WAS KILLED instantly. Nina, in the back seat, was thrown out; she hated seatbelts and fortunately had defeated hers. Terry was alive but badly injured; he managed to crawl out only because he was able to turn off the pain of movement. He lay stunned, realizing dimly that he was bleeding and must stop. As he took control of his physical processes in the way the mentors had taught him, his head cleared and he realized that the renewed pain he felt must be Nina's. "Nina!" called out. "Nina, where are you?"

"I'm over here," she answered weakly. He turned toward her voice and saw to his dismay that the wreckage near her was burning. There wasn't much left that was flammable but to be safe, he drew on his long-unused psi skill for extinguishing fire, thankful that Tristan had forced him to overcome his fear of pyrokinesis.

"I'm losing a lot of blood," Nina called to him. "I pushed the emergency button on my phone, but—"

"You'll be okay. We won't wait for the response team to stop the bleeding." He crept over to her and took hold of the arm from which blood was gushing. "Just relax; it will stop in a minute."

"No it won't, it's deep—" She broke off, staring at the slash from which the flow had abruptly ceased. "It just *stopped*! How could it do that?"

"Never mind. The pain will stop too, if you relax and squeeze my hand." His long experience in the neurofeedback clinic made ending it for her second nature to him. *Follow me, Nina! We don't need to suffer, we can go into a state where pain doesn't matter. . . .*

She met eyes, awed. "*You* did that, Terry! You turned off the bleeding and the pain! You—you *are* Aragorn, Aragorn was a healer—"

She still thought of him that way, several years after

their discussion about it. The stress of their injuries opened her mind to him, and he knew that she hadn't stopped imagining a parallel with the long-delayed union of Aragorn and Arwen. He could not let that continue.

"Yes, I'm a healer," he confessed. "As I told you long ago, I came from offworld. From a place where there are other healers who taught me. And I'm married, Nina."

"Married? But if you can't ever get back there, that surely isn't binding."

"It's binding to me because I still love my wife."

"I didn't believe what you said before," she whispered. "Now I've got to, because you stopped the bleeding. And I believe more than ever that you're destined to be king—not literally, of course, but to lead us. Elrond will see—"

"Elrond is dead," Terry said bitterly. "They killed him; they were afraid he might know too much. Perhaps they thought Guroff had informed him before the trial."

"Killed him? But how?"

"There was a bomb in the car," he told her. "It was put there when they made us leave it in the stack—somebody climbed up to its rack while we were meeting Elrond. Apparently they never intended to let him go."

"I don't understand!"

"It's complicated. The paramedics are here now, I'll tell you later."

Terry spent more than a week in the hospital, wishing for a mentor to heal his broken bones more rapidly than he could himself. After that, with a strapped torso and one leg still in a cast, he moved into Alison's apartment, which was located near the clinic and had a spare bedroom, so she could help him get to and from work. The arrangement worked well and he decided to give up his rented room, in which he had remained since arrival on Ciencia despite the fact that he could well afford a nice apartment of his own. He enjoyed eating his meals with Alison and relaxing in her company during the few minutes when he wasn't hacking. It was the closest he would ever be to having a home, he knew; he found he was thinking of her almost as if she were family. And he could talk more freely about the conspiracy with her than with anyone else.

During his hospital stay he had spent a long time thinking, deeply troubled by Elrond's murder. Though he'd known the government racketeers were ruthless, he hadn't thought they would go that far—after all, Elrond hadn't done anything to displease them. Or had he?

"I didn't see the whole picture till now," he told Alison. "The government doesn't really care what we read—the officials were all born here, and they don't have any idea of how powerful unscientific thought can be. That's why they haven't searched harder for our stuff on the Net. They themselves have never stooped to reading anything suggesting that the mind can do more than reason, so they've lost the founders' awareness that if people came across such material they might take it seriously. What they do know is that offworld contact could threaten stability here, which would mean a threat to their own power—and definitely the end of their smuggling racket. So they'll do whatever they have to do to limit communication with starships."

"Elrond didn't go to a starship," Alison said, puzzled.

"No—but at some point he must have communicated with one. I hadn't stopped to wonder how he set up our courier system originally. By the time I arrived, he had arrangements with captains who'd agreed to bring data chips from the starships he referred to as "the source." But Darrow didn't negotiate with those ship's captains himself. How did Elrond find out that they were willing to sell data, and how was the price determined?"

"It would have had to be through a local captain," Alison said, "if not Darrow, then one of the others."

"Yes—and I think it must have been Guroff. When Guroff was questioned in prison, he must have revealed that at some time in the past, he carried messages between

Elrond and the starship captain, perhaps even that Elrond was buying chips, something they didn't know when they framed him for selling cargo. They couldn't risk his doing so again. And they don't know who he was acting for or what became of the chips, so they killed him to send a message to the receiver. Either that, or they did know, and the bomb was meant for me, too."

"But why didn't they question Elrond in prison to find out what's going on?"

"Probably they did," Terry said sadly. "He didn't have time to tell us what happened in there, but Elrond was a lot tougher than Guroff." With remorse, he thought of how he'd worried that Elrond would want to take charge of the conspiracy; had he suffered to protect it? Had he earned the right to be reinstalled as its leader?

Alison, who could usually sense the gist of Terry's thoughts despite not being consciously telepathic, said, "If he held out to protect the other conspirators, it was because he'd come to believe what we're doing is important, that it will change the world. And you are the best person to accomplish that, Terry. You mustn't feel guilty because he died when you didn't."

Slowly, Terry said, "I had two close friends on Earth who were killed for the same reason Elrond was—they were trying to foster public acceptance of mind power. Even if Ciencia's government didn't know that was what he was doing, *he* knew. It was why he risked himself. I've got to do more than I have so far, Alison. We have to have a plan for making it happen."

"You couldn't do more than you already have," she pointed out. "You're killing yourself by working at it day and night."

"I can't spend more hours," Terry agreed, "but I could change the selection of texts a little. It's been mostly fantasy and books about spirituality or psi or the mind's role in health. I haven't been sending for political books. But people are ready now to start thinking about connections."

"That's a whole lot more dangerous," Alison protested. "The government isn't going to ignore political ebooks the way they discount unscientific speculation, and besides, it will be obvious that they come from outside."

"All the same, it's necessary—all the more so *because* the offworld connection will be clear. Most of our readers haven't ever wondered where the ebooks come from. They think contact with the outside is impossible, so they may assume we've got a bunch of gifted writers creating some sort of imaginary world that's different from the world we live in. They need to be told there's hope that we can change things here."

"I'm not sure there is, Terry. Just knowing facts that aren't taught here is important in itself. Changing the government's policy is probably more than we can expect to accomplish."

"It may be," he agreed, "but people should *want* it. They should share some symbol of wanting it."

Late that night, after he had finished catching up with the file changes that had backed up during his hospitalization, Terry inserted a new easter egg where his readers would be likely to discover it. "There is a ship," he wrote, "and its name is *Estel*, which means hope. Its captain came from the stars and his heart is there, but at times his ship descends to bring the knowledge that's rightfully ours. And someday this knowledge will no longer be hidden."

63

IT TOOK A WHILE, but eventually people everywhere were talking about the ship *Estel*, presumably orbiting Ciencia, which the police ships diligently sought but did not find.

"You're crazy," Darrow had told Terry. "To deliberately reveal that texts hidden on the Net are coming from space—"

"They would have figured that out anyway as soon as I started posting political texts that can't be accessed from standard references," Terry pointed out. "This way they've been misled into hunting for a ship that doesn't exist, and it's keeping them busy."

It was an effective means of distraction. The police knew *Estel* did not land and therefore must rendezvous, yet the routinely-monitored trackers on all the local ships, including those of the large mining companies, showed that no one rendezvoused with anything except the known starships to which cargo was sold. They would not, of course, have had any jurisdiction over a starship in high orbit; all they could hope for was to arrest whoever was bringing data from it. So periodically, they strip-searched incoming crews, whose captains could not protest the humiliation because of the racketeers' hold over them. Nothing was ever found, as Darrow was alert enough to destroy the chips the few times *Bonanza* was boarded. Actually, after the strip-searches started few texts were imported; the cloud already contained far more illicit material than anyone could read in a lifetime.

Occasionally officials located and erased some of it; they hunted now, but weren't knowledgeable enough about the subjects covered to find the easter eggs, which were accessed not by single words but by non-adjacent combinations. Terry had, of course, used suitable precautions to keep bots out of the files themselves. The inspectors looked for political books, which were in the minority, and since he reposted them with different access points as soon as they disappeared, the countermeasures were not damaging. They also searched for the name Estel and found it in an appendix to *Lord of the Rings* that he had deliberately left open to discovery for the purpose of confusing them; the discovery of the name Elrond in the same text looked promising, but since Elrond was dead and they already knew he had communicated with a starship, it yielded no new information.

Terry's biggest worry was that one of his backup hackers would be caught. However, they were people he felt were capable of withstanding pressure; he did not think they would betray anyone, and even if they did, the worst that could happen—apart from their personal fate—was that the bulk of the reading material would be lost. It would take decades to get all traces of it out of the cloud, and by that time it would have served its purpose, since it could never be gotten out of the minds of the thousands of people who had been exposed to it.

As for him, he was beyond suspicion. He gave up delivering cargo when he stopped picking up data at the spaceport and focused on his work at the clinic, for which he had become renowned. Inevitably, over time clients had caught on to the fact that his personal gift, rather than just the neurofeedback, was responsible for alleviating their pain. Many other neurofeedback clinics had opened after observing the success of Alison's, and they did not get comparable results. Alison herself did not get comparable results on the occasions when she had to take over for him. And much as he hated being acclaimed for his healing power, he had to concede that it was a valuable cover for his other activities. No one would guess that a celebrated healer spent his spare time hacking the Net.

To be sure, the government didn't approve of healing either, since it was considered fraudulent by science. But they couldn't arrest him for it as long as neither he nor Alison claimed that he did anything more than conduct standard neurofeedback sessions. Despite their knowledge that he was a former cargo courier, they ignored him. Because they assumed that any healing effects attributed to him were imaginary, they viewed him as a harmless crackpot.

So the years passed, and for Terry one was like another. He didn't give himself time to stop and reflect, for if his thoughts drifted to anything beyond the demands of his undercover work, he soon found himself remembering Maclairn, and *Promise,* and the happy days of his youth. And Kathryn, always Kathryn . . . sometimes during the night he dreamed she was in his arms, that their minds were about to merge, when suddenly he was torn from her and awoke, his body and soul aching with frustration over what he could not have. Then, if he couldn't go back to sleep, he got up and went from his small dark bedroom to the sitting room of Alison's apartment and stood by the window, looking out at the perpetual dusting of snow that surrounded the city buildings, their glassy walls reflecting the glow of the reddish night sky; and he thought of how above that sky there was a black expanse full of stars, as he had seen it so many times and never would again.

Often, when this happened, Alison too got up and came into the sitting room and fixed hot drinks, and they sat at the table, not talking, just feeling the comfortable companionship on which he came more and more to depend. Sometimes he sensed that she shared his longing to be free of this confining planet, that she ached to travel between worlds and see the wonders of space as much as he did, now that he had made her aware that to do so was a human birthright. Yet she did not speak of it; she did not want to stir the feelings that she knew were an ongoing torment to him. She seemed to know the limits of what he could bear.

Though she was a charming woman well-liked by her clients, Alison had little social life, and after the first few years he had known her, she had rarely gone out with men. Terry was mystified; she seemed to him far more appealing than less thoughtful women like Nina, and he couldn't see why men wouldn't be attracted to her. It was strange that she wasn't in a long-term relationship; perhaps, he thought, one had ended that she was still mourning. But whenever he tried to ask her about it, she seemed embarrassed and turned away, closing her mind to him.

He wished he could put his arm around her and offer sympathy, as she had many times shown sympathy for him; but for some reason he did not quite dare.

His only other close friend was Darrow, who was un-married and spent little time on the planet's surface. Whenever he returned from a mining trip they got to-gether for drinks or a meal, for although they were rarely bringing in data now, Terry liked the man. He had never imagined that he might choose a smuggler as his best friend, despite having acquired more respect for smug-gling than he'd had as a Fleet officer. But they agreed on politics, and Darrow was eager to hear what Terry knew of governments on other worlds as well as his hopes for change on Ciencia.

Still, Terry had never told him about his own past. They knew each other too well now for Darrow to think he was crazy, but he would undoubtedly envy his starship experience and understand his grief over the loss of it. He didn't want to put him through that, nor did he want the captain to take the risk of transporting him into space, as he might well do if he knew why he longed to go there. He knew that if Darrow suggested it, he wouldn't have the strength to refuse the offer. He had gotten used to the confining gray sky, but sometimes he thought he would die from depression if he couldn't see the sun or the stars just once.

He had been on Ciencia more than twelve years when Darrow was badly injured in a mining accident. He knew nothing of it until Darrow called him from the hospital, where he had been taken after a police ship rescued him and his crew of miners from the asteroid where it had happened. One of the officers had brought his ship down without cargo; it sat at the spaceport, abandoned.

Terry felt for him, but it was only a temporary ground-ing, after all; Darrow would recover enough to fly, though he might have to give up the physical work of mining, and so his deep depression seemed out of proportion to the situation. He visited him in the hospital daily, relieving his pain as he did for the clients at the clinic—an ability Darrow had heard he possessed but until now had not fully believed in. When he was released, Terry drove him to the rooming house where he lived while onworld, promising to return after work.

"Stay now, if Alison can spare you just this once," Darrow said. "I may have only a little time."

"A little time for what? You're not going to be doing anything until you recover."

"A little time before they arrest me."

"Arrest you?" Terry exclaimed, shocked. "What for? Surely they won't blame you for not bringing in money when you're unable to fly."

"You're my friend, and you have a right to know," Darrow said. "I've been duping the extortionists. Besides taking cargo up to the starship I've been selling platinum metals there—of course all the mining captains do that, and the government knows it, since they know how much ore we deliver to the orbiting refineries and how much metal they return to us, and they know what we sell to the city buyers. They overlook the discrepancies because they want their cut. Well, usually I don't sell quite all I've got, and nobody notices because I'm a better negotiator than some and my proceeds come within the expected range. I hide the rest of the metal in the ship, and then when there are several starships bidding up the price, I can sell more than the government thinks I've got, and keep the difference. I've been getting away with it for years—I thought I was smarter than Guroff because he just held back money and pretended he'd made a poor deal. I never stopped to think they'd find my stash if I was grounded.'"

"Maybe they won't. Your crew's not likely to report you if they haven't so far."

"My miners haven't reported me because they've been getting shares. What we dig out is ours, and the government racketeers have no right to profit from it; I hired people who agree with me on that. But they may not all be loyal. I'll be grounded for a long time and they won't get shares while I am, whereas any one of them could get a damn big reward from the government. It's been a long time since an example was made of Guroff, and another is past due."

"Oh, my God."

"It was the principle of the thing more than the money," Darrow said morosely. "I had to defy them somehow, I couldn't just sit back like a docile slave. I knew I might pay for it, just as you know you might pay for spreading information the government has no right to suppress. We're two of a kind, Rivera, but you've had more of a positive influence on the world. I want to say that I'm proud to have known you, since this may be my only chance to say it."

Life in prison. For a spacer like Darrow it would be worse than death. And he had risked it for principle rather than for profit. It mustn't happen, Terry resolved—not when there was a way out.

He said slowly, "If another pilot were to take your ship up now, tonight, and get rid of the stash by mixing it in with a new load of ore, there'd be no evidence against you. And since the crew would know there wasn't, no one would stick his neck out to report you."

"Sure, but there are no pilots who aren't busy with their own ships, and if there were, they wouldn't risk getting involved. The cut-throat nature of this business doesn't foster mutual aid."

Drawing a deep breath, Terry said, "Darrow, I haven't leveled with you. You must have wondered sometimes about my past—"

"I have," Darrow admitted. "You're the strangest guy I ever encountered, what you know, what you can do— superb at everything you try. Yet half the time your mind's off somewhere on other worlds."

"That's because I miss those worlds. I was born on Earth, Darrow."

Darrow stared at him in astonishment. "From anyone else, I'd take that for a fantasy or a lie. It would account for your being as well informed as you are—but all the same, it needs a lot of explaining."

"Yes, and I'll tell as much as I can of how I ended up here. But right now, what you need to know is that I'm a pilot, and I used to be captain of a jump ship."

64

HARD THOUGH IT was for him to believe, Darrow listened to the story with fascination and evident feeling. Terry didn't tell him about Maclairn, of course, or about the Elders, to whom he referred merely as "a powerful group of people." Since Darrow was all too familiar with powerful people interfering in helpless citizens' lives, he found that part entirely credible. The part about having been taught advanced mind powers aroused more doubt; still, he knew Terry was revered as a healer by clients of the neurofeedback clinic. The interstellar flight part was what interested him most, however. He was, as Terry had predicted he would be, envious.

"But Rivera," he said finally, "it's been over twelve years since you've flown anything. Do you really think you can take off in an unfamiliar ship like mine and land it on an asteroid?"

"You don't forget that sort of skill," Terry said. "I've landed on many asteroids. I've lifted off in a starship that had been grounded for two hundred years, and later I put it down on an ice world—an earthquake swallowed it after that, but there was nothing wrong with my landing. And I've flown more shuttles than I can count."

Darrow frowned. "I think you can handle it," he said, "and I don't really have anything to lose if you can't. But *you* do. You could be killed. And even if the flight goes well, you could run into trouble if you were caught transporting the stash. It's all very well to hope they wouldn't arrest you if you handed it over to the racketeers—but it's not as if they were honest. They care mostly about enlisting ongoing sources of money, and you don't have a ship to keep getting it for them. They could take the stash from you and then arrest you anyway."

This had occurred to Terry. But risking it was the only way to save Darrow—and besides, to fly again! To see the sun and the stars one more time!

Convinced that Terry was aware of the dangers, Darrow gave him the location of the asteroid on which his claim was staked and agreed to call out the mining crew. Terry made calls to his backup hackers, warning them through a prearranged code that he would be out of touch for some time. Then he went back to the clinic to complete the afternoon's scheduled neurofeedback sessions. He had to struggle to keep his mind on them, though the pain of his clients soon drove everything else from it. When the last of them had left, he went to the apartment to say goodbye to Alison.

He had decided to tell her the truth. He'd left Kathryn without a farewell, assuming he would soon be back to her, and had spent the past twelve years regretting it. He could not leave Alison in the same way, for there was no denying that what he was about to do might get him into trouble.

Alison was more worried than he'd expected her to be. "I know you care about Darrow," she said, "and it's admirable to risk yourself for a friend. But oh, Terry—" To his amazement she seemed personally upset—calm, collected Alison, who had always been poised, always an emotional anchor not only for her clients, but for him. She was fighting to keep her distress from him, but her resolve broke down and he could sense that she was on the verge of crying.

"Alison, what is it?" he asked in dismay. "Not just that I might be in danger, surely—I've been in danger all the time for years. At any moment I could have been caught hacking."

"But you were *here*," she said. "You weren't off in space where I might never see you again. I can't shut that out the way I do when we share the danger."

I'll be away for only a little while, he started to say, but that was what he had written to Kathryn. "I know my work here is important," he told her, "and I suppose it may be wrong to risk abandoning people in pain when I've promised to help them. But this is something I have to do."

"You think I care about the *clinic*?" She reached out to him and he found she was in his arms and her tears were wet against his chest. "Terry, you're so blind! You say you're telepathic, yet you've never even guessed how I feel—"

And suddenly he did know what she was feeling, what he would have sensed all along if he had not so firmly shut it out. *Oh God, Alison*, he thought, *I never meant this to happen, I never meant to hurt you. . . .*

Neither of us meant it to, she was thinking, *but it happened anyway.* "I tried to respect your memory of Kathryn," she told him. "But it's been more than twelve years for you, Terry! Would she want you to mourn for twelve years?"

Had Alison's love for him really been so much less obvious than Nina's? Terry wondered. Or was it just that he'd been more aware of Nina's because with her, there had been no possibility of his returning it?

He had not dared to examine his feelings for Alison. It was true that Kathryn wouldn't want him to mourn so long, and yet . . . the Maclairnans had said that having once experienced the merging of minds during sex, a telepath could never be satisfied by sex with a non-telepath. He could not say this to Alison. He could not bear to let her know that a relationship between them could never be to him what she had every right to think it would . . . that it might turn out like the frustrating relationships he'd had before Maclairn, before he knew he was telepathic. He could not face that possibility, and so he had lived in her apartment for years without letting himself suspect that he wished they could be more than friends.

In turmoil, he pulled away. "This isn't a time I can answer that," he said gently. "I have to go now. Please, Alison, don't be afraid for me! I'm a good pilot. It's not dangerous for me to fly."

"You *want* to fly," she observed, "more than you want to help Darrow, more than you want anything else in life. And I'm glad you've finally got your chance. But it's not the flying that scares me."

The spaceport was dark by the time he got there. Darrow had told him that when brought in by the police officer, *Bonanza* had been put down some distance from its usual pad in a part of the field where he didn't often go. He found it easily enough, and the three miners in its crew were there waiting for him. He turned on the pad lights and made a thorough preflight inspection, finding the procedure no less clear in his mind after passage of years than if he had done it yesterday. The ship was not too different from many large shuttles he had flown, though older and more battered. Darrow had assured him that it had no mechanical or AI problems.

He also inspected the interior of the ship. The crew did not watch, though they knew what was hidden there and where it was hidden. They had been with Darrow long enough to see stashed platinum metals brought out, a little at a time, during rendezvous with starships, and they had stuck with him because they'd known. They could not retrieve it by themselves in his absence, as they would have no way to sell it. Moreover, Darrow had promised to split the entire proceeds from the trip among them if they flew with Terry, and they therefore welcomed him with enthusiasm.

Everyone was aboard and Terry was about to close the hatch when the lights on the adjacent pad came on. A man stood there, hailing him. "Hey! What the hell are you doing there! That's not your ship."

"Darrow asked me to fly for him while he's laid up," Terry called back. He backed down the ladder and walked toward the challenger, realizing that for an unknown pilot to appear did look strange. "I'm a friend of Darrow's," he began—and then as the light struck the other man's face, he recognized him. It was Renssalaer.

Oh, God, Terry thought. In all these years he had never run into Renssalaer, who had told him he was a family man and probably didn't frequent the hotel's bar. Was he himself enough older to seem a stranger? No, for his mind training slowed aging; he knew he would be remembered because Renssalaer had almost hired him and an unemployed pilot was a rarity.

"I know you!" Renssalaer said. "You're a thief. It's lucky I caught you before you got away with Darrow's ship."

"If you remember me, you know my name is Terry Rivera," Terry said. "You can call Darrow at his home and he'll tell you I'm taking it up with his permission."

"That makes no difference, because I'll bet he doesn't know about your record. He'll be grateful for my warning—you stole platinum once, and you're no doubt aiming to steal some of his."

"As you know, that charge was dismissed," Terry said.

"On a technicality. In any case, you won't mind waiting while I call him, and we'll have the police here to take over if he changes his mind." He reached for his phone, and Terry saw that he pressed the emergency key before the number search.

He had to act fast. If the police came they might search the ship and find Darrow's stash. He ran for it, scrambled up the ladder, and sealed the hatch behind him, aware that by doing this he was virtually proving his guilt and might well be pursued. Yelling to the miners to strap in, he slid into the pilot's seat and started the liftoff sequence.

As the ground fell away a police car reached the pad. Terry did not have time to think about it when setting his course, and then for a while he thought of nothing except the thrill of breaking through the cloud barrier and seeing, for the first time in more than twelve years, the glory of the stars.

65

THE JOY OF flying again, and of being above the thick gray shroud that had imprisoned him so long, overcame any fear Terry might have felt at the thought of what awaited him at the flight's end. No matter what happened, even arrest, these days of freedom would be worth it. For the moment he did not care about anything else.

But eventually he shook himself back to awareness of his situation. Did the police know on which asteroid Darrow had staked his claim? If so they might be on his tail. And they soon would know if they didn't already, since claims were a matter of public record. Police ships were faster than this one; they might be there waiting for him when he arrived. Either way, he would have no chance to unload the platinum metals and mix them with enough ore to disguise the fact that they were already refined. Moreover, he might be accused of claim jumping, a far more serious offense than mere theft. It wouldn't help if Darrow verified his permission to be there; Renssalaer believed he had conned Darrow, and besides, that would substantiate the case they would have against Darrow himself.

Could he head for some other asteroid and dump the stash there? The ship's AI had access to standard charts. But he might be followed, and besides, all the nearby asteroids had undoubtedly been claimed—it really would be claim jumping if he allowed his miners to dig on them. And he hadn't enough life support to reach a distant one.

The only possible action was to jettison the metals into space. The miners wouldn't like that, but there was no alternative. Reluctantly he turned the ship over to the AI and got out of his seat to give the order.

"No way," announced the mining boss. "Are you crazy, man?"

Terry was shocked; as a captain he was used to hearing, "Yes, sir." Biting back a reprimand that he realized was not applicable here, he tried reasoning. "We've haven't any choice. If we wait too long the police may catch us; they'll board us and search. At any rate they'll find the stash when we land, so we've got to get rid of it."

"We damn well do have a choice. They may not catch us, in which case we can stick to the original plan—but if they do, we won't have lost anything we could have kept. I'll gamble on cashing in rather than throw the chance away."

"They'll arrest us for possession, if not for claim jumping."

"They'll arrest *you*, maybe. You're the captain; the rest of us aren't liable."

"They will arrest Darrow and send him to prison for life," Terry declared. "That's what we're here to prevent."

"It may be why you're here. We're here to get the share he promised us, and we're not going to let go of it unless it's taken away from us."

Terry said decisively, "We'll have no more discussion about it. As you said, I'm the captain, and you have your orders. Now get up and start loading the stuff into the airlock."

Nobody moved. God, thought Terry, how did mining captains enforce their orders? Darrow had never implied that they were armed. In any case he was not, and he couldn't physically fight them when it was three against one. And he couldn't jettison the stash personally, either, since the three could easily restrain him.

They were at an impasse. He stood helplessly, knowing that if he sat back down he would lose what status he had with them and be viewed as useful only as long as the ship was in flight. They wouldn't hesitate to turn him over to the police as instigator of a scheme to defraud if it came to that.

And then, to his astonishment, the long-range comm came alive. "Ciencia control, this is HS *Freerunner*, inbound from Earth, requesting permission to approach. Over."

Terry knew how that worked. Permission would be denied, which they expected; smugglers' starships broadcast the request on all frequencies when they arrived so that mining captains with something to sell would know they were there. "HS *Freerunner*, this is Ciencia Control," came the reply. "Negative, repeat negative, no ships are permitted to approach this world. You are instructed to jump out immediately."

They wouldn't jump; they would wait several days in high orbit to see what they were offered, as Control was aware that they would. The police didn't want to chase smugglers away. If they went after anyone, it would be local captains with whom they were displeased—but only after they had rendezvoused, and had been observed in the act of doing so. And right now the police ship on duty was busy chasing *him*.

It wouldn't hunt for him in the direction HS *Freerunner*'s transmission had come from, Terry realized, looking at the comm's readout. And all at once he got an insanely bold idea. Could he possibly reach the starship and sell the metals without being caught? The miners would back that plan. And if it failed, Darrow would be no worse off than he would be if the stash were discovered some other way, as it was bound to be if not jettisoned.

To be sure, he, Terry, would be a great deal worse off.

To have contact with a starship was the ultimate sin and the penalty was predetermined, whether any sale took place or not. Still, the thought of being back aboard a jump ship even for a few minutes was appealing.

He took up the comm, using the frequency reserved for commercial transactions, which he knew was intentionally unmonitored by the government. "HS *Freerunner*, this is IS *Bonanza*, do you wish to rendezvous? Over."

The reply came immediately. "Roger, IS *Bonanza*. Darrow, is that you? Doesn't sound like you."

Thank God it was someone who knew him. "Captain Darrow is recovering from an injury. This is Captain Terry Rivera, acting for him, in command."

"Have you authority to transact business, Rivera?"

"Roger, *Freerunner*. I have business to transact." They proceeded to agree on a rendezvous point.

It took five hours to get there, which the miners, with renewed admiration for Terry and happy expectations of receiving more money than originally agreed upon without even having to work for it, spent getting drunk. They were asleep in their seats by the time Terry completed the docking and he realized that it was not customary for mining crews to have any part in the sale of cargo. The less they knew, the better; only the captain was legally liable.

He had no idea of what price platinum metals should bring and was inclined to accept the starship captain's offer until he recalled the emphasis Darrow had put on negotiating ability as a factor in avoiding arrest. This meant that one wasn't expected to accept the first offer, and so he held out for nearly twice the amount, earning the respect of Captain Yakimov, who remarked that if he wasn't already in the smuggling business he would do well to consider it.

Smugglers took pride in their work, Terry perceived with surprise. It wasn't just that Darrow was proud of his ability to outwit government racketeers—even a brief conversation with Yakimov made him realize that they all viewed laws against free trading of goods as a violation of human rights. Smugglers kept their freedom, he thought wistfully. They flew from star to star as they liked—it was as good as exploring.

When *Freerunner*'s crew finished retrieving the stashed metals from *Bonanza*, his relief at the completion of his mission was mixed with regret that his stay aboard *Freerunner* was so short. And with sudden excitement he wondered, did it have to be?

Yakimov seemed to consider him a kindred spirit. He might agree to take him into his crew—they might welcome an extra pilot, especially if he revealed that he was qualified to handle jumps. It wouldn't be a bad life. It couldn't get him home to Maclairn, of course, but he could go to Earth, and if Kathryn still made trips in *Promise* . . . He wouldn't attempt to go where there were mentors—he had long ago decided that contact with mentors would make his past years of exile meaningless—but he might well have a chance to be reunited with Kathryn in secret. And at least he would be away from Ciencia, with its corrupt government and its dull forbidding sky.

It wouldn't be a betrayal of Darrow not to go back. He had enough credits banked to pay him for his ship, and if *Bonanza* was reported lost there would be no evidence that there had been a stash. Except—oh, God, Terry thought. The miners. They couldn't be left stranded and if the police were alerted to rescue them, it would become known that their missing captain had docked with a starship. There was only one reason anyone would take such a risk, so it would be assumed there had been cargo, and the miners had proven that they didn't care about protecting their employer. The evidence would be circumstantial, but if they were bribed or pressured into testifying against Darrow, it might be enough to convict him— or at least raise enough suspicion for the racketeers to use the evidence of smuggling they'd had on him all along.

Well, thought Terry sadly, he had never expected to escape from Ciencia. He had been resigned to his confinement for years now; a chance he must reject was not really worse than no chance at all. He said goodbye to Captain Yakimov and headed back into *Bonanza*.

As he left the airlock he glanced at the adjacent viewport and saw with cold, sick dismay that the police ship was approaching.

They must have taken the unprecedented step of monitoring the commercial frequency in order to catch him—they would have gotten here first, but they'd waited until his transaction was complete before closing in. For a moment Terry stood frozen, aware that there was no possible means of escape. Then, realizing that all his reasoning about circumstantial evidence against Darrow now applied, he hurried back into the starship.

"You're Darrow's friend, right?" he asked Yakimov.

"Sure. Done business with him for years; he's a straight dealer and a great guy."

"There's a police ship coming," Terry said, "and they must not find out that his ship carried cargo. If they do it will mean life in prison for him. So if they ask, deny it, and give this secretly to the mining boss on condition that he keep quiet about it." He handed back the credit chip he had received.

"I will, but they're likely to guess that you sold me something. Why else would you have come?"

"Leave that to me," Terry said. "And back me in what I say."

He knew there was only one thing he could say, one possible way to save Darrow; and as far as he himself was concerned it wouldn't make things any worse than they already were—his mere docking with a starship had already condemned him. He watched as the police officers boarded, savoring his last moments of freedom.

"You're a fool to have thought you could get away from us," an officer said, "and a brazen one to attempt selling what you stole to smugglers from offworld. Don't you know that offworld contact is a more serious crime than theft?"

"I am not a thief," declared Terry, "though I sometimes pretend I am, for cover. I didn't come here to sell. I came to buy."

"Buy? What could you want from offworld traders? There's no market here for anything they have to offer."

"I think you know what I buy. You've been seeking me for years, after all." At the officers' blank look he drew a deep breath and added, "I am the captain of *Estel*."

Part Five: Estel

66

TERRY WAS TAKEN aboard the police ship in handcuffs. At first the officers had laughed at his announcement, and they still suspected it was an idle brag. But Captain Yakimov had backed it, as Terry had requested. Ciencia's government could not touch Yakimov as he was not a citizen and not on the surface; the worst they could do would be to shoot his ship down if he was foolish enough to descend to low orbit. So he was free to say that he had sold information from the knowledgebase to agents from Ciencia over a long period of time. Terry realized that this wasn't mere fabrication. As a friend of Darrow, he was undoubtedly one of the smugglers who had been referred to as "the source."

"I won't name the people I dealt with," Yakimov had told the police, "and I never knew who the ultimate buyers were. I've heard rumors of a ship called *Estel*; whether this man is its captain, I can't tell. In any case its contacts seem to have taken over the text purchasing, since I haven't received offers from anyone for some years now."

"Where is your ship *Estel*?" an officer demanded, addressing Terry.

"Where you won't find it," Terry said honestly, "and in any case outside your jurisdiction. You can put me in prison, but you won't be rid of *Estel* so easily."

He hoped that this was true. The texts on the Net were well hidden through methods designed to propagate them; he did not think it would ever be possible for the government to delete them all, and they were influencing the lives of readers. That was some satisfaction, considering that his own life was effectively at an end.

He was resigned to spending the rest of it in prison, just as he had become resigned to his imprisonment on Ciencia. The time for raw anguish was past. He was no longer young enough to summon rage against fate; he was thirty-eight now, and too long accustomed to loss to be thrown by it. For a few minutes, aboard *Freerunner*, he had let himself imagine what it would be like to travel among the stars again, but even before realizing that Darrow would bear the consequences of his departure he had sensed that it wasn't going to happen—precognition, he supposed, like the flashes he'd had in his younger years. They had not come to him for a long time, perhaps because there had been nothing ahead worth foreseeing.

The thing that worried him most about his arrest was the possibility that it would lead to other members of the conspiracy being caught. He didn't really think they would be; he had covered his tracks when hacking, and his backup people were competent to do so as well. No new data had been added recently, and none needed to be. Few members knew names of anyone but their immediate friends, and the capture of the leader should have no bearing on the danger they faced. The prison authorities would, of course, try to make him name them; but he was well equipped by his mind training to deal with that sort of thing.

Still, he couldn't help fearing that some suspicion might fall on Darrow. The police investigators' assumption that Terry had conned him was his best protection; hopefully he would have the sense to see that and let them think he had known him merely as a cargo courier—a role he'd assumed specifically as a cover for their other dealings. Darrow was good at looking out

for himself and he knew nothing he could say would help
Terry. But if despite caution he was accused of complic-
ity, at least he would be no worse off than if Terry had
not acted to protect him. His vulnerability to arrest had
become a matter of risk, rather than a sure thing.

It was harder for Terry to confront the thought of
danger to Alison. He was her business partner and lived
in her apartment; they would surely question her. But as
far as anyone knew, to her he was simply an alleged healer
responsible for the success of their neurofeedback practice. Even if it was learned that his bank account had
been transferred to her, as he had told his backup hackers to do in case of his death or imprisonment, there would
be no reason to suspect he had told her he was involved
in conspiracy or discussed forbidden texts with her. On
the contrary, they would assume he had used his work at
the clinic as another cover. They would think his reputed
ability to heal was a con, too; it was unlikely that they
would open their minds to the idea that relief of pain
through mind power might be real.

But there was another reason why the thought of Alison tormented him. She would grieve for him, and now that
he knew why, the grief was mutual. He had left her just as
he had left Kathryn, assuming that he would return. And
then he had disappeared. Neither of them would ever see
him again—he knew Alison wouldn't be allowed to visit him
in prison, even if she found out he was there—and so both
had been hurt deeply. He cared too much for Alison not
to feel pain at the thought of her suffering as Kathryn
must have suffered ... and besides, he would miss her.
He would miss her more than anything else in the pseudo-
life that had replaced his real one. Waking in the darkness of his cell he reached out for solace, and while still
half-dreaming he thought of Alison in the next room as
for years now she had been—and that comforted him until he was jolted into awareness that she was not there.

The cramped prison cell was even smaller than

quarters aboard a ship and without such amenities as shipboard staterooms provided. There was no window, and he was not sure whether that was a bad thing or a good one. On one hand, the blankness of the walls was nerve-wearing, but on the other, he was not eager for another look at Ciencia's depressing gray sky. His surroundings had not mattered to him as long as he had a computer and hacking to do. Now he had nothing. The daily interrogation sessions by an arrogant police officer named Quaid were at least a diversion.

These sessions were conducted in a civilized manner so far, and probably would be until after his trial. The authorities were in no hurry; they knew the members of the movement he represented were not going anywhere. Some of them might turn up at the trial, in which case they might cause a disturbance if he didn't appear to be in good shape.

Quaid was a fanatic about the alleged corrupting effect of unscientific thinking. "The founders of this colony managed to keep out all the superstitious nonsense that has retarded human progress since the beginning of time," he told Terry. "It was the greatest social achievement in history, and I'll be damned if I'll let some fool pilot with a warped sense of his own importance lead the public astray."

"If the ideas that have come from *Estel* appeal to the public, that shows there's truth in them," Terry ventured.

"Of course it doesn't. Silly notions about extrasensory perception and life after death once appealed to the public too, and only the crackpots were taken in. The other stuff was, and still is, more dangerous because some of it sounds plausible."

"As to life after death, I don't know," declared Terry honestly, "except to say that historically, a great many people who weren't crackpots believed in it. Extrasensory perception, on the other hand, is a capability humans are known to have."

"That's a pernicious falsehood," Quaid stated. "All input to the brain comes through the senses. If people got ideas some other way, out of thin air, they couldn't keep their thoughts straight. They wouldn't be able to control the content of their minds."

This was a fairly accurate description of what bothered the people afraid to admit that psi existed, Terry thought. And it had deeper roots than fear of psi. Tristan had explained it to him, but he doubted that he could find the right words to explain it himself. Nevertheless, he enjoyed baiting Quaid so he made a stab at it.

"Just where do you think scientists get new ideas?" he asked.

"By reasoning, of course."

"No, I don't mean how they evaluate them. How do they get ideas to reason about?"

"By putting two and two together," Quaid declared. "That's a matter of logic."

"But if it were only logic, the universe would have been figured out long ago," Terry argued. "Any intelligent person can put two and two together. New ideas require intuition. And intuition doesn't get into human minds through the senses. Sometimes it comes through unconscious ESP and other times it just comes in some way we don't understand. That's true for everybody, not just scientists. If you rule out all the knowledge intuition provides, there couldn't be any scientific progress. So minds have more powers than reasoning, even here, and people have a right to use them. Even when they come up with ideas you guys don't happen to like."

Quaid frowned. "The trouble with you, Rivera, is that you're not only crazy but you want to make everybody else crazy along with you. I don't think you even have a hidden ship—you probably made the whole thing up. You admit you've been buying illicit texts from smugglers. By passing them off as having some mysterious origin you've conned people into thinking they've got value, just the way you conned Willard into thinking you had some magic words that could ease people's pain better than drugs."

Terry was not sure how many of his readers knew that *Estel* was imaginary, or whether officials other than Quaid suspected it was. But since he had indeed brought in most of the texts concealed on the Net—and had, albeit somewhat earlier, come from the stars—it was not really a lie to say so. He had no intention of confessing to deception, for Quaid was right that making a symbol of the ship encouraged people to read.

"Everything brought by *Estel* originated on Earth or some other world," he said. "That's no mystery."

"Yes, nonsense about mind and spirit has infected Earth throughout history—which is why its civilization never overcame conflict and is now decaying. It's too late for anything to be done about that. But as for other worlds, if there are colonies breeding superstition they should be wiped out! We didn't learn how to eliminate such ideas just to have them sprout again and reinfect advanced societies like our own."

My God, Terry thought, that sounds just like what the enemies of Maclairn advocate, the conspirators at League headquarters who'd tried to prevent contact with Maclairn even at the cost of violence. For the first time in years he let himself wonder if they had made any more attempts. Had more mentors been murdered? Had Maclairn and its goals been endangered when he was powerless to defend it? He'd been so overwhelmed by personal loss that he had not dared to speculate about what was happening to the plan for spreading acceptance of psi on Earth.

"Don't think we're going to let you contaminate this world," Quaid declared. "You're going to admit in public that you invented the *Estel* myth, and you're going to provide us with any information you have about the people who've been posting your trash on the Net. No freaking

megalomaniac with a savior complex is going to under-
mine the stability we've maintained here."

Quaid launched into such tirades more than once. So
far, they were only words. But Terry knew that within
the prison more sinister things went on. The lifers, among
whom he was already understood to be numbered, were
isolated from the rest of the inmates; he was not sure
whether they were allowed contact with each other or
were kept in solitary confinement. In any case, since from
most of them no information was sought, his case was
special. He did not expect that he would be accorded any
legal rights.

67

THE TRIAL WAS held three weeks after Terry's arrest. It
would, of course, be a farce—since he had already admitted his guilt, there was no jury—but the government authorities wanted publicity and so did he. Their aim was to
demonstrate that the man claiming to be captain of *Estel*
was an ordinary criminal of no account and the legends
about his mysterious ship were foolish. His was to prove
the opposite.

The authorities wouldn't be pleased by what he was
going to say, Terry knew. But even if it fell on deaf ears
he would take satisfaction in it, and there was nothing
worse they could do to him than what they were already
planning.

He was taken from the prison to the courthouse in
the center of the city, which like most of the larger buildings had outer walls that looked as if they were made of
glass. A product of chemistry, virtually unbreakable and
strong enough not to need much surrounding framework,
it let in more light than he was accustomed to seeing on
dreary Ciencia—less expensive buildings such as the one
housing Alison's clinic had less of it. Little as he liked the

view, Terry couldn't help wondering whether this was the last daylight he would ever see. Such exercise space as the prison provided was enclosed.

To his surprise, both the street and the courtroom to which he was taken were crowded. He'd had relatively few friends, after all, and as members of the conspiracy they could not take the risk of appearing. He supposed the government had promoted the trial as a sort of spectacle. Not until his telepathic sensitivity alerted him to the feelings of the people present did he understand what they were there for. They were pulling for him! These were strangers who believed in *Estel*.

He would be conducting his own defense; as Darrow had told him long ago, no lawyer would take a smuggling case, or any case involving contact with a starship. This didn't bother him, considering that he had been caught on board, which alone was enough to assure a sentence of life imprisonment. What he wanted was to convince people that the hidden texts on the Net were worth reading, and that, no lawyer could have done for him.

The prosecutor, a middle-aged woman who showed little enthusiasm for a case she considered already settled, presented it straightforwardly. She called police officers to testify that they had observed Terry lifting off in *Bonanza*, a mining ship belonging to Darrow; had followed it; and had found him aboard the starship *Freerunner*, a smuggler's ship illegally orbiting Ciencia. She also called Renssalaer, who stated that he called the police because he had cause to believe Terry was a thief, as well as the three miners, who testified that they had expected to work on an asteroid and—falsely—that they did not know why the starship had been visited first. It was obvious, said the prosecutor, that there must have been something aboard to sell. No doubt Terry, who was known to have a past history as a cargo courier, had taken advantage of Darrow's generosity in loaning his ship in order to dispose of stolen goods.

Terry, who was permitted to cross-examine, required the miners to state under oath that they had not seen any cargo aboard during the flight. This was simply to protect Darrow in case it later occurred to the police to wonder where the hypothetical stolen goods had come from; it would make no difference to the outcome of his own case. He knew the miners wouldn't volunteer that there was hidden cargo that they'd seen previously, for that would have implicated them in its concealment. As for its unloading, they truly had not observed it—they'd been drunk at the time, presumably because they'd been well aware that the less they knew about such transactions, the better.

Darrow was called next to testify that while recovering from his injury he had allowed Terry to pilot his ship, offering him a percentage of the proceeds. The prosecutor's purpose being to show that Terry had conned him, she avoided any questioning that might suggest that he himself had ever been a smuggler—that the government knew he had, and had therefore visited starships, was not something they wanted revealed as long as they were getting a good share of his profits. When she asked whether he had known the starship would be visited by Terry he replied truthfully that he hadn't, and that he had been astonished when the police informed him that it had been.

Alison too had been subpoenaed. As she took the witness stand, her eyes met Terry's and he was overcome by sorrow at the thought that this was the last time they would ever see each other. With some surprise he became aware that if they had met in a different life, if he had not been committed to someone else and had never known what love between telepaths was like ... but that was pointless speculation. Things were as they were. And now they would be separated in any case, no less irrevocably than he'd been separated from Kathryn.

To his relief Alison was asked only to confirm that he had worked as a healer. Although the prosecutor wanted to establish that she too had been deceived by him, that would have been awkward to pursue because she had benefited financially from their partnership. Instead, the police had managed to locate one of the few clients who hadn't responded well to neurofeedback and telepathic reduction of pain. This, Terry knew, was because she had been told by doctors that her pain was incurable and underneath she didn't want to believe medical science was not infallible. He had never claimed he could help everybody. This witness nevertheless testified, with some bitterness, that he was a swindler; and he could call no others to counter her because the police hadn't given him an opportunity to contact anyone.

"It has been demonstrated," said the prosecutor in summation, "that this man, Terry Rivera, is a habitual liar and perpetrator of fraud. Although the evidence that he attempted to sell stolen goods is circumstantial, there is little doubt that he did so. His status is that of a common criminal. In his defense he will make claims that if not deliberate lies, can be nothing other than delusions. Since he admits that he visited a starship, none of this would matter except that he has associated himself with a absurd legend that has been circulated on the Net. To make sure that no citizens are taken in by this legend, we have chosen to try him publicly even though he has pleaded guilty to the charge of offworld contact, the penalty for which supersedes all others."

Terry stood. Beforehand, he had feared that speaking out would be wasted effort, but by now the mounting emotions of the spectators had made plain that they were people who would listen to him. This was his last opportunity ever to do anything by his own free choice, and he would make the most of it.

"You've been told that I am not honest," he began, "and it's true that I've disguised myself at times. But I now tell you a more significant truth: I am the captain of *Estel*, and I was born on another world."

There were gasps; even Quaid had not guessed that he would claim offworld origin. "I was born on Earth," Terry repeated, "and I have visited many planets. And on all of them except this one, people are free to read whatever they like. All the books and stories that have been written are publicly accessible. All the vids that have been produced can be seen. You have not been informed that this is so. You are not permitted contact with offworlders, lest you find out. I will be imprisoned for the rest of my life because the authorities believe I am a Ciencian who has defied that law, but the rest of you are already imprisoned inside the shell of the restrictions they have placed on you. You may think you are free because you can live and work as you choose and spend your money as you wish—but you are not free as long as knowledge available elsewhere is withheld from you."

He could feel the listeners' surge of agreement and knew he was communicating telepathically in a way possible only because of his psi-giftedness, and that through unconscious telepathy, they were responding. He had felt nothing like it before except at the Ritual, and for the first time he understood the full power of mass mindsharing. And he knew, too, that during his years as a healer he had done more than help people who were suffering. Many of those people were here—as he became aware of this, he recognized them not only by faces he spotted among the spectators, but by the touch of minds once joined to his in the crisis of pain. They idolized him as he'd feared they might, yet it wasn't a bad thing, for when he himself disappeared into the oblivion of prison, they would remember what he was saying now.

"You may wonder what knowledge they have withheld," he went on, "though some of you may have read pieces of what I have hidden on the Net. It is knowledge of the power of the human mind. The mind can do much more than reason scientifically. It can perceive truth that today's science is unable to define or analyze. It can create stories that express such truth through metaphors, or acknowledge its existence through how their characters feel and act. And the mind can also do greater things that even on Earth are not fully understood. It can banish pain, as I helped people do in the clinic where I worked; it can perceive things the eye cannot see; and above all it can allow people to connect with each other without words, so that that they can understand what others are feeling and can live in harmony.

"The government does not want you to know these things because if you did, you would not give the dogma of science and its champions full control over your lives. You would use science for the good it can achieve, but you would also use the other aspects of your minds. As this would lessen the power of the authorities, they have, since the founding of this colony, taken drastic steps to keep it from happening. They have made offworld contact the most heinous crime that can be committed here, though everywhere else it's recognized that to travel between the stars is the destiny of humankind—that to explore varied worlds, and ideas, is the essence of our human heritage. People of Ciencia, don't remain blind to what's being withheld from you! Break through the clouds that confine you, and see the sun—"

The people in the courtroom were on their feet, applauding, and the judge was banging his gavel for order. As the police moved to restrain Terry and take him away, a woman ran forward, crying "Estel! We believe you, we're with you!" It was Nina, her face flushed with excitement. She alone among the conspirators had dared to come, the danger of discovery outweighed by her hopeless love for him. Inspired by her boldness, other citizens, knowing nothing of *Estel* beyond the hints they'd read, took up the shout: "Estel! Estel!"

And beyond the transparent wall of the room the people in the street were shouting, too, pressing close to the building's façade. A few were waving hastily-made signs bearing the slogan. Terry, at first bewildered, realized that the trial must have been shown live on the Net with the expectation that the legend of the ship *Estel* would be discredited, and that passers-by had been watching on their smartphones.

With unanticipated elation Terry saw that the idea behind the symbol he'd created, the desire for an end to suppression of ideas on Ciencia and faith in the powers of the human mind, had been firmly established in too many people for it ever to be extinguished. Thousands had seen at least some of the texts secreted on the Net; now hundreds more would find them every day. That might never lead to political change, but neither would the population of Ciencia remain unaware of what was missing in their world. *Estel*, hope, had become part of the collective unconscious.

68

"THAT WAS A foolish performance," Quaid said when they arrived back at the prison. "You'll regret it."

"No, I won't," Terry retorted. "The government will regret it, though. You may not find the public quite so docile as in the past now that they've laid eyes on an offworlder."

"Do you think I believe that nonsense?" Quaid demanded. "How could you have gotten here? How could your ID say you're a native Ciencian?"

"Well, as to the first," Terry said, "I'm a pilot, after all. A starship pilot."

"I've got to admit you managed to fly a mining ship and even rendezvous with a starship," Quaid agreed reluctantly, "though I don't see how you learned without there being any record of your flight training. But a starship pilot? Don't stretch your story too far if you don't want to lose credibility."

"As captain of a starship I've made a good many jumps," Terry declared, amused by fact that this was truer than Quaid, who assumed he meant *Estel*, could imagine.

"You'll lose your cockiness once you've told me who hacked the Net to produce these fantasies," declared Quaid grimly.

"I've already told you. I did."

"A sharp swindler, a psychic healer, a starship pilot, *and* the most skilled hacker the world has ever seen? Come on, Rivera. I am not as stupid as the people you've duped."

"Well," Terry confessed, "It's true I haven't done *all* the hacking. There was another man—"

"Now we're getting somewhere."

"A man named Elrond, who was killed by you or your cronies some years ago. I don't think you knew he was the hacker while you had him in prison; at any rate, you obviously didn't get him to name me as his accomplice. But since he was indirectly responsible for the existence of *Estel*, it may interest you to know now that he's beyond your reach."

Quaid was livid; evidently he hadn't known. For a moment Terry was afraid he'd said too much—Nina had spoken out at the trial, and she was Elrond's cousin. But she didn't have the computer skills to be a hacker, nor was she acquainted with the people who did. She had helped only with the pickups, about which no evidence remained.

"Ancient history doesn't interest us," said Quaid. "I want the names of your present accomplices, and I'm sure you know I have the means to make you tell me."

"What, don't you believe I have the power to end pain, either?"

"Of course not. You may have convinced some hysterical women that you do, but they evidently didn't have any real pain to begin with. You will."

As this was an issue about which he was totally

confident, Terry, thankful for the thorough training he'd received from Aldren, went on taunting Quaid throughout the man's attempts to break him. While it was true that the various methods employed produced far more severe pain than clients at the clinic had experienced, there was never any question of his suffering from it. Quaid, of course, continued to doubt that such a thing could be controlled by the mind, and eventually came to the conclusion that Terry's nervous system was physically abnormal. When he discovered that Terry could also control bleeding, his own nerve snapped and he retreated in fear that he was losing his grip on reality.

Which, Terry reflected, was the root of the fear that all opponents of mind powers displayed. He was glad Quaid had no contacts in the League and didn't know Maclairn existed, because if he had, he'd have been among those trying to find some malevolent way to prevent contact with it.

Though in most respects he was past caring what might be done to him in prison, one possibility did frighten Terry, so much so that he thrust it out of his mind whenever it began to emerge. They might subject him to drugs. Darrow had said long ago that uncooperative captains were intentionally addicted to drugs in prison and were thereby forced to become drug dealers. This was bad enough, but still more alarming was the question of what sort of drugs they were made to sell.

Psychoactive drugs, Darrow had said. Nasty ones that didn't exist elsewhere. Recreational drugs to be pushed on the streets of Earth, where due to blanket prohibition the demand was insatiable? Undoubtedly, but that was not the worst. Terry had heard rumors; he had seen allusions in some of the political texts he had posted; and his imagination was all too able to fill in details. If the government produced such drugs it might also produce other illicit biochemicals, and street dealers were not the only potential market—terrorists were another. And there were all sorts of uses to which they might be put by governments or agents of governments. He had read that in the past they had even been used for genocide.

Would his mind training enable him to overcome the effects of drugs? Terry wondered. He could control his brain's production of neurotransmitters, so perhaps it would—unless the drug interfered with his brain itself to extent of depriving him of volition. Hopefully, any drug powerful enough to do that would be useless to interrogators because it would render him unable to remember the information they wanted from him, but he wasn't sure of that; he recalled episodes from Maclairnan history involving narrow escapes from truth serum. And what if they used the drugs as a threat rather than directly, telling him that it wouldn't matter if his mind was destroyed, even permanently destroyed, if he refused to tell them anything?

There was a still more chilling possibility. Ciencia's scientists were extremely proficient in biochemistry—they couldn't produce unique substances if they were not— and there was no way they could have gained such capabilities without the use of test subjects. There were not many animals on Ciencia, since none were native to the planet; presumably they bred lab rats, but there was a limit to what could be proven with rats. People sentenced to life in prison, on the other hand ... The lifers were isolated and at least some were under the control of the racketeers. Nobody knew exactly what happened to them. Terry did not look forward to finding out.

He adjusted to the monotony of his surroundings. Whether the days passed quickly or slowly he could not tell, for his permanent cell was never either dark or bright; he existed in a sort of half-light that approximated dusk under Ciencia's gloomy sky. Quaid, he decided, had given up on him, as there were no more interrogations. No form of activity replaced them; he was locked up alone and he realized that the authorities wanted him forgotten.

During his years on Ciencia he had hated everything about the planet, from the unending snow and fog to the stark design of the closely-packed buildings that huddled together as if to conserve warmth. Installations on Earth's moon and on worlds without breathable atmospheres had never bothered him, although they were no less stark and considerably more compact—but they were oriented toward space, never allowing their inhabitants to feel isolated from the larger universe, whereas Ciencia was intentionally self-contained. It was merely a psychological difference, perhaps, but one he had never been able to forget. Yet looking back on the city now, he knew that he missed it. There was evidence of human aspiration in it, one-sided as that evidence was. And the current of Net communication ran through it, as through all inhabited worlds, carrying the shared thoughts and feelings of its people, far deeper and more vital than the limitations of the physical environment suggested.

He had no access to the Net in prison. That, more than the steel bars, was what confined him. All his life, except on Maclairn, he had been a loner, or thought he had; but he had lived actively on the Net, and he found he was terrified at the thought of being permanently cut off from it. Looking ahead, the life sentence began to seem worse than he had imagined it could.

To be sure, he was safer in prison than he would be if released. At least in prison they could not kill him; execution was contrary to Ciencian law and there were enough uncorrupted guards to get the word out if it happened. But outside, an accident could be arranged, as it had been for Elrond, and that would certainly solve the problem he presented to the government. It was, to his satisfaction, a problem that was growing.

The people outside were still demonstrating in support of *Estel*. Terry knew this because sometimes, when the walls pressed so closely that he was not sure he could bear it for another hour, he reached out with his mind and he saw them, not just with imagination but through the remote viewing skill in which he had long ago been trained. He had avoided using it during his years on Ciencia; not only would it have served no useful purpose, but he could not forget that it had been the cause of his losing everything. If remote viewing had not led him to seek out the Elders' ship, he would have had the fulfilling life he'd expected as a Fleet officer and defender of Maclairn. So he'd wanted nothing more to do with viewing; but now, in desperation, he turned to it and sensed that there were people, many people, who believed in what he had told them and who from time to time came to the prison gates with signs that bore the slogan he had created: *Estel! Estel!* And Estel meant hope—not for him, because he was past hoping, but for Ciencia and for the flame of belief in mind power he had kindled here.

He dreamed of Maclairn a good deal, and of Kathryn; and more and more he allowed himself to slip into the dreams even when not asleep. It was pointless to resist— why should he, when his life was over and the time on Maclairn was the only part of it that had been happy? The years on Ciencia held nothing he cared to remember ... except Alison, and Alison's grief was too painful to dwell on. As for the dream he'd once had of exploring the stars, he could not bear to think of it, knowing that never again would he even see them.

He was not aware that he had in fact been drugged into passivity until one morning when he realized his head was clear. He felt more alert than he'd been for a long time, and this continued for what he guessed was a period of several days, until he began to fear that they were readying him for a trial of a different drug for which they needed a fresh start. He felt like himself again; but with this came the torment of longing for action, and for freedom.

Finally, shortly after Terry had finished a more

adequate meal than usual, Quaid came to his cell. "Get up, Rivera," he said, motioning with his gun. "You're about to be useful to me."

69

SO THEY WERE going to use him for biochemical experimentation after all. Sick with fear, Terry followed, wondering why he had not been escorted by a guard, as before when taken anywhere, instead of by Quaid himself. To his surprise, they proceeded not to the medical laboratory he was dreading but to a narrow door in a deserted part of the prison, locked but not guarded. Quaid, who was wearing a flight jacket, handed him one like it and ordered him to put it on. Then, after handcuffing him, he unlocked the door and opened it. Astonished, Terry found himself looking out into a dark night and breathing cold outside air.

There was a groundcar parked near the door. Quaid told him to get in, and Terry complied with rising apprehension. No one else was around; obviously whatever Quaid was doing had not been officially authorized, and he certainly was not doing it out of kindness. Most likely it had been decided, either by Quaid alone or by the government in secret, that a prisoner around whom a legend had arisen should be quietly eliminated.

He expected that they would head for the wilderness, perhaps the logging road by which he had arrived all those years ago. It would be a fitting exit, he supposed. Instead, Quaid drove to the spaceport and on out to a pad in its most distant corner. It was long after midnight, Terry judged, because he saw no lights in the hotel and there was little activity on the field—but not so little that a liftoff would be considered abnormal if observed. The ship on the pad was an ordinary shuttle of the type used by large mining companies; no name appeared on it.

Quaid, who had been silent during the drive, turned to Terry. "I'm willing to grant that you're a competent pilot," he said. "I have need to reach a starship tonight, and I don't want it known that I went there. So you are going to take me and bring me back."

Speechless, Terry nodded his assent. "Just so you know," Quaid went on, "if you ever suggest to anyone, in any way, that this trip ever happened, you will die in the most unpleasant way our biochemists can devise. Is that understood?"

Again Terry nodded. It needed no elaboration. Inside he was bursting with joy at the thought of flying again, even under these less than inviting circumstances. God, he realized, past all hope he was going into space one more time!

After turning on the pad lights and convincing Quaid that no pilot could lift off without a preflight check, he performed it while still in handcuffs with his captor, gun in hand, at his side. All appeared to be in order. "But I don't know anything about the condition of the engines, or how well this ship has been maintained," he warned. "If anything goes wrong with it, that's beyond my control."

"I've been assured that it's spaceworthy. I assume you won't do anything to make it less so, seeing as your life is as much at stake as mine."

Quaid overestimated the value of life to condemned prisoners, Terry thought. He had half a mind to head for deep space and just keep going. That might be something to think about on the return trip—but perhaps there wouldn't have to be a return trip. Perhaps he could reach a different starship from the one designated and ask for sanctuary; Quaid didn't know anything about astrogation, after all.

"In case you've got any idea of fooling me," Quaid said, "you should know that this ship has only a few hours of air, no food or water, and no long-range comm.

Therefore it's not going anywhere except where I say it is."

"I can't locate your starship without long-range comm capability," Terry pointed out.

"You don't have to—it will locate you. Just get us off the ground and into the right orbit." He handed over orbital specifications, which Terry gave to the AI. Quaid must have agreed on an approximate time and attached a tracking device, he realized; once they were within range of each other, the rendezvous and docking would be automated. He sealed the airlock, strapped himself into the captain's seat with Quaid in the copilot's, and lifted off.

They were not in orbit long before the AI announced the presence of a nearby ship. The rendezvous was totally silent; Quaid would not allow him to use the short-range comm. There was no need for it, but it was customary for approaching pilots to greet each other and Terry found himself wondering what sort of errand would demand such extreme secrecy. And then, amused by his own denseness, he knew.

It was not unusual for the government racketeers to deal directly with smugglers without using a local captain as a go-between. Darrow had mentioned occasions on which he had not negotiated or even known the price, but had simply delivered sealed cargo for a fee very little larger than his expenses. Normally this was done openly, or at least as openly as the rest of the theoretically-illegal smuggling business. But in this case Quaid was apparently selling something without the knowledge of his associates, something so unique and valuable that he did not intend to cut them in on the deal. He feared, probably with justification, that he'd be in some danger if they found out about it.

Terry got a good look at the other ship on the viewscreen. The name on it was HS *Venture*. It was a small starship, about the size of *Picard*, but newer and more pleasingly designed, a beautiful ship that reminded him in some ways of *Skywalker*. He looked at it wistfully, thinking that it was just the sort of ship he would like to own if he were rich and free.

When the two ships were joined and the "docked" light came on, Terry asked, "Will you need my help unloading cargo?"

"There is no cargo," Quaid said, "I'm just delivering a message that I couldn't send through the ansible."

That was odd. Unless *Venture* regularly picked up cargo although he'd never heard it mentioned among those that did, Quaid must already have used the ansible to arrange the time and place of the meeting; so it wasn't that he lacked access to it—despite his disapproval of offworld contacts, he evidently had one himself. For a ship to be sent specifically to receive a further message on physical media seemed unlikely, to say the least, so probably Quaid was lying. But it was hard to image what could be carried on his person that would be worth enough to warrant a special interstellar flight.

"I'm not letting you out of my sight," Quaid continued. "I don't want to be stranded up here. So come along."

They passed through to *Venture*, where Quaid was met by two men who were obviously in charge. They did not look like typical smugglers—they lacked the rough edge of outlaws and seemed far too young to have the necessary bargaining experience. There was a sort of nervous intensity about them that Terry immediately sensed. These were men with a mission, and his psi faculties told him that it was not an altruistic one. At the sight of them he felt a foreboding that felt almost precognitive.

Immediately, they escorted Quaid to a stateroom, where all three remained for some time; evidently the transaction required discussion they didn't want overheard. As soon as they emerged they were joined by *Venture*'s captain, who appeared from the direction of the bridge. "The AI has processed the coordinates you gave me," he said to the tallest, a darkly handsome young man called Rafe. "There's something wrong with them—they point to a solar system that hasn't been visited for centuries. It's marked as worthless. There's nothing there unless you're prospecting, and we're not equipped for that."

"Don't worry about it," said Rafe. "You don't need to know why we're going there."

"Now hold on," retorted the captain. "You hired me to take you to Ciencia and back. Nothing was said about a side trip to some distant uncharted solar system with no inhabited worlds. I'd need a crew for a trip like that. I'd need extra consumables and people experienced enough to find more if necessary. It would be suicide to go without them, and I won't do it."

"You'll do what we tell you to do," declared Rafe. "It would be suicide not to."

"If by that you mean what I think you do, forget it. We're in high orbit above a planet that won't let us land, and without me you'd stay here till your life support ran out."

"Wrong," said the second young man, Yuri. "This guy Quaid brought along is a pilot. If you won't cooperate, he will."

"He's a local pilot—he can't jump through hyperspace."

This was an opportunity to be seized. Terry put in quickly, "I can jump. I've had a lot of experience at it. And I've explored uninhabited solar systems."

Rafe turned to him, looking thoughtful. "He might be our best bet, at that. He doesn't know where we came from or who our contact was. If anything went wrong, he couldn't trace us back."

"The man is a braggart with illusions about his own powers," Quaid warned. "He's a convict and we'd like to be rid of him, but he's got a following demanding his release and killing him would create a martyr. Frankly, I doubt that he's ever piloted a starship, certainly not as captain. But if you want to gamble, he's yours—just so your pilot takes me back to the surface."

"I'd rather do that than take these idiots on a suicide mission," said the captain. "But I understand that your world doesn't allow starships to come or go. I sure as hell don't want to get stuck there."

"Well, there are exceptional cases of contact with starships," Quaid said, "just as I've reached this one. Passage with a free trader could be arranged."

"A smuggler, you mean? What assurance do I have that I wouldn't be arrested when I got where he was going? And what about my ship? How am I going to get it back?"

"What we paid you up front for falsifying your flight plan would buy your ship twice over," Yuri declared. "We weren't planning to give it back. After our final jump we'd have rendezvoused with friends and turned you loose in a shuttle."

Terry felt for the captain, whose avarice had apparently led him to make what from the beginning had been a bad bargain; no matter how much he'd been paid it was unlikely that he could replace the ship. There weren't many to be had in anywhere near as good shape as this one. But his loss was Terry's gain. The two men were obviously up to no good and he'd have to watch his back, but as long he was their only starship pilot they couldn't dispose of him—and if they eventually turned him loose in a shuttle, he'd be free! In any case, whatever happened would be preferable to going back to prison. To escape Ciencia would have been worth whatever risk was involved, even if he weren't a prisoner.

Sensing the men's satisfaction, it dawned on him that the exchange might have been prearranged. Despite his expressed skepticism, Quaid could have believed him when during interrogation he'd claimed to have flown starships. Hoping to get him permanently out of the picture without making a martyr of him, he might well have realized that the men would want to get rid of the captain who knew their identity and origin. Terry wondered if they were really going to a system with no inhabited planets—where it was hard to see what business they could possibly have—or if they had handed the captain false coordinates to trick him into giving up his ship without a fight. Telepathically, he sensed more and more that they had some dark purpose no legitimate captain would have sanctioned.

Terry's heart swelled with excitement. Incredibly, his life—even perhaps something approaching his old life—had been given back to him. It would take a while to sink in, he knew. He felt as if he were waking from a bad dream, or perhaps sliding into one too good to be true.

"Let's get going, Rivera," the first man said after Quaid and the captain had departed. "You'd better have told us the truth when you said you can program jumps, because it's true that our destination's an uncommon one and we're in a hurry."

Terry went to the bridge. As he sat down at the captain's console, he was still dazed; to be at the controls of a starship again made him feel as if he had stepped backward in time into a memory. When he saw the figures still displayed on the screen, he was sure he had.

The coordinates the two men had provided were those of Maclairn's star.

70

DURING THE HOURS it took to get far enough from Ciencia's star to execute the jump, Terry struggled to stay in touch with reality. Reason told him they could not be going to Maclairn. For it to be a coincidence was just too incredible—yet no one on Ciencia had known that was where he had come from, even apart from the fact that only a select few had ever possessed its star's coordinates. And why would Quaid, who hated him, send him back? As hard as he tried, he could not make sense of it.

Yet here it was. The figures were in the computer, and real. He ran a number of tests to make sure there was no error, and everything checked out. Or did it? Perhaps the drugs he'd been given in prison had produced false perceptions. Perhaps it was all some horrible experiment to see if he could be rendered incapable of distinguishing between inner wishes and objective fact. The figures might have come from his memory along with the knowledge of how to pilot a starship. The men could be Ciencian agents in disguise, observing the result of their sinister research. He might not be in space at all—he might be strapped to a table in some laboratory with wires inserted into his brain.

But even if that were true, he had the ability to choose his course of action. They had not turned him into an automaton. He could go ahead as if this was really happening, or he could deny it and tell them to go to hell. It was a gamble either way. And looking back as cloud-shrouded Ciencia receded into the distance, he knew that he would go ahead. If it was all in his mind, it was better than what would be in it otherwise. It was better to believe in something, even a mere illusion, than to believe the human mind was a machine that could be manipulated. Was not *Estel* an illusion, and had not that symbol of hope done as much for people as a real *Estel* would have done?

He calculated the jump and recalculated it. He listened to the countdown with racing heart, too overcome with emotion to alter his pulse rate through volition. When the count reached zero, he gave the command to execute; and *Venture* was suddenly within a day's range of Maclairn.

The two men were in their staterooms by that time; Terry reported that the jump had been successful, then went to his own. He was too excited to sleep. Maclairn!

He had believed he would never see it again. He couldn't imagine how he had endured the thought of never seeing it. Through all the years he had agonized over his exile, he had somehow managed to hold back the fullest, most concrete awareness of what he had left behind. Now it was as if a light had come on, flooding scenes that had been mercifully veiled in mist. He walked through the streets of Petersville, entered Jessica's house, went hand in hand with Kathryn to their room. . . .

Kathryn. He was about to see Kathryn—and their son!

In his heart he knew that Kathryn was probably with someone else by now, and that meeting him, especially with his appearance altered beyond recognition, would be a major shock to her. It didn't matter. Just to see her, feel the touch of her mind, would soothe the pain that had paralyzed him so long. To love, even if there could be no physical expression of that love . . . Though on Maclairn, he recalled, love need not always be exclusive. Maclairnans felt no jealousy; as telepaths they were too sensitive to each others' feelings. He would not be jealous of anyone Kathryn loved—he wouldn't want her to be hurt by such a conflict. But he and Kathryn were still married. They had committed themselves to each other forever as lifemates. That didn't necessarily mean excluding others, but it shouldn't mean denying their desire for each other, either. . . .

And his son—Radnor. He had so often imagined what he looked like as he grew . . . now he would be twelve years old, only a year away from adulthood on Maclairn. He would soon begin his mind training. What did the boy want from life? Terry wondered. Did he admire Fleet officers and want to fly? Since he had been born to League citizens he could apply to the Fleet academy if he wished, though probably he would prefer to stay on Maclairn. Would he perhaps, like his parents, become a Steward of the Flame?

A Steward of the Flame—it was a long time since

Terry had thought of himself as that, yet it had meant more to him than any of his other experiences on Maclairn, excepting only his love for Kathryn. He had been a Steward for less than a day, but the commitment he had made still overrode all others, despite all that had happened to him since. Fate had torn him away and had offered no opportunity to prove that commitment, but his life wasn't over yet. Against all probability, all hope of reprieve, he was coming home.

To be sure, he could not act openly as a Steward or attend the Ritual, because that would require close contact with mentors. The Elders had believed he couldn't conceal what he knew from the mentors, and that for them to learn of it would be harmful to human evolution; and on the latter point he had been convinced. At least he had told himself that he had, but that might have been just because he couldn't bear the thought that his exile was meaningless. Since it had turned out not to be permanent, maybe he should reconsider the necessity for revealing his identity only to Kathryn and his son. He longed to resume his friendship with Tristan and with Aldren . . . surely they could keep the secret even if he couldn't. . . .

The questions whirled in Terry's mind, and the anticipation energized him so that he could not lie in bed any longer, could not keep still. He went to the bridge and sat in the captain's chair to check their position. The AI told him that they had passed the gas giant Five and he recalled the earthquake on Five-C, the loss of *Picard,* his first ship—a ship much like *Venture*, as it happened— and the rescue of his crew. Where were they now, he wondered? Were they still with *Shepard*? Had Drew and Mikaela married? They would have Commander rank by now, as he himself would have had. . . .

He would not see the other landmarks, Four and Corwin, as they were presently on the other side of the sun—which meant their sensor stations would not detect

Venture. Maclairn was next in line; naturally he had set his course for it. All of a sudden he was struck by the realization that he had not asked the two men where in this solar system they wanted to go. He had been so eager to see Maclairn that he'd given no thought to what their purpose here might be.

What was he thinking of, heading straight for Maclairn with passengers he knew to be evildoers? They couldn't be going there intentionally, of course; they could not possibly know it by name or be aware of the colony's presence. Nobody knew unless the secret had escaped during his absence; and if it had, if knowledge of Maclairn had become public, *Venture*'s captain wouldn't have said no worlds in the solar system were inhabited. And these men wouldn't get away to tell anyone—the ship would be intercepted by Fleet and its occupants permanently confined to the surface, as all intruders were. It might be warned off first; he himself wouldn't be recognized and, he realized with some nervousness, he would have to defy the warning and would perhaps be fired upon. But Fleet wouldn't shoot to kill; *Venture* would simply be captured, and he could straighten out his own status afterward.

Nevertheless, fully awake and clearheaded now, he knew he ought not to take outsiders to Maclairn at all. He ought not to have come to its star in the first place; he should have gone somewhere else even if they killed him for disobeying them. He was breaking his oath never to reveal that it existed.

What did they want in this solar system? To them, it was an uninhabited one. Unless . . . oh, my God, Terry thought. A few people did know about Maclairn. Its enemies at League headquarters, the ones who had arranged the killing of Corwin and Arthur Bramfield, knew its location. That was the underlying reason for the early warning system he had helped to deploy, the reason why he'd been trained in remote viewing. How could he have been so absorbed in his desire to return that he'd not thought about that?

These men were almost surely hostile. Still, Terry reflected, what harm could they do? There were only two of them, and they couldn't be armed with anything larger than sidearms. They were spies, most likely, who had come to see whether the League had been told the whole truth about the Maclairnans' capabilities. Evidently they were unaware that Fleet would not let them leave—but it wouldn't, so no information could reach their backers. And no damage would be done if it did, since whoever had sent them must already know that Maclairn existed.

He should not have come, but he was here now, and to go away forever when he was this close to Maclairn was too much for fate to ask of him, considering that two captured spies could do no harm.

When the men emerged from their staterooms they asked, as Terry had expected, how long it would take to reach the second planet from the sun. He told them, noticing that they seemed even more nervous than they had been before. "Will you want to land on it?" he asked.

"Yes," said the one called Rafe. "We'll take the shuttle down ourselves."

No, you won't, Terry thought. We'll be intercepted first. It was odd, he thought, that they hadn't mentioned before that they were shuttle pilots—not even to *Venture*'s original captain.

"We won't be needing you once we arrive," Yuri said. "We needed you only for the interstellar jump. Keep that in mind if you have any thoughts about interfering with us."

"You also need me to jump back," Terry pointed out.

"Maybe. And maybe we've made other arrangements—"

"What the hell, Yuri!" Rafe burst out irritably. "This guy hasn't any reason to cross us, and you're giving him ideas. Shut up and focus on what we're here for."

The men were silent after that. But as time passed

and he got closer and closer to Maclairn, Terry began to sense that something was very wrong.

He could feel the growing tension in the men even after he got back to the bridge; telepathically he sensed that for some reason they feared what was ahead. Why? They wouldn't have come if they'd known the planet was guarded by a cruiser. . . .

But they should have known, Terry thought, suddenly chilled. If they had been sent by any of the League officials in on the secret, they would know about Fleet's presence. Those officials were the ones who had authorized the cruiser's deployment.

Was it possible that the authorization had been withdrawn? It had been more than twelve years, plenty of time for political reversals. Perhaps *Shepard* was no longer there. Perhaps Maclairn had been left vulnerable to discovery, or even attack, from outside.

All the same, two men with sidearms could not attack; the potential danger wasn't immediate. He had only to make sure they couldn't get away to make public what they had seen. He would disable *Venture* once they were in orbit, Terry decided. He thought of Ivana, who had disabled *Picard* for the same reason—but of course it wouldn't require the drastic method she had used. He was alone on the bridge with no opposition; he could tear out the hyperdrive controls without melting them. Perhaps it would be enough to sabotage the AI portion, considering that Rafe and Yuri didn't know how to jump anyway.

It was too late for him to reverse his decision to come here, though more and more he felt it had been an unwise one. They were too close to the sun now to jump out safely. And where would he have gone? What good would it have done to refuse to come, since if he had, they would simply have hired some other starship pilot? Perhaps, he thought, it was a good thing that he'd acted impulsively, his longing for Maclairn overriding both his vow of secrecy and his common sense, because nobody else would have taken precautions to prevent their leaving.

All at once the comm lit up and with a gulp of relief Terry heard, "Unidentified ship, this is Patrol Leader Alpha from FHS *Shepard*. This solar system is off limits, Fleet is conducting maneuvers here. You are instructed to retreat to a safe distance and jump immediately, over."

Thank God, he thought. *Shepard* was still here after all. He would not have to worry about the men escaping, though he might well be in trouble himself until he could make contact with someone who knew him. He did not acknowledge the call, as there was nothing he could say.

"Unidentified ship, please respond. You must leave this solar system at once. Over." On the viewscreen Terry saw three patrollers closing in.

The bridge hatch burst open and Rafe appeared. He was holding a laser pistol. "Tell them we're in distress," he ordered. He didn't seem surprised by the patrollers' appearance.

If they had known they'd be met by Fleet, what had they hoped to accomplish? Terry sensed desperation in Rafe, and mounting fear. Evidently they realized they would be captured; a distress call wouldn't change that. Since it would do no harm and might prevent the firing of warning shots, he complied. "Patrol Leader Alpha, this is HS *Venture*. We are in distress and request assistance."

"*Venture*, what is the nature of your emergency?"

"Tell them we have illness aboard and require immediate hospitalization. Tell them to send a fast shuttle to take us directly to the surface."

But that was pointless, Terry thought in confusion. When they got to the surface it would be seen that neither of them was ill, and they would be in more trouble than if they pretended to have been unaware that *Shepard* would capture them. He turned to Rafe and asked, "Why?"

"That's not your concern," Rafe said coldly. "Tell them,

or I will. Now that they've seen us we don't need you anymore."

They had never intended to leave the surface, Terry perceived. And yet they were both terrified of going there. They could not have been more afraid if they had believed they were going to die. . . .

As he sensed this, full telepathic awareness kicked in and he knew beyond doubt that it was true. These men were certain that they would die, and soon. Which meant they were literally on a suicide mission. They were terrorists who expected Maclairnans to die with them.

71

LOOKING BACK IN the light of cold logic, it wasn't hard to make the connections. The enemies of Maclairn who wished it had never been discovered, who had repeatedly proven that they were willing to use violence to prevent its influence from spreading. Quaid, the fanatic who believed that all sources of "corrupting" unscientific thought should be wiped out. The surreptitious rendezvous above Ciencia. The care taken to make sure that Rafe and Yuri couldn't be associated either with him or with their backers. And the transaction behind closed doors, supposedly involving a mere message, which Terry now saw must have been an exchange of a considerable amount of money for some means of killing inhabitants of Maclairn.

What did the government racketeers on Ciencia have to sell to Maclairn's enemies? Anything hidden in, or beneath, Quade's flight jacket would have been too small for a weapon. At least not a conventional weapon. A weaponized product of biochemistry, on the other hand . . . Ciencia was known throughout the galaxy for its biochemical expertise and the officials at League headquarters were surely aware of that.

Under the spur of crisis, Terry's long-dormant psi

faculties were magnified, and through clairvoyance he saw what the terrorists carried. Vials, many small vials.... With horror he recalled that historically, biochemical substances had been used for genocide. Even in past eras, small amounts of such substances could kill large numbers of people. Ciencia's advanced biochemical engineering might well have produced even more efficient ones. The settlements on Maclairn were confined to a small region of the planet. Given a powerful enough biochemical or virus, it might not be impossible to release enough into the atmosphere to annihilate the whole population.

No doubt Maclairn's enemies had become desperate. In twelve years, the mentors must have made progress in teaching people to use their latent capabilities. All further attempts to prevent it must have failed, so that the opponents had resorted to stirring up the public's underlying fear of what psi might lead to. Evidently propaganda-driven hysteria had reached the point where they could recruit terrorists willing to die in order to combat the alleged threat to Earth's society.

Rafe and Yuri had taped the vials to their bodies as Quaid must have, correctly assuming that there would be no reason for Fleet to search the occupants of an intruding ship if they were captured before reaching the surface. Once on the ground, they would move fast. The substance in the vials couldn't kill instantly, or they wouldn't live long enough to open more than one. A delay would have been built into it, resulting in slow, agonizing death for everyone, or almost everyone, on Maclairn.

Which would mean an end to the plan for spreading acceptance of new mind powers. Laesara had said, *If that plan fails, your people's evolution will be set back for centuries, and may even be permanently halted.* And she had insisted that only through the influence of Maclairn could the plan be fulfilled before Earth's civilization collapsed. The Elders had banished him to protect it; had he now, unknowingly and ironically, defeated that aim in his eagerness to regain what they had taken from him? Had he brought about the death of those he loved—his friends, Kathryn, his son?

All this flashed quickly through Terry's mind, and he knew that he must act. Whether or not the potential holocaust was his fault, it was up to him to prevent it. But how? Oh, God, he thought, where were the Elders now that they were needed? Hadn't they been tracking his ship? Perhaps not; they were not omniscient, and they might be on the other side of the sun. Besides, they couldn't have foreseen this kind of threat; if they were watching, they would know that Fleet patrollers had found him, and their policy was to let Fleet deal with intruders when possible.

As Fleet undoubtedly could, if he alerted them to the danger. All he had to do was make sure that the terrorists didn't get into a shuttle; once they were aboard *Shepard*, he could expose them before they were taken to the surface. They would be neutralized, and the deadly vials would be destroyed. Maclairn would be safe, and so would he. He could go home. . . .

Except what if the captain of *Shepard*, thinking him delusional, refused to believe him? What if the biochemical weapon was slow-acting and contagious, so that Shepard's crew could be infected without anyone realizing that they'd become carriers? Or what if his effort to keep Rafe and Yuri out of a shuttle backfired? They might kill him if he tried to prevent them from leaving *Venture*, and then nothing could stop them.

Terry knew he could not take that chance.

"I said, tell them we need a medical shuttle," Rafe repeated, his voice harsh with anger and suppressed apprehension.

"We're too far out for a shuttle to reach us," Terry said. "We're beyond range."

"The patrollers reached us."

"The patrollers were alerted by the early warning system. And they never land, so they don't need to save power for that."

"Well, tell Fleet to get a shuttle ready and meet us half way."

Not daring to refuse, which might lead Rafe to shoot him before he could take any action, Terry spoke into the comm. "Patrol Alpha, we have a medical problem. We need transport to Petersville." He was taking a chance; he wasn't supposed to know about Maclairn, let alone the name of its capital. If the terrorists did know, they would suspect he was not the harmless pawn he seemed to be and would kill him immediately. But since they might kill him soon anyway, it was vital to tell *Shepard* that something was not right about the request.

"Petersville? What does that mean?" Rafe demanded, genuinely puzzled.

"It's a Fleet code word for emergency care," Terry lied.

"And how would you know any Fleet code words?"

"How do you think I learned to pilot jump ships? I'm a Fleet washout."

There was a pause while Patrol Leader Alpha, undoubtedly dismayed, contacted *Shepard*. Then he responded, "*Venture* captain, please identify yourself and your origin."

"This is Captain Terry Radnor in command, bringing a message from League headquarters." They would know this was a lie; the League would not dispatch an unknown ship, let alone a private one. And if his name was remembered after all these years, they would realize that anyone using it was trying to send a signal.

Rafe frowned. Terry, carefully but unobtrusively leaving the comm channel open, said, "Well, what did you want me to say? I assume you'd rather I didn't mention Ciencia."

"What's with the alias?"

"It's my own name. I used an alias on Ciencia, as what smuggler wouldn't?" There was no danger of Fleet—or Kathryn—believing it might really be him; if in doubt they would check voiceprint records, and his voice had been changed.

The patrol leader was young, however, and failed to grasp that the speaker was under duress. He burst out incredulously, "Terry Radnor? Not the one the planet was named for?"

God, Terry thought, they must have named Four after him, assuming he had died in the course of trying to protect Maclairn. As indeed he was about to; they had just been a little premature.

"No, not that one," he said over the comm. But of course Rafe now knew that Terry had had some previous connection with Maclairn. He would understand that an attempt was being made to thwart him.

"Patrol Alpha, our situation is urgent," Terry added quickly. "Make sure your captain gives it his full attention." Which by now the captain would already be doing, but that would not eliminate the threat. If the terrorists were suspected of being dangerous, they might reach a prison on the surface before the vials were discovered, and if they were left alone in a cell long enough to open them, prison walls would be no barrier to the spread of the lethal content.

No more time could be wasted; they were fast approaching Maclairn and once they were within shuttle range, the men could attempt to fly *Venture*'s shuttle past the patrollers. Somehow he had to get Rafe off the bridge so that he could alter course.

Making a move would be risky, yet there was no alternative. In desperation, Terry swiveled in the chair, reaching back to switch off the artificial gravity and grip a handhold. Before Rafe had time to recover from sudden weightlessness, Terry kicked out with both feet, propelling him out the hatch, and locked it behind him by voice command. His long-ago experience paid off; you didn't forget how to maneuver in zero-g. For the moment, the terrorists couldn't get to him. But they might well blast the hatch lock if given time.

Where to go? *Venture* was faster than the patrollers; they couldn't catch it, so there was no danger of being brought back to *Shepard*. It was a pity, Terry thought, that there'd been no chance of provoking Fleet into firing to kill; that would have been the best solution. There was no way he personally could kill two armed terrorists. The bridge was sealed and he might depressurize the rest of the ship, but they were not stupid and would be anticipating that; by now they were probably in spacesuits. And they had access to the shuttle. They were suicidal fanatics; they might take off in it, gambling that Fleet would pick them up instead of destroying it—as indeed Fleet would. He must get well away before they had time to try, for *Venture* had no weapons with which he could shoot them down.

He could jump, he supposed. That he was too near the sun to do so safely no longer mattered. But the AI required a long countdown to jump, and besides, jumping from here would take out the close-by patrollers. So there was no assurance that the terrorists wouldn't be in the shuttle before he could go into hyperdrive—and where would he head for, anyway? To ensure the terrorists' death and the destruction of the vials he would have to jump directly into a star, and that would take too long to program since the AI's safety lock would have to be overridden.

There was only one place he could go, Terry knew, and he had already set his course for it while considering less feasible alternatives. There was no choice. The AI had checked its current position and found it to be miraculously close to him: the asteroid where he had first landed on his very first trip as captain of *Picard*. Where he had placed the first sensor station, the one that had now, after more than thirteen years, proved its worth by alerting the patrollers.

The sight of it was familiar as he approached—a rugged mass nearly covered with rock crags. There was the level place where he had landed, the marks left by the shuttle still visible on the reddish surface. But now he was not in a shuttle, and although he might be able to land *Venture* as he had landed *Picard* on Five-C, that was not what he was going to do. There must be no chance of rescue for the terrorists. He could not land; he must crash.

He made no attempt to orbit, but went straight in. *Venture* was moving along the same path as the asteroid, however, and its relative speed was not great enough to cause its total destruction, considering the asteroid's low gravity. At least part of it would remain intact. He used thrusters to make sure that it wouldn't be the terrorists' part.

Memories of all that was past surged through Terry as the rocky surface loomed ahead of him, though the descent wasn't long enough for him to ponder them. *Kathryn,* he cried out silently, *Oh, God, Kathryn—* But then in the last moment before impact, the face that flashed into his mind was not Kathryn's but Alison's.

72

TERRY REGAINED CONSCIOUSNESS slowly amid the wreckage of *Venture*. It was on its side, tilted at an odd angle, and he was pinned under a portion of the captain's console; but the pressure seal of the bridge must have held since he was still breathing. The pain in his back told him he was seriously injured, but as his mind cleared he was able to shift into the appropriate state of consciousness to do away with suffering. He found he was able to move. Seeing that his shoulder was gashed, he stopped the flow of blood. Then he managed to lift the fallen console desk enough to free himself.

The bridge hatch was still locked, and of course he couldn't open it anyway if the rest of the ship was exposed to vacuum. The AI wasn't functional so the air on the bridge would soon be contaminated by carbon dioxide. He would die here trapped inside, without a last look at the stars.

It was an extraordinary destiny after all, he reflected—not the encounter with the Elders, not the long exile under a false identity on a world he despised, not even the legendary status he seemed to have acquired on that world, but the astonishing fact that if it had not been for these events he would not have been in the right place at the right time to save Maclairn from a disaster no one could have foreseen.

After a while he noticed that the captain's locker had fallen open and there was a spacesuit inside. He might be able to put it on, he supposed. Then he could get into the rest of the ship and perhaps crawl outside. The air tank would last for a little while. But why should he bother? What good would it do to live for a few more hours when he was dying anyway? No ship from Maclairn could reach him in time even if they knew where he was, and of course they didn't know. The patrollers hadn't enough range to have followed him and though Fleet knew the intial alert had come from the asteroid's sensor station, they would not expect an intruder to head toward it.

Maclairn ... it would be visible from here! Suddenly he knew that he could not let himself die without one more look at Maclairn.

At least not if he could get outside. In a moment of panic he feared there might be no power for unlocking the hatch, but when he pulled himself up to reach the switch he saw that some of the LEDs were still glowing. With difficulty, he stretched far enough to press it, and the green one over the hatch came on. Then, ignoring the suppressed pain intended by nature to warn of injury, he managed to stand up long enough to struggle into the suit and helmet. As soon as got it on he collapsed again and lay motionless, exhausted, for more minutes than he could count; but eventually he crept to the hatch and opened it. The remaining air on the bridge rushed out explosively and was wasted. It didn't matter; he would not need air very much longer. His trained sensitivity to his physical condition told him that his internal injuries would be fatal.

The bodies of the two terrorists, wearing suits but not helmets, lay sprawled on what had been a wall of the lounge. It had cracked open on impact and the gap was wide enough to see black sky outside. There was no knowing what had become of the vials, but even if accidentally opened their content could do no harm in the vacuum of space. It need no longer concern him. Slowly, by supreme effort, he crawled through the lounge area and out onto the surface of the asteroid.

Maclairn hung low over the horizon, a golden ball about the size of a full moon as seen from Earth—gold studded with azure jewels, surrounded by an infinity of sparkling diamonds. He stared at it, remembering how he had first seen it from a viewport aboard *Shepard* almost fourteen years ago in what now seemed another lifetime. From that moment it had been the focus of his inmost feelings, and it was still there, real, far more real than in the dreams since then during which he'd longed for it. And he had almost reached it. He had returned from exile to the threshold of the one place in the universe he had ever cared about, only to turn away. Having been forced to do so, he did not mind dying. There was nothing left to hope for, nothing to regret.

He had been wrong to curse the fate that placed him in the hands of the Elders, Terry realized. Fate had been kind, for it brought him beyond all foreseeing to the one point in space and time where he needed to be in order to save Maclairn from destruction. Nothing else could have saved it. If Quaid had not believed his following on Ciencia posed a threat, he would not have been taken aboard *Venture*. Had he not been aware both of Maclairn's ruthless enemies and of Ciencia's corrupt uses of biochemistry, he would not have perceived what the terrorists were doing. And had he not been so obsessed with desire to come home that he ignored his clear duty to reject the opportunity, they would have found another pilot and he would not have been present to thwart them. What would the Elders think if they knew of this second irony: only his defiance of their decree had given him a key role in the cause they'd believed it would serve.

He had come so close to seeing Kathryn again. He had thought that to die without seeing her would be the worst thing that could happen. But to his surprise, now in the face of death he found himself thinking more about Alison than about Kathryn. Kathryn belonged to a dream from the past—a dream he would always treasure were he alive to do so, but no longer part of his everyday reality. He had sworn that their bond would last beyond death, and perhaps it would; he supposed he was about to find out. And yet he'd stopped truly grieving the loss of it long ago. With surprise he realized that the finality of that loss caused him no anguish.

But Alison! His eyes stinging with tears, Terry became aware that the most unbearable part of dying was that he had left Alison without their having experienced what they should have had together.

What a fool he'd been to think they could not bond! Had there not been a link all along, no less real because she was not conscious of its telepathic basis? Why had he assumed she could not become a telepath without a mentor to teach her and the stress essential to formal training? Given their close companionship, would not sexual union alone have been enough to awaken her latent power? It had been he who resisted, not letting himself be aware that the barrier to full intimacy was a matter not of Alison's mind powers but of his own. That it was based on fear, fear that those powers would preclude an ordinary relationship and if they made love it would turn out like the brief liaisons of his youth, leaving him physically satisfied but with painfully frustrated emotions. Yet it could never be like that with Alison! He was sure it couldn't, now that it was too late.

He watched Maclairn drop below the close horizon, knowing that he hadn't much air left and would not live long enough to see it rise. He was alone under the stars he had sought all his life and had once believed he was destined to explore. And then, out of the darkness, another light appeared, and brightened.

It was a lander from the Elders' starship.

73

AT FIRST TERRY did not believe it was real. Very likely he was hallucinating; the gauge on his air tank might not be quite accurate, and he might already be experiencing oxygen deprivation. They wouldn't have been stationed closer than the orbit of Corwin; how could they possibly have found him in the short time since he crashed? Then he realized that they must have been tracking *Venture* after all, and unaware of what it contained, have decided to let Fleet's patrollers deal with it when they saw it had been intercepted. They must have identified him through remote viewing, for they would not have intervened in the imminent death of someone who didn't already know about them—after all, they could prevent thousands of deaths if their overriding concern for humankind's future did not bar them from revealing themselves.

The landing was swift and silent. Two figures—suited, of course—carried him to the lander, and he knew that he would neither see them nor hear their voices, for they would not be as humanlike as Laesara had been. Was she still among those guarding Maclairn, he wondered, after more than twelve years? He had no idea how her people measured time; if they had a long lifespan she might not have aged at all.

He had long ago stopped hating them for what they had done to him. By their strict standard of nondisclosure it had been necessary; though he had kept their secret from Alison, he was not at all sure he could have kept it from Kathryn or the mentors. As they took him aboard the starship, which was smaller than the one he remembered, he felt no emotion—not anger about the past, and not even thankfulness for the rescue. He was past feeling anything at all.

They healed his injuries and gave him clothing to wear while his own was being restored, and someone—a powerful telepath whose face was hidden—silently asked permission to probe his mind. Terry consented, not caring whether the experience would overwhelm him or not. It did, for the Elder drew the details of everything that had happened from him. Afterward they left him alone to recuperate.

He was stunned, numb. He had not expected to live, and was not sure he wanted to. What was left for him now? He had come home to Maclairn, only to find that it was out of reach; they would take him somewhere else. Probably not to Ciencia, for he was a convict there and after rescuing him they would not doom him to lifelong incarceration. Wherever it was, he would have to start over again from scratch—perhaps be stuck forever in a routine dead-end job. And he would no longer have a purpose to keep him sane.

He would not try to get back to Maclairn a second time. That part of his life was over; he'd been foolish to think he could regain the feeling of belonging that had meant so much to him. Jessica and even Tristan—and Aldren, if he had returned—might well be dead. His friends in Fleet would no longer recognize him, so never again could he fly. He would be a stranger to his son and as for Kathryn, if she was with someone else his reappearance would only cause her pain. All these years he had envisioned her as she'd been when they were young, but both of them had been changed irrevocably. He was painfully aware that it was Alison he now loved . . . Alison, whom he would never see again either.

He slept for a long time, and when he woke he was told that the Elders' flagship had arrived from another solar system and that he had been moved to it. He ate the food they brought him. Then, when he had recovered as much as he felt he would ever recover, they gave him a face mask and oxygen tank for passage through the alien air and took him to the familiar room in which he had once been imprisoned. And Laesara, now commander of their fleet, was there to greet him.

"I had not thought we would meet again, Terry Radnor," she said.

"Just Terry," he said. "I gave the name Radnor to my son long ago, even before you took it from me, and Rivera was never more than a pseudonym. Maclairnans use single names, as you no doubt know."

"And you still think of yourself as Maclairnan?"

"I don't know what I am," he admitted.

"You are a defender of humanity," she declared. "What world you happen to be on no longer matters."

He realized, to his astonishment, that this was true. He had thought he would not care to live, coming so close to the world he longed for yet unable to set foot on it. But now he felt no pain, only a kind of emptiness. From this day on, when he pictured Maclairn he would dream of his youth and of Kathryn, his first love; and it would always be his most cherished memory. But he couldn't go back—not just because the Elders would not allow it, but because it wasn't possible to reverse time.

There was only one thing he wished he could have

regained. Recalling the Ritual, remembering that magical night, his last on Maclairn, when he had touched flame unharmed and joyfully pledged to serve an important cause, he said, "I would have liked to remain a Steward of the Flame."

Laesara's surprise surged into his mind. "But Terry, you did. Surely you know—"

"I suppose saving Maclairn from the terrorists counts," he agreed. "But being a Steward meant something more than acting fast in a crisis. It was a long-term commitment, the same as the mentors made, to further the plan for giving mind powers to humankind."

She met his eyes. "It goes without saying that what you did a few days ago saved not only countless Maclairnans but the plan itself, which could not have outlasted the destruction of their colony. But that is not what I meant. Do you not realize that your work on Ciencia contributed more toward the achievement of Maclairn's goal than any mentor accomplished elsewhere? You lived in exile, as they do, and you opened the minds of many not only to psi but to the whole human heritage that is prerequisite to it. And besides that you had influence as a healer. In effect you *were* a mentor—and certainly as much a Steward as the rest."

"I didn't think of it like that," he protested in amazement. "I thought only of wanting to escape."

"But you cared about more than escaping, and you achieved what no one with less courage and capability could have. As I expected."

"You *expected* me to have an effect on Ciencia?" he burst out.

"We made the best of a bad situation, Terry," Laesara said. "We had to confine you somewhere, and where better than a world where you could further the cause to which you had committed yourself? We had recently observed Ciencia. We knew that the repression there was an even greater evil than the government's corruption and that it would delay the maturation of your civilization—even threaten it if their culture grew strong enough to spread—and we also knew that its secret exportation of deadly biochemicals under cover of isolation might present a danger. Yet to break our policy of not interfering with younger worlds would have been harmful. Then fate sent you to us. And when you revealed that Aldren sensed you had some extraordinary destiny, I knew that your coming had meaning, though I did not foresee anything as extraordinary as the saving of two worlds."

"I suppose telling me that losing everything might serve my true purpose would have been interference," Terry said bitterly. "You used me—I was just an unwitting tool."

"Only in the sense that we all are tools of circumstance; that is how human progress works." Laesara reached into a pocket of her tunic and drew something out. Against the golden skin of her hand he saw the gleam of copper—incredibly, it was a flame pin like those the Stewards wore.

"It is yours," she told him, "the one you swallowed long ago. It was recovered while you were unconscious and I kept it to remember you by, for I knew that you should be remembered."

His eyes blurred with tears as she pinned it to his shirt. "Wear it always, save in the presence of those who might know its meaning and seek to learn how you came by it," she said. "You have as much right to it as anyone else who honors what it stands for."

Though he intended to put the past behind him, he found he could not leave her without knowing one thing more. "Laesara—have you ever heard anything about my son?"

"I was wondering if you would ask. Your son Radnor is psi-gifted and hopes to someday become a mentor like his foster father, with whom Kathryn has lived for the past six years. She mentioned this to our agent, whom she believes to be Earthborn, the last time she visited League headquarters."

"She's still ambassador, then. And happy?"

"We have every reason to believe she is. Grief never completely passes; but like you, she has moved on."

He nodded. Aware now that the years of exile had not been wasted, he was free to look forward. "Must I keep working to enlighten Ciencia?" he asked, not liking the thought. "I'm an escaped convict there now, but I suppose you could alter my face and biometrics again."

"Is that what you want, Terry?"

"It's not. I want to go once, to see a woman named Alison, but not to stay. And I'm not sure she would recognize me if I were changed."

"She would recognize your mind-touch even if she is only latently telepathic. But there is no need. We observed Ciencia a short while ago; it can get along without you from now on, for a political party called the Estelans has arisen—you have inspired others to finish what you started. We will take you wherever you wish, as long as there are no mentors there; I think we can trust you not to seek them out."

"Then repair my ship," he said, "and give me a clear title and license under the name HS *Estel,* which I'm sure your agents can arrange. And change my ID as you did before, making me Terry Steward, a worldless star pilot. Flying is what I always wanted to do, and the task of a Steward is to spread belief in mind power throughout the worlds of humankind. I think perhaps Alison will agree to come with me. We may occasionally orbit Ciencia, but there must be many colonies where new ideas can be promoted along with merchandise, and smuggling is a less dishonorable trade than I once thought."

"One that ensures that you'll steer clear of Fleet," said Laesara with a smile. "Will you need help getting Alison away from Ciencia?"

"Well," Terry said, "it would be nice if your lander could put me down near the city in disguise and guard *Estel* while it waits in high orbit. We can ride back with a local captain who owes me a favor, and who may even want to sell us some cargo."

"That is little enough to ask," Laesara said. "It is a very small intervention, lesser than when we sent you to Ciencia in the first place, though I suspect your influence will be wide."

So *Venture* was retrieved, leaving false evidence of an intruder's destruction to be found by Fleet; and it was made spaceworthy under its new name *Estel*. And when the Elders' starship had jumped to Ciencia's system, Terry took leave of them and set out alone to orbit the world he would set foot on again but once.

He was no longer an exile, for *Estel* was his home, and wherever he took it he would offer hope: hope for the future he alone knew was awaiting humankind. For him, too, the future was hopeful. He thought now of Alison as he had not dared to think of her while with her; and he knew that at last he could love again—and that he had come full circle to a life of journeying between the stars.

About the Author

SYLVIA ENGDAHL is the author of eleven science fiction novels. Six of them are Young Adult books that are also enjoyed by adults, all of which were originally published by Atheneum and have been republished, in both hardcover and paperback, by different publishers in the twenty-first century. The one for which she is best known, *Enchantress from the Stars*, was a Newbery Honor book in 1971, winner of the 1990 Phoenix Award of the Children's Literature Association, and a finalist for the 2002 Book Sense Book of the Year in the Rediscovery category. Her trilogy *Children of the Star* was reissued in a single volume as adult science fiction.

Her five most recent novels, a duology and a trilogy, are not YA books and are not appropriate for middle-school readers, but will be enjoyed by the many adult fans of her work. In addition, she has issued an updated and expanded edition of her nonfiction book *The Planet-Girded Suns: Our Forebears' Firm Belief in Inhabited Exoplanets* (first published by Atheneum in 1974 with a different subtitle) as well as three ebooks of collected essays.

Between 1957 and 1967 Engdahl was a computer programmer and Computer Systems Specialist for the SAGE Air Defense System. Most recently she has worked as a freelance editor of nonfiction anthologies for high schools. Now retired, she lives in Eugene, Oregon, and welcomes visitors to her website www.sylviaengdahl.com, which contains many of her essays, including those dealing with her long-term advocacy of space colonization.

The Founders of Maclairn Duology

Book One: *Stewards of the Flame*

When burned-out starship captain Jesse Sanders is seized by a dictatorial medical regime and detained on the colony planet Undine, he has no idea that he is about to be plunged into a bewildering new life that will involve ordeals and joys beyond anything he has ever imagined, as well as the love of a woman with powers that seem superhuman .This controversial novel deals with government-imposed health care, with end-of-life issues, and with the so-called paranormal powers of the human mind.

Book Two: *Promise of the Flame.*

Three hundred people, isolated by choice on a raw new planet in the hope of fulfilling a dream, the dream that their psi powers will become the foundation of a culture that can someday shape the future of humankind. If they don't starve first. And if they don't lose heart in the face of hardships beyond any they imagined. Starship captain Jesse Sanders hasn't expected to be responsible for the settlement, but Peter, the visionary leader, has his hands full; so the job of ensuring its survival falls on Jesse. And in the end, he must stake his life in a desperate attempt to prevent the loss of all they have gained.

Children of the Star Trilogy

An omnibus edition containing the complete trilogy *This Star Shall Abide* (known in the UK as *Heritage of the Star*), *Beyond the Tomorrow Mountains*, and *The Doors of the Universe*. Noren knows that his world is not as it should be—it is wrong that only the Scholars and

Technicians can use metal tools and Machines. It's wrong that only those few have access to the mysterious City, which he has always longed to enter. Above all, it is wrong for the Scholars to have sole power over the distribution of knowledge. Unable to believe in the Prophecy that promises these restrictions will someday end, he declares it to be a fraud and defies the High Lew under which they are enforced. His family and the girl to whom he is betrothed reject him. Yet he cannot turn back from the path that leads him to the mysterious fate awaiting heretics.

YOUNG ADULT NOVELS FROM SYLVIA ENGDAHL THAT ARE ALSO ENJOYED BY ADULTS

The Far Side of Evil

Assigned merely to observe a young world whose people may soon destroy their civilization, Anthropological Service agent Elana finds that only she—at great cost—can prevent a war of annihilation.

Journey Between Worlds

When she reluctantly visits the thriving colony on Mars, Melinda Ashley finds love and a new way of life.

Enchantress from the Stars

A Newbery Honor book that can be enjoyed by younger readers than Engdahl's other novels, but was intended for teens and is also read by many adults. It is of interest to readers of the Captain of *Estel* trilogy because it is where the interstellar Anthropological Service first appeared.